"Despite your opinion of me, I am not a barbarian."

"That is not my opinion," Carolyn corrected.

"Oh? Then I see I have been too tame." Magnus came to her chair and, taking her hand, drew her to her feet. "I hope I have not left you with any misconceptions. Now, come and kiss me goodbye."

She started at his boldness. He chuckled. "In less than a week, we shall share more than that, Cara. Having second thoughts?"

"No!" she declared a little too vehemently. He was close and she found it difficult to breathe. And his hand resting high on her waist, just under her breast, was giving off a scalding heat.

There was some vague knowledge that he was toying with her, trying to shock her. Despite his tender courtship today, she must remember Magnus was the infamous Earl of Rutherford, of whom she had heard so much ill....

Dear Reader,

If you've never read a Harlequin Historical, you're in for a treat. We offer compelling, richly developed stories that let you escape to the past—by some of the best writers in the field!

We are delighted with the return of Jacqueline Navin, who is quickly becoming known for her wonderfully stormy Medieval tales with "to-die-for" heroes. Her first Regency, *A Rose at Midnight,* has the same passion and charm. When the powerful, roguish Earl of Rutherford thinks he is dying, he finds a wife to have his child. A penniless countess marries him because she secretly needs the money to care for her ailing brother. Neither realize that their fateful marriage of convenience will blossom into a profound love....

For Love of Anna by Sharon Harlow is the sweet, heartwarming story of a young widow with children who finds her happily-ever-after in the arms of a cowboy who is running from his past. Elizabeth Mayne's latest Medieval tale, *The Highlander's Maiden,* features a fearless female mountain guide who, by royal decree, must join forces with a mapmaker from an enemy clan.

And don't miss *Hawken's Wife,* book three of THE WEDDING TRAIL series by RITA Award finalist Rae Muir. Here, tomboy Meggie MacIntyre falls for an amnesiac mountain man whose past life threatens their future together.

Whatever your tastes in reading, you'll be sure to find a romantic journey back to the past between the covers of a Harlequin Historical® novel.

Sincerely,
Tracy Farrell, Senior Editor

Please address questions and book requests to:
Harlequin Reader Service
U.S.: 3010 Walden Ave., P.O. Box 1325, Buffalo, NY 14269
Canadian: P.O. Box 609, Fort Erie, Ont. L2A 5X3

A Rose at Midnight

JACQUELINE NAVIN

HARLEQUIN®

TORONTO • NEW YORK • LONDON
AMSTERDAM • PARIS • SYDNEY • HAMBURG
STOCKHOLM • ATHENS • TOKYO • MILAN • MADRID
PRAGUE • WARSAW • BUDAPEST • AUCKLAND

ISBN 0-373-29047-0

A ROSE AT MIDNIGHT

Printed in U.S.A.

Books by Jacqueline Navin

Harlequin Historicals

The Maiden and the Warrior #403
The Flower and the Sword #428
A Rose at Midnight #447

JACQUELINE NAVIN

lives in Maryland with her husband and three small children, where she works in private practice as a psychologist. Writing has been her hobby since the sixth grade, and she has boxes full of incomplete manuscripts to prove it.

When asked, as she often is, how she finds time in her busy schedule to write, she replies that it is not a problem—thanks to the staunch support of her husband, who is not unused to doing the dinner dishes and tucking the kids into bed. However, finding time to do the laundry—that's the problem. Jacqueline would love to hear from her readers. Please write to her at this address: P.O. Box 1611, Bel Air, MD 21014.

To family and friends
who have held nothing back in their support of me—
thanks for all of it.

Prologue

All actual heroes are essential men,
and all men possible heroes.

Elizabeth Barrett Browning

Magnus Eddington, the sixth Earl of Rutherford, was not a nice man.

People knew this, but they were drawn to him just the same. Men admired him, for he had an easy mastery of all things masculine: financial success, an excellent seat on a horse, women vying for his attentions. What made it all the more dashedly enviable was that the young earl seemed not to expend one whit of effort in any of these accomplishments. For this reason, among others, he had his detractors. Though fair, Eddington was a hard man who had not shrunk from making an enemy or two in the pursuit of his ambitions.

As for women, they were attracted in droves, much as moths to the flame, and most times just as tragically, for he was not prone to romanticism. He was arrogant, but they forgave him; he was inattentive, but they excused. He was handsome, of course, with a fierce look about him.

Dark brows hovered over intense eyes of emerald green, glossy rich hair so dark it appeared black curled loosely down to the nape of his neck, and his face was constructed of planes and angles to lend a most appealing aspect.

This accounted for his attractiveness to women, along with the air of tragedy that surrounded him like a subtle scent. Those of a more sensitive nature responded to it, intrigued. Yet no one knew the cause of this darkness, for he kept his demons well hidden.

His only spot of humanity, insofar as anyone could see, was his fondness for his younger brother. David was an exuberant, good-natured fellow and as simple a soul as his sibling was not.

When the news of Magnus Eddington's fatal illness reached the ears of the London social set, it was met with a mixed reaction ranging from weeping and beating of breast to glasses raised high in triumphant salute. As for the mysterious earl himself, he ingested the results of his latest medical consultation with the expressionless equanimity for which he was so well-known. The physician, the fifth and last member of that noble profession to whom he had submitted himself for examination, delivered the unfortunate diagnosis and then sat in the ensuing silence, wriggling like a plump grub on the end of a fishing hook as he contended with the earl's strange green stare.

"There is no mistake?" The earl's voice was a rich baritone. He could raise it with tremendous effect, shaking the rafters and jarring his listener to the core. Yet, when he spoke in this soft, even tone, the quiet innuendo of threat made it all the more intimidating.

The poor doctor cleared his throat. "Ah, ah, no...that is to say, there cannot be any other conclusion, based on my examination. The evidence is persuasive, and with the history of heart ailment in your family, there is no question, I am sorry to say.''

Magnus stood. ''Then allow me to thank you, Doctor. My man will show you to the door.''

The doctor all but leapt to his feet. His hands worried at the felt brim of his hat. ''There is the matter of my fee.''

''Send me an accounting of the charges, and I will pay on the morrow. Now, if you will excuse me, I wish to be alone.''

''Yes, yes, of course. Dastardly news, to be sure. It will take some time to adjust, I expect. Yes, well then, my lord. Call upon me any time you wish. Any time a 'tall.''

''By your own prognosis, I am going to be dead before long, Doctor. Time is not something at my disposal.''

Whether from the scathing tone Magnus used, or the withering glare he threw in for good measure, the doctor's tentative smile was quelled. ''Yes, quite right.'' He moved toward the door. ''I shall leave you, now. I will send my man round tomorrow.'' He hesitated, turning back to his patient. ''May I ask, if you do not mind…what it is you plan to do now?''

Magnus bestowed his laziest scrutiny upon his guest. He wished he would leave. He wanted a drink, badly, and as reproachable as his manners were, he could not very well partake without offering the doctor a similar indulgence and Magnus had no desire for company.

The diagnosis was not a surprise. The other four physicians had rendered identical decisions. Heart ailment, the same as his father. All the information these most distinguished healers had to offer was that the trend of his decline showed no promise of relenting and would, if it continued on its current course, lead him to his grave in less than a year. It seemed there would be no answers to the why of it. Only the when.

Magnus raised his eyebrows as he forced himself to speak civilly. "What shall I do? But of course, my good man, I plan to select a wife and marry as soon as possible. Then I shall plow the wench whenever my waning energies allow and with any luck I shall beget a child on her so that when I die, a small part of me lives on."

The doctor simply gaped at him.

Magnus felt a twinge of regret at his harshness. Devil take it, why had he spoken so? he wondered. He was feeling a subtle rage, though he was not at all certain to whom it was directed. Right now, the doctor was bearing the brunt, which was unfair. It was no more this man's fault than it was his own.

"Are you serious, sir?"

Magnus grinned lazily. "Deadly. Now, Doctor, if you would leave me. I wish to be alone."

After the doctor had scurried out the door, Magnus poured himself a tall glass of whiskey, threw it back in one swallow, and filled it again. Then he walked to the fireplace and stared at the cold embers in the grate. Sweet sounds of birdsong filtered through the open windows and cheery light flooded the room, contrasting sharply with his mood. He placed a hand on the mantel, letting his fingers trace the carved stone. It was beautiful. He had never really noticed it before.

Good God, he was becoming maudlin already! He drank deeply, reducing the brown liquid by half and savoring the way it burned in his chest. Pain was life. Not pleasant, but so much better than nothingness.

Maudlin indeed.

He was a liar. He didn't wish to be alone.

Was he afraid? To his surprise, he found he was, a little. Not of death. He had to admit, this was not from any great courageousness on his part, but rather the fact of his demise still being too far off to seem real. What he was afraid of was leaving nothing of himself behind. And though it was said with a defiant bravado, every word he had uttered to the doctor had been the truth. From the time the first physician had pronounced his death sentence, he had grappled with the most fundamental urge to not quit this earth without leaving behind a trace of himself. Each doctor he consulted had stolen hope that there could be some other way to interpret the strange attacks that had begun to plague him six months ago. In its place a strong desire grew, desire for the one thing—the last and only thing—of meaning.

A child.

It was a very basic aspiration, he supposed, just one to which he had never been subject before. He had always assumed those ambitions were reserved for men more worthy than himself.

Now, the need was growing into an obsession, and with it a sense of urgency. He was dying. He had precious little time.

He abandoned the pretense of the glass and sank into a leather chair with the bottle of fine whiskey in his fist, drinking steadily until David came in.

His brother said nothing. He took the other chair, sharing the silence until Magnus spoke.

"Find her for me, David. Find me a wife."

Chapter One

Rutherford, Cambridgeshire, England 1847

With back ramrod straight and chin raised to give her courage, Caroline Wembly lifted the heavy knocker and let it fall with a resounding knell. She cast a look over her shoulder in time to see the coach and four being led away, leaving her alone in the semicircular driveway of the grand manor of Hawking Park. Turning back to the massive door, she hitched a trembling breath and waited.

Not wanting to seem gauche in front of the coachman, she had tried to appear unimpressed by the stylishness of the phaeton in which she had just ridden. Likewise, her first glimpse of the enormous house had drawn no comment from her, nor did any of the other trappings of the Earl of Rutherford's fabulous wealth. Still, she could not deny utter shock when she noticed the knocker she had just made good use of was not brass, as she had first assumed, but *gold*.

The massive portal swung inward, and a tall serious chap with a thick topping of salt-and-pepper hair stood in front of her.

"Miss Wembly?" he inquired.

She inclined her head. The man stepped backward, a sign she was to enter.

Complying, she found herself in a large circular foyer that dazzled with light from the leaded panes of countless windows. "I am Arthur," the man said in his clipped, precise tone. "The master is expecting you. Follow me, please." Dutifully, Caroline trailed after the majordomo, down the long, vaulted hallway. Silent except for the click of her heeled slippers on the marble floor, they proceeded past a row of arched embrasures housing a series of exquisite sculptures, alabaster nymphs whose writhing naked forms skated perilously close to the edges of decency. She was shocked by the sensuous bodies, and had to keep her gaze averted until they passed through a groaning set of mahogany doors and into a palatial *salon*. Arthur indicated a chair, and Caroline seated herself.

"The master shall be in momentarily," he stated. He backed out of the room, closing the door without producing the slightest sound.

Blowing out her held breath, Caroline Wembly deflated, bowing her head and almost doubling over. Gloved hands dug into the brocade upholstery at her side, finding no purchase in the stiff cushion. Throwing back her head, she breathed deeply to steady her nerves as she looked about her.

Never had she been to a place such as this! As if her present mission were not harrowing enough, finding herself amidst all this mind-numbing grandeur nearly reduced her to a quivering mass of anxiety.

Praying the earl would not be arriving too quickly, she rushed to a gilded mirror to check her appearance. The crisp swish of her skirts seemed to echo in the cavernous room. A critical perusal in the silvered glass reassured her

all was in order. She ran her hands down the clean line of
her gown, frowned, then adjusted her bosom so a generous
swelling of each breast loomed over the top. It was, of
course, unthinkable to be showing one's bosom at this time
of day, but Caroline was determined to exploit all of her
assets to the best advantage.

After all, she mused as she adjusted a blond curl at her
temple, *if one is going to act the whore, one should look
the part.*

Her eyes caught their own reflection then. Blue orbs, so
deep in color they had been called violet by more than one
admirer, appeared overlarge, dominating her tense, pinched
features. Good Lord, this would never do! She looked pet-
rified. The image staring back at her from the glass was
of a pale-faced, round-eyed waif frightened out of her wits.

No matter if it were true by half, the Earl of Rutherford
would not want an awestruck ninny. It was worry over
James, written in her face, making her appear less than her
twenty-two years. Grimacing, she narrowed her eyes and
firmly turned her thoughts to her father—that wretch! It
was he who was most to blame for her having to come
here and prostrate herself in a most humiliating fashion in
front of a stranger. As the bitterness congealed inside her
chest, she watched her wan face harden. Her soft mouth
set, her eyes turned cold.

Satisfied, she shifted her attention to her gown. This was
the one detail where she was the least sure of herself. She
had purchased it only last week from Mrs. Rensacker's
shop in London. It had stood on the rack with the other
abandoned garments which had been ordered by frivolous
patrons and never collected. The material was a deep blue
silk, a shade which provided a striking foil for her unusual
eye color, and offset the paleness of her cornsilk-colored
hair. Caroline and her mother had labored around the clock

to rework the castoff into some semblance of style and fit for her slender form. However, neither she nor her mother were clever with a needle, and the niggling fear that she would split a seam was distracting. Even with this concern, the dress was lovely, truly worth every penny.

A pang of conscience at the cost hit her hard. She had spent nearly all of the proceeds from her great-grandmother's brooch. The sadness at the loss of such a precious keepsake was overshadowed by the thought of the amount of money she had invested in this insane scheme, money they could ill afford. Reminding herself it was all for James, she pushed the regret aside. No cost was too high for him.

She gave herself a last long look, deciding that she had, after all, turned out satisfactorily.

From behind her she detected a sound: someone—a male someone—clearing his throat. She whirled…and found herself staring at a darkly clad form of a man.

He had her pinned by a pair of iridescent green eyes that seemed to glow with an inner mischief. From the cut of his clothing and the haughty expression, Caroline concluded he could be none other than Magnus Eddington, Earl of Rutherford, himself!

But this could not be the earl. This man was not what she had expected.…

In fact, he was amazingly robust for a dying man, younger than she had anticipated—perhaps a score and ten. Caroline guessed he might stand a head taller than the average male, and thus herself, for she could meet most men on eye level. The crisply starched lawn of his shirt and loosely tied cravat seemed a gratuitous semblance of civility encasing a massive chest and shoulders as broad as the mighty Atlas. A carefully tailored morning coat stretched snugly across the breadth of these assets, showing them to advantage then tapering to accentuate a narrower waist and hips. Oh yes, a man in excellent physical health to be sure. Caroline was certain she must be mistaken.

"My lord?" she asked. Her voice sounded high and unnatural in her own ears. Goodness, she had suffered a shock.

He bowed slightly, almost mockingly. "Magnus Eddington, at your service, Miss Wembly."

This *was* the earl! His face was fascinating, for there was hardness in the cut of his jaw and the contemptuous curl of his nostrils, yet the strange green eyes, held as they were in frames of sooty lashes, looked haunted and the sensuous curve of his mouth belied a soft, sensitive aspect as if twin natures were at war within him, each claiming different features. A peculiar observation, as was the certainty of mystery, of something withheld, behind the aristocratic bearing and devastatingly handsome face.

That was another surprise. Her mental image of the earl had been of a frail, sickly man prone to vanity, for she had heard rumors of his amorous conquests and questionable reputation. A popinjay, perhaps; what used to be called a "fop" in her grandmother's day. The man before her was the quintessential opposite of such a dandy, for he exuded an air of unrefined masculinity that seemed to steal across the room and entwine itself around her, choking away her courage.

And he had seen her preening like a court peacock! Ignoring the shame flooding through her, she pulled herself up into a rigid posture and met his gaze head-on. It was an old reflex; just when she felt the most vulnerable did she become the most reckless.

"Miss Wembly," he said again as he strode into the room. "Please have a seat."

She was grateful to do so, for her faux pas left her feeling off-balance. She perched on the edge of the chair and watched as he moved, as stealthily as any feline, to recline comfortably in the opposite chair. Crossing his long legs, he cocked his elbows on the tufted arms of the chair and folded his hands in front of his chin. Saying not a word, he gazed at her mercilessly until she spoke to fill the void.

"You have many beautiful pieces." Waving an arm toward a pedestal, she indicated the gorgeous sculpture set upon it. She was mortified to realize the piece was a particularly *vivid* depiction of two unclothed lovers in each other's embrace. Quickly, she returned her hand to her lap.

The half smile reappeared on his face. "Yes, I noticed you admiring them." He meant, as she well knew, that he had seen her fussing over her appearance. It was this quip which caught her up short and enabled her to regain her head.

She forced herself to sit back in her seat and return his stare with what she hoped was a look of defiance. She would be damned if she would flutter and gab to fill the silence. After all, it was *his* interview. Let him take the lead.

Best not to think how desperately she wanted, *needed,* to win this position. How odd, to think of it that way, but it was the truth. She was applying for the position of his wife and future mother of his heir.

Forcing aside discomfort, she sat unmoving under that strange stare of his until he finally spoke.

"Please tell me about yourself, Miss Wembly."

She had prepared for this. "My name is Arabella Caroline Wembly, but I have been called Caroline since birth. I am twenty-two years old. I was born in London, and have lived there since I was a babe. My father was the second son of a marquess, and made his money in shipping, so we were somewhat well-off, though by no means wealthy. I was educated by a governess until the age of eleven, when I was sent to—''

"Why are you unmarried at such an age as twenty-two?" the earl interrupted.

The question was insufferably rude. Yet in this strange, almost absurd situation, common courtesies could not stand unaltered. Caroline drew in a bracing breath and answered. "I did have two seasons when I was seventeen and eighteen, but no one caught my fancy."

"But I'll wager you caught theirs, did you not?" He moved suddenly, leaning forward to peer at her more intently. How like a cat his movements were. A cat eyeing its prey. "How many marriage proposals did you receive?"

"Several," Caroline countered curtly.

"Several, meaning two? Or several meaning twenty?"

Caroline glared at him. The maddening way his gaze held her almost as tightly as a stifling embrace wore on her nerves. She notched up her chin and said, "I received nine marriage proposals, my lord."

"Good heavens!" he exclaimed, but she could see he was pleased at having baited her so well. "And did none suit?"

"No, my lord."

"May I ask why not?"

She gritted her teeth. "No, my lord, you may not."

He was deciding whether to anger or be amused, she could see. Damn him, and his impertinent questions. She wanted this so badly, but already he was prompting a most unattractive aspect of her nature to assert itself—pride.

He finally shrugged. "I was merely curious. Now, tell me, Miss Wembly, how is it you came to hear of my...predicament?"

This too, she had anticipated. "A friend of mine who is acquainted with a clerk in your solicitor's office was told your lawyer was making inquiries as to young ladies of good breeding and poor situation to consider a marriage of convenience. As I matched that description, I went round to see Mr. Green and eventually was persuaded to make my application."

She was surprised she could say all of this without fluster, for thinking of the studious grilling she had submitted herself to under that vile Caractacus Green was most unpleasant.

Think of James, she reminded herself, and managed a smile.

"Ah, good. I instructed him to be discreet. I am already the target of much gossip. Pray tell, what precisely *is* your unfortunate situation."

Caroline cast her eyes downward. It was not difficult to speak of her circumstances, but she must tread carefully, for the full reason behind her presence here today, he must never know. "Upon my father's death, my mother found his estates heavily mortgaged, and after the debts were settled, there was no annuity to provide for us. We had to sell our house and lease apartments in a modest neighborhood." She did not explain about her father's gambling debts, nor did she recount how the creditors had descended upon the house, swarming like a cloud of vultures and plucking up valuables like apples from a tree, before it, too, was taken. "I am presently employed at a bookseller's shop. There is no longer any money for my portion, so marriage to a man of breeding is out of the question."

He took all of this in, nodding as if he understood. He did not. No one could. Who could imagine what it was like to see one's life disassembled before one's eyes?

"All of your erstwhile suitors deserted you, did they?"

he said in a quiet voice that was almost compassionate. "Which leaves you to come to me, a man who will be dead within the year, most likely. A stranger, and a well-known reprobate at that. Which brings up an interesting point." He cocked his head to one side, affecting a look of helpless appeal. "Which of the rumors about me, if any, have reached your ears? It is important to clear the air of these matters, so please, feel free to tell me."

He was trying to charm her, and she had to admit the lopsided smile and soft-eyed expression were incredibly bemusing. Even as she named it for the manipulation it was, her heart started to beat faster.

"I have heard nothing," she lied. She didn't even care if he knew it.

They were interrupted just then by the arrival of a troop of servants.

"I took the liberty of ordering tea, as I assumed you would be in need of refreshment after your journey. Tell me, how do you find the accommodations at the Barrister's Ordinary?" He relaxed now, leaning back as the butler and a pair of maids rolled in the cart and began spreading all the essentials on the teakwood table between them.

"Very fine, my lord. It is a lovely inn."

"I trust your journey from London was not too tiresome."

"Not at all."

"Would you do me the honor of pouring out?"

Caroline almost groaned, fearful her hand would tremble and not only betray her inner feelings, but scald the man whom she was so trying to impress.

And not doing a very good job of it, she thought miserably. How she would have liked to stand right now and stalk out of this place with her dignity intact, but so very much counted on this...

Thankfully, she did not disgrace herself. After the servants had laid out silver teapot, sugar, creamer along with two sets of china cups and saucers so thin she could almost see through them, Caroline determinedly took hold of the pot and poured two perfect cups of tea.

Giving silent thanks for that small miracle, she settled back.

"So, you have heard none of the gossip, eh?"

"No, my lord."

"Not even the duel on the continent? I must say, I like that one. Rather dashing, I think. Completely preposterous, of course, but amusing."

"Oh?" she queried, angling a look up at him as she stirred cream into her tea.

"You will hear a number of things about me, most, if not all of them, unflattering. I am what they call a controversial figure, that is to say my associates cannot decide whether I am a rogue or a scoundrel or a bounder or a cad. The truth is I am all of these, and none, if you will allow such a statement to stand without explanation. Those who hold a good opinion of me will no doubt regale you with my virtuous qualities, none of which I can think of at the moment. Others, in fact most, would frighten you witless with tales of my misdeeds. It is, of course, relevant to mention the rumors of my criminal nature are greatly exaggerated."

Indeed, she had heard plenty about this man, including the incredible claim that he had been Queen Victoria's first crush. Some said it was for wanting of him the young monarch went into decline just before she met and married her precious Albert, and that she had allowed the earl to affectionately call her "Drina," a nickname from her childhood when she was the impoverished, isolated Princess Alexandrina Victoria. Caroline laid her silver spoon on the fine bone saucer. "And what of the 'duel on the continent?'"

He laughed, revealing the flash of strong white teeth and eyes that crinkled merrily and…impossible! Yes, there was one dimple in his right cheek. A dimple! The summation of all those attributes left her nearly breathless. Her cup stalled on its way to her lips and her mouth stayed open as she stared.

He really was a splendid-looking man! So, why had he found it so difficult to find a bride, even if he was dying—which was difficult to believe in and of itself, for never had she seen a man so hale and hearty. Surely a few score besotted souls would have vied for the privilege of easing his last days on earth and bringing forth his child.

"The duel," he said, raising one dark eyebrow in a rakish manner, "never took place. The story goes that a certain gentleman, with whom I had a…shall we say, *disagreement,* challenged me to a contest of pistols, and we traveled to the continent in order to do the thing legally. There, it is told, we chose our weapons, paced off the deadly field, and I killed him in cold blood. Depending on the teller, you may have heard versions where I spit on his corpse, or spent the following sennight in an orgy of carousing to celebrate the poor chap's demise."

She had to give him credit. He certainly hadn't stinted on the details. If she had been ignorant of this particular tale, which she was not, he had done a fair job of relating it.

"None of it is true." He was momentarily distracted by a small particle of lint on his arm. He frowned at it, pinched it between his thumb and forefinger and set it adrift on the air. "It is based on fact. A certain gentleman accused me of improper behavior with his wife. He did challenge me to a duel, and he did die on the continent while I was also there, but that is where the verity of the tale ends. In actuality, the chap went to Provence where I was supposed to have been visiting friends, for he intended to catch me there and throw down the gauntlet. I was still in Paris, however, and while searching me out, he fell in with a band of miscreants who slit his throat for the purse he held. Since attaching the murder to me was much more romantic, I am afraid the gossipmongers had their way, and it became a much more exciting story.''

Now it was Caroline's turn to question him. ''Would you have fought him, had he caught up with you?''

His expression was only a little surprised. He blinked, then smiled. ''I do not know, Miss Wembly. I suppose so. I am only glad I did not have to find out. Contrary to my reputation, had I needed to kill him in order to protect myself, I would not have enjoyed it. After all, the man was half-mad with grief.'' He paused, adding in a softer, almost penitent voice, ''and he did have cause...''

He seemed to catch himself, jerking his gaze back to her. Caroline took a long, thoughtful moment to sip her tea.

She peered at him over the gilded rim of the cup, her lashes shielding her eyes as she studied him. ''So then you do have a conscience?'' she asked.

''Now, there is no cause to be insulting,'' he replied as he shifted in his seat. Giving her a sideways glance, he added, ''I thought you said you had not heard tell of my vile nature.''

Caught off guard, she had to confess. ''I suppose I did hear a few things. I thought it unkind to mention it.''

He was staring at her again over his interlaced fingers. She hated herself for fidgeting, but she couldn't help it.

''How wise.''

She inclined her head in a regal fashion. She could

swear it amused him, drat the man. It seemed no matter how she tried, she could not manage to get the upper hand.

He continued, a smile toying with the corners of his mouth. "I offer this information, for it is important you have an understanding of my character as we are about to enter into a most...*intimate* business arrangement, and these matters are inarguably pertinent."

"It is kind of you to explain," Caroline stated. She caught the flash of pride in his eyes, could almost hear his thoughts: *Magnus Eddington does not explain himself to anyone!* She smiled, deceptively demure.

She had provoked him, it seemed. His brows slanted down wickedly as he leaned forward, rubbing his thumb and forefinger along his chin. "Tell me more about yourself, Miss Wembly. I hardly feel you have disclosed the equal of what I have shared with you, and it is I who am the one to make the choice of *your* suitability."

"I have told you of myself, all there is to tell." Setting down her cup, she was uncomfortably aware of the way his eyes could bore into her, seemingly able to plumb the depths of her thoughts and bare her secrets. She looked away.

"Your answer as to why you wish to marry a complete stranger was incomplete. In short, you never said why it is you desire to enter into this...what did Mr. Green call it? Ah, yes. 'Odd alliance.'"

She forced herself to face him calmly, but her hands grabbed fistfuls of the lovely blue silk dress as she said simply, "Money."

He liked her directness, she surmised, for he whooped in delight and rocked back in his chair. "And what, pray tell, do you wish with my money?"

It was a laughing matter, was it? Her temper raced hot and dangerous. How well the wealthy were amused by the grasping need of the less fortunate. They never had to go hungry, had they? Or wear dresses that hung threadbare and short, so tight across a burgeoning breast it was almost impossible to breathe. Or bury all dignity and come to an earl's house and offer oneself like a brood mare for a chance at life for someone they loved.

Her bitterness almost choked her. "Why does anyone need money?" she spat. "To buy things."

Things like medicines. Things like life for a dying child.

He narrowed his eyes, those seemingly omnipotent orbs that saw all. Good God, she had gone too far!

She would be foolish to forget her precarious position. Oh, what had made her think she could do this? She was hardly the deferential type—the very kind of woman whom the earl would desire, she had no doubt. Swallowing hard, she began to stutter an apology.

The earl cut her off. "Do not! Groveling does not become you." Stunned, she snapped her mouth shut. "I am not displeased by your strong character. It is an asset, for my son will need a firm hand to guide him through life since I will not be able to do it. I am not looking for an agreeable partner for myself, Miss Wembly, but a surrogate for myself in my child's life."

There was something chilling about his casual tone when speaking of his own death. It stopped her.

"You are being interviewed for the position of mother for my son, nothing more, nothing less."

Worried at this statement, she asked, "What if the child is female?"

"She will be likewise endowed with my fortune."

"What if there is no child?"

An odd look passed over his features. Pain. "It would be regrettable, but we can hardly control all of it, can we? We must merely do our best, and leave the rest to the

Almighty. Which brings me to the rather delicate matter of lovemaking.''

The word made her start. She actually jumped and a small sound like a tiny squeak escaped her. As if to calm her, the earl held his hands up. ''It must be discussed. I need to know the prospect of being intimate with me is not, how shall I put this? *Distasteful?*''

Suddenly, the swell of flesh gushing over her décolletage felt glaringly conspicuous and completely too much. She couldn't stop staring at his hands. They were large, capable, callused—now how did an aristocrat acquire calluses?—and wondered what it would be like to have him touch her, hold her in the manner in which, as she understood it, a husband holds a wife. He was not a tender man. Submitting to him…that way, well, it could be unpleasant, she imagined. Yet her blood raced and a strange heat stole up her neck as she continued to stare.

Thankfully, he did not seem to notice her inconvenient diversion. ''It must be stated openly that though this is a marriage of convenience for both of us, there can be no question of separate bedrooms or continued chastity. Nor, until my death, shall there be any lovers, discreetly met or otherwise. Are you agreed?''

She snapped her head up, focusing on his handsome face. Taking refuge in a haughty look, she answered, ''Sir, I assure you I am well aware of the process by which babes are made. I would not have troubled you with my application in the first place if I were not prepared to submit to such doings, knowing as I do the importance of a child to be conceived before your death.''

He eyed her speculatively. ''You say you are knowledgeable about the act of sex. I must respectfully inquire if you are a virgin.''

She bristled. "I said I was aware of the process, not an expert. Yes, my lord, I assure you I am a virgin."

"Good," he asserted, "there can be no question of another man's child precluding the conception of my seed. And now, I must inquire if you are in good health."

"I am."

"Is there any history of madness in your family?"

"No, my lord."

"I will require a detailed accounting of your family history. Do not worry, I shall commission an agent to research it. I merely ask you to cooperate fully with him."

This was good news. She had much in her family heritage to recommend her. She just hoped he didn't dig too deep and find out about James.

He continued, "Again I must broach a delicate topic. Are females in your family prone to ill health? Are they typically fertile? Do you have what the doctors refer to as 'childbearing' hips?"

Caroline did not blink. He had only inquired as to the health of the *females* of her family and so she could answer honestly, "No, yes. And…" Realization of his last query dawned. Had he actually inquired about her *hips?* "I—I do not know." She paused, struggling with a hot flush of humiliation and an overwhelming urge to… She lost the battle. "Would you like to examine my teeth?"

Good Lord, there was that smile again. Devastating. "Perhaps later," he drawled.

She had the notion she had impressed him favorably, this in spite of her many gaffes. He was staring at her again, with that same intent concentration. It was most disturbing, as was its potent effect on her. She found herself trembling, her body atingle, and her heart seemed not to want to beat a steady rhythm. She was acutely aware of him as a *man.*

All of a sudden, she was very angry with herself. Why, she was behaving like an idiot! How well she knew the temperament of men, having been adequately acquainted with the dominant sex through the example of her father. At his knee she had learned of the callow nature of the male beast, his selfishness, his inability to allow another's need to supersede his most capricious whim.

Yet this man, with bald need and strangely pained eyes and soft mouth made her feel so strange, sparking to life something unidentifiable, yet not unpleasant. No, not unpleasant. But frightening all the same.

"Well," he said somewhat loudly, slapping his thighs and rising, "I must say, I am most pleased with our interview, Miss Wembly. May I have the references I requested? Ah, thank you. These appear to be in order. Yes, well, I shall be in contact with you as soon as the tasks are completed."

She rose, taking her cue to leave. The interview was over, and amazingly, he was telling her he would be proceeding to the next step.

"Thank you for seeing me, my lord," she said, moving to the door. As she did so, it was necessary to pass close to the earl, who seemed to be watching her with that unusual feral look he favored. As she did so, she caught a breath of his scent—a hint of soap from his morning shave and masculinely pleasant. It was then she was aware of a pressure at her waist as his large hands came to rest at the place where her skirts just started to swell. She jerked her head around, too shocked at first to protest. Firmly, he ran his hands down along the gentle flare of her hips.

"Slim," he murmured, his lips only inches from hers. "Hmm. I must speak to the doctors about this."

Outrage crept upon her as she realized he was groping her to feel if she had hips wide enough for birthing! Without thinking, she drew back her hand and let it fly, landing a smart slap upon his left cheek. His head snapped back, but otherwise he did not react.

They both froze. Caroline was horrified by what she had done—what he had done, was still doing, in fact, for his hands remained on the sides of her derriere.

Through gritted teeth, she snapped, "I am afraid I will not permit a trial tumble, my lord. I come to you a virgin, and will remain so until properly wed."

His breath fanned her face as he laughed softly. "I expected a fiery answer, and you do not disappoint me. Quite right, a proper mother of the future Earl of Rutherford should never allow a man to handle her so." This said, he stepped back, releasing her. "Still, those hips are quite narrow... Ah, I shall speak to the authorities on these matters and decide. Until then, I trust you will be well taken care of at the inn."

Every nerve screamed to unleash another blow and wipe that infuriating look off his face. Instead she calmly met his eye. "As you wish, my lord."

He laughed at her docility, seeing it for the act it was. "You are a spitfire, Miss Wembly, and I think you could give me a fine, spirited boy." He reached out and picked up a small bell from the table beside her and rang it.

"Arthur will show you out. I look forward to our next encounter, Miss Wembly." He bowed. "Until then."

Arthur materialized in the doorway and waited for his charge.

"Thank you, my lord," Caroline said and followed the manservant out of the room.

And there it was, all so very correct. A perfectly respectable farewell. Who would have thought they had just discussed her virtue, bandied about the topic of lovemaking and suffered through gropes and blows?

As Arthur arranged for the carriage to be brought round, Caroline cast a look about her. The magnificence of Hawking Park no longer daunted her, for it could not hold a candle to the man who owned it.

Chapter Two

When the earl's phaeton dropped her at the door of the Barrister's Ordinary, Caroline headed straight through the common room and up the stairs. She knew her mother and brother would be anxious for her return.

The Earl of Rutherford had arranged for a suite of rooms for Caroline's use. The parlor and two bedrooms were welcoming and infinitely pleasant after the crowded place where they had been living in London's meanest section.

Inside the room, Caroline only glanced at the small, thin woman by the window before moving quickly to the bed. James was sitting up, propped with a half-dozen goose down pillows behind him. His blue eyes sparkled with excitement. The splash of color from his auburn curls was beautiful against the crisp white linen. Every tense line of his small body spoke of his anticipation, as did the brilliant smile he gave her when she entered. From her spot by the window, Caroline's mother took a step forward, as if to intercept her daughter, then stopped. Her hands grasped one another under her breasts as she looked her over.

Avoiding her mother's assessing gaze, Caroline sat on the bed. "Well, how are you doing?" she said cheerfully

as she took the seven-year-old's hands in hers. "You look
wonderful. Did you eat today?"

"I felt grand today. I ate a whole bowl of porridge and
even some cheese," James answered. He was exuberant,
a state which delighted Caroline. His small face had a flush
of color and the dark circles under his eyes had faded
considerably. "I think it was all the excitement. It made
me hungry. Now, please Cara, tell me what happened. Are
you going to be a countess?"

Feigning a lighthearted laugh, Caroline gave her
brother's hands a reassuring squeeze. "It went well,
James." She darted a glance up at her mother, who still
stood motionless, before she continued. "Very well indeed. The earl said he wanted to examine our family and
contact the references I gave him, but otherwise I believe
he was favorably impressed."

Audrae Wembly gasped and turned away, her short
steps clicking loudly on the bare floor. James glanced over,
then leveled a wizened look at his sister. "She doesn't
know if she should be happy or sad," he explained solemnly. "She doesn't want you to have to marry him, but
we need the money."

A feeling so powerful it was almost blinding came over
Caroline—pure love, exquisitely bittersweet. It actually
hurt.

They often teased James about being an "old soul," for
he had wisdom and perception beyond his years. Perhaps
it came from so many years of illness, or from the unhap-
piness in their home when Father was alive. However he
had accomplished such uncanny maturity, it never ceased
to amaze and humble his sister. It frightened her as well,
for she could not help but think—only at night and when
she was feeling particularly anxious—that a child as

unique and wondrous as James was too unearthly, too perfect, too precious to dwell long in this world.

"Yes, perhaps," she replied, "but had you seen Hawking Park, James, you would know there is no cause for any such reservation."

"Is it very beautiful?" he asked excitedly. "More beautiful than here?"

"Yes, it is. It is the most grand place I have ever seen. Why, it is like a palace." She told him all about it, the towering columns and marble floors and beautiful objets d'art wherever you looked. She even told him about the unclothed nymphs, which made him gasp in shock and clamp a small hand over his mouth. Delighted giggles escaped just the same, warming Caroline's heart.

If she had any misgivings about today's business, they were gone now that she was in the company of her brother. He listened with rapt attention, asking only the occasional question as he digested all of the details as if it were some fantastic fairy tale come true.

Caroline noticed he was most keenly interested in the character of the earl himself.

"I wonder why he does not appear ill," he mused, his brow furrowed. "You did not discuss his sickness?"

With a start, Caroline realized she did not even know the nature of the malady which afflicted the earl. "You know, I didn't think to. I suspect I was a bit overwhelmed. It is a good thing I have you to remind me. I shall ask him the next time we meet."

His little chest puffed up, so pleased was he that he had been of service. "When will that be?" he inquired.

She could see from the heaviness of his eyelids James was starting to tire. She tousled his hair. "He told me he will review my references, and I suppose there is the family to be looked into. When these things are accomplished, he will send for me.''

''Oh, Cara! How can you wait? I wish to know right now if we are going to live in a palace!''

Caroline glanced nervously at her mother, who looked away. She had not mentioned James to the earl, and with very good reason. In order to make the best appearance possible, she had decided that the earl should not know about him. Oh, certainly his inquiries would reveal that she had a brother, but it was almost impossible for him to learn of James' consumption. It was imperative that he not know of it. Not only did she fear that if her possible future husband thought her encumbered with such a heavy family obligation as a sick child, he would look disfavorably on her, thinking perhaps that she would not be able to devote herself completely to her own child, but there was also the question of James' illness tainting the purity of her heredity.

''You are tiring,'' Caroline said. ''I'll wager you did not nap all day, did you? Now, rest, my darling, and when you wake, we'll talk more.''

Yawning, James protested. ''But I'm not tired at all.''

''No? Hmm. Perhaps I was wrong then. Well, settle back and I shall tell you more.'' Caroline smiled, softly speaking of the sleek phaeton and the other wonders of the day as she rubbed gentle circles at his temple. It was an old trick discovered when James was a babe. He could never seem to keep his eyes open for long when sleepy and the featherlight touch was applied to the side of his face. Within minutes, his eyes drifted shut and his breathing slowed, deepened, as he slipped into sleep.

''Thank goodness,'' Audrae whispered beside her. ''He refused to rest. He was so determined to be awake when you returned.''

"I'm glad he was able to do it. They are so important to him, these little victories."

The two women exchanged a long look. Without speaking, Audrae turned to leave. Caroline lingered, gazing at the angelic face of her brother. His cheeks were flushed, his small mouth like a tiny rosebud. His lashes were dark where they lay like small fans against his cheek. She frowned as she fingered his red-gold curls. His hair was too long. She must see about cutting it for him....

Her fingers froze and she withdrew her hand. A pain that was jagged and familiar lanced through her body. Her eyes blurred, obscuring the vision of James cradled in slumber, such an innocent, so very precious and fragile—she *had* to marry the earl. They needed the money so desperately!

Blinking away the moisture from her eyes, Caroline followed her mother into the other room.

"Now," Audrae said definitively as she closed the door, "tell me about him."

Caroline drew in a deep breath. Her mother was a good five inches shorter, and slight of frame, yet she held herself with an air of uncompromising authority that brooked no hesitation. She had been a beauty of renown in her day, whose looks had weathered a disastrous marriage well, but not unscathed. Her once fiery hair was now almost gray and lines of worry had been etched across her brow and around her mouth. Still a handsome woman, strong and sharp, she nevertheless wore the burdens of her unhappy life.

"He was very forthright, Mother. He conducted the interview like any for a position for hire, asking me pertinent questions and offering some explanations as to his own character." She recalled some of those questions, then went on quickly, "He explained his need to foster an heir, as he has had no issue. He was polite overall, if a bit challenging at times. I have no idea how many women he has interviewed, but I believe I did well. He even said so.''

Her mother's shrewd eyes missed nothing. "Why did you blush just now?''

Caroline silently groaned. By nature a private person, she could however never keep a thing from her mother. Except one secret. The darkest secret of all she had kept in utter solitude for ten years.

"I am afraid the position of wife—or more precisely mother of his future heir—did necessitate some unorthodox topics of conversation.''

Her mother's eyes snapped wide. "Did he make untoward suggestions?''

"No, no, nothing like that, Mother. He did ask some…unconventional questions regarding…well, my virtue.'' At her mother's incensed look, Caroline rushed, "Which was completely understandable, given I could be a woman who found herself in an inconvenient *condition*, and saw this as an excellent way to salvage her name and bring legitimacy to her unborn babe.''

Audrae narrowed her eyes. "What other improprieties did he commit?''

Caroline waved her hand ineffectually in the air, trying to appear casual. "He wanted to know about my hips.''

"You…your…he…hips?''

"You know, for birthing the babe,'' Caroline explained, attempting for all the world to sound as if this were the most natural curiosity for any prospective husband.

Her mother was still sputtering when Caroline let her shoulders slump and gave up. "Oh, all right, if you must know it was wretched. But Mother, what does it matter? It could have been far worse, and still I cannot regret it. We have been given a marvelous opportunity. And the earl was not bad, not at all. A tad arrogant, perhaps, and more than a little imperious, but had he been a demon I would still wed him and gladly.''

Audrae controlled her trembling lip with a quick sniff. She held her hands out for her daughter. Caroline moved into the embrace. It was familiar and soothing. She lay her head upon the slight shoulder, remembering the comfort that coveted place had afforded her through the years. Yet, now it seemed so small.

Audrae smoothed the silken strands of Caroline's hair and sighed. ''Ah, my beautiful child. I wanted so much for you, so much more than this.''

''Hush, Mother,'' Caroline said bravely, pulling away with back straight and chin held high. ''We are blessed to have this chance to save James. So, don't think of it as any hardship for me. Think upon how wonderful it all is.''

Her mother gazed at her with eyes shining. She opened her mouth to speak, then thought better of it and simply smiled, nodding, then turning away. ''I have waited luncheon for you, Cara.''

''Very good.'' In truth, Caroline was not the least bit desirous of food. What she wanted more than anything was to be by herself. To think. To ingest what had happened this morning at Hawking Park, let it settle in her brain. To reflect on the enigmatic and incorrigible man who just might become her husband.

Hawking Park was dark when the midnight hour struck, save for a miserly gas lamp in the library which was turned way down low. Magnus prowled among the shadows, traveling the length of the book-lined shelves, rounding, then heading back to his desk. The remains of his meal were littered among an untidy scatter of papers. He picked up a particular document, brushed off some crumbs and fingered it thoughtfully. Miss Wembly's preliminary history, he saw. He had read it already, twice in fact. Tossing it back onto the desk, he watched dispassionately as it fluttered onto the mess of documents like a feather settling after a brisk ride on the wind.

He sighed, turned away and refilled his glass with three fingers of whiskey. It burned its way down to his stomach, warming him.

Miss Wembly. Just a girl, really. Only twenty and two, she had said. Not so very young, then, but making him feel, at three and thirty, like he was robbing the cradle.

Well, he thought as he threw back the last drops of his drink, *turnabout is fair play. After all, she is robbing the grave!*

God, he was in a foul mood tonight. He sat down at his desk and shuffled through the papers, thinking the work would distract him. It didn't.

Why was he feeling like smashing every priceless object in the house? He should be delighted! The report on Miss Wembly was promising. He had been given a thorough review of her background—quite august—her family— blessedly small, and her character. Everything had shown her to advantage. This was a tremendous relief after the two applicants he had interviewed so far. Completely unacceptable, both of them. One, a thin wisp of a woman who looked as if the sight of her own shadow would send her into fits, and the other a strange, quirky girl of good breeding who had the annoying habit of twisting her nose, as if she were smelling something foul. Miss Wembly was far and away the best candidate.

Not only that, but he was favorably impressed with the woman herself. Perhaps too much so. He might as well admit it. Might as well also admit he had known she was the one from the first.

Well maybe not from the *very* first. When he had caught her gazing at her own reflection, he assumed she was some vapid, inadequately-bred chit. What he found on subsequent acquaintance was a woman who could match his wit. A woman who wanted his money, but was brave enough to say so directly. She had not breached propriety, yet neither had she fainted when he had laid his hands on her, showing herself able to handle herself in difficult situations.

And she could set his blood on fire.

That was what had him on edge tonight. Miss Wembly.

Lovely Miss Wembly, who dressed like a siren, acted the prig and yet looked at him with such challenge. An excellent choice to bear his child.

Miss Wembly who could tempt a saint with her pouting mouth and flashing eyes and who was—damn her—making him feel a new and terrible dread of leaving this world.

He pushed the thought away, crossed quickly to the decanter and splashed more whiskey in his glass. He downed it in a single swallow.

He must not think of dying. He would lose his focus, his mission. He would lose himself.

Glancing at the stack of papers on his desk, he swiped them off with a growl. Dishes and scraps of food scattered onto the floor, ruining the documents.

It made no difference. Caroline Wembly would be his wife. Waiting had merely been a formality, and his investigation of her halfhearted. It did not matter if a dozen full-blooded princesses wanted the position. He had decided. Miss Wembly's mother could sport a cockney accent and her dead father turn out to be a fishmonger, and still Magnus knew he would have no other.

Impatiently, he unfastened the studs at his collar, opening the fine lawn shirt to midchest. He was growing warm.

Perhaps he had drunk too much. Even as he thought it, he knew otherwise.

His suspicion was borne out when he began to sweat and his stomach curled gently, a teasing premonition of what was to come.

This is how it always started. His pulse quickened, as if his blood had grown thick and unwieldy in his veins. His heart felt ready to burst out of his chest, he struggled to his feet. He needed to call Arthur. Assessing his position quickly, he saw he was closer to the door than to the bell-pull.

He made his way to the hallway, advancing only a few steps before he was able to go no farther. Cursing himself for waiting too long to summon help, he stumbled as his legs began to buckle. He was falling. Reaching out, he grabbed at a marble pedestal, knocking it askew and bringing the Chinese vase which had been set upon it down with him. The sound of it breaking into countless shards was satisfying, and sufficient to wake the entire house. He smiled wryly. He had been wanting to break something all night.

A young parlor-maid, Wendy, was the first to arrive. Arthur was fast on her heels, barking for her to return to her room. The manservant called for two burly footmen who hurried out of the attics in their nightshirts. With the efficiency and care of much practice, they hauled Magnus to his feet and bore him to his rooms.

"Get me the chamber pot," Magnus managed to say. Arthur cleared the room, locked the door and brought his master the basin, holding it as Magnus retched in violent spasms. He was on fire, feeling as if his skin were suddenly too small for his organs. It was a nasty attack, one of the worst. How many more would he endure? When he felt well, he could scarcely fathom the fact that he was ill, but in these moments when his whole being screamed in torment, he knew with certainty he would not survive long.

Arthur gave him his paltry measure of laudanum. The beneficial effects set in immediately. The valet was summoned and undressed his master, laying Magnus carefully on the bed. Cool cloths were placed on his feverish skin. He slept, occasionally waking to vomit and shiver and wait until it was safe to administer another dose of soothing medication.

It went on like this throughout the night and most of the next day. In his waking moments, Magnus could think only of the woman who had sat with him in the grand salon. He feared he would never have the chance to act on the carnal desires which she stirred in his blood, making him crave a lifetime of such pleasures as she offered. Worse, if he died now, he would not be given the opportunity to lay his seed in her belly to take root and bring forth his redemption.

Chapter Three

Magnus straightened the pile of papers on his desk before answering the knock at his study door. "Come," he said, leaning back in the tufted leather chair and watching as the slender woman entered. He smiled. "Miss Wembly."

"My lord."

"Please have a seat." He indicated one of the two tapestry chairs situated in front of his massive desk.

She was dressed more soberly today, and Magnus was grateful her décolletage was more in keeping with convention. A modest fichu of starched lace frothed at her throat, crowning a simple gown of fawn muslin. He would not be distracted by that enticing swell of exposed breasts, at least. Yet, his mind savored the taunting memory even as the corners of his mouth drew down in disappointment.

"Thank you for coming so promptly," he stated without inflection. "I have completed my investigation of your application, and can inform you…" Here he paused, conscious that this was no way to propose to a woman. "Of my decision to accept you as my wife."

She was silent. Stunned, probably, but she recovered quickly. "Th-thank you, my lord."

She didn't smile. He wanted to see her smile. Ever since

he had first laid eyes on her a week ago, he had wondered what that gorgeous face would look like lit up with laughter. He had seen her angry, wary, prideful and bristling with indignation, but he had not seen a whisper of happiness on those striking features.

"Are you not pleased, Miss Wembly?" he drawled.

"Yes, I am, of course, my lord."

"You seem as if I just asked you if you would stop stepping on my foot."

A faltering smile, which was worse than her seriousness, appeared. "I apologize. I suppose I was simply surprised. I thought it would take longer."

"I began the necessary inquiries when your application was first made. Other than your family history, everything I require has been completed, and after some preliminary investigation, I have decided not to pursue it. I really do not see the need to wait, as time is of the essence."

Her mouth made a small O, but she said nothing.

"I have taken the liberty of applying for a special license from the Archbishop of Canterbury, who is an excellent friend. The dispensation will be granted posthaste, and we will be free to marry anytime after that. I would, of course, wish to have the ceremony soon so that we may begin our wedded life."

His pulse quickened just thinking about the implications of those words. He could see she was reacting too, a little, by the pink tinge which spread up her neck to those delicate ears.

My God, he was like a randy youth hot after his first woman. In fact, his body was responding much as it had in his adolescence at the sight of a desirable female. He was grateful he was seated safely behind the desk.

Her next words offered another explanation for the

pretty flush of color. "There are some arrangements I need to discuss, of course. Financial arrangements."

Like ice water, those words killed his brewing desire. "Of course," he said crisply. He withdrew a document from a stack of files. "You remember Mr. Caractacus Green, the solicitor handling this transaction? I have asked him to draw up an agreement by which all will be made clear to you. In addition, I am giving you a copy of my will, so that you will know exactly the settlement I have arranged for you and the child upon my death."

"And if there is no child?"

His mouth tensed. "You will be given a generous annuity, which I have arranged with David, who will inherit the title. It is all explained here." He proffered the document.

Slender hands reached out and took it from him. She perused it. "It does not mention a specific amount."

Coldness settled in deeper. "No," he said. "We can amend that if you prefer. I simply thought we would leave it open. I do not imagine there are any expenses I cannot afford. However, if you feel the need to have it stipulated clearly..."

"I do," she nodded definitely. "What amount had you in mind?"

He laced his fingers in front of his chin, regarding her steadily for a moment. "You name a figure."

She was startled, and he grinned maliciously. He wanted her off guard, uncertain.

His glee at forcing her to ask for a monetary amount was cut off when she named a figure no larger than one of his footman's salaries. She sat unmoving under his glare, and only by her preternatural stillness could he detect the crucial nature of these proceedings. He didn't understand it. Not yet. But, Lord, she did intrigue him.

He reached out his hand for the document. Taking up his quill, he inserted an addendum. "I'll double it," he stated as he scrawled the amount, still remarkably small to his way of thinking, on the contract.

When he raised his head, his heart stopped dead in his chest and his arm, halfway extended to return the document to her, suspended in midmotion. She was staring at him with the most exquisite expression, a mingling of joy and gratitude, with a sheen in her eyes as if there were tears building. He had not thought it possible for her to be lovelier than when she had hissed and spat at him like a cornered she-cat, but there it was.

After a long moment, her hand came up to take the document, and the spell was broken. He let out the breath that had caught in his throat and busied himself with shuffling papers while she read over the rest of the agreement and affixed her neat signature. He in turn impatiently scrawled his own name.

The deal was done.

"Now," he began, "there are some details which we have to contend with. Namely, the disposition of your mother. I would prefer if she did not reside at Hawking Park. I am a private man, and my illness makes me more so."

"About that," she interrupted softly, "your illness, I mean, I was wondering…that is, I do not know…"

Something gentle made him save her from the discomfiture of her question. "Is it the nature of my illness you wish to know about?" She nodded. "I am afraid I cannot tell you that, Miss Wembly." At her self-conscious glance downward, he explained, "I do not know for certain, nor do any of my physicians. My symptoms indicate a weak heart, but the weakness does not follow the usual course. It is generally agreed that it is an atypical disease of the heart. However, there is one aspect upon which there is complete agreement. The attacks are coming more frequently, more severely, and will in time result in my heart ceasing to function. Just as my father's did. It is hereditary you see—a wretched curse. How lucky for you that you come from healthy stock and have nothing to worry about.''

There was a long, broad silence. She simply returned his regard with a strange look on her face and the unexpected desire to know her thoughts registered in his brain.

''I am so sorry,'' she said at last.

God, there was true regret in her eyes! ''There is nothing to be done about my condition. As for my most profound wish, you are providing it for me, so do not apologize.'' His tone was harsh, and he immediately regretted it. ''About my condition,'' he continued, unable to disaffect the curtness in his voice, ''there is one expectation we have not discussed. I hope it will not be a hardship for you, but I will wish you to attend me during the episodes of my illness.''

She blinked, seeming to be taken aback. ''Attend you?''

''As a nurse. A companion, really, for there are servants to do the more onerous duties.'' For an instant, her gaze melted into his, and he knew she understood. He himself had not anticipated the desire to have her close to him at his death, but it was there as a sudden, urgent need to not die alone. She nodded and said, ''Of course.''

''Thank you. Now, are there any questions you have?''

''Yes. If my mother is not allowed at Hawking Park, where shall she live? I was hoping she would be provided a better home than the place where she presently resides.''

He considered her request for a moment. ''There is my London house, which is quite spacious, and a staff of servants remain year round. Also, I have a lodge in the Cumbrian Lake district. It is a more than modest residence and also comes with an intact staff.''

"Someplace close, if you please,'' she asked, biting her lip as if she hardly dared request more than was already being so generously offered.

"Hmm. Someplace close.'' He thought for a moment. "I cannot think of a thing. Unless…''

"Yes?''

"Until something suitable can be agreed upon, or until my death, I will continue to make the suite at the Ordinary available to her.''

It was then it happened. The smile he had wished for, fulfilling the promise of all he had dreamt it would be. She clasped her hands together and nodded, as if speech failed her.

It certainly failed him. There was a long pause as he studied her unguarded delight. Recovering, he cleared his throat. "Very well, I will make the necessary arrangements.''

When they had signed the papers, he called in Mr. Green, whom he had kept waiting in the parlor, much to the solicitor's obvious and abundant displeasure. The sour-faced man looked over the adjustments, giving Caroline a slow, disdainful perusal when, Magnus guessed, he came to the annotation about her allowance. Shifting his gaze to his client, Green opened his mouth and was about to say something. Magnus bestowed a quelling glare, stopping the objections before they were spoken. With a snort and a "Harumph!'', Green stuffed the papers into his portfolio.

"I shall see to these, my lord,'' he said, darting one more disapproving glance toward the future countess before taking his leave.

Caroline visibly relaxed in his absence. Catching Magnus's eye, she gave a sheepish smile. "He does not like me, I am afraid."

But I do, Miss Wembly.

"He is merely looking out for my interests," Magnus explained. "Come, I shall take you on a tour of the house. My brother said he would be arriving today, and with any luck he will be here in time to join us at luncheon."

"Oh," Caroline said, surprised.

"That is, if you do not have other plans?" He meant his tone to communicate she would certainly break any other commitments should that be the case.

"No, as a matter of fact I had nothing other than returning to the Barrister's Ordinary to take luncheon with Mother."

Pushing his chair away from his desk, he rose. "I will send a man to inform her you are spending the afternoon with me. Would that be acceptable?" Before she could agree or disagree, he came to take her elbow and proceed with her out into the corridor. "Would you care for tea now?"

"N-no," she answered. "I am not hungry just yet."

"Excellent. Then we shall start on this floor and work our way up."

She stopped. "Up?"

He turned. Her eyes, those magnificent depths which had seemed indigo or violet or some indefinable color he had never witnessed before, were in fact a deep blue shot through with swirling gray, rather like a storm cloud. Thickly fringed with dark blond lashes, they possessed a haunted, otherworldly quality. She stared at him now, her features signaling mild alarm.

He chuckled. "I assure you, Miss Wembly, I am content to wait out the week until you are my wife, properly wed.

The tour is not a ruse to compromise your sterling respectability.''

Those eyes he had just studied flashed blue fire. Ah, yes, they *were* nearly violet. ''Are you mocking me, sir?''

''Not at all. Simply trying to reassure you I am not half the reprobate I am reputed to be. Have I not acted the gentleman thus far?''

She seemed unsure. ''Yes,'' she admitted.

''See? It is just that my circumstances defy propriety's dictates. I haven't the time to import my great-aunt, who is the reigning matriarch and acknowledged authority on the family history. Thus, I must do it myself. Besides,'' he said, pausing as he gave her a lazy look, ''it will give us time to become better acquainted.''

She regarded him for a moment, her face unmoving and unreadable. At last, she said, ''Very well, my lord.''

They started in the huge, circular entryway with its two-story Palladian windows and Ionic columns. As they wandered, the earl kept up a running monologue of the history of the house.

''This is my mother's salon, which you've seen. She used to gather with her friends here each day. They were all artists and musicians—Bohemian types. That is why there is no music room, it was incorporated as part of this one. Now, down here is the grand dining room. I rarely use it.'' He paused, looking about. ''Come to think of it, I have never used it.''

He showed her the other rooms: a smaller dining room, a cozy parlor, a large mirrored ballroom with so much leaded glass and gilt it made her dizzy. He introduced her to every servant they came across and even took her into the kitchens where his appearance was met with an enthusiastic reception from Mrs. Bronson, the cook.

''Mercy, aren't you a love?'' she cooed to Caroline,

smiling and clasping her pudgy hands together. "It's wonderful, we all say. What a lovely thing, the two of you meetin' like that and decidin' to marry right off. Oh, terrible romantic it is!"

Caroline's eyes rounded and shot to Magnus. He merely grinned back at her and purred, "Yes, isn't it?"

"Oh, heavens, you poor ducky, you've gone all pink. Well, of course she has, my lord, when an old woman rattles on at her, don't ya know. All right, I'll get back to my puddings. I hope you're hungry, miss. I'm whipping up a rack of lamb."

"For luncheon?" Caroline asked, her voice almost a whisper, having not yet recovered from her former shock at hearing how she and the earl were so enamored of each other.

Magnus beamed at the older woman. "Mrs. Bronson is a wonderful cook. She loves to spoil me."

"Ah, be gone with ya." Mrs. Bronson blushed, shooing them out of the kitchen. She could be heard fussing to the scullery maids as they headed down the corridor.

"My lord?"

"Magnus."

She paused. "Pardon me?"

"Please call me Magnus. It is unseemly for you to be referring to me as 'my lord' all the time."

"Yes, well," she stammered. "I-I shall call you...M-Magnus."

She was unsure of herself, a new facet to her he had not glimpsed before, and he enjoyed the girlish way her teeth worried at her bottom lip.

"I wish you had informed me you planned to put out the story that we were...ah..."

"In love," he supplied.

"Yes, exactly."

"My dear Miss Wembly—or may I call you Caroline? I think it would be best. Caroline, why else would we wish to marry in such a hurry if not for the sheer impatience of true love?"

The dripping sarcasm in his tone caused her to flinch, and in an instant of pure understanding he knew this was a woman who had always thought to marry for that most tender of emotions. Love. Magnus was not certain if he even believed it existed. It hardly mattered, having no relevance in his life. There was duty, there was need, there was pleasure. Love was not a part of any of it.

"I see," she said, choosing her words carefully. "I am not criticizing. I only wish you had told me. I was caught unawares."

"You are correct, of course. You should have been prepared. I apologize."

She seemed relieved, and even slightly amused. "Tell me, my lord—" She stopped. *"Magnus,"* she corrected with determination, "where did we meet?"

He laughed. "Don't you recall? A mutual friend of ours in London presented us to one another at a small gathering."

They ascended the grand staircase, Magnus pointing out various paintings and describing the painter, the subject, and the manner in which each was either obtained or commissioned. It was all too much for Caroline to take in, and she told him so.

"You are not expected to learn it at once, but I should like you to try to remember as much as you can. When the child is born, he shall wish to know these things."

"Yes, of course."

"I will not bother to show all the guest rooms. Your rooms, however, you must be anxious to see. Here we are."

He swung open the double doors. They entered into a sitting room, elegant, plush, exquisitely furnished in shades of yellow and rose. "Beyond there is the bedroom, and a large dressing room which connects to my apartments. There is a water closet through there."

She was openly gaping, which satisfied Magnus. For himself, he was having a difficult time acclimating himself to his surroundings. He hadn't been in this part of the house in years. Since his mother's death. And he had lied to Caroline. His rooms were not through the connecting dressing door. He had never taken his father's place in the master's chamber, but he would have to now, as was fitting. What an irony that it was only in death he found himself worthy to do so.

He had had the room redecorated when he had first decided to take a wife, so everything, from the plush carpet to the silk draperies to the last embroidered pillow, was new. As Caroline walked about, studying this aspect or that, he waited. At last, she swung toward him, almost knocking him senseless with another of her smiles. "It is beautiful, my lord."

He felt his heart do something queer in his chest. "Magnus," he corrected, his voice almost a croak. He cleared his throat.

"Yes, I am sorry. Magnus."

He caught himself staring and said roughly, "Come. All Mrs. Bronson's talk of lamb has stoked my appetite. You will want to see the nursery before we go."

"Yes, yes of course," she said, and for the first time, Magnus saw the spark of excitement in her eye. As she passed him, he caught her scent, a gentle hint of rose water mingled with musk. His body tightened slightly, and he smiled as they continued the tour.

Chapter Four

The formal dining hall was set with leaded crystal, Limoges china, crisp linen and brilliantly polished silverware. Caroline was a bit astonished at all this fuss just for luncheon. As soon as the thought registered, she chided herself. Really, she must stop acting like an awestruck child every time the earl's wealth showed. She hoped it was not obvious, and endeavored to appear relaxed and comfortable as Arthur pulled out her chair and placed her napkin on her lap.

"The weather is quite cool," the earl said. His rich baritone carried over the length of the table. He was seated at the opposite end, gazing at her in that way he favored, with his fingers laced at his lips as if studying an intriguing specimen.

"Yes, rather," she agreed. They were served soup, and a piping hot loaf of bread was placed on her plate along with a cup of sweet butter. Her mouth watered. This alone was a meal to her—more than enough by the standards she had grown used to in the lean years since her father's death.

The earl said, "Unseasonably cool."

"Winter is not far off," she replied, picking up her spoon.

When the majordomo had gone, she heard a low chuckle. "Now that we are clear on the state of the clime, and—not incidentally—alone, perhaps we can discuss matters of some consequence."

"Yes, my lord?"

He paused, frowning. Caroline stared back at him, puzzled, until she realized what was the matter. "Pardon me. Magnus."

"Much better. You know, it sounds quite nice coming from you. Your voice is husky, as if you have a sore throat."

"I am in excellent health," she assured him.

His eyes danced. "Yes, I know, Caroline. Anyone can see that."

He was mocking her again, and she lowered her gaze to her bowl. As she ate, she heard the clatter of china and looked up to find him gathering his place setting. To her amazement, he carried his bowl and plate down to the seat on her right, returned for the other items, then settled himself at his new place.

"Much cozier, don't you think?"

"Certainly." She concentrated on her meal. "You were correct about Mrs. Bronson's cooking. This is delicious."

"Good. Now, as I was saying, there are certain matters I wish to discuss with you, namely the wedding."

She stiffened. Was he reconsidering his decision? "What about the wedding?"

His shrewd eyes narrowed. "I merely meant the details, Caroline. We must limit it to a small gathering, as there is no time to invite guests nor prepare for a gala celebration. However, I have determined it should be an occasion of note and you will be properly outfitted—" He cut off as the servants came in to collect the dishes and lay out the second course. The earl's changed seat caused some dismay, which he ignored. When the food was in place, the servers filed out, leaving them once again to themselves.

"As I was saying, I will have some sketches sent to you, and some scraps of material so you can choose a proper wedding dress. You and your mother can take care of the gown and all the other various and sundry accessories. Also, you must choose the flowers. I shall take care of arranging the ceremony and a small reception here at the house. Just your family, the parson and a few of those who live close by should suffice. And David, of course."

"David? Oh, your brother."

"Yes," he said, glancing at the clock on the sideboard. "I wonder where he is. Ah well, I shall tell you more tales of my ancestors. Boring, I know, but necessary for you to learn. Now, there was the first earl, my great-great... I cannot recall just how many greats, and in fact he was not at all great from the stories that have survived him, but my grandfather just the same."

Caroline found herself smiling. She was surprised to observe he possessed a certain charm, and she had to admit she found him more than passably engaging.

The meal was delicious. Though comfortably sated, she found she could not forego the lamb. It was spectacular, seasoned to perfection and complemented with the subtle taste of mint.

The earl continued to relate stories of his family in his quirky, almost self-deprecating way, then switched to outline his plans for her installment as his wife. He seemed to have thought of every detail. It was quite overwhelming and she was glad to let him take the lead, carefully nodding in agreement while her mind wandered.

She still had to marvel at the miracle of it all. The earl

had chosen *her.* And the best of it was that he had agreed to allow her mother—and James—to stay at the Barrister's Ordinary where they would be close by. Why, she could visit every day!

"Caroline?"

She was suddenly aware he was addressing her. "What? Oh, yes, my lord. Magnus. I am sorry, I am afraid I became a little lost."

Emerald eyes raked over her. "I suppose it is a great deal to take in at once."

"No, it is not that. I—I simply was—"

"Nonsense, Caroline, there is no need to explain. It is my terrible sense of urgency, which cannot be helped. It must cause much confusion. I shall have my secretary draw up a schedule and deliver it to you."

"Thank you."

After coffee and dessert, which was a thick slab of butter cake soaked in heavy cream and topped with fresh berries, Magnus offered to show Caroline the gardens.

"I don't know if I can move. I am afraid I am quite full," she said as he drew out her chair for her.

"Then a bit of exercise should be just the thing."

They walked through the library to the glass doors. Arthur brought in her cloak and Magnus drew it around her, the fleeting brush of his fingers on her shoulder sending a shiver coursing down her spine.

"Chilled already?" he inquired.

Did nothing escape his notice?

"Fleetingly." She gave him a smile. "I shall be fine."

"Splendid." He led her out into the flagstone porch. A soft breeze played among the turning leaves. It was only September, and although cool, the bright kiss of the sun lent a lingering memory of summer as they walked across the well-tended lawn and into the formal garden.

He pointed out the different flora, displaying acute pride in the tranquil place. From time to time he would stop to finger a wilted flower or faltering perennial. He seemed most enthusiastic about the plethora of rosebushes, blowzy things with their sagging blooms and naked branches, saying how lovely they were in the spring. It was the sadness in his voice—just a trace—which caught her attention, and Caroline was struck with the realization that he would never see them bloom again.

And suddenly her delight in her fantastic good fortune faded. Angling a covert glance at him, she felt a pang of stark regret. He seemed so invincible, strong and handsome, profiled against the azure of the sky as he surveyed his beloved garden. Noble, mysterious, and today he had shown he could be charming. Dangerous, too, she reminded herself. This was no weeping philosopher. This was the infamous Earl of Rutherford. Yet, in this moment, she had never seen a person look so vulnerable.

Then he turned and the moment was gone. His green eyes caught hers, perhaps read the sympathetic look, and he said, ''All this will be yours shortly. Not bad for a few months' work, eh?''

She was saved from having to make a reply to that outrageous statement by the call of a new voice. ''Halloo!''

Caroline turned around to find a lanky young man coming toward them. He waved. She felt the possessive grasp of Magnus's fingers at her elbow and his low voice whispered in her ear. ''David.'' Her flesh tingled as she tried to suppress the shudder caused by his caressing breath.

''So this is the delightful Miss Caroline Wembly of whom I have heard so much good,'' David said as he drew up to them. Caroline noted his boyish good looks, ready grin, and lean, graceful form. She mentally compared him with his elder brother, seeing a resemblance, but the differences were far more striking. Where Magnus was broad and tall, this man was rather rangy and elegant, almost dandified. His dark hair was not as lustrous as the earl's, and his eyes were an ordinary brown. On the whole, he appeared to be a thinner, more amicable and somewhat lesser version of his commanding brother.

"I am pleased to meet you," Caroline murmured. David bowed. When he straightened, he took her hand in his. "Who would have thought old Caractacus Green could do such a marvelous thing as find you?" He swung toward the earl. "I apologize for not being here for luncheon, Magnus. I set out later than I had planned."

"Mrs. Bronson was disappointed. She cooked enough for an army."

"I shall ask her to fix something for me later. And I will not be able to stay but overnight." Turning back to Caroline, he smiled. "Not to worry, sister-to-be, I will be on hand for the wedding."

They began to walk back toward the house. "I have been meaning to ask you about Mr. Green," Magnus said. "Chiefly, I am wondering why you chose such a disagreeable old coot for this job."

"You did not get on well with Caractacus?" David gasped in mock horror. "I chose him for his agreeable nature, of course." Caroline stifled a giggle as they entered the house. She liked this man, with his easy wit and bedeviling manner. Yet something about his good humor gave her the impression he was trying too hard. To impress her, or ingratiate himself with his dour brother? Caroline wondered. Or perhaps, she silently amended, it was the forced cheerfulness people sometimes used to patronize the ill. Goodness knew she was guilty of the same with her own brother.

David crossed the library to fling himself onto one of

the leather chairs. "I thought the two of you might have a small conflict of wills. Bossy fellow, isn't he? But he fills two very important qualifications which you specifically asked for. One, he is not in our usual circle, and therefore unlikely to have any clients who might know you." Looking to Caroline, he explained, "Discretion is a valuable asset in a solicitor, but not always a realistic one."

"What was the second qualification?" Caroline asked.

"He was willing to do the job."

Magnus scowled. Turning his back to them, he walked to the large window as David broke into peals of laughter. Awkwardly, Caroline shifted her gaze between the two. Magnus grumbled, "His fees are outrageous. For a solicitor not in fashion with society, he has an awfully high opinion of himself."

"Oh, Magnus," David said when he had sobered, "Lady Sarah Gleason has told me to send her regards, as well as her wishes for a speedy recovery. She was distressed when she heard you were ill."

Magnus merely grunted, apparently unimpressed with Lady Sarah's concern. David continued, "And Carstairs was asking after you. Did I tell you about the railroad he has invested in? Made him a fortune." As David launched into a report on the latest London gossip, Caroline relaxed. For the first time since she had come to Hawking Park, she was free of the earl's intense and undivided scrutiny. Indulging her curiosity, she studied her future husband.

He was standing perfectly still, looking out of the window. Since their walk, he had been pensive. She sensed him withdrawing into himself as if beset by a deep melancholy. Yet there also was an edge to him, hinting at a keen, biting rage just below the surface.

How difficult it must be for such a man to lean on others. Even his brother, with his lighthearted manner, did not understand this. Magnus Eddington was proud to a fault. It was something Caroline could understand. And identify with. When the bottom had fallen out of her world, she had carried on with nothing but stubborn determination to get her through.

He looked over just then, and caught her staring. His face was, for once, blank and open. Unreadable. She wondered what he was thinking.

David was still talking about their society acquaintances when Magnus cut in. "Miss Wembly wishes to return to the Barrister's Ordinary."

David stopped in midsentence. "Oh. Of course. Do you want me to take her there?"

"No need. She is quite accustomed to my phaeton."

David shrugged. "Surely she would prefer companionship for the ride."

"It is only a half hour to the village," Magnus countered.

"Even so, she may enjoy it better—"

"Gentlemen!" Caroline cut in. "*Miss Wembly* is standing right here, and is not an incompetent. Therefore, your disagreement over my preferences can be easily resolved simply by asking me. Yes, I am quite used to the ride and do not mind taking it alone, but I would welcome company if you are so disposed, Mr. Eddington."

"Excellent," David declared, jumping to his feet. "It shall give me the opportunity to tell you all the stories of my brother any future bride of his is in need of knowing."

"That was what I feared," Magnus mumbled. "Very well, David. Send Billy to fetch the phaeton."

David gave a short bow and exited, presumably to find Billy.

Magnus came to Caroline's side. "I shall arrange to

have the items we discussed sent to the Ordinary. Also, I will have my man come round to make arrangements as to the flowers. If you need anything else, simply send me a message and I will see to it. I will be in the village later on this week, so I expect to visit you then.''

She nodded, still a bit put out with the detached way he and his brother had discussed her. What did she expect, when she was merely an employee of sorts—a wife-for-hire?

''Do not sulk, Cara. It is much too attractive on you.'' He smiled, a hint of his earlier charm softening the harsh lines of his face. ''With that luscious mouth all tense, it makes me want to kiss you.''

A strangled, shocked sound came from her gaping mouth. Sulk? Luscious mouth? *Kiss* her?

And how had he known she was called Cara?

Playfully, he reached out a finger, set it under her chin, and with a twitch, closed her jaw. ''Now go.''

His fingertips brushed her face, not quite by accident. All at once, she was aware that in a week's time she would lie with him. He *would* kiss her then. And touch her. How could she bear it when only the slightest contact sent such wild tremors through her?

He raised one brow when she did not obey. ''Unless you are waiting for that kiss?''

She took one step back, her fingers touching her lips, betraying the fact that he had, indeed, read her thoughts. ''No!'' she declared.

''Then good day, Caroline.''

''Good day, Magnus.''

She was almost at the door when he called, ''Caroline.'' Pausing, she did not turn around. ''Yes, Magnus?''

''When you choose your gown, make certain it is grand,

and do not mind the expense. You must have something worthy of you.''

She shot him a glance over her shoulder. He stood with his feet braced apart, hands clasped behind him, looking every bit the aristocrat. ''I mean worthy of the Countess of Rutherford,'' he amended.

Chapter Five

"So, how do you find my brother?" David asked once they were bumping down the dirt road to the village.

"Quite agreeable," Caroline answered.

"Agreeable? Magnus must be dusting off the old Eddington charm. Hasn't used it in years. Usually in a sulk, is Magnus, at least until he sets his sight on a beautiful woman. Then, he's formidable." He seemed to catch himself, casting her an apologetic look. "Sorry, bad form to mention that sort of thing. Anyhow, the Eddington charm is actually inherited from our mother, which would make it the Coulter charm. Now, *she* actually worked at it. Had a bevy of sycophants who adored her. Oh, nothing improper. She just attracted admirers in droves. We grew up with it, so it seemed quite natural."

"Did your father not mind?"

"He tolerated it. You see, he was besotted himself."

Caroline smiled slightly. "I see you have a touch of your mother's charm as well."

"Ah, bless you. Now, tell me about you. You are a Londoner."

"Yes." Caroline's guard went up. Was this friendly escort simply a ruse to delve into her life on Magnus' behalf? "I have lived there all my life."

"I love the town. So much to do. How is it we have never met?"

"I had two seasons several years ago. Since the death of my father, I have been working at a bookseller's shop."

"What? Not as an old lady's companion? I suppose your looks made that impossible. Governess, too. No wife wants a beauty hovering about. How awful—I have made you blush."

She was. She could feel the heat on her face and at the tips of her ears. She said, "Actually, the reason I took the position of clerk was to be able to be close to my family."

"Oh?" She had raised his curiosity.

"My mother needs me."

"Ah." Whether he was satisfied with that or tactful enough not to pursue it, David allowed the matter to drop. However, his next question was even more unsettling. "Do you like children, Miss Wembly?"

She blinked as he chuckled. "I only ask because it will make a great deal of difference to my nephew—or niece. Magnus hates children as a rule. He has none of his own. By-blows, I mean. You must have wondered. Am I shocking you? No, you are made of sterner stuff, aren't you?"

"He hates children?" she asked.

"He is not cruel to them, if that's what you're thinking. Just doesn't particularly care for their company. Me, now, I find their crafty little minds charming. Refreshing to have them come right out and tell you what's what. I like that."

"Children are very honest," Caroline agreed.

"That they are. You mustn't worry about Magnus. He is a good man, and he will do his duty and beyond for his child and you."

"He has assured me of it." She didn't mention the contract.

"Magnus is a man of his word."

The conversation turned to lighter topics, helping to pass the drive until they pulled up to the Ordinary. David sprang out of his seat and leapt to the ground, gallantly holding out his arm to hand her down. "Allow me to take you safely to your rooms."

"Thank you, Mr. Eddington, but I can find my way from here. It was good of you to accompany me. I enjoyed it most thoroughly. I hope I will see you again soon."

"Yes, Miss Wembly. I suppose you shall. At your wedding." He took her hand, bowed over it and brushed a light kiss to her fingers. "You will be lovely, I know."

"Thank you again. Good day, Mr. Eddington."

"And to you, Miss Wembly."

When she entered her room, her mother's face was lined with concern.

"Yes, Mother. He asked me to marry him. We are to be wed in a week's time."

The only response her mother made was a hard swallow. "So it is to be." She drew in a breath and let it out slowly. "Was that he who brought you home?"

"It was David Eddington, Magnus' brother. How is James?"

"He is sleeping." She gave her daughter a measured look. "Magnus?"

"The earl. He insisted. And Mother, he called me Cara. I didn't tell him to. He just knew."

Her mother's eyes narrowed. "Caroline, darling, he said he was going to thoroughly check your background. It was probably a fact he uncovered." She motioned for Caroline to sit with her over by the small hearth. Two chairs and a soft, overstuffed settee clustered about a deep fireplace, creating a cozy grouping. "Now tell me everything."

"So much happened, Mother." Caroline began with the curious exchange over her allowance and related everything. When she reached the part about James and she being allowed to stay at the Ordinary, Audrae clasped her hands over her mouth and her eyes shone.

"Goodness! It is such an expense!"

"And he was rather charming today. Not so dour. He said he would be coming to the village later on this week, so you shall meet him then."

A small voice cut in. "Can I meet him, Cara?"

James was standing at the portal to his room, hair mussed, eyes puffy with sleep. His small bare feet peeked out from under his nightshirt.

Caroline jumped to her feet. "James, darling, what are you doing out of bed?"

"I wanted to hear more about the earl. I want to meet him. Can I?"

Kneeling in front of his slight body, Caroline lightly grasped his shoulders. "Listen to me, James. I need you to understand something which may seem quite strange to you. The earl is very ill. He is dying. He has arranged for me to be his wife, and he told me today he wishes me to attend him when the sickness is upon him. Now, I know I can help take care of you and still have plenty of time for the earl, but I am afraid he will not think so." She didn't like the furrowing of the little boy's brow. "Now you mustn't worry. It is only that we must keep you a bit of a secret. So the earl will not consider he has made a bad bargain. Do you understand, love?"

His head bobbed solemnly. "Yes, Cara. He does not want me about."

Caroline cast a helpless glance at her mother. Audrae

stepped forward. "You mustn't pout, James. I know you are disappointed at not seeing the earl, but Caroline has met him and has decided this is best."

His frown deepened and his lip quivered. "Then, I am not to live in the palace?"

"No, not at first," Caroline said. She smoothed his tousled hair and chucked him on the chin. "But only for a little while. Then you will live there forever and ever!" He still seemed uncertain. Caroline had an inspiration. "You know, this is like a grand adventure, don't you think? It is as if you are a secret prince, whom we must hide while we fight to restore you to your kingdom so you can rule from your lovely palace."

It worked. His eyes lightened. "Hurrah! And can I fight with a sword?" He paused, perplexed. "Who are we fighting?"

In truth, the only person who stood between James and his "palace" was Magnus, but Caroline was not about to say so. "A legion of dragons!"

Catching the excitement, James exclaimed, "Oh, yes! And they have a sorcerer to do their bidding, who has cast a spell on me to make me ill!"

Caroline's breath caught. "Y-yes, darling. Come, let me carry you back to bed, and I will tell you the whole story."

It took hours to hammer out the elaborate plot, but between the two of them they conjured a wondrous fantasy. Audrae stood beside her children, sometimes listening, other times looking lost in thought. They ate dinner and played a lively game of cards, after which James was exhausted. Caroline went to change for bed while her mother crooned a lullaby in her soft, lilting voice.

Alone, Caroline reflected on David, whom she found to be a congenial fellow, and she hoped she had made a friend. The servants were well-mannered and polite, with ready smiles for her and respectful curtsies. And the house was magnificent. Overall, she was quite satisfied with what she had learned of Hawking Park.

Yet, most of her thoughts this night were of Magnus Eddington. She could still see him in her mind's eye. Dragging his bowl and water goblet down to sit by her. Guiding her proudly through his ancestral home. Or silhouetted against the sky as he studied the garden he would never again see in its glory.

She was feeling less than elated when her mother came in. "Mother," she began, "do you think I am doing a terrible thing?"

Audrae's voice held surprise. "Why, child?"

"To benefit from this man's tragedy. It seems wrong."

Audrae walked to the bed, pensive. She sat with a sigh. "The Earl of Rutherford will die. His tragedy exists with or without you, Cara." Turning to her daughter, she patted the space beside her. When Caroline sat, she held her hand. "I know I have had my doubts about all this, but they were doubts about whether this was the right thing for *you,* darling. For the earl, I truly know you will indeed be a blessing to him in his last days, for he has a chance to leave this earth knowing his most heartfelt desire has been realized."

"I know," Caroline whispered.

Audrae nodded, giving Caroline's hand a pat. "You are a good girl, Cara. And smart. Smarter than I. I married your father because I confused lust with love, and I thought I knew everything the world had to offer. I was such a young fool, and forgive me for speaking ill of your father, but I lived to regret it so."

"Oh, Mother." Caroline knew her mother had been miserable with Louis Wembly, but they had never spoken so openly about it before.

"I tell you this not for sympathy, but so you know you could be doing far worse than a dying earl. God forgive me, but I thank the Lord for taking Louis, for he grew more dissolute each year. Drinking and gambling, and there were other women, you might as well know, a string of mistresses."

Caroline gasped in rage. "How dare he spend a farthing on other women when his own family was in need!"

"He cared for no one but himself. Nothing that man did would surprise me."

That last statement slammed into Caroline's brain. Her eyes snapped wide and she stared at her mother, wondering if Audrae were trying to hint at something. *Does she know?*

Audrae continued. "So you see, I have made peace with your decision by telling myself of the advantages of widowhood. As the countess, you would have power and money, and with it, something no woman achieves alone— the right to your own destiny. Your life would be your own."

Her heartbeat slowed as Caroline realized her mother suspected nothing.

"You just make certain the earl is kind to you." Audrae wagged her finger at her daughter, as if she were but eight years old and caught pilfering a biscuit before supper. "If he does anything to harm you, or humiliate you, or cause you strife, you come home."

Amused at the heated admonishment, Caroline grinned. "Yes, Mother."

Catching herself, Audrae stared at her finger and offered her daughter a baleful look. "Habits die hard."

They fell to laughing then readied themselves for sleep. It was not long, however, before Caroline's thoughts turned once again to the earl. The image of his proud, handsome face would not leave her, following her into sleep and haunting her dreams.

On Wednesday morning, Magnus sent a message requesting she receive him at one o'clock, and invited Audrae to join them at four for high tea in one of the Ordinary's private dining rooms.

"Finally," Audrae said. "Now I shall see him and judge for myself. It is about time he instituted some semblance of propriety. I know this whole marriage is unconventional, but I believe I should at least meet the man who is to be my son-in-law before the actual wedding."

Caroline set about choosing something from her meager wardrobe. He had already seen her in the fabulous blue gown she had worn at her first interview, and subsequently in the more sober muslin, which was her second best. That left the drab gray wool skirt with its matching short jacket. Once elegant, it was now downright shabby, a bit too short and only still wearable because the loose-fitting white shirtwaist did not pull across her breasts, as all her other old dresses did.

She knew the earl did not expect her to be glamorously dressed, as her needful state was precisely the reason she was marrying him, yet she did not want to shame him. She told herself this was the reason she fussed with her toilette and spent much longer than was her habit dressing her hair.

The maid came up to tell her Magnus was waiting below in the hall.

"I shall see you at four," her mother said. Her eyes swept over Caroline critically. She adjusted an errant curl at Caroline's temple and said, "You are lovely."

"Thank you, Mother." Her hand came over her stomach to still the wild fluttering. Taking a deep breath, she descended the stairs.

He was waiting for her at the bottom. Dressed impeccably in dark waistcoat and breeches, he looked every inch an earl. Caroline faltered, and he glanced up just then, his gaze flickering over her in a quick assessment. Self-consciously, she smoothed her hands down her skirt, wishing it were not so plain, or worn, or outdated.

"Good afternoon," he said, reaching his hand out for her.

She placed her fingers in his broad, warm palm, feeling a tremor of reaction shoot up her arm. "Good day, Magnus."

His lips curled with approval at her having remembered to use his Christian name. "My phaeton is waiting outside. I thought an outing would be enjoyable. The day is fine. There won't be many more like it."

He seemed unaware of the double entendre of his words. She said, "I don't see your driver. Do you have a chaperon for us?"

"Caroline, we are going to be married in three days."

He was right, of course. She was being silly, and needlessly conscientious. "Let me get my cloak."

He had the reins firmly in hand when she joined him several moments later, clambering up onto the driver's bench beside him. He watched her inelegant movements, his green eyes dancing and that broad, sensuous mouth compressed into a hint of amusement.

"Ever resourceful," he commented.

"As you have already mentioned, Magnus, it is one of the reasons why you chose me. I do not play the helpless female, and neither do you attend me like a chivalrous suitor."

Snapping the reins to get the horses started, he said, "You aren't disappointed, are you?"

"Not in the least," she sniffed. "It would be ridiculous for us to carry on so."

"Just so," he agreed. "And you are correct. I very much like your independence. A most necessary quality."

He flashed her that smile, and her insides felt watery all of a sudden.

He made no more conversation as he drove her to a lovely horseshoe-shaped lake. Pulling the sleek conveyance to a stop, he pointed out the heap of stone in the center of a promontory jutting out into the water. "This used to be a castle and the lake was its moat," he explained. "The builders were very clever in channeling the nearby stream, so the water was always fresh and the castle refuse was washed away. Too bad they weren't as insightful about the foundations. All that is left of the keep is a few crumbled walls. You can still make out some of the different buildings, if you know a little about castles. It helps if you have a good imagination."

Caroline stood and fairly leapt out of the phaeton. "Let's go see!" she said. Picking up her skirts, she began to run along the lakeshore toward the ruins.

"Hold up!" he called, catching up with her easily. He took hold of her wrist and tucked it in the crook of his arm and they strolled more sedately the rest of the way.

"Is this an old home of ancestors of yours?"

"No. But I used to come here as a boy. I loved it there on the rocks, dreaming of knights and dragons and rescuing a fair maid." His voice trailed off as he lost himself to memory. Caroline wondered what he was like as a child. It was so difficult to imagine his chiseled features and broad, muscular body small and gangly with the awkwardness of youth. Yet, sometimes when he smiled, she saw a hint of the boy he had been. His dimple, she supposed.

Magnus demonstrated his knowledge by pointing out where the stables had been located in the lower bailey and the deep scar in the ground that still existed, most likely the location of the smithy. Taking her to the large circle of a shallow wall, he explained how the staircase in the keep always wound on the right side so the knights would have the wall to their back when descending to fend off invaders. This gave the advantage of having the enemy forced to fight upward and perilously close to the sheer, railingless drop off the stairs.

"That's fascinating," Caroline said. They were sitting quite comfortably on the weathered sandstone in the area, Magnus had informed her, of the old hall.

"Yes, well, I am a font of worthless information," he answered.

"You must have been a delight to your professors. Did you attend University?"

"Oxford. I was sent down during the Michelmas term during my last year."

He said it without inflection. Curious, Caroline asked, "Do you regret it?"

"What? Doing the deed, or getting caught?"

"Not finishing."

He paused and studied the sky. "Sometimes."

His eyes flickered to her, and he grinned. "But it was worth it. Had a professor, a wretched fellow by the name of Blecher, who was a pompous jacka—fool. Absurdly proud of his mustaches. Always stroking them and curling them. Idiotic things were out to his ears. He was vain, but worse, he was a vicious chap, always saying the most humiliating things to us and all the while he would laugh in this twittery little voice. One day, he went after a certain fellow I happened to like very much. Said some things about his mother. Well, this fellow's mother had died the previous term, and much to my friend's shame, Blecher's words made him cry, right there in front of all to see.''

"What did you do to him? Blecher, I mean,'' she inquired.

"Snipped off his mustaches while he slept. Would have gotten away with it, too, if I hadn't acted on impulse and glued the things to his portrait in the dining hall. Got caught and that was that.''

"Were your parents very upset?"

He got a strange look on his face. "My mother hardly cared about it. She was happy to have me home, actually. But my father was…deeply disappointed.''

Something somber drew his features into an odd look. The impulse to reach out and touch his arm was hard to resist.

He lifted a hand to indicate the low angle of the sun. "We should be getting back for tea.''

They were late, as it happened, and Caroline's mother despised tardiness. However, it took Magnus only five minutes to charm her until she was laughing and blushing like a schoolgirl.

When the earl said it was time for him to take his leave, Audrae tactfully excused herself.

"You were civil to my mother.''

"Of course I was. Despite your opinion of me, I am not a barbarian.''

"That is not my opinion,'' she said.

"Oh? Then I see I have been too tame.'' He came to her chair and, taking her hand, drew her to her feet. "I hope I have not left you with any misconceptions. Now, come and kiss me goodbye.''

She started at his boldness. He chuckled. "In less than a week, we shall share more than that, Cara. Having second thoughts?''

"No!" she declared a little too vehemently. He was close; she found it difficult to breathe. And his hand resting high on her waist, just under her breast, was giving off a scalding heat.

"It was a pleasant day, Cara *mia*. I can't remember the last time I spent such carefree hours." Long, tanned fingers touched her jawline, making her shiver. "I enjoyed showing you the mysteries of the castle ruins."

There was some vague knowledge that he was toying with her, trying to shock her perhaps. Despite his tender courtship today, she must remember Magnus was the infamous Earl of Rutherford, of whom she had heard so much ill.

"It was an excellent outing, Magnus. I thank you."

"Pretty words, Cara, but I was thinking more along the lines of your *showing* your appreciation."

Her heart lurched, but before she could think of anything suitable to say, he had slipped his hand to the slender column of her neck and dipped his head. When his mouth touched hers, it was not gentle, though neither was it an assault. His lips moved lightly, eliciting a pleasant yearning inside her which was too frightening to indulge. A tangled coil of delightful sensation tingled in her belly and her knees buckled. Magnus caught her up with his other arm, pressing her much closer than was proper, but she didn't resist. She gripped his massive shoulders, her palms wanting to explore the broad expanse and feel the way his powerful body moved.

Slanting his mouth, he deepened the kiss, opening her lips to the intrusion of his tongue. Stunned, reeling, she gasped a short intake of breath when it touched hers. He made a low, soft sound in response, causing her to shudder with some indefinable sensation.

His lips broke contact with hers, but he held her still

pinioned against him. "In three days' time, I will take you
to bed with me, and you might as well know I find you a
very desirable woman, Caroline." His voice was husky.
Distracting tremors raged through her body, leaving her
limp, devoid of will or thought. "I am looking forward to
making love to you. And judging by your kiss, you are
anticipating it as well."

He must have felt her stiffen, for he grinned. "No, do
not get prissy on me. Whatever bit of pleasure you felt at
my kiss is nothing to the feelings you will experience that
night."

Aghast, Caroline tried to pull away. He held her tight,
then suddenly released her so when she yanked back, she
stumbled into her chair where she landed with a plop.

"One more thing," he said, "We shall outfit you completely once this wedding business is out of the way." He
leaned over, fingering the collar of her jacket where it was
just starting to fray.

At this new humiliation, spoken on the heels of his outrageous promise of pleasure, Caroline was certain her color
was a deep shade of burgundy. She didn't even attempt to
speak, for her mind seemed too shocked to function.

Gathering his hat and driving gloves, he cast over his
shoulder, "Until then, Cara *mia*."

She didn't move for a long time, sprawled rather hap-
hazardly on the chair with her mouth agape, until her mind
began to recover. An image surged into her brain of a tiger
she had seen once, languishing gracefully in its cage. It
had been so beautiful, she had longed to touch it, feel the
softness of its fur. Then, angered by some missile tossed
in its cage by an imbecile in the crowd, the beast leapt to
its feet, its eyes suddenly deadly, and gave off a low,
threatening growl. The vision of those teeth had awed her.
Something of the same feeling filled her now. Her future

husband was like the tiger. Beautiful, appealing and at times harmless, as he had been by the ruins. Always, there were tragic underpinnings; a great beast caged by his mysterious illness. Yet there was a deadly side to him, one he would unleash at the slightest inducement. She would do well to remember this.

The only question she could not settle was: what had she done to provoke him?

To Magnus' mind, the tempting piece he had chosen to wed had done plenty. Nothing intentional, nothing criminal, but so very disturbing all the same. Today, on the old castle motte, with the past all around them, she had made him forget. Not just the illness. Everything.

Like old companions, his demons were familiar baggage. Today, they had eased their terrible burden in the presence of Caroline Wembly. But not for long and not forever. They had, as they ever would, returned with a vengeance.

Which was only part of the problem. The most unforgivable thing was how she had made him anxious all week in anticipation of seeing her again. And how the bottom had fallen out of his heart when he had glanced up the stairs and seen her looking indescribably lovely, even in that ridiculous outfit the most conservative Puritan would eschew. Most unpardonable was how she had taken such innocent delight at their outing, reclining in the sun and making him wish the day could go on forever.

He did not have forever. And he wasn't courting her, damn it all. Theirs was a business arrangement. Nothing more.

The woman was only marrying him because he had one

foot in the grave. The chit wanted his money, nothing more.

And he... He wanted a child. It was so simple. Ridiculously simple.

He must keep that in mind.

Chapter Six

Magnus was painfully aware of the curious faces of the folk lined up in the pews. Thus, when Caroline was escorted down the aisle of the village church, resplendent in a stunning cream silk confection and smiling brilliantly on the arm of his brother, Magnus made a great show of gazing tenderly at his bride. For the sake of the smattering of guests, he appeared besotted, but he had already made up his mind to steel his heart against Caroline Wembly's dangerous appeal.

Caroline's strange indigo eyes studied him as he repeated his vows sotto voce. He kept his own gaze cool when her soft, slightly husky timbre promised herself to him. *Until death do us part...*

He kissed her briefly, reining in the urge to linger at the softness of her lips. When he pulled away, something flashed in her eyes—a sadness, perhaps? Did she regret her bargain already? Then David, who had doubled as his best man, wanted to shake his hand, and Magnus turned away.

At the reception afterward, he was studiously attentive, introducing her to the vicar and his wife, the local squire— an insufferable boor who possessed, oddly enough, a pert, pretty wife who seemed to adore the man—and some other minor landholders from the area. Caractacus Green was there, staring from under his hooded eyes as if the entire matter were distasteful in the extreme. David, of course, was his usual sociable self, elevating the mood to one of high gaiety. Even Audrae Wembly smiled and chatted comfortably. Frowning, Magnus realized Caroline's brother was not in attendance. When he asked her about it, she shrugged. "He is shy, and boy enough to think all things having to do with marriage are utter foolishness."

"Do you know, I have never met him?"

Caroline sipped lightly from her champagne flute. "Really? Your invitation didn't include him when you came to the Ordinary, so I suppose Mother assumed he wasn't invited."

"No, not at all. It was just an oversight. Ah, Grenville, how are you?" Distracted by the well-wisher who came up just then, he dropped the matter of his wife's absent brother.

The guests did not stay late, for which Magnus was grateful. He grew weary of the role of doting bridegroom. More accurately, he was an anxious bridegroom. With his new countess so close, her subtle perfume was like a siren's song in his head. He was consumed with anticipation.

Devil take it, he felt warm. Loosening his cravat, his eyes searched out Arthur. The servant caught his eye and frowned. Magnus shook his head. *Not yet.*

He strode to the open window, inhaling the fresh air.

Please, no, not tonight. He had never staved off an attack before, but if sheer dint of will would do it, certainly now would be the time. To his utter relief, he began to feel cooler. He flashed his manservant a quick smile and a nod to indicate the alarm had passed.

Probably just overheated from inhaling that damnable

scent. What was it, anyway? Some kind of spicy concoction, nothing cloying or flowery. Completely unique. And sensuous.

He had better stop this train of thought. His temperature was rising again.

Off in a corner, he spied Caroline with her mother. Audrae was speaking in urgent tones to which Caroline nodded solemnly.

Something about the tender scene angered him. No doubt, the elder woman was giving the traditional "Submit, be meek and don't complain when it hurts" lecture properly prudish brides get just before the rending of their virginity.

If she was nervous about the night to come, he was not any less so. Having plenty of experience bedding women, Magnus was not at all unconfident. The women whom he had known, however, all possessed a quality his blushing bride did not. They were willing. Caroline Wembly—nay, Eddington—was not. She was merely granting him access to her body, not out of desire or for the purposes of pleasure, but singularly for the begetting of a child. In exchange for money.

What a harsh thought. He was brewing up a foul mood. Caroline was no different than every aristocratic bride since the dark ages and beyond. Marriages of the upper class were always about money or power. That their arrangement was a bit more baldly stated than most did not make it any less honorable.

Pulling aside the housekeeper, Mrs. Gervis, he instructed her to invite the new countess to retire. Then he strode into his library and shut the door, leaving his guests to take the unsubtle hint and leave.

Caroline had not had time to purchase a suitable night-gown for her wedding night. Luckily, her best and prettiest was still in good state. It had been freshly laundered and the few flaws carefully mended. Laying now across the bed, it awaited her as Lillian, an upstairs maid just promoted to attend her, brushed out her hair.

"My goodness, ma'am, yer hair is luv'ly. So thick and smooth it is. Bee-yoo-ti-ful color. I don't think I ever seen the like, 'cept what come out of a bottle." After a moment of horrified realization, Lillian rushed, "I wasn't sayin' yers come from there. Anyone can see it's nat'ral."

"I knew that, Lillian," Caroline answered with a smile. "It's a lovely compliment. Thank you."

Blushing, Lillian nodded. She helped Caroline into the nightdress, fluffing the pale blond hair attractively about her mistress's shoulders when she had settled her in the bed.

"The master, he be comin' soon. G'night, ma'am."

After the door closed, Caroline sat in silence, wondering how long she would have to wait until Magnus arrived.

She wasn't dreading the act of sexual intercourse. Her mother had explained it thoroughly, and though it seemed more than a bit distasteful—not to mention embarrassing—she was fully prepared. So, why was her heart beating quick and hard, like the flutter of a bird's wing?

The sound of a door shutting in the adjoining room warned her that Magnus had entered his chamber. Only moments later the connecting door between their suites opened.

He stopped in the doorway and stared at her. She sat among the pillows, clutching the coverlet to her breast, with her back perfectly straight. Belatedly, she thought of offering a welcome. She forced a smile.

Holding a decanter of some deep amber liquid in one hand and two stemmed glasses in the other, Magnus nearly took her breath away. Never had she seen a man appear more…elemental. He had removed the ebony studs from his shirt, so the cuffs and collar hung loosely, baring his forearms up to his elbows and his chest almost to his navel. Dark skin showed, brushed lightly with a furring of smooth, black hair. He still wore his shoes and breeches, thank goodness, keeping him from true dishabille, but the remnants of formality did nothing to civilize the raw masculinity that seemed to fill the room with crackling tension within moments of his entrance.

All at once, those handsome features broke into a smile…and he laughed!

"You look like a damn lamb eyeing the butcher!"

Nothing could have cut her deeper. He thought her ridiculous! With the heedless swell of rage moving her limbs, she shot out of bed and squared off against him, hands firmly planted on her hips. "What a terrible thing to say to me, you brute!"

His eyes traveled an insolent journey from the top of her head to the tip of her toes, lingering on her breasts. Indignant, she snatched her wrapper to her. He shrugged and turned away, setting the glasses on the table and filling them. "I didn't say that you don't look positively delectable. Lamb is one of my favorite dishes. With mint sauce. Do you not recall our luncheon last week?"

So he was in one of his moods, wanting to goad her? As cowed as she had been moments ago, she was more irritated now. Sauntering up to him, she said tightly, "I remember our luncheon. You were kinder then."

He turned, his green eyes gleaming as he handed her a glass. "Did you notice how I devoured every last morsel?"

She narrowed her eyes back at him. "Did you? Or did you merely push it around on your plate? Sort of toying with it?"

He flashed her a grin, showing that dimple that never failed to intrigue her. "You are observant, Cara *mia*. Will you drink with me?"

She raised her glass to his. Tilting his head back, he scanned the ceiling for inspiration. "Ah, let me see. To lust. Fruitful lust."

Hiding her reaction, Caroline gently clinked her glass with his. "Hear, hear. A wonderful salute, Magnus. Inspirational, I would say, particularly to a nervous bride. So very kind of you to show such sensitivity, courteously dispelling my fears." With a sweet smile, she sipped. It was an excellent sherry. She sipped again.

He watched her, his eyes hooded. Once again he raised his glass. "I am duly chastised. Imagine that, wed less than a day, and already I have earned my first scolding. At this rate I shall be henpecked before the week is out." Though he was still teasing, he had lost that dangerous edge. Again, as on many occasions in the past, she had the feeling he was mocking himself more than her. "And so I am redeemed." Just before he sipped, he curled one corner of his mouth. "And your fears are dispelled."

Astonished, Caroline realized he was correct. Anger had replaced trepidation.

He stared at her over the rim, pinning her in that way he had. He must practice, she thought distractedly. It was far too effective to come naturally.

Something shifted in the air between them, and an odd thought occurred to her. *Playtime is over.*

He reached out and took her glass from her fingers. After setting it out of the way, he took her hand in his and pulled gently. "What are you expecting to happen tonight, Cara?"

His left hand moved to her hair, lifting a handful and letting it fall in a cascade. Looking at the effect as if it were some fascinating marvel of science, he said again, "Tell me what you expect."

"I—I..." She had no idea why he was asking such a ludicrous thing. Deciding on boldness, she answered, "You shall h-have intercourse with me."

His gaze didn't shift as he continued to play with her hair. The effect was wickedly pleasurable, and Caroline's eyelids started to droop. Slowly, Magnus shook his head from side to side. "Weren't you listening when I promised you pleasure? I am not simply going to douse the light and lift your nightgown. What I shall do may shock you, it might embarrass you at first, but I assure you, you will come to enjoy it. I am going to make love to you, Cara."

His eyes watched her tongue as she ran it over her lips, suddenly gone dry. He handed her her glass, and she downed the contents in a single gulp. Unable to keep the smug amusement from showing, he took the empty glass with a catlike grin playing at the corners of his mouth.

His hand started to wander, touching lightly here and there. Caroline noticed how the languid feelings his caress elicited were starting to muddle her thinking. "Now, understand I am not unconfident in my ability to do exactly as I say, but neither am I a braggart. One of the reasons you were so excellent a choice, Cara, was your physical appeal. I was attracted to you from the beginning. I wanted to kiss you, taste you, since the moment I first laid eyes on you. And when I finally did, I knew I had found a matched desire. You don't know it yet, but you want me. Either that, or you are an excellent actress."

"What do you mean?" His long, sun-browned fingers were fiddling with the blue ribbon at her breast. One tug and the wrapper would fall open. When he did it, she offered no more than a soft gasp.

The low rumble in his chest sounded like a distant thunder. "No, darling, don't think I suspect you of artifice. I know a genuine primal response when I see one. Or feel one, as the case may be." He had somehow managed to get the robe off her shoulders. It fell to the floor in a silken puddle. Then his hand slipped to the small of her back and pulled her forward.

He was so gentle now, seductive and exciting, titillating her with his words as well as his unpredictable touch. She felt like an instrument in a master's hands. A part of her brain warned her not to be lulled too far off guard. She already knew he was capricious. Tonight his mood had run the gamut from rampant belligerence to tender desire. And they had been in each other's company less than half an hour.

But her mind seemed unaccountably sluggish, unable to comprehend these cataclysmic events. The barrage of sensations he was eliciting shook her to her core, leaving her dazed.

"I am going to kiss you," he murmured, lowering his head and doing just that.

He had been gentle the first time. Now, he extended no such courtesy. His mouth captured hers in fierce possession, sparking a hunger that compelled her to moan softly and arch against him, answering without thought. Pure instinct reigned as his tongue invaded, plunging deep into the recesses of her mouth, stroking, parrying until she was aquiver. It felt like madness. Maybe it was the sherry, she thought fleetingly as his mouth left hers, trailing a hot path to her earlobe.

"Ah!" she cried at this new sensation. His voice, a soft, husky whisper, tickled her enough to raise gooseflesh. "Do you like this?" he asked.

"Ummm," was all she could manage to answer.

"And this?" His tongue traced the delicate shape of her

ear. She whimpered, but he demanded, "Tell me what you like."

"I like that!" she said before she could stop herself.

"I am going to lick you like that everywhere. And yes, even the parts you are saying to yourself right now 'surely he doesn't mean *there.*' Most especially there. All in good time, and when you are ready."

Oh, dear God! It was impossible to feel this way. She thought she might expire, for the exquisite passions he commanded were unbearable. "What are you doing to me?" she gasped.

He had traveled to her neck, making good on his word to apply his outrageous kiss to every inch of flesh in his path. "I am making love to you," he said huskily. "Exactly as I promised I would."

She clung to his shoulders, wanting him to stop. It was too intense. Her stomach hurt, her body danced with live sensation like lightning in her veins and a strange achy yearning was asserting itself in her most intimate parts— a shameless desire to be touched.

In perfect harmony with her sensate overload, Magnus pulled upright and stared down at her. His eyes had darkened to the color of jade, holding her for a moment before he reached for their glasses. "More?" he asked as he splashed a generous portion of sherry into his.

"I don't want any more sherry. It's making my head all fuzzy."

He chuckled. "That's not the sherry, sweet. Come to the bed, and I will get you some water."

Her limbs were rubbery feeling, but she managed not to look ridiculous as she obeyed. Magnus returned with a glass of water, as promised.

Dear God, he was a handsome man. His dark, glossy curls fell in soft disarray over his forehead and down the nape of his neck, barely touching his collar. Her hand itched to feel its texture. She wanted to kiss him the same way he had kissed her, make him weak and gasping for air as he had done to her.

"Touch me," he said, reading her thoughts yet again. *How did he do that?* He took the glass from her, then grasped both her wrists and brought her trembling hands to his chest. His gaze was fastened on her mouth, leaving her feeling self-conscious. At her first touch, her inhibitions ebbed away. He felt glorious. Under her fingertips pulsed warm flesh covered with crisp, feathery hair. His skin was surprisingly soft, smooth over rock hardness beneath. He moved his arm and muscle shifted under her questing hand. She trailed her fingers over his breast, across his massive chest to the wide reaches of his shoulders, opening his fine linen shirt farther for her perusal of his masculine form.

His body was magnificent. As her hands slipped under the material of his shirt, he closed his eyes and his broad, sensuous mouth fell open just a little bit, a sign of reaction. It turned her innards to aspic to see it, and emboldened her as well. She stroked his back where granite-hard muscle rippled against her palms. With a low growl, he grabbed her arms and dragged them away. His eyes opened, fixing her with a steady stare. Bringing her hands up, he kissed each palm, first one then the other, then traced tiny circles with his tongue in the exact place his lips had touched.

"So, Cara, are you still afraid?" His voice was as soft and smooth as a purr.

Caroline blinked, trying to focus on his words. "My lord husband," she nearly gasped, "I am more terrified now than I ever was."

He grinned impishly. "Now, isn't this far better than

some clumsy groping in the dark? Tell me, love, what do you think of the joys of the marriage bed so far?''

''I think it is heaven,'' she breathed just before his mouth possessed her once again.

Chapter Seven

Magnus was in hell.

Had he been flayed alive, his body would be in less torment. Every nerve screamed, every inch of flesh danced with unendurable fire. The places where her touch had been felt singed. His gut churned and his manhood was hard as stone, aching with insistent need.

He had only himself to blame. It had started as another of his games, a game of mastery. To overcome his distaste at having to take a cringing bride to his bed. When he had walked through the door tonight and seen her sitting bolt upright, staring with round eyes and tightly compressed mouth, something inside him had rebelled against a wife who would submit her body only out of duty. Thank God he had the presence of mind to laugh. As much as she had chafed under his mockery, it was better than the blinding rage that flashed in his brain for an instant.

But he had *made* her want him, made her whimper and moan and go limp at his touch. For the past week, he had wanted her like this, but all he could envision of their first night together was her lying under him in resolute sub-mission, eyes squeezed shut, thinking about all his lovely money while he rutted over her still body.

Well, she was not thinking about money now, he was willing to wager. Since he had first kissed her, he had known she was capable of this, yet even he was not prepared for how potent it was, this passion between them. And now, as he possessed her mouth with harsh thrusts of his tongue, she answered with soft parries of her own. His hands kneaded her shoulders, slid down her back to mold the contours of her tight little bottom.

She was losing herself to him, and he was in control of her senses.

The problem was, he was not in control of his own.

Had he ever felt skin this soft? Had he ever seen so erotic a vision as Caroline in her girlish nightdress with white-blond hair falling about her like a curtain and her perfect features stained with the flush of desire?

He pushed her back on the bed, laying her ever so gently on the tufted counterpane. Her hair spilled across the pillows, catching the candlelight like the purest, palest gold. His breathing grew shallow, and he could only stare for a moment. She was so lovely....

Her gaze flickered to the bedside candelabra. "Are you going to douse the lights?"

He was about to say no, for he wanted to experience every nuance of her reaction, every sweet, soft inch of her flesh. Yet, she was a virgin, he must remember, and surely he had already pushed her modesty beyond her expectation. Grudgingly, he blew out the three candles. As he visited the others about the room, he began to strip off his clothes.

His hands trembled as he undid his trousers and tossed them on the floor, there to join his discarded shirt, shoes and stockings. Easing next to her, he marveled at how small she seemed. His large hand easily spanned her waist and her hips... Ah, he remembered how they curved. On

their first meeting, he had groped her crudely and joked
about the slimness of her long, lithe figure, but the truth
was it excited him to feel the supple flesh so firm and lean
under his hand.

She stirred. Perhaps she was growing restless with his
lazy exploration. His eyes adjusted to the darkness, and
there was enough moonlight coming in the windows by
which to see. Her eyes were closed, and that luscious
mouth parted slightly to facilitate her quickened breathing.
He groaned and covered her, crushing his mouth over hers,
devouring her while his hands moved swiftly to drag the
hem of her ridiculously modest garment to her waist. Leaning back for an instant, he pulled her upright and jerked it
off over her head.

His mood had changed from languorous exploration to
greedy need. When she brought her hands up to cover her
breasts, he grabbed her wrists and held them at her sides
as he tumbled her back onto the bed. Now, flesh to flesh,
he came over her once again, and her sharp hiss of surprise
whispered against his own lips.

"Magnus... Is this... I-Is this... proper?"

"Lovemaking has nothing to do with proper, Cara *mia.*
Intercourse is proper and dull, but this, what we are doing
tonight, is wild and wicked and the only rule is," he
paused, touching his tongue to the fluttering pulse at the
base of her throat, "there are no rules."

His hand slid up her side, stroking the beginning swell
of her breast. She made a sound like a whispery "Ah,"
and stiffened. Bolder, he closed over the warm, round
flesh, rubbing his thumb over the hardened nub of her nipple. The sounds she tried not to make nearly reduced him
to insanity. Sampling the other, he played while his mouth
nibbled and kissed her jaw, her shoulder, then lower until

he took one of the hard tips into his mouth and sucked gently.

She arched violently, hands on his shoulders to push him away. "Magnus, no, you mustn't. Oh, God, what are you doing?"

He smiled and moved his hand over the flat of her stomach, down to her hip to caress her thighs. She was a tall woman, her legs exquisitely long. She clamped them together protectively as if anticipating his intended destination.

"Open your legs for me, Cara," he whispered, straightening so he could gaze into her face. He was certain she was as heedless as he was, but her inexperience made her shy. He cautioned himself to control his impulses enough to be soothing, to ease her into the intimacy he was determined they would share. "I want to see if you are ready for me."

"I—I am ready," she stammered.

He kissed her lightly. "Not only in spirit, love." Obediently, hesitantly, she allowed him to nudge her thighs apart.

"It's time," he whispered at her ear. "Trust me, I will be gentle. I cannot take away the pain, though."

Raising his hips, he positioned himself at her entrance and slowly, slowly eased inside.

She stiffened, resisting this unfamiliar intrusion. Though he had no doubts she understood the mechanics of intercourse, her reaction at this first time was natural, he supposed. He had never taken a virgin before. At least he had spared himself that one depravity. Yet, for him, the sensation of her slick heat was madness itself, and he gritted his teeth against the insistent urge to bury himself inside her.

He felt the barrier, meant to pause, then it seemed to

give way of its own accord. Going deeper, he was all at once sheathed inside sheer sensation. She hadn't made a sound, no cry, nor had she flinched. He looked down. "Are you all right?" His voice was strained, barely a rasp. "Did I hurt you?"

"Was that it? It hardly hurt at all." She sounded amazed. And relieved. What dread the weaker sex must feel in anticipation of the rending of their precious membrane. He felt her body ease in his arms. Tentatively, he pulled out. Then, again slow and easy, he slid inside.

Her hands began to move, running short trails down his back. Her touch was featherlight, creating tremors of feeling that radiated throughout his body like ripples on a still lake. His hips thrust, harder this time, and her fingers curled into muscle. He wanted to bring her pleasure, but his body was about to explode. He had never craved release like this before and as he moved rhythmically, it became inevitable. Swift, sharp, almost violent, his climax slammed into him, wracking great shudders as a deep, hoarse growl escaped from his throat.

He lay still, braced on his elbows, head folded into the curve of her shoulder, until his body returned to some semblance of regularity. Regularity. He felt certain he would never feel the same again.

"Caroline," he murmured gruffly.

"Yes." Her husky voice sounded so sensual, still breathy and tinged with uncertainty.

"You didn't feel release, did you?"

"Ah… I don't know what that is."

"The pleasure, I know you felt that." Silence answered, and he knew she was too timid to comment. "It builds toward a kind of crescendo, a completion. Did you experience anything like that?"

"Like what happened to you?" she asked. He nodded, rubbing his cheek against her hair. "No," she said.

"I will teach you how to enjoy the act, and I shall endeavor to give you that ultimate pleasure."

"Tonight?" came her weak, nearly baleful cry.

He almost chuckled. Having assaulted his poor, innocent bride with all manner of fleshly sensation, he had quite overwhelmed her senses, it seemed. He hauled himself up on one elbow and smiled down at her as he traced his fingers over her lips. "When you are ready. And I didn't forget my promise to taste every inch of you, but, again, not tonight, love. You have had enough new experience for now." He withdrew and stretched out next to her, lying with his head propped up on one hand and twirling her hair with the other. "Sleep, Cara *mia.*"

Settling the sheet around her, he watched her nest into the softness of the bed. "Magnus?"

"Yes."

She paused. He sensed whatever it was she had intended to say, she decided against speaking it. "Good night."

"Good night, Caroline."

It was not long until her breathing fell into a deep, regular pattern. The moonlight waned, and the room darkened, but Magnus' eyes remained fixed on the slender female beside him in the bed. After a while, his body began to rouse, wanting to repeat the fiery union they had shared a short while before. Even in sleep the siren called out to his flesh, and it answered with ready desire.

By God, she was a terrifying creature! He rolled onto his back and folded his hands under his head while he stared into the darkness. He had wanted to stir her passions, give her pleasure, so she would never come reluctantly to his bed. Only his cunning had worked so well, it had ensnared him as well. He had felt like a callow youth, aquiver and overcome in the presence of the object of his infatuation.

Again.

He closed his eyes, but the memory would not be stayed. He mustn't equate his bride with that unfeeling bitch. It had been more than twenty years since he had succumbed to such intense feeling. The wash of remembrance emerged, unbidden and full of long-suppressed emotion.

She had been one of his mother's friends, so lovely he could think of nothing else for months. Then the depraved object of his obsession noticed him, a boy of only fourteen years but already showing early signs of a tall, well-formed frame and strong, regular features. She had set her sights on seducing him. Although his mind yearned for poetry and flowers and the gentle romanticism of idealistic youth, his body was ripe for her enticements. One night she bade him come to her chamber. There she initiated him into what she termed "the arts of love." It had been so beautiful, so tender, he had wanted to weep afterward. What he did instead had been a disaster. He had told her of his devotion, his love. She had merely stared at him and then, to his utter humiliation, she laughed.

In that single instant, he realized in retrospect, he had had a choice. Leave in unspeakable shame. Or laugh too, and thereby turn his back on everything tender and good inside him.

And so he had pretended he intended the joke to amuse her, and something inside him died. It was his first step in becoming the brazen wastrel everyone knew him to be. "Come, Magnus," she had cooed, "Come love me some more."

They had laughed as he had climbed on top of her, and this time it was not beautiful. It was sordid and base and mere primal need for release. Over the years, he had learned many tricks in bed and become adept at giving and taking pleasure. He had experienced debaucheries not even the most vicious gossips had the courage to repeat. He had followed the road taken those many years ago, when a sex-sated jade had laughed at his heart. Yet, never had he experienced the same wonder, the same reverence, the same ecstasy as he had tonight.

Beside him, Caroline stirred. He glanced down, able to see her in the first pale streaks of dawn creeping into the room. As his long-ago countess had defiled him, did he now corrupt his new wife? She was all the things he had never allowed himself to have.

He was a rake, a scoundrel, a cad of the first rank. With a hellish temper. An insatiable sexual appetite. A viciously brutal wit and a cold, remote manner. No one could touch him.

All true.

Except, behind it all, he loathed himself more than any of his countless enemies. More perhaps, than had his own father.

Caroline woke up alone in the elegant chamber. She blinked, trying to shed the hazy cobwebs of slumber. All at once, memory descended and last night, in all of its vivid detail, exploded into her brain.

Oh, yes, last night.

Releasing a protracted breath, a hint of a smile touched her lips. It had been wonderful. She had never imagined such feeling existed, and Magnus had been kind and tender, yet exciting. Unpredictable. He had taunted her outrageously, touched her where she had never thought a man would dare, and brought her as close to the brink of sanity as she had ever feared to be.

Catlike, she stretched, running her hands over the

crushed bedclothes next to her. They still bore his masculine scent, stirring alive a not-so-dormant longing. He had been with her through the night, she knew, for the unfamiliarity of his presence had brought her out of sleep several times. Yet, it was a comforting, pleasant knowledge, and each time she had contentedly drifted back into her dreams.

Rising, she examined the sheets. There were no stains on them, but her thighs bore a few flecks of blood. The ending of her virginity had been surprisingly painless.

Suffering through a quick hip bath with the cold water in the basin, she yanked the tapestry bellpull to summon Lillian.

Her toilette did not take long. Donning the prim muslin and instructing Lillian to dress her hair in a plain chignon, she rushed downstairs. She got lost trying to find the small dining room, until a parlor-maid showed her the way.

Magnus and David were already seated. She watched for her temperamental husband's reaction, trying to gauge his mood this morning as he looked up and caught her eye. He seemed closed, reserved. David, on the other hand, leapt to his feet and ushered her to her seat.

"Ravishing, simply ravishing," he fussed as he played footman and fluffed her napkin and placed it on her lap. "First thing in the morning, and she looks like a dew-kissed flower. That comes from righteous living, eh, brother?"

Magnus continued his steady look. "Food's on the sideboard. Help yourself. Cook'll get you eggs if you like."

"Just toast," Caroline murmured.

Was this the passionate man who had set her flesh on fire only hours ago? She would never understand his mercurial moods.

And, strangely, it hurt more than a little bit to have him look at her with such dispassionate eyes.

"So, sister," David said, "What are your plans for the day? Being a London girl, you will no doubt find country life dull. I know I do," David said.

Magnus' deep timbre cut in. "I think it best if you spend some time with Mrs. Gervis, the housekeeper. There are duties you will be expected to take over, and she can instruct you. David and I have business to attend to, and perhaps after luncheon, we'll take the horses out."

It wasn't a request. Caroline understood his conversational tone was only a courtesy. She nodded in assent.

He never looked up from his paper again. When the meal was over, they dispersed—the men into Magnus' study and Caroline in search of Mrs. Gervis.

At the housekeeper's monologue on the working of Hawking Park, Caroline felt as if she were back in the schoolroom, but she endured in polite and attentive silence. It was late in the morning before she had a chance to steal away and dash off a message for her mother. Finding a footman, she asked him to dispatch it to the Ordinary.

In it, she had written only one line: *No money yet.* Magnus had not mentioned when she would begin to receive her allowance. If he didn't bring up the matter soon, she would have to.

After luncheon alone, David came to say his farewell before returning to London.

Holding her hands in his, he said, "I am so glad to know you are here, Caroline. Though he would never admit it, Magnus needs you, and I am pleased he is in such good hands." In the face of his unfamiliar seriousness, Caroline only nodded.

Magnus strode out of the study. "Still here, David?"

"I'm leaving." He clicked his heels together and bowed

low over her hand like a Prussian prince. "Just lingering in the presence of beauty."

"Yes, well, get out."

David grinned. Caroline noticed Magnus was never truly vexed with his brother. Rather their rude and teasing interchange seemed a comfortable repartee between siblings deeply fond of one another.

Magnus looked to Caroline. "Are you ready to go riding?"

"I have no habit," she answered. Actually, she had, but it was so dated and small she would never have let him see her in it.

"I never understood that convention. It's merely a skirt, no more practical for riding than any other dress. You will wear what you have on. No one shall see us, anyway, for it is all my land."

Caroline shrugged. "Very well."

He grabbed her cloak and led her out to the stables, inquiring, "Do you enjoy riding, Caroline?"

Just last night, he had called her Cara. He had made it sound like a cry from his soul.

"I do, though I am not very accomplished." She mimicked his attitude, keeping her voice cool and abrupt.

His hand touched her waist. It was warm and the gentle gesture of possession was decidedly pleasant. "The country out here is beautiful, and Balthazar and I love to roam."

"Balthazar?" Caroline queried.

Magnus held up his hand. "Balthazar."

Caroline swung her head in the direction he indicated to find two horses saddled and waiting in the stable yard. There was no question which one was Magnus's Balthazar. Midnight black, sleek and beautiful, the proud stallion was indeed noteworthy.

"I am no equestrian, but I know enough about horse-flesh to see that is an extraordinary animal!"

"He is," Magnus agreed. Approaching the stallion, he caressed his velvet nose. The horse responded affectionately, drawing a chuckle from his master. "And not only fine-looking, he has an excellent temperament and great intelligence. Not to mention he is an astute judge of character."

He continued to nuzzle the majestic beast. "Balthazar shall miss me when I am gone, won't you, friend?" Emerald eyes shifted to Caroline. "Not many shall."

His gaze flickered away. "Lord, I am getting morose. Please believe that I am not normally like this."

She did move then, laying a gloved hand lightly on his arm. "I think you are very brave, Magnus. I don't know how you have the courage to face each day."

A quick frown of pain darted so quickly across his features that she almost missed it. He swallowed. "Caroline, you misunderstand me. There is nothing brave about me. You do not understand. There is nothing to live for. Only to die for. The child, the one you will give me, is what gives me courage, if indeed I have any."

She shook her head and smiled. "You are a poet, Magnus. I'm never quite certain I understand you."

"Ah," he laughed, folding his hand over hers and leading her to her mount, "if you ever do, let me know of it. I'm afraid I still do not understand myself."

"There!" she giggled playfully. "You did it again."

He was lighthearted once again, his features softened with the twinkle of merriment in his eye and strong, white teeth flashing in the sun. "Very well, you have my permission to call me on the carpet every time I say something inexplicable." He paused, cocking his head. "What a novel idea for seduction. It is liable to increase my maudlin musings, not the opposite.''

"Then let us confine the calling onto the carpet to the figurative," Caroline suggested.

"Not nearly as enjoyable as my idea, but as you wish."

He introduced her to the pretty mare as if it were a formal presentation at a London soiree. Then they mounted and rode in the direction of the river.

It was the perfect autumn day, Caroline reflected, with large billowy clouds racing across a steel-gray sky. Riotous color surrounded them as they skirted the forest: cherry-red, burnt orange, vibrant yellow. The breeze was cool, whipping Caroline's hair out of its pins as they cantered along the path.

Magnus was being charming once again. The aftershocks of last night had lessened, and Caroline was restored to her normal temperament. She had been a bit numb, she realized, knocked off-balance by the devastating feelings she had felt in his arms. In addition, daily life as the mistress of Hawking Park was a new experience, and she wasn't too proud to admit she felt more than a bit intimidated.

Yet, all seemed well as they meandered through the wooded path to a small stream that fed into the river.

"There's a beautiful spot just ahead," Magnus called.

Following the stream, they came upon the small delta where the land opened up once again and the darkening sky was visible. "We may get a soaking," Caroline commented, glancing upwards at the gathered thunderheads.

"Very likely," Magnus answered. He squinted at the sky. "Do you wish to return?"

Caroline tossed her head bravely. "I? Afraid of a bit of water? How many times have you commented that I am no shrinking violet?"

"Good enough," he said, pleased, as he kicked his horse onward. They traveled down to where the countryside fell away, and a vista of brilliant color and intricate pattern lay before them. Plots of ground were visible as squares and rectangles in various shades of green bordered by clusters of magnificently crowned trees dressed as gaudily as a band of gypsies. Through all of it, the crystal blue of the river cut a meandering swath.

"My God, Magnus, it's beautiful!"

He paused, taking in the scene. "Let's dismount and rest here awhile."

They tied the reins to a low branch and walked a little way. Magnus picked up a handful of rocks and skipped them on the calm water. Devilishly, Caroline selected a few choice flat stones and taking careful, very low aim, astounded her husband by skipping one four times before it disappeared.

"A multifaceted woman," he stated with approval. She bowed her head in exaggerated humility, and they laughed.

They stopped where the river descended quickly, the swiftly moving water spewing white against the rocks.

"It's called the Witch's Cauldron," Magnus said. He was standing very close, behind her and off to one side. The sound of the rapids was loud, but his deep voice carried clear.

"Is this another of your childhood haunts?" Caroline called back.

"Actually, I always dreamt of making love to a very special woman right here in this spot."

Her stomach plummeted in reaction. She turned to face him, already trembling. He gave her a quick shake of his head and pointed upward. "Don't look so frightened. The weather would not cooperate even if we were so inclined today."

"Are you trying to shock me?"

"Did I?"

She sighed. "Yes, actually."

He touched her chin with warm fingers. "Cara, you are no prude. Last night you were unabashed and passionate." At her flush, he raised a forbidding finger. "No, no. No belated modesty. I can't think for a minute you have any regrets. Though I do."

Despite herself, she had to ask. "What regret do you have?"

"Your pleasure, madam," he grinned. "As much as I would loved to have petted and teased you all night long, I didn't think your delicate new-bride sensibilities would take so much."

Petted and teased? Her belly convulsed, sending ripples of shivery delight through her. Oh, God, what was he doing to her with mere words?

"Come here," he said. "Now you have made me want to kiss you."

He pulled her close, and she stepped willingly into his arms. If he had tossed her onto the ground and realized his fantasy, she would not have uttered one word of protest.

Was it only a game to him, she wondered as his lips brushed tantalizing kisses over her mouth. A game of power?

The sound of thunder brought his head up. "I think we may have outstayed our welcome."

The first few spatters of rain confirmed this. Magnus grabbed her hand and they hurried back to the horses. They mounted, riding at full tilt as the heavens unleashed their burden. It was exhilarating to ride helter-skelter through the storm, and Caroline laughed at the sheer joy of being so reckless. And being with Magnus.

Chapter Eight

The grooms were waiting at the house, as was Arthur, fretting at the front door as Caroline and Magnus dripped all over the fine Aubusson carpet.

"Right upstairs," Magnus ordered, grabbing Caroline's elbow. "Hot tea, Arthur. And tell Mrs. Gervis to send up plenty of towels."

"Yes, your lordship."

A mere fifteen minutes later Caroline was wrapped in Magnus' dressing gown—it was larger and thicker and therefore warmer, and he had insisted—with her feet tucked up under her, nestled by a roaring fire in the sitting room of her apartments. She had both hands around her teacup as she sipped the steaming brew. Outside, the storm was going full force. Raindrops pounded against the leaded glass and grumbling rolls of thunder rippled through the air.

Magnus came through the connecting door, dressed in fresh clothes and rubbing a small towel over his still damp hair.

"Shall I pour you a cup?" Caroline asked.

"Yes, thank you." He sat on the sofa opposite her chair, his long legs crossed ankle over knee. A loud clap of thunder sounded close. "I hope David pulls off the road some-where. Horses can be unpredictable in this kind of weather."

"Why does David travel back and forth so frequently? It's not a terribly long journey, but still time-consuming."

"I need him here." Magnus grew serious as he stared into his teacup. "He is starting to take over some of the business." He didn't explain further, but Caroline could imagine how difficult it must be for Magnus to hand over his duties to his heir. It was admitting weakness. Defeat. "And," he continued, "he despises being away from Lon-don for too long, thus the travel."

The lovely mood of only moments ago dissipated. Thun-der roared again, and talk of business had reminded Car-oline of an unpleasant duty.

He had picked up a strange-looking pastry, a sort of knotted bread. Seeing her look at it, he explained. "I am afraid I have a wicked sweet tooth. Mrs. Bronson makes these just for me. They are so sickeningly rich, no one else can take them." He took a huge bite, giving testimony to his enthusiasm for the odd things. "Would you like to try it?"

She couldn't have forced a single bite past her con-stricted throat as she thought about the awkward request she was about to make. She shook her head.

"Magnus, I need to ask you about something. Or, rather, remind you. That is…there is the manner of my allowance. As thoroughly as everything was explained, it was never made clear when I would receive this first…ah…"

"Payment," he supplied.

It was barely noticeable, the darkening of his eyes from emerald green to murky jade. The tenseness about his mouth was slight, but she was waiting for a sign of his displeasure, and so she saw every nuance. She sat unmoving as she awaited his answer.

What she would give to have had their carefree afternoon not be spoiled by talk of money. Or payment. But she was not in this house, this room, to while away pleasant hours with its lord. She was here for money. Money she needed for James.

"How much would you like?" he asked at last.

"All of it, please." She said it quickly before the words could choke her.

He hesitated, and for a panicked moment, she though he would refuse. Then he stood and said curtly, "I'll get it at once. Of course the money is yours, and you can have it right away, if that is what you wish. You earned it last night."

Her head snapped back as if she'd been slapped. His look was brittle and cold before he turned away and left the room.

Alone, she blew out a long, tired breath. She could not blame his shifted mood on his capriciousness this time. It was her own doing that had ruined the lovely day.

But what was she to do? Even as she had ridden like a fury through a storm, and gazed at beautiful scenes and kissed her husband by wild rapids, her brother had languished in a bed, as he did every day, be it a good or bad one. She was here for *James*. She was not here for love.

The thought startled her, and she groaned, knowing it was true.

Oh, yes. She could easily fall in love with Magnus.

Burying her face in her hands, she tried to think. Falling in love with Magnus was something she must never do. Magnus was *dying*. She absolutely would not allow herself such a disaster. The fear of losing James was bad enough—unbearable, unthinkable. Would it be any less excruciating to lose a beloved husband?

She was not in love with him, not yet anyway. He was merely charming, when he set his mind to it. And, yes, handsome, and a passionate lover. She was simply confusing the wonderful desire he had awakened in her with a more lasting emotion. Oh, assuredly, when he passed on, she would miss him, but she could carry on without him. She certainly would.

Arthur arrived within a quarter hour of Magnus' abrupt departure and set a covered silver tray on a table. When Caroline opened it, a stack of bank notes lay neatly on the salver.

Guilt stabbed at her soul. She wished she could explain that the money was desperately needed to save a life. She couldn't do that, of course, but still, a pressing desire to see him made itself felt, and she slipped into a tattered patterned muslin and went down to his study.

He was there, as expected, striking an insolent pose when she knocked at the half-open door. "Is there something else you require?" he asked, his voice sounding bored. Her instincts flared. He had retreated behind aristocratic ennui once again.

She entered the room, feeling as if she were entering the lion's den. "Magnus, I wanted to explain. About the money."

"You do not need to explain."

"I want to. My mother has debts, and her moneys are nonexistent."

"What do you mean? She lives at my expense."

The statement hit her wrong. "It is ill-mannered of you to brag of your generosity."

His face darkened, and he said stiffly, "I merely mentioned it because I have no idea why she could be in such dire need of funds.''

''Did you ever think of clothes?'' she shot back. She swept her hands demonstratively down the front of her nearly threadbare dress. ''Do you think my mother would dress me like this and reserve finery for herself? I tell you, her wardrobe is much worse. And there are other things she will want to purchase, small items, like perhaps a toy for James. He is only seven, and has nothing with which to play. For Christmas last, my mother used rags to fashion him a gaily colored pillow. It was his only present besides mine, which was a book that had been damaged at the shop. He could barely read it.''

She found herself standing squarely in front of him, hands fisted at her sides and fully in the grip of a fine rage. He watched her from under heavy lids. ''Very well, you have explained. You have your allowance.''

''Yes, but you are angry with me because I asked.''

His lip curled lazily. ''I am not angry, Caroline. I assure you, when I am angry you will know it. In fact, there will be no doubt....'' He trailed off, shutting his eyes for a moment. Shaking off the strange distraction, he looked at her once again. ''Go on to bed.''

She gave him a questioning look. ''It is early.''

''Then go read in your room or write a letter or something!'' he snapped, loosening his collar.

''You are angry! I don't—''

''Caroline,'' he snarled. He went to his desk and leaned on it, palms flat on the cluttered surface, head hanging down. ''Get out. Right now.''

It was then Caroline realized the truth. ''You are ill!'' she cried.

''Leave me.'' His voice was growing hoarse, strained.

''Magnus, let me help you!''

"No! Get Arthur. Quickly." He raised his head. His pallor shot a jolt of panic through her. There were beads of sweat clustered on his brow. "Please," he said, eyes blazing.

After a moment's indecision, she said, "Yes, yes, of course."

She ran out of the room, flying down the corridors as she yelled most unseemingly for the very proper major-domo. When she found him, she said only, "Magnus—the master—he's in the study" and the servant was off in a flash.

She followed, lingering outside in the hallway. Arthur was barking orders to several people within. Then two footmen came out, bearing Magnus' limp form up the stairs. Caroline shrank into the shadows.

Tears spilled onto her cheeks, and her whole body shook so violently her teeth chattered. Magnus...so helpless. Dear God, is that what it was like for him? The image of that proud, magnificent man being borne away like a limp rag doll was too horrible.

As she crept up to her rooms, Caroline wondered how she was going to abide watching Magnus Eddington die.

Safely ensconced in his old room, Magnus stretched experimentally. He did not want to be near Caroline, not when he was like this, so he had kept this room as a retreat for when his illness struck. Rising shakily to his feet, he waited for the dizziness to subside before shuffling over to the washbasin.

This attack had not been a bad one, but he knew better than to be heartened by that fact, nor to interpret it as any sign of recovery. There seemed to be no rhyme or reason to their occurrence, duration, or intensity.

The water was bracing and he felt much better after

washing. A yank on the bellpull signaled the kitchens he was ready for a very late breakfast. He was ravenous, as usual. While he waited, he wandered over to the windows and began drawing the brocade hangings.

A gray, overcast day met him, but Magnus liked the majestic gloom. It matched his mood. This window overlooked the gardens, and a movement drew his attention downward.

A cloaked figure moved among the dead shrubs. There was no mystery as to the person's identity. It was Caroline. He could never mistake that willowy form and the grace with which it moved. He watched her as she picked her way down the cobblestone path.

He closed his eyes against the quickening of his heartbeat. What had she thought when she saw him succumbing? Had she witnessed him being dragged through the house like a useless, defenseless...? *Had she been disgusted?*

He groaned, laying his forehead against the cold glass.

She turned, paused, and as if beckoned by the force of his thoughts, glanced up. She saw him. At least he thought she did. Her face remained toward him, a slight frown on the lovely features.

"Here are your eggs, your lordship."

Magnus didn't turn around. "Thank you, Arthur."

Arthur came up to look over his master's shoulder. "She has been very quiet. Mrs. Gervis has looked after her today."

Magnus grunted. Moving away from the window, he let the curtain fall back into place. "Make certain she is never to come near me when it happens."

"Yes, my lord."

He gave Arthur his instructions. Then he finished his meal and went back to bed, giving up on the hope of spending time with his bride. His body just wouldn't follow his will, and as he reclined in obedience to his fatigue, he was surprised to discover he missed her.

Caroline handed her cloak to a parlor-maid and asked for the fire to be lit in the small parlor. When it was done, she sat at the lady's desk and wrote a quick letter to her friend, Lucy, who had worked with her at the bookseller's. After that she was still restless. She went in search of Arthur.

When she located him in the pantry, she asked, "How is my lord?"

Arthur blinked. "Well, my lady," he answered after a moment's hesitation. "He is recovered, but resting."

"Will he be at supper tonight?"

"I do not believe so, my lady. Would you like me to give him a message?"

"No. Yes. Please tell him I hope he is feeling better very soon and that he is in my prayers."

"Yes, my lady, as you wish," was his correct response, but Caroline detected a softening in his face, and his lips quivered just a bit in something suspiciously like a smile.

Thinking to amuse herself with a book, she entered the library. The smell of leather and dust was thick, but it was a pleasant, masculine scent, combined with the sweetness of the oil used to polish the furniture and floors. She found several of the latest popular novels, as well as some old favorites. She chose a few and brought them up to her room.

She started three of them before giving up, for her mind refused to settle into any of the stories. She dozed out of boredom, then woke feeling cross.

A knock at the door sent her heart leaping in hopes it was Magnus. She had a great need to see for herself that he was well. When she flung the door open, she was met by Mrs. Gervis.

"My lady, I have the dressmaker here."

Caroline frowned in confusion. "Pardon me? Dressmaker?"

A large woman breezed past the housekeeper and declared, "You remember me, don't you, Lady Caroline? Oh, of course she does. Come along"—this to a trio of heavily laden servants who bore in chin-high towers of material. "Do not be all day! Oh, madam, wait until you see what I have brought for you!"

Caroline did indeed recognize the overbearing woman as Mrs. Dungeness, the seamstress who had created her wedding gown. She had had a devil of a time with the woman, whose tastes ran to the more ostentatious rather than elegant. Caroline had had to fight to attain the artful, dignified style for her wedding gown, fretting the whole while that she would end up at the doors of the church looking like a magnificently attired tart. Mrs. Dungeness had surprised her—pleasantly—for the gown had been flawless and exactly as Caroline had stipulated.

Caroline had no idea, however, what the seamstress was doing here in her room.

She would have asked if another servant hadn't appeared at that moment and handed her a folded piece of paper. Opening it, she read: *You need clothes. Mrs. Dungeness will be visiting your mother as well.*

It was signed simply "M."

The seamstress was upon her. "Here, you must look at these sketches. Have you ever seen anything like that? And this—no, that is not quite the thing, but look! It would be magnificent for you. In purple brocade!"

Caroline quickly became absorbed in the project of acquiring a new wardrobe. Refusing to be bullied by the other woman's persuasive comments, she chose several day dresses to be made up in muslin, a few more formal gowns from the heavier silks and brushed wool, a riding habit, dainty nightdresses of a sinfully sheer batiste and various undergarments, stockings, gloves and a smart wide-brimmed hat topped with a jaunty plume.

They had worked through tea, and as a result, Caroline was famished when they finished. It was already dark, but Mrs. Dungeness seemed not to mind at all the late hours. "I will send over the dresses as they are made instead of waiting to fill the whole order. His lordship said they had to be finished as soon as possible." She clapped her hands together and Caroline guessed she was being paid handsomely for a timely delivery.

Exhausted, Caroline ordered her meal sent to her room. She ate little, then retired. When morning broke, she rose early, feeling a bit sluggish. It was her normal warning of her monthly courses. After breakfast, she fixed a tonic her mother always gave her to ease the discomfort and tried to interest herself in one of the books she had borrowed. This time, the story entranced her and it was already luncheon when a knock sounded and Lillian entered.

"Ma'am," she said with a perfunctory bob that was her abbreviated curtsy, "Mrs. Gervis wanted me to tell ye 'is lordship is askin' for ye. 'E's waitin' luncheon—"

Caroline was on her feet in an instant, her book falling onto the floor, forgotten. Lillian dressed her hair, pulling it loosely away from her forehead and curling the gleaming blond tresses into an artful twist. There was no help for her clothing, not until her new dresses arrived, so Caroline simply pinched her cheeks and bit her lips and hurried down to the dining room.

Chapter Nine

The smaller dining room at Hawking Park could hardly be called cozy, yet Magnus much preferred it to the other. He waited impatiently for Caroline, growing annoyed at the delay.

When she swept into the room, flushed and smiling, she fairly took his breath away. Caroline exuded life. It vibrated from her in every nuance of her moods, for she never did anything by halves. And now, from her face and the way she moved toward him, he could tell she was pleased to see him.

"Magnus, you look well!" she exclaimed. Almost as if she had been concerned. His heart gave a curious flop.

"I am much improved," he said. His hand itched to reach out and touch her, just her arm or hand. He *needed* to establish some contact, and it was the intensity of this need which frightened him. He curled his fingers into fists at his sides to stifle the urge.

"Thank you so much for the clothes. They are going to be lovely, and much appreciated. I cannot tell you what that means to me that she is to visit my mother as well. You are too generous!"

Was that why she was so delighted with him then, for

the few pounds he had laid out for her wardrobe? The bitter thought almost made him groan before he pushed it away from his mind. Outwardly, he merely shrugged. "We will outfit you properly when we go to London."

"London? When are we going to London?"

He led her to her seat and held her chair. "I haven't made the arrangements yet, but it will be soon. It is necessary for you to become established with fashionable society. We don't want any disparaging gossip about you or our marriage. It will reflect on the child."

She was silent, apparently thinking on this latest revelation of his plans. Though she made no objection, he sensed she was disturbed. After a while, she asked, "Will we stay long?"

"A month, perhaps. The opera a few nights, and a ball or two. When the season starts, perhaps earlier. I detest the crowds and all those glaring matrons sizing you up for son-in-law potential."

She laughed. "I hardly think you will be troubled on that account any longer."

"What an idiot I am!" he declared, chuckling, too. "Thank goodness those endless interrogations shall be no more."

"See," she teased, her eyes dancing. They really were a fascinating shade of blue-violet. "I am of some use."

His look must have showed something of what he was thinking, for she blushed and turned away.

Schooling himself, he gathered his wits together and addressed the meal in front of him. He was burning for her. Their one night together had far from sated his desire, for the memory had driven him nearly mad all day yesterday as he waited for his body to gain strength. Tonight could not arrive fast enough as far as he was concerned, and though he himself saw no reason to have to wait that long, he was determined to have consideration for her inexperience.

"I was in the garden yesterday," Caroline said in between bites. "And I noticed it looked a bit neglected. Your gardener needs to cut back the perennials and dig up the annuals, and some of the shrubbery should be trimmed before winter."

He paused, his fork suspended in midair. "How do you know gardening?"

"I don't, really," she admitted. "I have never done it myself, but I do admire gardens, and I ask a lot of questions. Most of the groundskeepers for the London parks run when they see me coming."

He laughed. "You are incorrigible, then?"

She pretended offense. "Knowledge, sir, is a valuable thing."

"Well, I shall be glad to let you test that knowledge. I tend the garden here, at least most of it. I find it relaxing. It can be backbreaking work, but it is one of the few interests a gentleman is allowed, besides horsemanship, that can physically challenge. And there is the aesthetic side of it, as well. I enjoy beauty." His eyes flickered over her in a way that told her of his appreciation of *her* beauty. Though she colored in response, she didn't look away and the hint of a smile tugged the corner of her mouth.

Dinner was another enjoyable meal, made more so by the ease of her company. His nerves were taut, strung to their limit with the single-mindedness of wanting her. Too often during their lively conversation, his mind drifted to irrelevant preoccupations such as the perfect shape of her breasts or her tiny waist. When at last the clock in the small drawing room chimed ten o'clock, he nearly jumped out of his chair.

"Shall we retire?" he said. She nodded, rising. He almost managed to behave respectably—almost. At the last minute, as they were about to exit into the hallway, he could resist no longer and captured her around her waist and spun her around.

She only gasped, melting against him as his mouth descended on hers. Without having spoken a word, he communicated the urgent press of need. Her arms twined around his neck, and when he pulled her in tighter, he could feel the swell of her breasts against his chest.

"I want you," he whispered, trailing kisses to her ear. He felt her shudder. "I have missed you, Cara. Come, let's go upstairs."

She stiffened, and as he made to lead her to the door, she pulled back. He gave her a questioning look. "I can't," was all she said.

Puzzled, he said, "I don't understand."

She slipped out of his slackened grasp. "I am fatigued tonight, Magnus. Please do not ask me. I…"

A rage so huge it nearly blinded him descended like a landslide. The little idiot was denying him! Even as his reason warred with irrationality, a niggling voice hissed in his brain: *she saw you, helpless and repulsively ill. And now she abhors you!*

Fighting the unbearable urge to shake her, he snarled through clenched teeth, "We discussed this thoroughly, Caroline. You are to be at my disposal. Have you forgotten the terms of our agreement? I kept my part of the bargain. I paid out every shilling. Now I expect you to keep yours."

Those delicately arched brows drew together fiercely and she clasped her hands together, working one over the other beneath her breasts. "Magnus, I know. I promise, another time…" Perhaps his face showed enough of his inner fury, for she stopped. Unable to meet his gaze, she studied the floor as she said in a very small voice, "I am sorry. I...I am...indisposed at the present time. I shall be recovered in a few days.''

At first the meaning of her words did not penetrate his inflamed state of mind. Then slowly, realization dawned. He closed his eyes and grimaced, unable to believe his stupidity.

When he opened them again, he saw that Caroline looked miserable. Chagrined, he reached for her. "Cara, don't be so ashamed. We are married. You can tell me these things.'' Albeit reluctantly, she allowed him to draw her back into his arms.

God, he was humiliating her further. He was behaving like an idiot, first throwing a tantrum because he thought she was spurning him and now shaming her beyond reason by referring to the unmentionable. True, he was her husband. Also true, he was a stranger, known to her a little over a week.

"We will not mention it again,'' he murmured into her fragrant hair. She stirred a bit, seeming to nuzzle him in silent pardon. He wished he could cherish it, but he was too filled with self-disgust. He had embarrassed Caroline because of his damnably prickling pride, and suddenly that old tired voice which had stated his defects so succinctly in his mind resounded with new force.

These were demons to be wrestled with later. Gently, he disengaged his wife and tilted her face up to his. "Go to bed, Cara. I shall see you in the morning.'' He set her away from him with determination. She still wouldn't look at him. Nodding, she hurried from the room.

In the silence after her departure, Magnus went to the window and gazed into the black void. He used to love the night, used to crave the excitement of its entertainments. Filling the dark hours with drink and women and divesting his friends at White's of their last shilling had actually seemed...fun.

Now night was simply the end of the day and without his anticipated evening with Caroline, it was cold. And lonely.

It always had been, he noted. All the diversions of his useless life were merely a way to dress his loneliness. But like a crone decked in queen's finery, it had never worked, never filled the emptiness. He was only recognizing it now, but he had known it. Perhaps that was why he had so doggedly pursued infamy.

Perhaps. That, and to prove his father right. Useless, depraved, obscene—these were the words the gentle man uttered against his son in his last hours. And, too late, Magnus had realized that this man's opinion, above all others, was the one that mattered the most.

Now there was Caroline, whose sweet face and flashing gemstone eyes made his pulse race wild and his soul ache. He was starting to need her. And he was proving himself to be no better to her than he had to his father.

Seated with her mother the next day in the sitting room at the Ordinary, Caroline's mind was leagues away from their conversation. She didn't know how long it had been since her mother had ceased talking, only becoming aware of it when she felt the weight of her stare.

"Tell me," Audrae commanded.

Caroline sighed. "Mother, this isn't going to be as easy as I thought."

Audrae nodded solemnly. "It is difficult to see anyone suffering, darling. Especially someone you care about."

Caroline whipped her head around to stare at her mother's implacable face. The statement hung in the air.

Finally, Caroline broke her gaze away. "How is the medicine working? Has it helped James at all?"

"It is too early to tell. The doctor was going to inquire about a sanatorium."

"Mother, those places are too expensive. As generous as Magnus has been, we cannot afford it."

"The doctor is looking into it," Audrae said calmly, putting the matter to rest.

James woke from his nap, and the women turned to cheerful topics, namely the exciting prospect of the new wardrobes provided by the earl. It seemed James was to have several new suits and a parcel of play clothes. Audrae ordered only two gowns from the crestfallen Mrs. Dungeness, asserting she would purchase others in due time, with her own money, thank you very much. They all three indulged in a hearty laugh at the giddy seamstress and her abominable taste.

It was past midday, but Caroline postponed her departure to play a game of chess with James, watching his small, pale face for signs of improvement. She saw none, but she allowed no disappointment showed as she teased and laughed with her brother, letting him fatally corner her king.

When she returned to Hawking Park, she took to her room. Thoughts of James kept her awake and restless until finally she gave herself over to tears.

She wished she could curl up and sleep, and in sleep shut out the horror. James. And Magnus. Death was all around her.

When her grief was spent, she rose, washed her face and donned a fresh dress before going down for dinner.

Magnus was pleasant company, if withdrawn a bit more than usual. It amazed Caroline how unfazed he seemed by his illness. He looked no worse for his recent bout. Unlike

James, whose pallor and gauntness only increased. This last thought brought a fresh wash of pain.

"Cara?"

She gasped, blinking into awareness of her present. Magnus was staring at her, a shadow of concern over his handsome features.

"Am I boring you?"

"No! No, I am sorry. Please excuse me."

His eyes darkened to gray-green as he studied her for a moment. Caroline became acutely aware of every plane on that angular face, from the strong nose to the square jaw. At times like this, when he leveled one of his penetrating looks, she felt a tremor of fear that he could somehow plumb her secrets.

"Is something disturbing you?" he asked.

It would be foolish to deny it. She cast about for some excuse. "I suppose. I was only wondering when my dresses would be ready."

She was rewarded with a scowl, and seeing her error, she rose. Acting on impulse, Caroline walked toward him. "And I realize I have been remiss." Stopping at the side of his chair, she leaned in close. "I have not thanked you properly. As I recall, you prefer demonstrations of gratitude." With that, she brushed her lips against the smooth-shaven cheek.

The texture of his skin felt wonderful and she lingered. It came as somewhat of a surprise to know she wanted to kiss him, and not just in this daughterly manner. He did not move, staring straight ahead with his lids drawn down over his eyes to shield their expression. At his lack of response, she made to move away, but his large hand caught her wrist and yanked her onto his lap.

"If you are going to kiss me, Cara, do it properly," he said as his mouth came down over hers. The thrill of it sent shudders rippling through her body and she relaxed, cradled securely and braced by steely arms. Slipping her hand into the soft curls twisting at his collar, she sighed.

There were words unborn in her breast, things she wanted to say, but she didn't know what they were. She wanted him. Her body ached for the feel of his hands, and the desire to be with him, to taste again the wonders of passion, was overwhelming.

A cry and crash brought them both up short. Caroline looked up to find a wide-eyed maid standing gawking at them, pastries scattered at her feet. With a squeak, she whirled on her heel and fled.

Caroline turned her head slowly to Magnus. They both grinned and fell to laughing.

"You are shameless," he sighed. "Now get off me before we shock the entire staff into giving their notice."

The fortuitous arrival of the servant had doused the burning fog in Caroline's head enough that she responded immediately.

Magnus stood beside her, clearing his throat and breathing deeply. She busied herself arranging her skirts, and he wandered away, leaning his head back to study the mural on the ceiling. After an awkward interval, he gave her an admonishing look. "Unless you want to test the sturdiness of this dining table, not to mention my restraint, I suggest you refrain from such doings in the future."

She grinned impishly. "You don't want me to kiss you?"

He slanted a glance at her and made a low, warning sound. Coming to take her arm, he led her to the door. "Come with me."

Caroline allowed him to lead her to his study. The cozy room had a well-lived-in look, cluttered with papers and bound volumes of ledgers. On his desk, a messy scatter of various documents obscured the surface.

She had been in this room several times, but never to enjoy its comforts. Magnus indicated a plush tufted leather chair, and she sat.

"I think it is absurd for you to retire after dinner on your own while I sit and drink port alone," he said. "We are the only two here, so we can dispense with the formalities, don't you agree?"

Caroline nodded.

"There is something I want to give you." He went to a hip-high cast-iron safe, knelt, and twirled the combination knob with a few quick flicks of his wrist. Swinging open the door, he brought out a flat black box about the size of his hand. "I had this brought here to give to you on the occasion of our wedding." He held it out to her. "I had forgotten about it up to now. It seems I am not very good at thinking of others. A fault of mine, I have been told."

She glanced questioningly up at him, and at the quirk in the corner of his mouth, took it. "I have no gift for you," she said.

He gave one small chuckle. "On the contrary."

She knew what he was alluding to, but cast her eyes downward rather than tempt his control by making a sporting reply. The box certainly contained some trinket, jewelry probably. She lifted the lid and froze, her eyes fastened on the brilliant array of diamonds laid out before her.

Lifting the piece, she held it up to see what it was. A choker necklace comprised of four strands of diamond-encrusted gold dazzled like fire before her eyes. Several large stones were set in a medallion at the front, with a modest fringe of dangling gems at the bottom. Looking to

Magnus, he saw he was studying her again, watching closely for her reaction. Intuitively, she knew he was waiting for some sign of greed.

"If I am not to kiss you, then how shall I thank you?"

He ignored the question. "It was my mother's. She wears it in the painting in the grand salon."

"I don't remember," Caroline said, returning her eyes to the fascinating play of light among the brilliant stones. "I shall have to go view the portrait." Looking back to him, she smiled. "Magnus, thank you, truly. I shall take excellent care of it, and when our son marries, he shall present it to his bride."

Immediately, she knew she had said something terribly wrong. Magnus' stricken expression and quick retreat made her curse her thoughtlessness. Placing the necklace back in its box, she set it aside and stood up. "Magnus, I am so sorry, I only wanted you to know that I shall treasure it—"

"No," he said without turning around, "do not apologize. You said nothing wrong." He glanced over his shoulder, flashing a quick, unconvincing smile. "I am glad you like it. Now, go to bed, Cara. Tomorrow you can try it on for me."

She wished there was something she could say, or retract the words that had caused him pain. Answering simply, "Yes, Magnus. Good evening," she retrieved the box and went up to her room.

Chapter Ten

The new medicine seemed to be working with James, for Caroline's next visit saw him somewhat improved. His doctor was convinced the sanatorium was the only way he would fully recover, but the expense was exorbitant. Audrae comforted Caroline, pointing out that the treatment was helping, and perhaps, at a later date, they would have the funds. Unspoken were the words that the "later date" was after Magnus' death, when Caroline would have access to the Eddington fortune.

Despite the good news about her brother, Caroline was miserable. She felt listless and sad, longing for something for which she had no name. David had come for a few days' stay, and Magnus was busy with him going over business. He was courteous, but distant, thrown into a funk, no doubt, by her tactless words about the future. Even the arrival of some of her wardrobe did not cheer her. As her worry over James abated, her empathy for the man who dominated her thoughts grew, and it was with a certain amount of irony that she reflected she had not lessened her heartache by marrying Magnus. She had simply traded one nightmare for another.

Would Magnus ask to return to her bed, or should she approach him? Would he think her forward if she mentioned it? Was he waiting for her to say something?

The truth was, she felt anxious herself. They had had only one night together. Though she wouldn't have admitted it for all the Templar's gold, she wanted to experience those exotic feelings again. Thus she made up her mind.

She took a delicate negligee out of the wardrobe. Mrs. Dungeness was remarkably talented, Caroline mused as she examined the artful way the sheer lemon-colored fabric gathered in coy folds over her breasts and flowed like a spun cloud to her feet. When she moved, tantalizing glimpses of flesh could be seen only to disappear when the fabric shifted. Drawing a silk dressing gown about her, she went to the connecting door and knocked.

She knew he was within, having heard the sound of someone moving about. Belatedly, she thought it might be Arthur, or perhaps Magnus' valet, but before she could retreat, the door swung open and Magnus stood before her.

He stopped and she froze, their eyes locked.

Caroline opened her mouth. "I—I wish to thank you properly." She tried to smile at her joke, but it wilted under his stern countenance. He looked angry, and she thought perhaps she had misjudged. Then he took a single step to clear the threshold and crushed her in his arms. His mouth came down over hers in an onslaught of desire. Parting from her lips only long enough to sweep her up into his arms, he bore her to her bed and laid her upon it.

Dazed by the intensity of his response, Caroline watched with growing ardor as he unfastened his cravat, then undid each stud and stripped off his shirt. She didn't ask him to put out the candles, for her eyes were hungry for him. The

sculpted contours of his male body were revealed in full
illumination as his trousers came off, followed by the last
of his undergarments, until he stood naked, bathed in the
golden glow like some glorious god of myth.

Wild surges of desire left her weak. His eyes seared her
with emerald heat as he gazed down at her. She held up
her hands for him, wanting to feel his flesh against her
own. Instead, he caught her hands and raised her to her
knees before him on the bed. Her eyes never left his face
as she shucked the dressing gown. When her hands came
up to slip off her nightgown, he brushed them away.
Slowly, his fingers tangled in the thin straps and hooked
them down her arms. Tracing light patterns, he edged the
garment farther until her breasts were revealed. Her nipples
were hard and aching for his touch. He seemed to be taunting her, hesitating, so she captured his hands and brought
them to the swell of her needful flesh.

The contact broke the lazy, tantalizing spell he was
weaving. He followed quickly with his mouth, tasting, biting, sucking at each sensitive tip until she writhed in his
arms, chewing on her lips to keep from crying out. He
spoke no words as his hands ran down her body, shedding
the negligee and boldly stroking up the inside of her
thighs. She arched, sighing, when his fingers explored her
woman's flesh.

"This time, you will know full pleasure," his harsh
voice whispered into her ear.

The elusive tendrils of sensation swirled to life inside
her. His mouth was once again at her breast, then trailing
kisses of insidious flame across her belly, moving downward.

He tumbled her back onto the pillows and bent over her,
his mouth finding the spot he had just caressed to life. She

gasped, thinking to protest this impossible intrusion, but the shivery feelings his tongue evoked enslaved her instantly. She relaxed as he began to summon a shocking response from her body. A mindless yearning took possession of her and she strained against his wicked kiss, craving the pleasure, craving release.

It came, and she cried out as a thousand shards of pure delight rained through her body. Every inch of flesh, every nerve, writhed with pulsating pleasure until the intense sensations crested, holding her aloft for what seemed an eternity.

He came over her, penetrating the swollen flesh before she had fully recovered her senses, and the sensation of him filling her was ecstasy. She couldn't think, only feel the deliciousness of each plunge. Her hands slid to the flexing muscles of his back, daring lower to the tight controlled movements of his buttocks as he thrust into her. Swiftly, then slower, he moved until at last he stiffened and groaned, finding the same fulfillment he had just given her.

Breathless and spent, he rolled her into his arms and shifted so they were side by side. Smoothing damp strands of hair from her forehead, he smiled with a devilish twinkle. "I told you I would lick you everywhere."

She gave him a lazy, contented look. "You really are a scoundrel, aren't you?"

"It's true," he said. "I've never denied it. Complaining?"

"Me?"

"Ummm," he groaned as he nuzzled her neck. "You nearly drove me out of my mind, you realize."

"What—oh!" His teeth were nibbling gently at her earlobe. "What did I do?"

He chuckled, low and throaty. "You *breathe,* Cara."

She wanted to say she felt the same way, that he aroused the same feelings of desire in her as he professed to have. Yet despite their physical intimacy, the words refused to come. She didn't understand him, and knew better than to trust his moods, but in one realm at least they were perfectly attuned. Tentatively, her hands began to roam.

He jerked his eyebrow up. "Am I to take it you haven't finished with me?" She stilled her explorations.

"I didn't mean to... I just wanted to feel you. Like the way you touch me. All over."

"Yes," he answered, his lids drawing down. "I want you to."

She watched her fingers as they splayed over the thick bulge of muscle in his upper arm, then trailed her fingertips up to his shoulders, across his back to feel the hewn musculature that was as well-defined as a Michelangelo sculpture.

"Your body is beautiful," she whispered.

He stared at her for a minute before he smiled. "That is an extraordinary thing to say. I know you are inexperienced, so allow me to instruct you. It is I who am to ply you with all manner of compliments, which you take in as your due, and then allow me to touch that which I have just admired."

She laughed. "I have never been good at playing by others' rules. I simply say what I think. You said you liked it."

"Yes. I do, Cara *mia.* And you are working miracles with my stamina."

His statement sent a lightning bolt of desire through her. She hesitated, wondering if she dared act on the impulse, then slid her hand downward to grasp his aroused member.

He reacted, hissing a sharp intake of breath, closing his eyes. She kissed his neck, tasting the salty-sweetness and breathing in the wonderful masculine scent that was his.

"Good God, woman, what are you doing to me?"

She smiled against the warmth of his skin, remembering their wedding night when she had asked him the same question. Recalling his answer, she said, "I am making love to you."

He chuckled, and rolled onto his back. "By all means..."

Caroline watched him sleep, studying the handsome face in repose and loving how boyish he looked without the signs of stress furrowing his brow.

They had made love again, and Caroline had been amazed at her boldness. She liked pleasing him. It thrilled her, actually. She just wished she could do it more often— out of bed. Sexually, they were more than compatible, they were combustible. Which was a fine blessing as they were to concentrate on getting her with child.

Rising from the bed, she slipped on her silk wrapper and went to the French doors which opened onto a small parapet. The night was too cool, so she shut the doors and locked them, then went out to the sitting room where she lit a lone candle to keep her company.

Lifting the cushion of one of the chairs, she reached into the springs and pulled out the black box containing her diamond necklace. Old habits die hard, and as ridiculous as it had felt to hide the box in a sofa cushion, she had done it because she had wanted to secrete the wondrous gift away, treasuring the knowledge that this gorgeous piece now belonged to her. Holding the choker in her hands, she watched the dazzling sparkle of white fire.

Yet ever since Magnus had given it to her four days ago, she had fought a battle of conscience.

This single piece of jewelry could pay the fees for the finest sanatorium in Switzerland, but could she bear to betray her husband?

She wondered if she should simply tell him about James. If there was one thing she had learned, it was that Magnus was a kind man, with a well-developed sense of responsibility. Surely, upon learning of his brother-in-law's condition, he would wish to help.

But would he hold her deception against her?

She had misled him. She had done more than that—she had openly lied to him. Caroline was not foolish enough to believe all men were like her father, but she couldn't help think of Louis Wembly and how he had coldly, unfeelingly dismissed everyone else's feelings and needs as unimportant. He had been a disgusting man, consumed with himself, so much so he had committed the most despicable act of depravity a person could dare.

Magnus was not like him, not the Magnus she was discovering. But there were the rumors. He was a jade. He didn't even argue that point. Being called a scoundrel only made him chuckle. And his moods were unpredictable, his good will unreliable.

True, he was generous. Even caring. He had, at times, been vicious as well.

If she told him, and he turned her out—if for nothing else than for not having been completely forthcoming from the beginning—then her brother's life was forfeit. As much as she was growing to care for Magnus, as much as she might admire him, she could never trust him that far, not with something so precious.

Gazing at the necklace, she realized she hadn't yet tried

it on. Perhaps she was afraid if she did so, she wouldn't be able to part with it. Rising, she went to the looking glass and attempted to fasten it around her neck. A shadow shifted behind her, and warm fingers brushed hers aside.

"When I decided on this particular piece, I confess to having delighted images of seeing you in it, and only it."

Magnus finished closing the clasp and grasped her shoulders, placing a light kiss on the back of her neck. Loosing the tie at her waist, he opened her dressing gown and slipped it off, leaving her naked in the moonlight.

"You are so very lovely," he said breathlessly, brushing his lips behind her ear. His eyes locked with her reflection and she stood transfixed by the smoldering gaze. Reaching around her, he grasped her breasts, then traced lightly over the flat of her stomach, testing the gentle swell of her hips, stirring her passions with one sweep of his hands.

Whirling, she threw herself into his arms.

Life settled into a pleasant routine at Hawking Park. Caroline's days were filled with her duties as mistress, her nights with her duties as wife. Magnus was a fabulous lover—tender, passionate, experienced, inventive and intuitive.

She hadn't even realized he had suffered no attacks in a great while until she was seated across from him at the breakfast table and saw a trickle of sweat run down his temple. He loosened his cravat, still trying to concentrate on his newspaper.

"Henry!" he called. At the servant's appearance, Magnus ordered, "The fire is too high."

Henry looked puzzled and Caroline frowned. The weather held the typical chill of October, and the room was in want of the comforting warmth emanating from the hearth. She stood and said, "Thank you, Henry. I will take care of it."

Magnus looked up from his paper. Caroline said, "Magnus, come over here by the window, if you would."

He might have thought she wished to show him something. Folding his paper, he stood, then stopped, wavered and sat back down.

"Call Arthur!" he demanded.

"Magnus, let me—"

"Call him! And get the hell out of here! I don't want you to see me like this."

"But you told me you wanted me to attend you when you were sick."

"I changed my mind! Now get—damn it!" He broke away to lay his head in his hands. His muffled voice sounded. "Arthur—get him!"

Caroline rang the table bell and sent Henry in search of the majordomo. But she was determined not to leave.

Back at her husband's side, she said, "Do not waste your strength. I am telling you right now I am not going to leave you. You are not to be ashamed, Magnus. You are ill. I am your wife, and my place is with you. You need me."

He didn't speak, just shook his head. Arthur arrived. Caroline explained, "He started sweating and feeling overwarm only a few moments ago. Should you call the footmen to take him upstairs?"

"I can do it myself," came Magnus' hoarse reply, preempting his manservant.

"Let me help you, my lord," Arthur said, draping Magnus' arm about his shoulders.

"Get her out of here," Magnus said, but the strength of his voice was fading. Caroline stepped up to take the other arm on her slim but sturdy frame. As she struggled under the weight, she said, "You might as well tell him to conserve his energy, Arthur, and quit arguing about it. He may be larger than I, but he is not at his best right now, and I am determined to stay by his side."

Arthur nodded, and the two of them concentrated on helping their unwieldy burden up the stairs. Arthur started down a corridor which led away from the master suite, and Caroline corrected him. "I know he goes to another room when he is sick, but as I shall be attending him, I think his normal apartments would be best."

"Arthur!" Magnus growled weakly.

Caroline ignored his feeble protests. They succeeded in getting him into the room, stripped, and into the bed. Caroline had seen no cause to involve the valet, convention be damned.

"What is normally done for him?" Caroline asked of the manservant.

"He has medicine, which I shall fetch. Just cool cloths and keep him clean."

Magnus' voice was barely a croak. "Arthur, get her out!"

"Shhh," Caroline soothed as Arthur went to see to his duties. "I am with you, Magnus. Do not worry, you shall recover like you always do."

He said something she didn't understand. "What?"

"Chamber pot!"

Caroline reacted quickly, getting a small dustbin to him in time to avoid soiling the bed.

"All right, lie back now," she crooned when he was through. A servant arrived with water, and Caroline immediately began swabbing his sweat-soaked body with a damp cloth.

"Medicine."

"Yes, Magnus, Arthur will be here in a moment with it."

She touched the cloth to his legs and arms, his torso and neck and forehead—everywhere where the flesh burned with fever. Arthur arrived and administered the dosage which sent Magnus into blessed oblivion.

"I'll stay with him now, ma'am," he said.

Caroline shook her head. "No, Arthur. I am here." At his hesitation, she said, "Go on."

The servant didn't argue, seeming to approve of Caroline's taking control.

By the time Arthur left, Magnus was sleeping quietly, the soft, even sound of his breathing familiar and reassuring to Caroline's ears. He looked peaceful, as natural as when he slept by her side. The clamminess of his skin told her the fever had broken. Arthur had mentioned this attack did not seem bad, so Caroline hoped the worst was over.

Nevertheless, she sat on the edge of the bed, unable to still her hands as they smoothed the thick locks from his patrician brow or traced the contour of his cheek. He was such a beautiful man, she marveled. She leaned over to press soft kisses on his forehead, curling up next to him, murmuring soft words of reassurance as she drew the coverlet over his nakedness.

When he roused a few hours later to retch and shiver and tell her to get the hell out of the room, Caroline held him, gently settling him back and calming his temper. Before he fell back under the effects of the laudanum, he muttered, "Just you wait until I'm well."

Caroline smiled at the threat. He would certainly have more than a few words to say to her, she knew. She—and Arthur as well, poor soul—would have hell to pay for her insubordination. But she would not leave him, not even for fear of what he would do later.

As the day wore on, she remained. When night fell, she had a servant bring in a large chair close to the bed. There she slept lightly, aware of every breath Magnus took. Sometime before dawn, he opened his eyes. She came instantly awake.

Magnus said, "You, my dear, are in a great deal of trouble."

Chapter Eleven

Magnus made good on his promise to punish her for disobeying him by being disagreeable, disgruntled and downright nasty for the next week. He stated emphatically, and at least once every time they were together, that Caroline was *never* to invade his privacy when he was ill again. These admonishments she took with implacable calm, which incensed him all the more.

"I will set you out without a farthing if you *ever* dare such a thing again!" he thundered one evening at dinner.

She bestowed upon him one of her cool perusals that so annoyed him. He almost came up out of his chair. "Don't give me that superior look," he snapped. "I know what you're thinking—you'll do what you please since I won't be in any state to argue. But I promise you, if you so much as step foot in my rooms when I am…*sick,* I'll have your bags packed and you will be back at the Ordinary so fast your head will spin!"

Daintily chewing a morsel of chicken, Caroline stated, "You cannot do that. It is not in our contract."

"Contract?" He did come out of his seat. "*Contract!* You little minx, I'll show you to flout that damned piece of paper before me, try to blackmail me with it!"

Calmly, she speared another bit of meat. "Actually, quite the contrary was stipulated. You expressly asked me to attend you."

His mouth worked in mute outrage. Caroline seemed completely unperturbed by his rising temper, eating sedately with no more than an occasional polite glance to acknowledge he was speaking.

Stalking away from the table, Magnus rubbed his hand over his mouth and squeezed his eyes shut. Devil take her, he had never felt so close to throttling a woman as he did now.

He was unaware she had come up behind him until he felt her hand on his shoulder. "Magnus, please do not upset yourself. You may bring on another attack."

He didn't turn around. "Isn't it enough that this illness is robbing me of my life? Of any future? Of seeing my child even born? Must you allow it to unman me, Caroline? Can't you at least leave me my dignity?"

There was a long silence. "There is no loss of dignity in being ill, Magnus," came her gentle answer. "You have nothing to be ashamed of."

"Nothing to be ashamed of?" He angled a glare her way. "Perhaps you haven't been paying attention. My whole life is something to be ashamed of. And if I had an intact brain, I might have sense enough to feel badly about it. Too much debauchery, I'm afraid, has damaged my mind. Now, I shall reap my just rewards. Dying slowly, unfinished… Well, there are some who would say it couldn't happen to a more deserving fellow."

"I would not say that, Magnus!" He was surprised at the vehemence in her voice. "You have given me so much. Let me give back something to you."

"You do, Cara *mia*. Every night."

Her eyes flashed, and her nostrils flared wide. "Yes, I

do, don't I? I never refuse you from my bed. I give all, and when I am with child, I will have fulfilled my part of the bargain. In return, you give me gifts. Necklaces, clothes, money." She took a step back. He was horrified to see the sheen of unshed tears in her eyes. He had never thought to see this woman cry, this strong, invincible bit of femininity who had taken his worst and given it right back to him with nary a flinch. Her next words were barely a whisper. "That makes me a whore, then. Doesn't it?"

He recoiled. God, he hadn't meant to say those things. "Caroline, don't…"

"It's true. If not your wife, then what? If I am not to be a part of you outside of the bedroom, then I am nothing more than a simple harlot. How you must despise me."

Despise her? Dear Lord, didn't she understand it was himself he despised?

She turned away and he reached for her. She didn't resist. God, she had never resisted him, not once. She had always done exactly as he required.

Yet, a small, tortured voice inside him urged, she was not so innocent and giving as all that. She had demanded an allowance, and had asked him for it when he had neglected to pay on time. She had not demurred at any of his generosity, not even prettily for effect. And—how could he forget?—she had only married him for his money.

He let his hand fall away. He couldn't make this right with words.

"And how you must hate me in return," he said. Her head came up. "If you think yourself a whore, then it is I who have made you one. And a martyr to boot."

"You know nothing about me, Magnus. For all of your thorough investigation, you do not know me. Or why I need to be with you when you are ill."

His mouth was suddenly dry. "Why, then?"

She gave him a long, haunted look. "If I told you, you would never accept it."

"What would you tell me?" he ground out viciously, aware that she was treading desperately close to his most vulnerable fears. "That you *care?*"

She took in a quick breath and let it out. "Yes." She was watching him like a cornered doe. "I do care about you, Magnus."

Something inside of him snapped. "And would you continue to care so much, I wonder, if the money stopped? If you were still running around in rags? Or if your family were shivering this winter in whatever hovel you came from?"

Her hand moved so quickly, he never saw it coming. Her flattened palm landed with a loud whack on his cheek. The sting shocked him. She had hit him again.

"Congratulations," she snarled. "You have finally succeeded in convincing me you truly are the mean-spirited, obnoxious boor you seem so proud of being. If you wish me to admit my fault, I shall. I was wrong about you. Wrong to care about you. I hope you are fully satisfied."

Whirling on her heel, she stalked toward the door. Magnus' flesh still tingled from her slap, and a blinding rage was fastening its talons around his heart.

She stopped, turned, and added, "And the month is almost up. Please do not be late with my allowance. I would not like to ask for my *fee* a second time."

That last comment broke him. Magnus was in motion before he realized it. In one fluid movement, he grabbed her and took her with him to the closed door, pinning her against it and pressing himself upon her until he could feel every feminine contour. "If you want your fee, madam, you will have to earn it like every other whore must. On your back."

She swung, but this time he caught her wrist and jerked it behind her. This caused her to arch, a position perfectly suited for his mouth to come down over hers.

To his utter shock, she bit his lip! His head snapped back.

"Get away from me. I hate you!" she cried.

"Ah," he said dangerously, "how contrary you are. A moment ago, you profess to care, now you hate me. Well, at least in this you are not alone. My detractors are legion."

"Why are you doing this?" she flung. "Why do you have to act like such a blackheart?"

"Because that is what I am," he uttered, his lips crushing hers once again. She struggled only for a moment. Slowly, her mouth responded, and with a weak, breathless cry, she surrendered in his arms.

He would ravage her right here, he would, if some shred of sanity hadn't remained, born of the need to protect her from shame. The servants were in and out of here all the time. Even as he ached to punish her, he would not allow such a thing.

Dragging her upstairs by her arm was no better, but they were lucky enough not to come across any of the staff. Magnus all but flung her into his chamber before locking the door behind him.

She faced him like a wild thing. Her hair was coming loose, pale tendrils falling seductively in her face. Lips parted, luscious, tempting him beyond thought. Regret slammed into him, nearly bringing him to his knees, but he could not turn back now. His blood was on fire, out of control, thundering in his ears and filling him with need. He closed the distance between them in a few short strides, and she held out her arms to him, welcoming him even now.

"Dear God," she breathed against his lips. "You are a fiend." He covered her mouth, crushing the words. He knew they were true. He was an unutterable, loathsome coward. His deft hands divested her of her clothing, lingering at her breasts, at the cleft of her legs. God, he could not help himself. She tugged at his clothes, helping him off with his garments. Naked, they tumbled into his large bed. Her hands gripped his hips while a soft, urgent moan sounded in the back of her throat. Without preamble, he slid inside her, the sensation a bone-jarring searing of pleasure and a homecoming at the same time. She moved, rocking her hips to stroke his embedded shaft, and he rose and fell in time to her motions. Pleasure exploded, consuming him, lifting him, bearing him to fulfillment as he heard her quickened breathing. He felt her stiffen and give a small, sharp cry.

He fell beside her, gulping in huge lungfuls of air.

Caroline lay staring at the ceiling. Without looking at him, she said, "Are you done with me, my lord?"

He almost groaned. "Caroline, I..." He what? What could he tell her? He didn't even know himself what lay in his heart.

She rose, gathered her clothes and left him.

The first thing Caroline did when she reached her rooms was go to the chair where she hid the necklace. She took it out, and without looking at it, stuffed it in the pocket of her cloak. Tomorrow she would see about selling it, Magnus and his mother be damned. James was going to the sanatorium. It was what she was here for, after all.

The next thing was to scrub her body with the frigid water left in the basin while her mind worked.

What was wrong with her? she wondered. How could she respond so strongly to him when he had behaved little better than a beast? He was odious, he was horrid, a dreadful, terrible monster who had no human feeling.

Then why did she desire him so? What drew her to him, after all the vile things he had said, whetting her physical hunger beyond reason?

Because she had foolishly thought there was more in his heart than the cruel selfishness she had witnessed that night.

She would never understand him. Nor herself, whom she hardly recognized anymore. She had become so absorbed in Magnus that she was forgetting her duty to James. How had she ever hesitated, even for a moment, over selling the necklace and sending him to the best facility money could buy? She had to get hold of herself, and quickly. Before she was lost forever.

Magnus never suffered from a guilty conscience. Never.

This is what he told himself, anyway, as he stared at his wife's empty place at breakfast.

A long-ago memory welled to life, a voice sounding as close as a whisperer at his ear.

Vile.

He pushed away his neglected meal and marched out of the room.

The familiar confines of his study brought no more relief from the uncomfortable pricking sensation than the dining hall had. Or his bedroom before that. He opened the French doors and walked out onto the flagstone terrace.

The wind lifted his hair. It was cold, bearing winter upon its wings. His feet took him to the symmetrical pathways of the formal garden, his haven of the past. It looked neglected, abandoned, with dead flowers and dried leaves littering the ground. His shoes crushed the refuse under heel as he wandered.

Hateful.

He could apologize to her. He should. He had said dreadful things. Unforgivable.

Hedonist.

He tried to tell himself this self-recrimination was absurd. Why should he care whether he had hurt her feelings? But the devastated look on her face haunted him, and just that expression wounded him to the quick.

Nothing he had ever done in his life had been worthwhile. So, why start dwelling on his failings at this late date? That he didn't like himself was no revelation. That this fact bothered him was.

It was dangerous to want more, which was why he never allowed it. Now there was Cara, and maybe he couldn't resist. She was temptation, but what she offered was forbidden, a soft refuge for other men, but not for him.

Wasn't it?

Looking down at a particularly shabby bed, he sighed. He hunkered down and gathered together the bracken with his bare hands. After a moment, he stood and pulled off his coat and got down to it in earnest.

Three hours later, he was still at it.

Chapter Twelve

Mrs. Judith Cameron sipped her tea. Caroline held the plate of pastries up to her. "You really should try these, they are Mrs. Bronson's specialty."

"Oh, really?" The plump woman eyed the sumptuous array of scones, lemon tarts and fried dough. "Well, just one, perhaps."

Caroline watched her pile three on her plate. Mrs. Cameron was the vicar's wife, a gentle, sweet soul who had come to visit, she had said in a timid, explanatory tone, to see how the new Countess of Rutherford was faring. Caroline had been prepared for a delicate grilling, but Judith displayed an amazing lack of curiosity. It had taken only minutes to realize she had not come for gossip, but out of her own sense of duty.

She had brought with her a healthy appetite. "Have you been missing London?" Judith asked between bites.

"Not so much. I do miss my family, though. They were with me until recently, but have gone to visit friends."

Actually, Caroline's mother and brother were in Switzerland. At the finest sanatorium in Europe, so James' doctor had said. Using the Barrister's Ordinary to post a letter, Caroline had contacted a jeweler in London about the necklace and the man wasted no time in coming to Cambridgeshire at the promise of so singular a treasure. Nearly salivating when he saw it, he had met her price with only a modicum of haggling and within days, James and Audrae departed, neither suspecting the nefarious means by which Caroline had come up with the funds.

"How lovely for them. It must be sad to have them gone, but a married woman must learn to be content in her husband's house."

Magnus' house, Caroline reflected silently, was an odd place. It was as changeable as its master, some parts cold, like the grand salon, and others charming. She particularly liked this parlor, and her bedchamber was cozy and welcoming.

"Hawking Park is such a lovely place," Judith was saying. "All this priceless marble and statues—oh, it tends to take one's breath away."

"I know what you mean," Caroline smiled, averting her eyes tactfully as the other woman licked strawberry jam from her finger.

"Oh, Lord Rutherford," Judith said, her glistening finger poised just before her pursed lips. She looked shocked.

Caroline looked up to see her husband dressed in plain wool trousers and loose-fitting shirt. It hung open, revealing much of his neck and more than a glimpse of broad chest. His hair was windblown and there were dirt smudges on his temple.

Caroline waited, not knowing what to expect. If Magnus had been unpredictable before, he was a positive enigma of late. He watched her all the time, sometimes with a soft longing in his eyes, sometimes with a harshness which hardened the green depths to deep emerald.

"Magnus," she said, rising. "Do you remember Judith Cameron?"

She held her breath, waiting to see what mood he would favor. One of his most engaging smiles graced his handsome face. He came forward to take the vicar's wife's hand and bend over it. "Of course. Mrs. Cameron, how are you?"

So he had decided to be charming, Caroline noted. He looked at her, the grin deepening and a devilish sparkle lightening his eyes. A warning quickened in her breast. "Darling," he said by way of greeting. In one step, he was beside her, his fingers burning a trail along her waist as he bent his head and brushed his lips against hers.

There was nothing she could do, short of push him away. It was not that it was unpleasant. Far from it. But Mrs. Cameron was watching, no doubt choking on that last scone, as the irrepressible earl lived up to his reputation and kissed her with all the intimacy of their bedroom.

He lifted his head and faced their guest. "Do pardon me, Mrs. Cameron. I have been in the garden. Bracing weather we are having." His tone was insolent and patronizing all at once, yet so subtle the vicar's wife never noticed.

"Quite chilly, yes, my lord." She wiped her hands on her napkin, a gesture that made her look nervous and fidgety. "Working in the garden, you say?"

"Yes. Nothing like the outdoors." He still had his hand about Caroline's waist, which meant she could not resume her seat. This put Judith at a distinct disadvantage, one she quickly remedied by standing and announcing she should be returning home.

Magnus said goodbye and strolled over to the tea tray and grabbed a pastry. Looking over his shoulder at the women, he shrugged. "I have a monstrous sweet tooth, and I've worked up quite an appetite."

The way he stressed the last word, making it ambivalent

as to which "appetite" he was referring, coupled with the slight widening of his eyes, put Mrs. Cameron to flight. When Caroline returned from seeing her to the cloakroom, she stood inside the doorway with her hand on her hips. "Are you quite satisfied with yourself?" she demanded in a steady voice.

Magnus leaned back, bringing his left ankle to rest on his right knee. "Yes, actually. I am." He took another bite of lemon tart.

She threw up her hands. "I am tempted to squash that pastry into your hair!"

"I am becoming quite alarmed, Cara, at your recent penchant for violence."

"Why were you so rude to Mrs. Cameron? She's a lovely woman."

Magnus shrugged. "She's a bore."

Caroline took a threatening step forward. "No, Magnus, *you* are a bore."

His eyes narrowed to slits. "Not to worry, my darling wife. You shall not have to endure my company much longer."

Stamping her foot, she shouted, "And don't try to play on my sympathies!" Whirling, she left, flying up to her chamber and slamming the door with enough noise, she hoped, to wipe the supercilious smirk right off his face.

Winter deepened. A harsh season was heralded by early snowfall which kept David stranded at Hawking Park for three days. Magnus' irritability had led to more than one quarrel between the brothers, arguments that could be heard echoing down the hallways and driving the earl into seclusion.

For Caroline, however, David was good company, and she was grateful for the buffer between Magnus and herself. He played chess with her, teased Magnus and generally brightened the chilly atmosphere.

In the parlor one evening when a north wind whistled with shrill urgency outside, Caroline and David sat across the checkered board from one another. Magnus had locked himself in his study. Caroline was happy not to have his brooding presence about, and yet she found she missed him. Or at least missed the way he had been once.

David rubbed his hand over his mouth as he studied his dwindling black pieces, and Caroline was struck with the similarity in gestures to his absent brother.

"It's check in three moves," Caroline said.

He flickered a glance at her that barely disguised his annoyance. "I know it." To her surprise, he was seriously vexed. This was the third game she had won.

It played out as she had predicted. David said, "Shall we do another?" He began lining up the ivory statues.

"Perhaps tomorrow," Caroline demurred, resolving to let him win the next time. But she was weary tonight.

His eyes snapped up, and he glared at her for a moment before blinking and forcing a smile. "You can't leave me out a loser this many times. What do you say to a small wager?"

Caroline laughed nervously. "I never gamble, David."

"Just something small. To make it more interesting."

His intensity was disturbing. "Really, no," she insisted. "We shall have a rematch tomorrow night."

"But I am planning to leave in the morning, if the weather permits. You must give me a chance to redeem myself."

"All right," she conceded. "But no wager."

They were three moves into the new game when a shout outside the parlor door brought them both to their feet.

"What the devil—?" David started to the door.

Caroline flew past him, racing into the hall. "Magnus!"

Both the parlor where she and David had been and Magnus's study opened into the huge circular center hall. The door to her husband's domain was open, and several men were just now rushing inside.

She took a step toward the study, then stopped. Uncertain, she turned to David. His face was ghostly pale. Someone within the study shouted, "There's blood! Call the doctor!" which was followed by a distinct growl voicing disagreement with that course of action. Magnus.

Blood. That unfroze Caroline's feet without a second thought of the consequences. She rushed forward, then stopped when her husband, borne between two footmen, came out and the three headed for the stairs. He was barely conscious, but he had seen her and given her a look that left her feeling as if she had just received a blow. She hesitated but a moment, then moved forward.

Magnus' hoarse voice ground out, "Get her out."

Caroline knew she was mad to ignore his repeated orders not to come near him when he was like this. Yet, what worse could he do to her? And if there was blood... Resolutely, she stepped closer.

Sweat poured down his face. Without thinking, she grabbed a handful of her dress, a lovely brushed wool in vivid rose, and wiped his brow. He gave her a damning look. Caroline whispered, "Let me help you."

He lifted a weak hand out to her, and Caroline's heart leapt. But all he did was touch his palm to her shoulder and give her a feeble shove.

Crushed, she stepped away, turning her eyes from the sight of him being half carried, half dragged up the stairs.

David came up and put his arms around her. "He'll be all right. He always is. I am sure this is the same as all the others."

He took her back to the parlor and poured her a deep glass of brandy. "Drink it," he ordered, then threw one back himself.

After a space, Caroline asked, "How long has he been like this?"

David stood by the fire, staring into the flames. "Not quite a year."

"Has he seen a doctor? Perhaps—"

"He's seen several," David cut in. "None of them worth a damn. All they have told him is that it is his heart. It is weak, you see. Like our father. He died almost ten years ago, from failure of the heart. His symptoms were the same."

Caroline took a deep breath. "How long…"

David studied her for a moment. "For my father, the illness lingered for years. However, Magnus seems to be… It has accelerated faster. They do not give him long."

Caroline dropped her eyes to her hands twisted on her lap.

"Mistress?" Arthur's voice cut in. Caroline's head came up. "Please come," Arthur said.

David stepped in front of her, body rigid and face a mask of fear. "Is Magnus dead?"

The majordomo shook his head. "No, Master David, it is not that. He is restless. This is a bad one. If the mistress would come, be with him, it may help."

Caroline rose and asked hopefully, "Did he ask for me?"

Arthur looked at her with regret. "No, mistress, he did not. But I think it would be best. If he is angry, then it shall be with me."

Caroline nearly wept for this dear man's concern, and braving his master's dark temper to do what he felt was right. "I shall go to him," she reassured, "and if he rages at anyone, I am sure it will be me. I shall not mind in the least."

She nearly ran up the stairs, with Arthur puffing behind. He indicated the rooms that adjoined her own, and Caroline went in.

Magnus lay unconscious with the sheet tucked around his waist. His chest was bare. Her touch at his forehead roused him slightly. He was burning with fever. His eyes opened, glazed and unfocused, and he tried to lift his head up from the pillow.

"Who—?

"Shhh, Magnus. It's me. Please relax. I am with you now."

He fell back. Caroline picked up the bottle of laudanum.

"Do you want your medicine? Have you had it already?" He didn't answer. Caroline did not want to risk an overdose, so she put the tincture down.

Magnus thrashed, kicking off the covers. His naked body gleamed with perspiration in the candlelight. Fearful he would catch a chill, she tried to cover him.

"You are a siren," he groaned. "Why won't you let me be?" He squinted at her. "Natasha?"

"It's me, Magnus. Caroline."

"Why did you laugh at me? I was just a boy."

"I never laughed at you. Magnus, it is Caroline. Your wife."

He closed his eyes and swallowed. "You were so beautiful. I loved you so much…"

He fell into a fitful sleep. Caroline kept watch over him, soothing his brow and murmuring soft words. Jealousy stung, and she fought with the burning question—who was Natasha?

She sponged him with a cool cloth and spoke to him in a low tone, trying to effect a calming influence. He went in and out of lucidity. He cried out for his father and said in a voice that almost broke her heart that he was sorry. Caroline pretended she was the old earl and, without a qualm, pardoned him for whatever it was that pricked at his conscience. It was enough to allow him to fall asleep, his breathing shallow. But he was quiet, she was satisfied to see.

She lay her head on his breast, as she had done so many times after making love, and heard the strong heartbeat. How is it such a powerful, vital man could be flawed? A weak heart. She knew enough to realize such illness could strike down the most robust, stealing strength and vigor. Magnus would waste away like that. Slowly fighting every step of the way.

She stayed awake through the night, keeping a faithful vigil. In the morning, she spooned a thinned broth past his pale lips and cooled him again, trying to keep the fever at bay. He opened his eyes briefly. "Cara?"

"Yes!" she said, stroking his cheek, happy that he finally knew who she was. It was a sign the delirium was over.

But his eyes were still glassy. "You are beautiful. Tempting. I shall miss you. So much." Then his gaze focused for a moment, and he smiled. "You *are* here."

"Yes, I am here, Magnus. I will never leave you, not as long as you will allow me to stay."

"Do not leave," he muttered, and Caroline wished she knew if he were in the grip of the fever or not. What she would not give to hear him say those words in truth. He subsided again, and she leaned toward him, whispering close to his ear. "I do care for you, Magnus."

He uttered something she couldn't decipher, and then he was gone once again in sleep.

Caroline opened the drapes and let the cold winter sunshine in. It was a beautiful day, and her eyes filled with tears thinking that she and Magnus should be out riding.

The same rage at the injustice of illness that she used to feel when she thought about James took hold of her now. She stemmed it, knowing its futility. On its heels, she thought of Natasha. He loved her, he had said. Why had he not married her? Caroline wondered. Who was she, and where was she now?

No wonder he had not wanted her caring, she mused miserably. He yearned for another.

Chapter Thirteen

"**Y**ou are awake!" Caroline declared.

Magnus didn't answer. He still felt weak, though not so much to fail to notice his wife looked especially beautiful this morning in a pale lavender gown sewn perfectly to conform to her thin waist and high, full breasts. Her skirts swung in an alluring way as she came to his bedside.

She was smiling, and he wanted so badly to kiss that gorgeous mouth. She said, "Oh, but you look better." Reaching a hand up to his forehead, she brushed aside a lock of hair. Her fingers were cool and pleasant against his skin.

"Were you here all night?" he asked.

"Yes. I came in after Arthur had you settled, so the work was done. All I did was sit with you."

He placed his hand to his head, probing gently where a faint headache pestered. It was a typical aftereffect of the opium tincture. He was so used to it now, he hardly felt more than a mild annoyance. "I don't remember anything."

"You became ill the evening before last—"

"Two days? I have lost two days?"

"Hush. Yes, I'm afraid so. It was a particularly bad attack. You were unconscious most of the time."

He watched the way the sunlight glanced off her hair, turning it almost white. It was such a glorious color. Unusual and lovely, like the woman herself. "Most of the time, eh? I had some outrageous dreams. I can't really remember them, but a few images keep flitting around my brain, skirting away before I can fasten onto them."

"You had delirium," she explained.

Magnus groaned. "What did I say?" The Lord only knew what unguarded statements might have escaped when he was out of his mind.

She shook her head. "It was mostly unintelligible. The rest was the usual ramblings." She was so nonchalant, he relaxed. Tentatively, she added, "I am glad you are not angry. Magnus, I wanted to be with you, as any wife would. Can't you allow that, if not for you, then for me?"

He was silent while he considered this. "I admit," he said slowly, "it was a comfort to me to know you were here." He lifted his eyes to the ceiling. "And since you are a disobedient, stubborn wife who will not listen in any event, I suppose I must concede."

She nodded, hitching up her leg like a tomboy and perching on the edge of his bed. "You know, I was thinking about the stream. Remember the spot you showed me by the delta, overlooking the flats?" At his nod, she continued, "I was thinking of how lovely it must look in the snow, and thought we might take the horses out as soon as you've recovered."

He gave her his best insolent look. "Are you inviting me to make good on my offer to make love to you there?"

The high spots of color on her cheeks amused him, but she surprised him by smiling. "It's freezing!"

He brought her fingers to his lips. "I promise you will not feel it."

She laughed. He did, too.

Surprisingly, he was only mildly resentful of her having disobeyed him.

It was hard to accept her caring, yet somehow not as much as it had been weeks ago. The decision had been taken out of his hands, and for the first time in a long time, he was truly dependent on someone who was not paid to attend him. His pride rankled, but another, softer part of his being was at ease. The change, as inexplicable as it was, was not unwelcome.

Caroline's fair brows furrowed. "Magnus, I am so sorry. I did not conceive this month."

It was a disappointment, but he didn't let her see it. "Well, perhaps we shall just have to try harder."

She touched his shoulder in an instinctive gesture of affection. "Yes, well, I can see where your mind is headed. If you are planning so much exertion, you had better get your rest."

"I hate being coddled," he protested. "I'm starving, and I am disgusted with this bed."

"I'll order you something to eat, and then you must rest. The sooner you gain your strength, the sooner you will be out of bed."

He opened his mouth to protest but she held up a single finger to forbid it.

Easing back, he crossed his arms behind his head. For some insane reason, he liked the way she tried to boss him. She was positively adorable with her chin jutting out and a stern expression on her classic features. "Very well," he conceded. "If you promise to go with me to the delta as soon as I am up to it."

She held her hand over her heart and nodded before

getting up to reach for the bellpull. As delightful as he found her companionship, Magnus wished she would leave him alone for a while. He needed time to think, assimilate the strange feelings that had followed him out of his illness. It was as if some wretched barrier was starting to crumble. Wouldn't half of London have a fine laugh if they knew the Earl of Rutherford was allowing himself to be nursed by this sweet-faced beauty? And, quite amazingly, not disliking it.

He ate under Caroline's watchful eyes. "Do you always consume so much after you recover?" she asked.

"Usually," he answered between bites. When he was finished she took the tray and exited the room, finally leaving him to the solitude he craved.

Yet the moment she was gone, he wanted to call her back. His thoughts crowded in his brain. His pride had urged him to keep Caroline at arm's distance, and perhaps a bit of self-preservation as well. Leaving this earth would not be easy, but leaving Caroline was impossible. If he allowed himself to get too close to the intoxicating woman who was his wife, it would only make things more complex.

He had hated needing her. So, he had hurt her. Pushed her away, said savage, unthinkable things and used her body to slake the undeniable desire that ruled him in spite of his attempts to rein it under control. He was no better than he had always been.

And the absolute worst affront he had committed was when she had told him she cared, and he had berated her for it, all because *he* could not bear it, because it was precisely what he yearned for with all of his heart.

His weak, cursed heart. He had laughed when the doctors had told him their diagnosis. A diseased heart. "I am surprised I still have one, after all," he had quipped.

Well, he did have one. And it was aching in more ways than one.

It was an exhilarating, terrifying notion.

He slept, waking feeling stronger already. David came to see him. "Gave us a scare, old boy," David said with a tremulous attempt at a smile. "See you don't do it again."

Caroline allowed them a half hour before she came in and shooed David out. As much as Magnus enjoyed her impertinent little self bustling importantly about his room, he would have none of her fussing. He ordered a bath, then dressed and insisted on eating with the rest of the family in the dining room.

The snow had melted enough to allow travel, and David informed them he was planning to return to London the following day. "Providing you are still on the mend, brother."

Magnus grunted, "I am fine. I don't want you lurking about like a ghoul waiting for me to take another attack."

It was the type of thing he always said to David, yet the younger man grew pale and Magnus could see his Adam's apple traverse the length of his neck as David swallowed hard. "Right," David said. "Then I had best be on my way."

Caroline told him about her latest letter from her mother, which reported James was enjoying the family's stay with…cousins, was it? On the continent somewhere.

Her face transformed as she breathlessly related how the boy was the envy of the other relatives' children for the lovely model boat and tin soldiers he had just acquired. Putting the missive down, her eyes shone as she thanked Magnus for his generosity in providing the boy's treasures.

Magnus felt a curious sensation in the nether regions of his chest. It was a kind of warmth, mixed with a bit of a thrill. He realized, after much analyzing, that it was the feeling one gets when one has done a good deed and sees the fruits of their labor.

He pleaded fatigue and retired early. As he had hoped, Caroline followed shortly thereafter. Entering her room, he took her in his arms and felt the hot spread of wanting flood his veins.

He loved her slowly, taking his time to reacquaint himself with the wonders of her body, reveling when she returned in kind. And when it was over, he wrapped her snugly in his arms and stared at the ceiling.

"What would you have done if I had not asked you to become my wife?" he asked.

Caroline was quiet for a moment. "I don't know. I would have done something else to help provide for my family. Whatever I needed to." She looked up at him, resting her chin on his shoulder. "Why did you choose me?"

He ran his finger against her full lips. "Caroline, you were the only one who applied for the position who was in any way suitable."

Those lovely blue-violet eyes widened, then blinked. "How can that be? Did Mr. Green send no one but me?"

"What need did I have to interview others when I had already made my decision? Not to mention there was not precisely a glut of applicants. Green's discretion may be part of it, but no society maven would covet me as husband." He gave her one of his most wicked smiles. "Have you forgotten the rumors?"

She arched a finely etched brow. "You mention them often. Is it that you are so proud of them, then?"

He threw his head back and laughed. "Of course I am proud of them. They do me justice even if they are untrue."

''There you are talking in riddles again!''

He wanted to kiss her, but he supposed he should explain. ''Ninety-nine out of every hundred comments passed about me are untrue. And the one in a hundred that is based on fact winds up being so unrecognizable after the rumor mill has churned it around that it might as well be false.'' He took a deep breath, reflecting that this was going to be harder than he thought. ''But I am no saint, Caroline. I have not exactly led a life of restraint or decorum. However, I am a very private man. I am a rascal, true enough, but a discreet one. I never cheat—not at cards, not in business—but I don't flinch even if it means cutting someone out. And I have not, I am afraid to say, been above helping myself to a tempting female's favors when offered. Yet, I have never uttered a single word to implicate the particular lady. Any innuendo of an alliance would strictly have to have come from her.''

She was watching her finger as it traced light, exciting circles over his breastbone. ''So you never made love to a duchess in the fountain of her garden in the middle of a ball given by her husband to celebrate her thirtieth birthday?''

''It was her thirty-fifth birthday,'' he answered blandly. ''And it wasn't a ball. The only reason anyone knows about the fountain is because *she* told fifty of her closest, dearest friends. She was quite proud of it.''

''But she was married.''

''To a jackass who hated her and slept with any woman who would have him—ah, hell, why am I trying to explain? I told you I deserved my reputation, even if it is built on lies. The truth, I suppose, is just as bad.''

She shook her head. ''I don't understand why you would want to live such a quiet life. Here, in the country, with me. Do you miss London? Your friends, all the fun you had?''

He didn't hesitate. ''No, I think I hated it, even when I was leading the whole pack of us straight to hell. I was merely fulfilling my destiny.''

''What?'' she cried. ''You must explain that one!''

He couldn't. Not yet. ''Perhaps some day, I will. I told you once before that dying didn't seem as hard as living. When I found out about my illness, I suddenly knew very clearly what it was I needed to do.''

''Have a child?''

''Marry. Have a legitimate child with a woman who would be strong enough to rear him in my absence. If heredity has its way, I am afraid you will have your hands full, should the boy—or girl!—have any of my traits. Poor Caroline. I am afraid you are finding out what a bad bargain you have made.''

She refused to be distracted. ''If you were so clear on what you should do, why did you wait until you were ill to pursue a family life?''

He ran his hand over the alabaster creaminess of her shoulder. ''Like most men, I thought I had time. I was a wastrel, after all. I had made up my mind to be the best damned wastrel there was. Came close to it, too.'' He sobered. ''A family of my own seemed like something out of my reach, too far into the future to foresee. Maybe even something I didn't deserve.''

Her voice was soft, thoughtful. ''Perhaps you really didn't want it.''

He leveled his gaze to hers. ''Perhaps it is what I wanted most of all.''

She studied him for a minute. ''Do you really hate children?''

''What?''

"David told me you hated children."

"He told you—?" Magnus sighed. "I don't hate children." He stopped and considered this statement. "Well, only disagreeable ones, and hate is too strong a word. Dislike perhaps. They are forever whining and interrupting and demanding you look at some silly scribble they've made with a piece of charcoal and you are to 'ooh' and 'aah' over it as if it is some masterpiece."

Caroline was staring at him and he was struck all at once at the shallow words he had just uttered. Good God, he was a cad!

"Ah, hell, Cara, I'm not a family man. I'm a self-absorbed rotter obsessed with my own gratification. That left little time to appreciate the precious cuteness of children."

Caroline was suddenly angry. "Who told you that?"

"What?"

"That you were a self-absorbed rotter obsessed with self-gratification?"

Her face was screwed up prettily in his defense. He wished he could tell her, and just as that thought registered, he heard his own voice saying, "My father," before he could check it.

She let out an indignant huff on his behalf. "Well, that is a terrible thing to say. I should think a father would have something more constructive to tell his son."

He closed his eyes and smiled, grinning like a fool at her innocent taking of his side of the matter. It felt good, so good in fact, he didn't bother to tell her that his father had been correct.

Chapter Fourteen

November passed quickly, closing with the disappointing discovery that Caroline was not pregnant. That and the letter from her mother requesting the next month's fees for the sanatorium put her in a state of despair as the advent season began.

All of her moneys had already been allocated to James, with only a little held back for a Christmas gift for Magnus. She had no idea what he would like, and there was certainly nothing he needed. Therefore, she chose something completely frivolous. She found it at a village shop. It was an exquisitely carved ivory tiger placed atop a gold leafed box. The inside was lined with red velvet. She bought it because of the graceful figurine more than anything, for the combination of beauty and danger so often reminded her of her husband. As Christmas neared, she alternated between satisfaction with the trinket and thinking it a silly idea, but as she had nothing else to give him, she did not make an exchange.

Magnus' health was doing splendidly, suffering one mild attack while out riding with David. It only put him down for the rest of the day.

The Christmas season came upon them and the magnificent house was decked with boughs of holly and mistletoe. A great twelve-foot fir was dragged in and set in the grand salon. Caroline helped hang the candles and bits of leaded crystal from an old chandelier she scavenged from the attics. She wrapped Magnus' present in gaily colored paper and hung it from a sturdy bough.

Magnus came in to admire her work. "Ah, the *tannenbaum.* A wonderful German tradition brought to us by our revered Prince Consort."

"Do you like it?"

Magnus shrugged. "It has a certain charm."

"What other Christmas traditions do you celebrate at Hawking Park?" she asked.

He told her about the Yule log, the wassail and the carolers who came on Christmas Eve from the village. Services were held Christmas morning, and Mrs. Bronson always prepared a plump stuffed goose for dinner.

Absently, he picked up some decorations and began to help her, talking all the while about Christmases of the past. "My mother always had a house full of guests. My father stood off to one side, watching her as she held court, everyone exchanging presents. That is how I remember them. She the center of attention, and he skirting the fringes, looking on as though he ranked lower in importance than her fawning admirers. A stranger coming in would never guess it was he who was lord of the house."

"David told me she was charming," Caroline said, her mind wandering to a different picture of her own home during the holiday. Her mother would look at her father with a tight-lipped reserve that contrasted with her forced gaiety as she tried desperately to make a jolly time for Caroline and James. And Louis, always worse for drink, shouting orders and finding fault and generally being his usual disagreeable self.

"She was able to inspire adoration, which was fortunate, for she seemed to need it as much as anyone needs air." He fell silent, looking off as if seeing faraway times come alive in his imagination.

"You adored her, too." Caroline took a step closer and touched his arm.

"Of course," he answered. With a deep breath, he focused on her, smiling. "She would have liked you."

Her heart swelled at the compliment. "I am sure I would have liked her as well."

Laughing, he said, "I don't know about that. Mother was a rather eccentric person. Her charm had its drawbacks. She was completely self-absorbed, and a terrible judge of character. In point of fact, she thought I was a delightful lad."

"Stop it," she said without rancor. "You are forever making these cryptic self-deprecating remarks. I know your father had some ill-chosen words for you, but you are not as bad as all that."

The corners of his eyes crinkled. "Oh, really? And you know me, do you?"

His arms had slipped around her waist. "I think I do. You are a fraud, I think, my lord husband."

"A fraud?"

"Yes, indeed. You prowl and snarl ferocious words, but you really don't mean any of it."

His eyebrows rose to convey his amusement. "And so I am harmless as a lamb?"

"No, I believe I was the one whom you referred to as a lamb. You, Magnus, are definitely feline. Stealth and cunning, beauty and unearthly grace. A tiger."

She waited to see if he laughed. Cocking his head to one side, he squinted. "A tiger, eh? I suppose if that is the way you see me, then I shall have to live with that." She was delighted he had accepted her musing. Perhaps he would enjoy her gift after all.

He pulled her close. "And what of you? I fear the image of the lamb no longer fits you, if it ever did."

"I?"

"Mmm-hmm. I fear I have married a wolf in sheep's clothing."

"A wolf and a tiger and a lamb. Hawking Park is sounding like some sort of zoo."

"Ah. The wonders of animal behavior are fascinating. Particularly of interest are their *mating* rituals. Shall I demonstrate?"

She pushed at his hard chest. "You really are wicked."

"You admit it, then. You see? Now, put those things aside and let me take you upstairs. I shall show you how wicked I can be."

She giggled as his lips brushed against hers. "I have already seen that demonstration, and so I shall allow that you can indeed be quite wicked."

"Who's wicked?" David's voice cut in. Caroline sprang out of Magnus' arms and smoothed her skirts. David said, "I do love a good gossip."

"How do you like our tree?" Caroline asked, hoping to divert him.

"Hmm? Oh, it's fine indeed." He surveyed the room. "You know, I never come in here anymore."

Magnus hid his disappointment at being interrupted. "I was just telling Caroline how Mother always entertained in here. Since she's been gone, it's hardly used. I don't do the sort of entertaining she did, and without all those people to fill it up, it seems rather cold."

"Yes," David agreed. He picked up a Dresden figurine. When Caroline saw the perfectly formed piece of porcelain, she felt a pang of insecurity about her gift. It was nothing so fine as this.

"All Mother's treasures," David mused. He put the figure down and touched a huge leaded crystal bowl. "Do you remember this? When we were boys, we thought it was a birdbath!"

Magnus stiffened, then turned away. David continued, "I remember the Christmas Mother received it. From that Russian princess or something. Do you remember her, Magnus? God, she was gorgeous."

Honing in on the word "Russian," Caroline instinctively sensed this might be the beautiful Natasha. She looked anxiously at her husband. Magnus waited a moment before turning to glance at the ornate piece of Waterford. "I always hated that thing."

David shrugged. "Well, it's worth a fortune if it's worth a penny, I'll say that much. Ah, here is the little shepherdess." He touched a dainty figurine painted in bold pinks and greens. "I got the thrashing of my life when I set my soldiers around her in a huge battle scene under the grand piano. It was a Helen of Troy kind of thing, and the chaps were there to rescue her. See, she still bears the scars of battle."

Caroline moved closer to see the chip in the dress. "Your mother must have been furious."

"Oh, Mother laughed. She thought me inventive. It was Father who gave me the switch."

Having recovered from his momentary descent into irritability, Magnus gave his brother a critical perusal. "Father never laid a hand to you. You were the one he took pride in."

"He thrashed me just the same. Said I had to learn to respect Mother's belongings, that they were precious to her."

"How odd," Magnus commented, "Mother cared nothing for any of these *things*. It goes to show he never understood her."

"Nevertheless, I got my hide tanned." Swinging to Caroline, David said, "How we must be boring you."

Caroline denied it. In fact, she wished they would talk more of the days when their mother entertained. Perhaps she would glean more information about the Russian princess, whom Magnus had loved.

The growing need to know, accompanied by the pang of pain—a sensation akin to a heavy boulder being placed on her chest—were undeniable signals of a certain undesirable emotion. Despite this abundance of evidence, Caroline flatly refused to admit, even to herself, the unpleasant feeling which accompanied thinking of her husband with another woman was jealousy. Natasha was the one he had called for.

"Caroline?"

"Yes? Oh! My goodness, my head was a million miles away."

Magnus was looking at her, a warmth in his green eyes. "Considerate of you to leave your body here. It is more than passingly agreeable to my eyes, and since my brother has arrived, I am afraid looking is all I will be able to do." He had spoken for her ears alone, yet Caroline still blushed and cast a worried look to David. He seemed not to have heard. Magnus said, "David suggested a sleigh ride. Would you like that?"

She said she would, and went upstairs to put on her woolen pantaloons and a heavy velvet dress. Magnus appeared in the connecting doorway, which stood open as it always did these days. "Come on, do not dally or you will give me ideas." He had changed into heavy trousers and boots and was just now pulling on a frock coat of gray flannel.

"Let's stop in the kitchen and have Mrs. Bronson heat us some chocolate to take with us," she suggested. It was second nature to take his arm as they descended the stairs.

"Go and arrange that and I shall see how the hitching of the sleigh is progressing. Meet me in the stables."

Without any forethought, Caroline nodded and reached up on tiptoe to drop a quick kiss on his lips. His arm caught her, holding her against him briefly before relaxing. A lazy smile curled his sensuous mouth, and his green eyes were half-hidden under heavy lids. It was a look full of passion, and her insides convulsed in response. "Go ahead," he urged softly.

Mrs. Bronson was delighted to provide the hot beverage. "My goodness, yes, of course you need something hot to warm your innards on a day like this. Oh, a sleigh ride's just the thing, isn't it? Lovely day for it, and if we get more snowfall, it'll be as pretty as a picture out in the woods."

Caroline thanked her, then took the basket with the tin of chocolate and honey cakes and goodness knew what else stuffed in. "We are not camping for a week!" Caroline laughed.

Mrs. Bronson smiled broadly, duly complimented for providing such a generous repast. "Men do work up appetites, you know. Can't have them going hungry."

"Mrs. Bronson, that would be impossible with you around. How Magnus and David have not grown fat is an amazement to me."

David and Magnus were waiting for her, the sleigh all hitched up and ready to go. "I thought I was going to have to bring a cart," Caroline said, indicating the heavy basket. Magnus chuckled, taking it from her and loading it in the sleigh. "Mrs. Bronson takes food very seriously," he explained.

"Good thing for us," David said, peeking under the linen napkin. "Honey cakes!"

They set out, gliding easily over the snow-covered paths that snaked through the hushed woods. Magnus managed the team expertly, bringing them to a frozen lake. David hopped out and began crunching through the snow.

"Do you want to get out?" Magnus asked.

"I don't think skirts are as functional in the snow as trousers," Caroline answered.

"Are you warm enough?"

She was quite warm with her thick cloak and the several rugs Magnus had tucked solicitously around her. Her feet rested on a warming pan. However, she only shrugged, giving him a satisfied look when he sidled closer and put his arm about her shoulders.

"You are hell-bent on torturing me, aren't you?" he murmured. His lips pressed light kisses against her forehead. She nuzzled closer. He said, "No matter. I shall simply have you make it up to me later."

"Pray tell me what it is I am doing that needs making up for?" she asked innocently.

"Driving me insane with wanting you, that's what."

She smiled a secret smile. "That is certainly unforgivable. How shall I make amends for such a heinous thing? Perhaps I should slowly massage your back until you are quite relaxed, and then I shall remove all of your clothing. Then—"

"That is quite enough," he interrupted tightly. She giggled and he laughed with her. Bringing his lips to her ear, he whispered, "Remember, my little minx, it works both ways."

His breath tickled, and she gasped. He gave a satisfied grunt.

David returned, saving them both from the temptation to goad their appetites further. Caroline poured out the chocolate and they sat nibbling honey cakes and drinking as the sun angled low in the sky. Magnus' eyes on her were like a caress, and Caroline knew she had never felt this warm, this content, this happy in her life.

They made their way home, David treating them to boldly-voiced renditions of his favorite carols. Even Magnus seemed lighthearted, and Caroline's spirits soared.

They arrived home to an early dinner, and Magnus announced he was retiring early. Taking her cue, Caroline offered David an excuse, one which, judging from his tight, barely-controlled smile, he saw for what it was.

Magnus was waiting for her, already reclining on the bed, propped up on one elbow and legs crossed at the ankles. "Ah, so you have decided to finally put an end to my misery," he grumbled. Caroline evaded his outstretched hand, reaching out to tumble him back on the bed.

"I believe I made it quite clear, my lord husband, exactly how I intended to make up to you my thoughtlessness in stirring your desire—as unwitting as it was, I maintain—and I intend to do it just as I described."

Magnus grinned, watching under hooded eyes as she undressed him, cooperating fully when she rolled him onto his stomach and began to gently knead his muscles.

"If you think this is easing my discomfort, you are mistaken," he muttered after a while. His voice belied the complaint, for it was low and almost slurred from deep relaxation.

"Do pardon me," Caroline replied. She tugged at his side, indicating he was to roll over. Touching him had heated her blood. When he stretched out on his back, she smiled at his ready state. Slowly, she undressed for him, forbidding him one touch until she was as naked as he, but she lost control of their play the minute she stretched out onto his waiting body. He tossed her on her back, and took over from there.

Chapter Fifteen

Caroline withdrew the letter from her mother and stared at it. For the thousandth time, she wondered what Magnus would say if she told him about James' illness and asked him for the money they needed for the sanatorium fees. And for the thousandth time, she dismissed the thought. As much as she longed to be truthful, she could never tell her husband that she had deceived him. She could not risk his rejection. Not for James' sake, nor her own.

Thus, the problem of how to get the money was uppermost in her mind as she descended to the breakfast table. She had suffered more than a few attacks of guilt for having sold the diamond necklace. It had been done in a fit of pique. Feeling no such emotion now, she didn't know how she could bring herself to do what she had been thinking of to cure her need.

"Good morning." Magnus' voice and eyes were welcoming. David waved his fork at her in greeting, his mouth too full of kippers to speak.

"Yes, good morning," she said. Trying to act casual under Magnus's scrutiny had never been easy, but after last night, the heavy weight of his gaze nearly reduced her to a blushing mess.

Thankfully, David had swallowed, and he launched himself into the conversation. The mood lightened as Caroline selected toast and scrambled eggs from the chafing dishes and settled at the table.

The men adjourned to discuss business. Caroline rose and squared her shoulders. Before she could change her mind, she went into the salon.

The Dresden lady and the china shepherdess were in their place. The Waterford bowl, however, was not.

She frowned, remembering Magnus saying he hated it. Perhaps he had removed it. It was not important, however, since it was too large for her purposes. She could hardly pilfer such an unwieldy thing.

She picked up the Dresden lady and carried it to her room.

Once in her chamber, she shoved the expensive statue under her bed and dashed off a quick note to Mr. Peterson, the man to whom she had sold the diamond choker. It read: *If you were pleased with the jewelry, I have another object which may interest you.* She included a proposed meeting date and sealed it, giving it to a footman to post.

She sat for a long time, feeling wretched. Her mood worsened when the thought occurred to her of what Magnus would do if he ever found out she was stealing from him.

Christmas Eve was begun by the assembling of the staff. Magnus dispensed the envelopes to each one, taking time to mention a few words of appreciation for their good service. He had never given it much thought before, but his staff was loyal and efficient, and deserved to be told so. Judging by their faces, they were quite surprised to hear him expressing such sentiments. Once again, he was struck with what a thoughtless idiot he had always been.

Arthur took the envelope stoically, and the words Magnus uttered in a voice perilously close to breaking caused him only to frown and nod. Mrs. Gervis blinked rapidly and inclined her head. When given her envelope, and a heartfelt statement of gratitude for her cooking, Mrs. Bronson's lips trembled and she sniffed loudly several times. When it was done, Magnus felt a sense of satisfaction at having settled his accounts—in more than just monetary ways—with these people who had been with him for years. He would probably not see another Christmas, and it was good to have said something of what they had meant to him—things he hardly realized himself until he heard his own voice speaking the words.

When the staff was dismissed, David, Caroline and Magnus retired to the salon where the candles on the tree had been lit. It was almost cozy. Magnus reflected, sitting back with unaccustomed contentment as David went to the pianoforte and struck up a tune. Beside him, Caroline sat comfortably at ease, a half smile of pleasure playing on her lips and a faraway look in her eyes as they listened to David playing "Adeste Fideles." As if called by his thoughts, she looked over and her smile deepened. A small, thrilling tremor ran up into his chest. Who would have thought a rake like himself would find such simple pleasure in a girl's smile?

He was well aware he was slipping into the very territory he had been determined to avoid from the beginning. He was becoming far too fond of his wife. Yet, he hardly cared. He, who had guarded his heart so jealously since that long-ago day when an overblown countess had shattered his tender innocence, was finding married life to be infinitely diverting.

As David played, Magnus's eyes traveled around the room. It was as if it had come to life again. The only difference between this year and last was Caroline. And that ridiculous giant fir propped near the fireplace, ablaze and glittering with a myriad of lights so that it looked bedecked with diamonds.

Which reminded him. Frowning, he touched Caroline's shoulder. "You have not worn the necklace I gave you. I thought for certain you would do so for Christmas."

Her lashes descended to shield the violet depths. "I forgot. I'm not used to having jewelry."

The sound of voices interrupted them. The village carolers had arrived. Arthur swung open the front door and the snow-flecked group gathered in the great hall. They sang "God Rest Ye Merry, Gentlemen," and "Silent Night," then everyone went into the salon where Mrs. Bronson's holiday wassail was waiting.

On other years, Magnus had stood off, much as his father used to do, and watched the proceedings in a detached manner. Tonight, however, he found himself laughing and conversing with the rowdy crowd, realizing for the first time how delightfully eccentric they were.

When they left, he pulled Caroline aside and said, "I have a gift for you."

"Oh, I have something for you as well."

He pulled a small package out of his pocket and handed it to her. "You were supposed to hang it on the tree," she chided. Reaching into the feathery needles, she withdrew a gaily wrapped package for him.

"You first," he said.

She opened the box. Inside was perfume, an expensive blend of spice and flowers, in a long, elegant atomizer. Attached to the bottle was a satin ribbon which was knotted around a ring. Caroline's eyes widened and her hands stilled. Magnus untied the ribbon and slipped it on her finger.

It was a wide filigreed gold band studded with a stunning array of tiny sapphires and diamonds. "It's so beautiful!" she gasped. "Is it another of your mother's?"

"No, I had this one made just for you. Blue is your color, but these paltry chips of stone cannot hold a candle to your eyes."

She gave him a doubtful look. "Since when is your tongue so glib?" The eyes he had just praised danced, entrancing him. "Thank you, Magnus. Now open yours. I am afraid it is nothing so grand as these."

He complied, amused at the skitter of anticipation in his breast. The mere fact of her making the selection made the unknown object in his hands exciting.

It was a box with a beautifully carved tiger prowling across the lid, and he smiled. The tiger. She had told him he reminded her of one, and so the trinket held a special meaning. The miniature animal was stunningly crafted, its feline beauty shown to full advantage.

Caroline said, "I don't even know if you have need of anything like it. It is more a decoration than functional, I suppose, but you could use it to keep your shirt studs in."

"Cara," he said, "I like it very much. It is a very thoughtful gift, more so than mine." There was a hardness in his throat he could not swallow away. "The tiger, eh? Thank you. I'll treasure it."

"Really? You like it?"

"Yes, of course I do, you silly thing. Ah, look! Here we are under the mistletoe and you haven't kissed me yet."

She gave him a haughty look. "You have not kissed me, either."

"Shall we compromise?" he offered, yanking her to him. She laughed, a flash of white teeth showing before his eyes closed and his mouth moved over hers. She always tasted delicious, like some feast out of a mythological fantasy where the more one consumes, the more one craves.

David, with his usual absence of tact, interrupted them. "Mistletoe?" he said, angling a critical glance up at the sprigs hung overhead. Reaching for Caroline, he threw a mischievous grin at Magnus. "May I?"

Magnus endured seeing his brother give his wife a chaste peck, marveling how that innocent kiss could make his insides burn with possessiveness. He was seized by an insane notion that perhaps David would marry Caroline after he was dead, and it made him want to roar with impotent rage.

Pushing the thought aside, he went over to the long French doors and gazed out on the night. Snow blanketed the lawn and clung to the spindly branches, glowing in the moonlight with ethereal light of its own. He struggled with the surge of unpleasant emotion, willing it under control so as not to ruin their fine evening.

He glanced back at his wife and brother, feeling left out somehow, which the rational part of his brain recognized as ridiculous.

This was *his* house. Caroline was *his* wife, and she had never made an untoward overture toward David. In fact, she had shown uncommon affection to Magnus, something he had not expected from the arrangement. Looking about the room, he tried to find some means to pull himself from his disturbing thoughts.

It was then he noticed the Waterford bowl was missing. It would not have registered except for David commenting on it only a few days ago. And the Dresden figure was gone as well.

Odd. He turned to ask his companions if they knew anything about it, then stopped. He wasn't certain why.

Something nagged at the back of his brain, something not right. His mother's things had remained untouched all the years she had been dead. For two objects to suddenly go missing without explanation was more than coincidence.

With an effort, he forced himself back to David and Caroline. His brother had her laughing at some silly jest. His eyes narrowed, and he could not stop a cold bitter feeling from rising up to lodge in his throat. Next Christmas, when he was not here, would they laugh and toast and make merry together? Would it be David in the master's chamber and Caroline in hers—and would the connecting door remain open as it now did?

Caroline turned to him, her delight fading from her lovely face. "Magnus, is something wrong? Are you ill?"

"No," he said, then forced a reassuring smile. "Nothing like that. Shall we retire?"

"Very well," Caroline agreed, coming to slip her arm through his. A sharp pang affected his heart, for he realized how unkind his thoughts had been. He was wallowing in one of his selfish sulks again. This woman had done nothing to merit his fractious suppositions. She had been only compassionate and giving and flawless in her devotion to him. She had even said she cared.

As they made their way upstairs, Magnus relaxed. He could dispel his fears with the knowledge that Caroline was honest and pure, and she had never done anything to deceive him. It was his own jaded past that made him suspicious, looking for the bad. Caroline was completely trustworthy. That he knew.

Magnus took ill late Christmas night, but the attack was not severe. Caroline stayed by his side, holding his hand while he slept and keeping vigil that his condition didn't worsen.

David stepped into the room. Caroline pressed a finger to her lips. "He's sleeping."

"Is he doing all right?" David whispered.

"He's on the mend already. It wasn't a bad one."

David came to stare down at his brother. "Thank God." He was silent for a long while, and then he said, "I know it is considered unmanly for me to say this, but I love him. More than just brothers. I idolized him growing up, and I suppose I still look up to him." His chin dropped to his chest. "I can't stand this, Caroline."

Caroline rose and put her arms about him. "Hush, David. It's going to be all right."

He looked at her, his brown eyes full of pain. "Do you promise? Oh, God, Caroline, I am so frightened."

Breaking away, he walked a few steps off while he struggled for control.

"David?" Magnus' voice was weak.

David's head came up and he paused a moment before swinging around, a smile neatly in place. Caroline was astounded at the speedy transformation, appreciating his brave face. David would not want Magnus to see his grief.

"Feeling better, old boy?"

"You still here?" Magnus croaked. Caroline put a cup of water to his lips and he drank.

"Just leaving. Came to say goodbye."

Magnus lifted a corner of his mouth ever so slightly. "I don't want you missing any parties on my account."

"Right." David made for the door. Caroline went with him, pulling on his sleeve. "Do you have to go soon?" she asked.

"I have to get out of here," he said sharply, and pulled away.

In the wake of his exit, Caroline felt a twinge of disquiet. Many people could not cope with illness. It made them too uncomfortable. David was one of these. He always retreated when Magnus suffered an attack. She should understand, but it made her angry. She knew what it was like to watch a beloved brother grow weaker before her eyes, yet she could not see abandoning him because of her own pain.

As her mind touched on James, she gave a silent prayer of thanks that he was doing well these days. Her mother's last letter thanked her for the generous funds she had sent and reported that James was increasing in health at an alarming rate. Caroline missed him so much.

She had sold the Dresden figurine. Who was she to judge David, she thought miserably. He had no backbone to face Magnus' illness, it was true, but he was not a thief.

"Are you hungry?" she said, but Magnus had fallen back asleep. She paused, looking down at his handsome face, so peaceful. Her hand came up over her belly, spreading over the flatness. If what she suspected were true, she would have wonderful news to tell him when he awoke. Knowing she must wait until she was absolutely certain, she sighed. She wanted so badly to please him. She wanted to tell him it was true—she was at last with child. She wanted...so much. More than just to fulfill her part of the bargain.

She wanted a lifetime with this man. She wanted to see him with their son hoisted on his shoulders, romping about like a fool. She wanted to see him in his garden, shirtless and sweating and smiling in the sun as he gazed on his precious roses. She wanted to see him gray and bent with age and still looking at her with desire in his eyes.

Oh, God, she had fallen hopelessly in love with him. She had tried not to, but it had happened all the same, beyond reason and beyond wisdom.

Admitting it to herself didn't help. It only made it more

real. The situation was hopeless, and she powerless. She wished she could, like David, run away, but where could she run to? The only place she wanted to be was at Magnus' side.

Her troubled thoughts kept her company until he awoke a few hours later.

"What day is it?" he asked, his voice hoarse and groggy.

"It is still Thursday. You were not out long."

"Mmmm." He sat up, rubbing his temples.

"Headache?"

"Not bad. This was a short one?" She nodded. "The past few have been easy ones."

She leapt at hope. "Has this happened before?"

"No. It usually varies. Since you've come, the attacks have been less frequent. And aside from the one severe one, they have on the whole been milder."

"Perhaps you are improving. Shall I call a doctor in?" Perhaps he could evaluate you again—"

"No doctors!" Magnus said. "They are a bunch of ninnies. Don't know a damned thing and always wanting to bleed you!"

"But if the condition is lessening, we must know immediately!"

He shook his head. "Maybe it's just my imagination. Or perhaps my will to live has finally awakened. But it won't stave off the inevitable forever. No, Cara, I consulted the best physicians." He paused, looking at her as if in wonder. "You really do care, don't you?"

"Of course I do!" she declared.

He reached out a hand to brush his fingers across her face. She caught it and pressed her cheek into its warmth, wanting so badly to share the depth of her feelings.

"Sweet Cara," he murmured. "I'm starving."

She giggled. The way he recovered so quickly always amazed her. It was so strange to see him ravenous and hearty mere hours after having been completely unconscious. "I'll tell Mrs. Bronson. She's got something marvelous prepared for you, I'm sure."

He relaxed against the pillows and Caroline went to order his meal. While she was downstairs, she met up with David and several servants who were laden with his luggage.

"I thought you had gone," Caroline said.

"Just now. I had some business papers to get together for Magnus."

"I know what a comfort it is for him to have you to help him, David," Caroline said, laying a hand on his arm. He almost flinched. "It eases his worry to know you are handling his affairs."

"It's you who has made all the difference, Caroline. Ever since you came, he has changed. I suppose if anything good has come of all of this it has been you."

"Thank you, but I've done nothing," Caroline began.

David cut her off. "You've done everything." He patted her hand. "I'll be back soon. Until then, take good care of him."

"I will."

They said their farewells and Caroline went in the kitchen. Mrs. Bronson looked up from the scrubbed oak table. "Is he ready for a feast?"

Caroline laughed, lighthearted and excited at the lingering optimism from knowing Magnus' condition was definitely improving. "He is always ravenously hungry after a bout, so pile on everything that you have."

"Bless him, the poor man." Mrs. Bronson fussed as she bustled about, "never knowing what to expect. Just when a body starts to think it's all over, he goes into one of his fits. Like his father did, but worse. Terrible it is. Such a fine man, too.''

''Yes,'' Caroline agreed quietly, ''he is a wonderful man.'' She looked at Mrs. Bronson hopefully. ''Did you know Magnus' father?''

The cook bobbed her head as she sliced some cold beef. ''I did indeed. Wonderful man, too. Very quiet. Such an odd match for the mistress, but he doted on her. He loved his boys, too. Gentle but stern, he was.''

Caroline sensed this woman didn't mind an innocent gossip, so she asked, ''Did he and Magnus have a falling out? Magnus mentioned some unkind words exchanged, and I think it wounded him quite a bit.''

''Oh, the master Magnus, he was a wild one,'' the older woman chuckled. ''When he was young, he was handsome and sensitive. His mother called him her little poet because he was always wanting to be around her friends. Then as a youth, he changed. He became colder, less happy, irritable. The old master, he didn't like it.'' She ladled gravy onto some potatoes. ''Never said anything, but you could tell. Then, after the mistress died, the old master, he went into decline. His heart failed because it was broken, I always said. He was so lost without his Esmine.''

She shook her head in sadness, apparently at the poor departed Esmine Eddington. ''That's when the master really went wild, staying in London and carousing like the devil. He hardly ever came home. When his father died, though, Lord Magnus was here. That was a sad day, indeed. It affected him more than I would have thought. He stayed up in his room for a good long time, then went back to London, and from what I've heard, tried to kill himself with late hours and drinking and all manner of uncivilized living. Oh, he has grief in him, that one.'' Her big eyes filled with tears and she brushed them away while arranging hot bread on the platter she was preparing. "One never understands the good Lord's plans when you see a man like that with so much heartache."

"So he came back to Hawking Park when he became ill?"

Mrs. Bronson bobbed her head and said, "Right after he met you, I reckon, though he kept you a good secret at first. Never mentioned a word about you, then suddenly, you were getting married." Her large form shook with mirth. "I'm sure many have been waiting to see if you are 'increasing' as they say, after all that rush."

"It did happen rather quickly," Caroline agreed.

Mrs. Bronson rubbed her hands together as she surveyed the results of her labors. "Well, here we go. That should keep him for a while. I'll have Tim bring it up for you."

"Thank you, Mrs. Bronson. For the talk, I mean. There is much about my husband I don't know, and I hate to ask him if it would cause him distress."

"I know you worry about him, dear. I do, too. We can always pray for a miracle."

Caroline nodded, unable to speak.

She was going to lose him. Magnus, who was infuriating and noble and exciting and exasperating all at once was the most important person in her life. She wondered if she could bear it.

Oh, God, she thought, *I do need a miracle.*

Chapter Sixteen

Magnus' recovery was quick and complete, and within days he resumed his normal routine. He was fond of riding the snow-laden woods on his beloved Balthazar. Sometimes Caroline joined him on the well-trained mare, and these were the times he liked best. With her cheeks cold-kissed and rosy, her corn-silk hair flying in loose tendrils and dark violet eyes sparkling, she looked like an angel by his side as they roamed the forests.

She was delightful company. She could make him laugh and within an instant, look at him in such a way that he would go weak-kneed with desire. He took her to the delta often, and they would watch the changes as it lay blanketed in white, then melt away to shades of brown and gray.

Often, he would dismount and test the frozen ground, arching a speculative brow at his wife. She would giggle and shake her head. "Too cold," she would say, and they'd laugh together. It became a frequent joke, yet Magnus' blood would race every time, for he had full intentions of one day laying her down on the soft spring grass and peeling away her clothing and making slow, maddening love to her under the lacy canopy of new leaves. In the spring...

Perhaps he *would* see another. He hadn't thought to, but he was feeling well so much of the time, and despite his protests to the contrary, a fledgling hope was coming alive that perhaps he would not die before too long. And life was becoming very precious of late.

It was after one of these excursions when they were warming by the fire in the parlor and sipping tea that Magnus noticed Caroline behaving strangely, as if her thoughts were far, far away. Upon reflection, he noted she had been a bit distracted today, in fact for the past few days.

He studied her as she stared into the fire, disgusted at himself when uncharitable suspicions began to assert themselves in his brain. He was a bounder to think it, but the idea she was wondering how long it would take him to die flashed in his mind. He had been doing so well, she had even said so herself, yet she had not bargained for so long a commitment.

He pushed the horror away, but the stubborn notion stuck to the fringes of his consciousness.

"Magnus?" she said at last, ending the long silence.

She turned to him, uncertain and unable to meet his eye. His doubts flared anew. His voice was cold. "Yes?"

"I was going to wait to tell you, but I believe it's fairly certain. That is, I am almost sure. Well, very sure. I think."
He waited. The sound of his own heartbeat thrummed in his ears and all feeling drained from his body. She had her head bent, her eyes lowered. Then she glanced up at him.

She said, "I am with child, Magnus. My courses are almost a full three weeks late, and I am beginning to experience the other signs." She paused, her breath catching. "I would have waited to tell you until I spoke to a physician, but there was no way to see him without telling you first. I hope it is true. I think it is. I would not want to disappoint you if I'm wrong.''

The world narrowed to a singular pinpoint of vision, and all he saw was Caroline's face. Lovely, hopeful, filling his head while her words echoed with perfect clarity. He stood abruptly, walked a few paces away and turned back around. Caroline was on her feet, a million questions written in her expression. He was mortified to feel a stinging in the back of his eyes, and a knot constricted his throat.

He turned his head.

He couldn't think. His brain was numb.

The hard slam of conscience almost brought him to his knees. This woman was preparing to tell him his dream had been fulfilled, and he had been thinking horrible thoughts of her. He might remember in the future, he thought wryly, not to judge her by his own standards.

Oh, God, a child.

Soft footfalls on the thick carpet told him she had come to stand just behind him. He waited until he was sure he wouldn't embarrass himself, then turned and took her in his arms.

She smiled, her own eyes shining. Magnus held her closer, burying his face in the fragrance of her hair. He wanted to fold her into himself, surround and protect her without end.

''Thank you,'' was all he said. Regret and elation blended into a soul-shattering emotion that left him nothing else to say.

She murmured, ''If I'm correct, the baby should be born next fall.''

Almost a year to the day of their meeting. Memory sprung to life, of her sitting in the salon with that ridiculous dress, her breasts spilling over the neckline like a sumptuous soufflé. Looking brave and struggling to remain composed, she had not been able to hide the fear in her eyes. He had acted like a satyr and she had put him in his place without a moment's hesitation.

He felt an insuppressible impulse to laugh. It started as a distant rumble, then blossomed into a full-throated guffaw. He laughed and laughed until tears streamed down his face, the release he had held at bay for so long flowing forth at last unchecked.

Caroline looked astounded, and then he cupped her face in his hands and she laughed, too. A beautiful sound, mingling with his own like a melody.

His child. His legacy.

He closed his eyes, and murmured a prayer of thanks. It had been a long time since he had last prayed. Apparently, the Almighty hadn't forgotten him in his absence.

He kept Caroline close as he led her upstairs. He wanted her, to love her and tell her with his body, his hands, his mouth how he felt—all the things he had no words for. Halfway into their chamber, he stopped.

"Can we—? Is it safe to make love?"

Slipping her arms about his neck, Caroline pressed her slim form up against him. "I am led to believe it is quite all right, Magnus."

"If there is discomfort, let me know," he cautioned.

She nuzzled his ear, nipping the lobe. "I assure you it's fine."

He groaned and caught her up to him, then ushered them into his rooms and locked the door.

Magnus began making plans immediately to go to London. He even seemed excited about it, which surprised Caroline. She had rarely seen him enthused about anything, yet since the news of her condition, he was like a different man. It was as if the darkness had lifted from him. Almost. The mercurial moods had evened to a steady pleasantness, but a sadness still clung to him. He would look at her sometimes, and she could almost read his thoughts.

He was wondering if he would live long enough to see his child born.

Yet he was never morose. When he lectured her about how the child was to be raised, she would roll her eyes and complain and he would catch her to him and kiss her soundly, sometimes, if they were alone, tumbling her onto the bed.

He marveled at the changes in her body, astounded he had not noticed before the darkening of her nipples to dusky pink and the plumper, tighter form of her breasts. If she bemoaned the imminent increasing of her waistline, he would admonish her, saying that when it happened— though no sign appeared yet—it would be the loveliest, most exciting thing he could ever imagine.

And so Caroline was utterly lost to him, loving him secretly as he transformed before her eyes into a man almost unrecognizable from the glowering Earl of Rutherford she had met not so long ago. When she told him so, she quipped that had it not been for his dimple, she might not know him at all. And he showed her he still had enough wickedness in him to fascinate her.

It became easy to love him. She longed to tell him, but she didn't dare. He was ecstatic because she bore his child. She knew she must never forget that. It had nothing to do with her.

Sometimes she forgot. Those were the best times.

The worst was when James' fees were due again and Caroline summoned the jeweler once again to the village. This time she stole the crystal candlesticks.

* * *

"Arthur, who cleans the salon?" Magnus inquired.

The majordomo's eyebrows shifted ever so slightly upwards at the unusual question. "Maggie, sir."

"Is she the only one?"

"Mainly. Gillie helps her, I think, when it's time to move the furniture and wax the floor, but Mrs. Gervis trusts only Maggie, my lord."

Magnus rubbed his hand over his mouth. "How long has Maggie been with us?"

The brows elevated a fraction higher. "Six years, my lord."

"How old is she, about thirty, would you say?"

"Perhaps. She worked for the Dorristers before us."

"Does she have a young man?"

The silvered eyebrows shot full up at that. "I am sure I do not know, my lord."

Magnus was oblivious to Arthur's shock. "Find out. Is the salon always locked when not in use? Yes, I thought so." He blew out a long breath and frowned.

"Is there something troubling you about the salon, my lord?"

Magnus sat perfectly still for a moment. "Several things are missing, Arthur. The Waterford punch bowl, the Dresden figure, some crystal candlesticks, and now a small Chinese vase. I have been watching them slowly disappear. I think someone is stealing from me."

"Perhaps the countess has moved them to other rooms, in order to enjoy them better if they pleased her," Arthur suggested.

"I looked and could not find them, though I did not ask her." He was not about to mention the nagging doubt in the back of his head, mostly because he was ashamed of this wretched jadedness. "I would rather she didn't know."

"Very good, sir," Arthur said, but there was more than a hint of disapproval in the old man's voice.

"We leave for London in three days. I want no one to go into the salon when I am gone, not even to clean." He paced a few steps away, thinking aloud. "There are treasures all over this house, but the salon is where my mother's gifts are kept. The room is rarely used, and these items are less likely to be missed, whereas the other items, while worth more, would be instantly noticed as having been taken. Someone is being very clever, Arthur, but I do not intend to lose another memento."

"I shall take care of it."

Magnus made his way to his and Caroline's adjoining chambers. Excitement stirred in his chest just at the thought of seeing her. It was so silly, he reflected, and completely out of character. It was as if he had never lost that part of himself that could take utter joy in the company of a woman he admired. As if Natasha had never taken it away.

Caroline was with Lillian, discussing what to pack. When he entered, his wife swung toward him with a welcoming smile. "Magnus, I am so glad you've come. Will I be needing a ball gown, do you think, and do I still have time to have Mrs. Dungeness make one? What about the opera? Do you think we shall attend? I have nothing suitable, except the deep blue silk I wore on my first visit to Hawking Park. I am afraid my lack of skill with a needle would be apparent and I would shame you to death with its shabby workmanship."

Magnus crooked a smile, liking her breathless excitement and the faint flush in her cheeks. "As I recall, I had no complaints about that gown."

Her teeth caught her bottom lip, and she chewed thoughtfully. "Do you think? It will be nighttime, after all. I hate to have anything made up, it just seems so frivolous."

"Yes, darling, you mustn't get anything new," he agreed. "Despite Mrs. Dungeness's inarguable talent, we shall visit the finest London dressmakers and have them create worthy confections for your debut as the Countess of Rutherford."

She was taken aback, but pleased. "Oh, no, Magnus, it is too—"

"I insist. Now, I will hear no more of it."

She giggled, catching his light mood, and shrugged. "I know nothing about what is fashionable at the moment."

"Neither do I," he said, "but I suspect it will be easy enough to educate ourselves."

"And enjoyable," she said. "I suppose I will be needing larger gowns soon enough."

"Ma'am, yer still slim as a youth," Lillian interjected. She was the only servant Magnus had ever encountered in his home who joined in the conversation as if she were an equal. Surprisingly, he found he didn't mind in this instance. In fact, he agreed with the maid, and said so.

"Not for long," Caroline reminded him. "And I am looking forward to it."

That absurd warm feeling began again. He watched his wife as she dealt with the servant, ordering which gowns would go with her and their companion accessories. After a while, she turned to him. "Don't you have some business or something, or are you suddenly interested in women's clothing?"

He was about to counter with a quip when he remembered Lillian's presence. For Caroline's sake, he suppressed it.

"Actually, I have paperwork to do. I have been feeling well enough lately to take over much of what I had previously delegated to David, and there is a lot of catching up."

"Then go catch up," she smiled, "because you are making me nervous."

Again, a wonderful retort went unsaid.

Chapter Seventeen

In the two years since her father's death, Caroline had come to hate London. Its overcrowded streets, the soot and fog and perpetual damp. The smell.

But she had never lived in Magnus' London. The Palladian-style house in Mayfair, right on Park Lane across from fashionable Hyde Park, was gorgeous. Not far away, Constitution Arch heralded the pastoral entrance to Constitution Hill, and Buckingham Palace just beyond. Within hours of their arrival, she persuaded Magnus to have the cabriolet brought out of the carriage house for a drive down Grovesnor Street. They crossed to Berkeley Square, then back to Bond Street for a quick perusal of its exclusive shops, then back up Piccadilly toward home.

It was still London. The smell was a bit better than the east end, where she had lived on a crowded, squalid street after the sale of the family's modest home, and traffic was horrendous, especially on Piccadilly. But it was a clear, dry day and not a trace of haze marred the crisp views of this, the poshest section of the city.

"Where to now?" Magnus asked as they drew to a halt in front of Eddington House. "Care to have a stroll in the park?"

She would have loved it, but the truth was she was exhausted. "Tomorrow. I promise."

He brought her into the house and right up to their chambers. Caroline would have never imagined she would love being fussed over so much, but Magnus's attentions were sweet and comforting.

"Rest, now," he said sternly, "and don't argue."

"I don't want to sleep through dinner," she protested.

"I'll wake you," he assured her. She knew he wouldn't. Sighing, she lay back in the huge four-poster that dominated the room they were to share. No master suites in this house, or if there were, Magnus had not utilized them. They were both ensconced in the spacious room situated at the front of the house with three sets of French doors leading to a long portico overlooking the park. It was lovely, dressed in hues of blue, green and deep violet. Magnus did not call for Lillian, drawing the brocade draperies himself and standing in the shadows until she slept.

As she had suspected, he left her to awaken on her own. It was late when her eyes fluttered open and the room enshrouded with twilight. The fire still burned steady, attesting to the fact someone had tended it while she slept. It was not long until Magnus appeared, informing her that he had arranged for dinner to be served in their apartments. Caroline allowed his solicitude. The way he looked at her, she was quite content to play the coddled wife.

"Tomorrow we shall go for an early ride in the park," he suggested when they were lounging in the chairs by the fire after the meal, "and then on to Bond Street to get you started on those gowns. There is a Madam Bouchert who is reputed to be excellent. We shall visit her first."

"I don't wish to tie up your whole day, Magnus. I know you have a great deal of business to attend to."

"Actually, I postponed my appointments until next

week so I would have the entirety of this week to spend with you. I have told Kenneth not to hang the knocker. Perhaps that will discourage callers until you've recovered from the journey.''

"Really," she protested prissily, "I'm not a porcelain doll."

"Oh?" His eyes danced. "You look like one. Perfectly formed, with just the right blush to your cheek and jeweled eyes."

She laughed, for he was being dramatic to tease her. "You sound like a poet!"

He stopped then, looking at her as if she had uttered some epithet. Glancing away, he attempted a smile. "I suppose I do. My mother used to call me that. Her poet. Well, actually, it was her *little* poet, but a man is not fond of such descriptors as that, even in recollecting youth." It was a poor attempt at humor, helped along by his lopsided smile.

Caroline remembered Mrs. Bronson's telling her about Esmine's nickname for her son. She wished she had not mentioned it.

"It's something about myself I haven't allowed in a long time," he said at last. "Not since I was very young."

He fell silent again. She wanted to know more. "What happened, Magnus? Is it something to do with your father?"

He drew in a deep breath and let it out slowly. His eyes stayed on the snifter of fine brandy that lay in his upturned hand. "There was a woman, a Russian countess, when I was a boy. Boy? I was almost a man. At least my body had begun to look like one, but my heart was still immature. I was infatuated with her. She was very beautiful, but she was cold. She seduced me. When I told her...I thought

I loved her, she laughed at me. I pretended I didn't mean it. I was too much of a coward to do otherwise."

"Natasha?" Caroline asked.

Magnus froze. Caroline explained, "You called for her once in a delirium. You merely spoke her name, thinking I was she." It wasn't completely true, but she could spare his pride. "It made me jealous," she confessed.

"Never be jealous of her," he snapped. "She was a whore." He caught himself, clamping his jaw together. Still frowning, he continued, "I threw myself into the life of debauchery which Natasha had shown me. I felt like such a fool. I wanted to prove to myself that my hurt didn't matter, that I *was* a man of the world."

Gently, she asked, "Was that when you and your father fought?"

"We never fought. It is hard to explain how it was. My mother was indulgent. She would laugh, or sigh and ask me when I planned to grow out of such things. But it never truly troubled her. Father, on the other hand, said nothing. He was always silent in his disapproval. It was only when he was dying that he spoke of his great disgust of me."

The timbre of his voice shifted lower, hoarser, heavy with emotion. "He had, it seemed, been waiting ever so patiently for me to change. To become the son he wanted. To become a man in truth, for he said—quite rightly—that I had never accomplished anything manly in my life. He wanted me to marry and take my duties as the future earl to heart as a sacred trust, just as he had done. Produce heirs. Give him the security of knowing the house of Eddington would not perish, thrown away on a wastrel's depraved extravagances."

"Oh, Magnus. How horrible for you."

He shot a look at her. It was almost feral in its intensity. "Why?" he snapped. "It was true enough. I had never done anything of value. When he passed on, I went a little mad, I think. Decided if he thought I was a no-good profligate, why then, I'd apply myself to be the best—or worst—one in London, in all of England for that matter. When my conscience pricked me, I told myself I had time, and I pushed it away. Then I got sick. And I ran out of time.''

She rose and went to him. Kneeling beside his chair, she took one large hand in both of hers. ''You are married now. And the house of Eddington will have an heir. You have done all your father wanted of you.''

''But I shall not live to see it, Cara. It's justice, I know that, but goddamn it all to hell, it's bloody awful.''

Reaching up to smooth a dark lock from his brow, she said, ''Let us steal what we can, then. Come to bed and let me make love to you.''

His strong hands curled into her shoulders, yanking her to him with a small groan. His mouth covered hers, hungrily seeking the sweet promise of her words. Artlessly, he pulled her to her feet with him and they stumbled to the bed, never breaking the kiss.

With reverent, slow movements, she removed his clothes, touching his beautifully masculine body as it was revealed to her. He was impatient and needful as he quickly divested her of her gown, her petticoats, her lacy chemise. She slowed his pace, taking time to tantalize and arouse, teasing him until he growled with impatience and need.

He rolled onto his back, grabbing her legs so she straddled him, one knee on each side. With a firm tug on her bottom, he pulled her over his arousal. ''You want to take charge, do you?'' he said, guiding her hips lower. Her mouth opened, and she gasped as he sheathed himself inside her. ''Then have your way.''

Her head fell back, spilling streamers of pale hair onto his lap. He reached up for her breasts, brushing his fingers against the sensitive peaks until she cried out. She moved her hips, stroking his manhood slowly, taking him into herself and withdrawing over and over again until she had spun a dizzying crescendo of pure ecstasy.

"Ah, Cara," he muttered, "you make me forget everything."

She gazed down at him, his heart-stopping look of desire mixed with pain making her wish she could tell him how much she loved him. It hurt not to, the ache within her heart mingling with the pleasure of her body in exquisite union. Leaning down, she claimed his mouth, slipping her tongue inside to mate with his. He moved under her, quickening the rhythm as the tension mounted to nearly unbearable heights. Wave after wave bore her aloft, lifting her toward fulfillment until she felt herself reach the brink, then spill over into wondrous sensation.

She felt Magnus stiffen underneath her just before he thrust powerfully again and again. He gasped her name as they rode out the harsh cadence of his release.

Breathless, weak, she collapsed on him, savoring the replete laziness that followed in the wake of their pleasure. His arms came to lock around her, holding her snugly against him.

She waited until his breathing had softened and slowed before moving. Drawing up the coverlet, she tucked it around his waist. When she touched his face, his breath caught and he turned his head away. He was deeply asleep.

She curled up against his back with her arm across his chest. Pressing a kiss to his shoulder, she said quietly, "Goodnight, Magnus. I love you."

It did make her feel better. She lay her cheek against his back and smiled.

* * *

The following days were filled with shopping and sight-seeing. Caroline had lived all her life in the city, but she had never visited the Athenium, nor had she perused the masterpieces of the Royal Academy of Arts. With Magnus, she did all these things, as well as venture into the quirky delights of King's Road, a highly entertaining shopping district of questionable respectability. With her husband as her guide, everything was exciting, for he had endless stories—some of them quite shocking—for every corner of London.

He took her to the finest milliner, the most exclusive haberdasher who showed her fabulous undergarments in an array of satins, silks and lace. The shoemaker was commissioned for seven pair of slippers to match the gowns Magnus had ordered for her, and two pair of boots. Even the grocer had a smile on his face when they left his shop, laden with all of the wondrous delicacies Magnus had selected. On the evening of their sixth day, Magnus announced he would be taking her to the opera the following night.

"If you are up to it," he amended.

"I will be if you would cease dragging me all over the city and purchasing things for me."

"You lazy chit," he drawled, "I suppose I shall have to allow you one day to lounge about."

"I hate being so tired," Caroline pouted.

"Cara *mia,* I was only teasing. Of course, I have been hatefully cruel to have not thought of your fatigue sooner."

"I've had a marvelous time this last week. I only wish I had the stamina to keep up with you."

"You must take care of yourself. And the baby. Tomorrow, I order you to stay in bed until it is time for the theater. We shall not even go to a late supper, but come immediately home."

She didn't like his constraints, and told him so. "I am not feeble, just pregnant," she insisted.

He gasped, "Madam! You do shock me with such vulgar reference to your delicate *condition*."

"Oh, I am sure," Caroline said drolly, "that your sensibilities are offended."

He chuckled devilishly, and they laid out their plans. As it was to be Caroline's launch into society as his wife, the circumstances had to be carefully chosen. After Magnus went into the library, there to begin addressing his business concerns, Caroline went to examine her rapidly expanding wardrobe to choose just the right gown. When she had selected a lovely peacock blue with a long, straight skirt that helped hide her slightly thickened waist, she and Lillian fussed like schoolgirls over the array of accessories until they had laid out the entire ensemble.

"Yer goin' to make all the rest of them ladies turn green!" Lillian crowed.

"I doubt that." Caroline shrugged. "Just so I do not shame my husband." It was easy to talk to Lillian as a friend. She was only a few years older than Caroline, and she had a no-nonsense quality about her that Caroline liked.

"Shame 'im! My ladyship, I hope yer teasin'. If ye could see the way 'e looks at ye, ye'd know you could never shame 'im."

"Looks at me?"

"When ye don't see. Anyone could tell 'e admires ye terribly. It—" She broke off, dropping her eyes. "I shouldn't be goin' on like that. Never know my place, that's what my problem is."

Caroline wanted to beg her not to stop. What was it Lillian saw in Magnus' eyes when she wasn't looking?

Of course, she could do no such thing. She thanked Lillian, and the maid left. Alone, Caroline pondered the possibility that Magnus could return her affection and, like herself, be afraid to admit it.

She could never imagine Magnus afraid of anything. Yet he had told her a little bit about himself, enough for her to understand that he had been gravely hurt as a young man, so much so that he had buried his vulnerability behind the facade of a scoundrel. The only question was, how deep did the facade go?

Of late, he was almost a different man, so full of caring and tenderness that she could almost believe he did harbor some true feeling for her. Or was it because of the babe?

She mustn't underestimate the power of her having his child. It was everything to him. She, as the baby's mother, was precious to him. That she knew. But was she cherished for herself?

To be loved was something she had never thought to want. Perhaps because she had considered it unattainable. Her father had taken that away from her when she was but a child. He had shown her no example of loving husband. And when he had touched her in that horrible way, he had shown her that men would love only to get what they wanted.

Louis Wembly was not all men. He was not Magnus. In her mind, she knew that. In her heart, she still could not trust, at least not completely.

Thinking about her father's depraved overtures brought no discomfort. Not even anger. She had gotten over the rage long ago, focusing it on the one who deserved it. Louis had been shocked indeed when, on the first occasion of his trying to slide his hand into her dress to feel her

newly-developing breasts, his twelve-year-old daughter
had told him in no uncertain terms that he was never to
do such a thing again. Oh, of course, Caroline had been
terrified, but the fierce example of her mother, who had
fought so doggedly and so often on behalf of her children
and who had, in spite of her resignation to her disastrous
marriage, never allowed her husband's sickening life-style
to make her less a lady, had given Caroline the courage
she needed.

Louis was like a different person after that. Even as
debauched as he had been, he had enough humanity left
in him to be ashamed of what he had done. That was just
luck, Caroline had the good sense to realize, and so a day
didn't pass that she would not forget to utter a prayer of
thanksgiving. If he had reacted differently to her rejection,
her life would have been ruined.

She had not told her mother, a carefully considered decision she made based on the knowledge of the heavy burdens of worry her mother already bore and Louis' surprising reasonableness about the matter. As her father
declined, Caroline enjoyed a certain smug satisfaction in
knowing she had been instrumental in showing him what
a disgusting piece of refuse he was. She liked to think it
bothered him, and perhaps it was that which brought on
his slow deterioration. As it turned out, it was disease. At
his passing, Caroline had felt nothing but relief, as if a
malignant presence had been removed from her life. Yet
after his death, she and her mother and James had been
plunged into worse circumstances than any of them would
have dreamt they would ever face.

That nightmare was over. Now, they had food and clothing and a decent roof over their heads—all their material
needs were now seen to in abundance. More importantly,
Mother's frequent letters reported fabulous improvements

in James' condition. Audrae was even hopeful they would be able to arrange a visit soon, if the doctors would agree. The knowledge of her brother's health growing gave Caroline a distinct sense of peace. Yet so much of her remained restless and unsure.

Chapter Eighteen

Magnus thought that his wife's enforced day of rest would be an excellent opportunity for him to run several errands he had been putting off. He ordered the cabriolet to be readied, and he set off just after breakfast.

It was a horrid day. The fog was thick and yellow. He hated the way it seeped into even the sturdiest wools, seeming to penetrate the flesh to one's very bones. There was no wind, which was both a blessing and a curse. It would have cleared the fog, but the added chill would have been uncomfortable.

He was not deterred, however, from his appointed tasks. Heading first to Caractacus Green's office, he braced himself for an unpleasant encounter. He had never liked the man, but since David had done most of the interacting with him, he could hardly complain overmuch. As it turned out, the solicitor was out of the office. Magnus headed back to the fashionable part of the city.

"Rutherford!" a voice called, penetrating the clatter of the horse's hooves. Magnus looked up to see one of his old cronies headed his way.

A strange reaction settled in his chest. It was Garding, a friend from Oxford. They had caroused together, raising hell and a lot of eyebrows for more years than Magnus could remember, yet Magnus could not muster an ounce of enthusiasm for his old friend.

"How the devil are you?" Garding roared, giving Magnus a fraternal embrace.

"Better these days, and you?"

"Ah, it is taxing carrying on the traditions without you. There are more whores to service, more fools to fleece without you to help. Why the bloody hell didn't you tell me you were in town? Come to White's tonight, everyone will be there."

"Not tonight."

"Why the blazes not? My God, won't they all just die to see you?" Oblivious to the tactlessness of his words, Garding's face was full of hope. "Come on, it will be just like old times. We'll work off a few demons."

"I've run out of demons," Magnus answered. He took a step away, a sign of dismissal. "I am taking my wife out to the opera tonight. You are welcome to join us, but only if you promise to behave yourself."

Garding whooped, "Not a chance, old boy. Sounds like you've got yourself at least one demon left—it would take a she-devil to tame you. The opera!"

Garding's laughs echoed behind Magnus as he continued down the street. Strange he had never noticed how annoying the sot was. It was only eleven in the morning and Magnus had smelled liquor on his breath. Choosing not to remember how many times he might have been in the same condition, he proceeded on his way.

Aimlessly, he glanced at the shop windows as he passed. He felt buoyant as his thoughts turned again to his wife. Tonight he would introduce her to everyone who was someone in the city. He was looking forward to it with relish. And pride.

It seemed the fog was thinning and the sun was glowing hazily, trying to burn some of it off with its meager mid-winter warmth. It might even turn out to be a pleasant evening, weather-wise.

His eye caught something in the window, and he was a full three paces away before what he had seen registered in his brain.

The Dresden lady.

He retraced his steps to the window and took another look. It *was* his mother's Dresden lady. Or one exactly like it.

If it was the very one, he had been correct. Someone was stealing from him. But how had the object gotten to London? He went into the shop.

"Oh!" a heavyset man exclaimed as he rushed around the counter. "May I be of service, your lordship?"

"The Dresden figure in the window. I was interested in it."

"Ah, yes, a beautiful piece. Let me get it for you."

Magnus gave a quick look around the interior of the store while the man fetched the figurine. Magnus looked it over, frowning. "Do you have any Waterford? A large bowl, suitable for punch?"

"No, your lordship," the shopkeeper said regretfully.

"Hmm." Magnus tried to remember what else was missing from the grand salon. "What about a Chinese vase?"

"No, but I can contact my dealers and ask them if you wish."

"No. I need it immediately. Do you have any cut crystal candlesticks, perhaps?"

"I did, your lordship, but I think they've been sold. Let me look for you."

He hurried to a glass case which was crowded with all

manner of bric-a-brac. Magnus's mind raced. Two items from Hawking Park—if the candlesticks were also here—made it certain someone had stolen them from the grand salon. That cleared Maggie, or any other servant, for they would have no means by which to barter with a London-based merchant. He had no visitors, certainly no one who had access to the salon, so that left David. Or Caroline.

Suspecting Caroline was absurd. She never left his side.

Except when her mother was at the Ordinary. She had visited quite often.

No, the vase had been taken only recently, and Caroline's mother and brother were off visiting friends. She had not left Hawking Park but for a few hours, and very infrequently.

David, then. David was always traveling to London.

The merchant returned with the news that the candlesticks had been sold.

"I'll take the figurine," Magnus said.

"Don't you want to know the cost? Of course you don't, my apologies, your lordship. I'll wrap it for you!"

Magnus brooded, wandering the shop as his mind turned over the possibilities. Leaning on a glass display case, he fought an inner war of mistrust and incredulity. *Could it be David?*

"Oh, your lordship, may I show you some jewelry?" Magnus was startled out of his thoughts to notice an array of gems lay under the case upon which he was leaning. The shopkeeper thought he was interested in them, almost salivating at the thought of another sale. "I have some very interesting pieces. Let me show you."

Magnus ignored the man, taking no notice of the necklaces, bracelets, earrings and brooches the shopkeeper piled up in front of him until— *No!*

Lightning-quick, his hand shot out and grabbed the sparkling object.

"Oh, yes, your lordship, excellent choice. It is a rare piece, look at the workmanship..."

Magnus crushed the necklace in his grip. His world narrowed, collapsing in on itself as he wrestled with the terrible implications of what lay before his eyes.

He wanted to snarl and growl and demand answers, but he knew he had a better chance at success by staying calm. "Yes, I see that. My wife will love it. She saw it in a painting once and always admired it."

"Yes, it's very old. Diamonds like that are rare."

"It would be especially delightful if it were the same necklace. I wonder if it could be. Tell me, where did you get it?"

"A lady in Cambridgeshire sold it to me," the stupid man gushed, too overjoyed with the prospect of his customer's total climbing higher to be sly. "It was hers, but beyond that I don't know its history."

Caroline. It was Caroline who was stealing.

Of course, how stupid could he have been? She had only married him for money, after all. Despite her sweet pretense at caring and the lush welcome of her body, theirs was only a business arrangement based on a fair reckoning of silver. When her allowance had not come in fast enough, she must have helped herself to the treasures littering Hawking Park.

Perhaps he wasn't dying fast enough for her.

"The same lady who sold you the other items? The candlesticks and this Dresden?"

The man was immune to the significance of Magnus's interest. This indicated that the transaction, at least from his end, had been honest. "Why, yes."

A cold feeling curdled Magnus's heart. "Include this and give me the total."

"Yes, your lordship. Oh, your ladyship will be pleased with this, you can be sure!"

Magnus stared at him, but he didn't see the bright, beady eyes nor the wide grin bristling with overlarge teeth. He doubted Caroline would be pleased at all. He paid the man, and waited an excruciating five minutes until the items were safely wrapped and bundled.

Magnus cut short his other errands, returning home and going directly to the library. He locked the doors, unwrapped his parcels and sat staring at them.

Why? His mother's necklace, for God's sake. Could she not have at least respected what it meant to him? And all his mother's trinkets, mementos he cherished. How dare she?

More pressing on his mind was the question as to why she would be in such desperate need of money?

There was some mysterious motivation, not just simple greed, at work here. With her family housed at the Ordinary and a new wardrobe for everyone, Caroline's monthly allowance was more than adequate for anything further they would have needed. There had to be some other need for money about which he was not aware. Something urgent, something that would spur her to thievery. What the devil was it? Blackmail? Debt? Revenge?

Rage welled up inside him, nearly blinding and so intense he could scarcely breathe. With a growl, he began to pace.

Her reasons mattered, but the fact was that whatever the cause, she had betrayed him. *Goddamn her.* The woman had done to him what no other had. Not even Natasha, damn her black heart as well. Natasha had never pretended to be different than she was. It had been his youthful inexperience which had prevented him from seeing it at the time. But Caroline had played him false. Intentionally. Played him like a fiddle. And a fool.

With a crash, he sent the Dresden lady across the room. It exploded against the paneling, raining a thousand shards of porcelain over the carpet. Agitated, he looked for something else to destroy.

She had penetrated his deepest parts. She had drawn him out of the safe chrysalis of defeat and resignation. The most unforgivable thing—she made him want to live. He had wanted a lifetime with her, to talk with her, to ride the forests and laugh and tease and fight and challenge. To love, night after night, until that unattainable day when he would feel it was finally enough. She had made him desire, not only her body, not only herself, but life.

He overturned a chair, taking savage pleasure in reducing it to kindling.

What moronic idiocy had it been that had allowed vulnerability? How it must have amused her. Perhaps she even laughed with her accomplices, "Oh, you should see him, the fierce Earl of Rutherford. He is positively besotted."

He cleared the library table in one swoop of his arm. The sound of it all crashing to the ground was deafening.

God, he *was* besotted. What he could not put to word—and thank the Almighty for that one bit of mercy—he had tried to show, demonstrate in action and tone. He had cherished her with his body, delighting in her pleasure, hoping his touch, his kiss, his tenderness would communicate what his voice could not.

A pounding at the door brought him up short. "Master, the door is locked! Are you well?"

"Get out of here, I am not sick. I am not to be disturbed."

There were no more sounds, and no one came when he yanked a portrait off the wall and stomped it into a mangled mess.

It took several hours to calm down. The room was reduced to a shambles at the end of it. As his reason returned, and he ran out of things to decimate, he began to formulate his plan.

He called in a manservant and instructed him to deliver a message to Mr. Green, directing the solicitor to reopen the investigation into his wife's background. Then he went upstairs to Caroline.

Caroline was delighted to see Magnus. "Thank goodness, I have been going mad shut in here all day," she said as he entered the room.

He stood watching her. "Have you missed our shopping excursions?"

"I have missed *you*," she purred, coming to slip her arms around his neck. He stood stock-still as she pressed her lips against his.

"Have you selected your dress?" he said, unmoved by her kiss.

She leaned back in his loose embrace, fingering the soft lock that curled at the nape of his neck. Something was wrong. "The peacock blue," she answered.

"Does it have a daring neckline?"

She arched her brows. "Are you asking because you would like me to wear a low décolletage, or prefer I do not?"

"I was wondering what jewelry you will wear. I have not seen the diamond choker on you. Well, only once, but it hardly counts since it was in the dark. I would like you to wear it tonight."

She took a long breath, paused, and let it out in a sigh.

"Oh, I—I think I must have forgotten it at Hawking Park. I didn't even think to bring it. I am not used to such fine things." Realizing she was over-explaining, she snapped her mouth closed and studied the smooth skin of his neck. "I'm so sorry, Magnus."

There was a long pause before he answered. "No matter. I have other pieces from my mother's collection stored in banks here in the city. I'll have someone fetch them and you can make another choice."

"Oh, no," she rushed, feeling much too guilty to allow him to give her any more of his family heirlooms. "The dress is enough without any jewels."

"Nonsense. Every woman at the opera will be strung up with as much glitter as a chandelier. You must have something worthy of your station. You aren't poor any longer, Caroline. You are a countess. You must act like one."

Did she imagine the reproof, or had he simply uttered some ill-chosen words? Magnus wasn't usually insensitive unless he meant to be, but there was no reason for him to be angry at her. Not that she was aware of, anyway.

"I shall endeavor to do you credit." She stepped away from him and pulled herself upright, showing him she was a little stung.

"Good," was all he said. He turned on his heel and headed back out the door. "I'll be up to dress after dinner, which I'll take in the library. I'll have yours sent up. Make certain you rest sufficiently." He didn't wait for her response before disappearing around the corner.

Caroline stared after him for a moment, puzzled. Then she shrugged. Something must have happened today to make him cross. She wouldn't let it spoil her day, for she was looking forward to this evening far too much. Whatever it was that was bothering Magnus, it had nothing to do with her.

The queue of carriages in front of the Royal Opera House moved slowly and the black landau made excruciating progress. Caroline leaned back in her seat, letting out a long, exasperated breath. "Is it always this crowded? We shall miss the beginning if we do not hurry." Like a jack-in-the-box, she sprang forward and craned her neck.

Under any other circumstances, Magnus would find her childlike excitement enchanting. He still couldn't help feeling a touch of admiration. Caroline looked magnificent. Her gown was an unusual blue with a plain, daring neckline that left much of her high, full breasts exposed. The skirt was caught up in the back in an elaborate array of blue and lavender ribbons, creating a cascade of horizontal folds across the front. She looked like a queen, creating a delicious contrast with her unsophisticated behavior.

The charm of his wife was wearing on him, making him more irritable. The uncertainty throbbed in his brain as he fingered the necklace in his pocket.

She sat back again. Glancing over at him, she was sobered by his reserve. "Magnus, what is the matter? You've been troubled today."

"Nothing."

Her eyes widened. "You aren't feeling ill?"

"No," he answered curtly. Devil take her, she looked so very convincing. As if she did care. Probably worried she would miss the gala night, a chance to show off that dress, he thought sourly.

He had arranged to have the other jewelry fetched to Eddington House, and now cold fire surrounded Caroline's neck and wrists and flashed at her ears. A full set of diamonds and sapphires with a huge pendant that hung almost to her breasts. His fingers held the memory of touching the ice-cold stone as it lay against her warm flesh. The contrast had sent a jolt up his arm.

He shifted in his seat, watching her every move. She craned her neck out the window. "Oh, this is going to take forever."

"Shall I tell Donald to simply pull over and we shall walk?" he asked drolly.

"That wouldn't be quite proper, would it?" She giggled, oblivious to the subtly patronizing tone in his voice.

Eventually, they arrived at the door. Magnus alighted and handed Caroline down, aware of the pleasure he had anticipated in this moment when London Society got their first glimpse of his wife. Now, he could barely summon a smile for the people who clamored to greet him and steal a closer look.

She was perfect, as he knew she would be. Pleasant but not gushy, dignified yet demure, she struck just the right chord to leave them gaping as they moved to take their seats in the premier box.

Sitting at attention, as if it were some military exercise, Caroline was entranced by the drama on stage. A dangerous temptation flirted with his anger as he watched her, a searing ripple of pain which he promptly squelched. At intermission, he excused himself, going down to the lobby alone.

He needed to breathe. He felt like running. No, he felt like digging, hauling, lifting, *throwing*. Christ, he needed a drink. Like a panther, he moved through the press of aristocracy, making his way to the bar.

Had he been less preoccupied, he would have noticed the angular man lounging against a nearby column.

"Rutherford, I thought you were dead."

The voice was immediately familiar. Magnus didn't need to look up to see who it was. "Not yet."

"What a shame. I can hardly wait to celebrate."

Magnus turned and faced the man. Frederick Cannon was an arrogant, ignorant rotter who was a cheat at cards and a sore loser to boot. Magnus had stripped him of an elegant schooner several years back in a poker game at one of the less reputable clubs. That night, Magnus had also ended up with the sweet little piece of skirt Cannon had been eyeing. Ever since, Cannon made no secret of his hatred, setting up a one-way rivalry. Magnus marveled that he kept at it, for he only seemed to get himself in deeper. After several challenges to reclaim his ship, Cannon had given up trying to attack Magnus at the card table. But he never passed up a chance to do so away from one.

"Well, you can invite half of London, and have a merry old time. But I'm afraid you'll have to wait a little while longer, unless you'd like to do something to hurry me along to my greater reward?"

Cannon glared. He was all sharp edges, jutting cheekbones, bony shoulders, pointed nose. "Oh, I'd like to all right. But justice, for once, is on my side. I can wait."

"Well, that is a relief," Magnus drawled. He purposely sounded bored. "I want to find out what happens in the second act."

He left his enemy behind, taking his drink out the arched doors and onto the street. It was a cold night. The dampness had returned. He downed the whiskey and wiped his mouth absently on his sleeve.

The cold wasn't helping. The whiskey wasn't helping. The distance from Caroline wasn't helping.

Blast. Intermission was nearly over. He went back inside and climbed the red-carpeted stairs back up to the box.

When he drew back the curtain to enter, there was a strange man sitting in his seat.

Chapter Nineteen

Caroline was startled, her gaze lifting up to meet blazing green fire. William stood immediately. Caroline did, too, though it annoyed her to find herself acting as if she had gotten caught doing something wrong.

"Magnus, I ran into an old friend. May I present to you Lord William Linny."

William bowed. "Your lordship."

Magnus made no move of acknowledgment. "How did you 'run into an old friend' here in our box? There is very little room for collision."

"I am certain the countess meant it figuratively, your lordship. Actually, I knew Caroline—I mean, the countess. Your wife…" William began to squirm. "I knew her a few years ago, and could not help myself from coming to pay my respects when I spotted her. It is such an unexpected surprise to see her again."

Magnus had that predatory look she hadn't seen in a long time. Caroline was as tense as a mouse with a cat in the room. No, it was William who was the mouse, and she the observer, knowing the great danger that lurked just beyond the poor prey's awareness. "I knew William from my two seasons before Father died," she explained.

If she had any hope Magnus would behave himself, it was dashed with his next words. "He wasn't one of the young fools who asked you to marry him, was he?"

Caroline went weak with shock. Reaching behind her, she felt for her chair and sat down.

"Well," Magnus demanded, turning to William, "were you?"

"A-actually, y-yes, I did have the honor of requesting Car—, the countess's hand in marriage." Sweet, brave William.

"Hardly an honor if she turned you down." Magnus took his seat, leaving Linny standing by the door. "Did you ever find someone to marry?"

Linny blinked rapidly several times, but he was too well-bred to show any other reaction to Magnus' outrageousness. "No, your lordship." Turning crisply to Caroline, he said, "Countess, it was delightful to see you again. I hope I have the honor again soon."

Caroline forced a smile, thinking, *Not likely. You will run like demons are at your heels when you see me.*

"Thank you, William. Give my regards to your mother."

"I will. Good evening, Countess. Your lordship."

Magnus grunted, not even turning around.

In the wake of William's departure, Caroline was seething. Before she could utter a coherent sound, Magnus turned to her. "So, is he the one you will take up with after I'm gone?"

She had nearly worked herself to full temper, but that comment set her back. "What?"

"I'm not going to be around very much longer. Is he waiting for you, is that why he is still unmarried?"

"What refuse is this?" she whispered as the lights were doused in preparation for the second act. "William is a lovely man. I declined his troth because I did not love him."

"Hah!" Magnus thundered. Several heads turned to look for the source of the rude sound. "You did not love me, yet you did not decline my troth. Poor William has the disadvantage of health. He should know it is widowhood you are after."

"What has possessed you tonight?" she flung in a repressed whisper, too aware how easy it was to draw stares. The music had started, thank goodness, and the curtain was going up.

He didn't answer her. She let the matter drop, but the evening was ruined for her. The lovely music which had carried her into another realm only a little while before sounded hollow, annoying in its distraction. She wanted to be home. She wanted to know what had Magnus so upset.

That the rude, arrogant man she had first met could grow into a gentle lover was not hard to imagine. She had witnessed it and believed it. That he could regress back, she had never anticipated.

During the next intermission, he took her for refreshment. Barely polite, he introduced her to everyone he met, but it was hardly the enthusiastic presentation she had dreamt of.

A fellow named Garding seemed to surprise Magnus. He introduced her to him, and Caroline took an instant dislike to him. Perhaps it was the way his eyes slid up and down her body. Perhaps it was when he said, "I had to see who caught the great Earl of Rutherford. Whew! Magnus, she is something." Even Magnus scowled and took Caroline by the elbow and steered her back to their seats.

She refused to speak to him. But when she got him home, she would have plenty to say.

On their way out, Garding came up to Magnus once

again. "Care to change your mind and join me at White's, old man?"

Magnus flickered a glance at Caroline. "Maybe I will at that. Let me see my wife home. I'll catch up with you there."

When they were in the landau, Caroline said, "If you think to avoid explaining what that was all about tonight, you are wrong. I want to know what you thought you were doing."

"I thought I was taking you to the opera. What did you think I was doing?"

"Don't be such a sarcastic cad. You know very well what I am talking about. You were outlandishly rude to William, you practically ignored me—"

"Please cease your complaints," he snapped, the detached amusement gone in an instant. "I purchase you dresses and festoon you with jewels and take you out in public so everyone can 'ooh' and 'aah' over you, and still you aren't happy."

"You were rude and uncivilized, and you humiliated me tonight." In the confines of the carriage, Caroline could not get the distance from him she craved. Instead, she crossed her arms over her breasts and stared out the window. She could feel Magnus' eyes burning into her.

"Do pardon me, countess. I forgot how you were used to so much better."

He was out for blood tonight. She glared at him, her chin tilted up in defiance against the stinging hurt he was so effectively doling out. "I have more breeding than you displayed tonight. I was poor, Magnus, but I was no mannerless urchin."

"But you are not poor any longer, are you?" he said savagely, his face jutting closer. Caroline could see, even in the darkness of the carriage, his eyes were fierce and a dull pulse throbbed at his temple. She shrank back as he spit out the words. "Thanks to me you have jewelry dripping about your person. You have gowns to show off your gorgeous breasts and that willowy slimness you wear with ease. Fine clothes, everything the best. So if you have to put up with my less than satisfactory company, then you shall simply have to bear it. If it depresses you, you have only to think on the fact that I can not hang on forever. It should cheer you."

Silence. Caroline whispered, "What has happened to you? Magnus, please tell me. I know something is wrong."

"Something wrong? Why yes, there is a great deal wrong. Why don't you tell me, Caroline?"

"How would I know why you are acting this way? I'm begging you to tell me what it is!"

He snorted and turned away. "Never mind."

The carriage pulled up to Eddington House. Magnus brought Caroline only as far as the front door. "Gregory will see you in. I am going to White's."

Before she could stop herself, she reached out for him, pulling at his arm. She had an irrational fear of his leaving her. "Please come inside with me, and let's talk about what's bothering you. If I've done something to offend you, I want to know. Let me make it up to you."

He gave her a long, slow look. It was filled with sadness. However, all he said before he turned to go was, "You do that well, Caroline. One would even think you meant it."

Magnus languished on a brocade-covered sofa, one arm flung across the back, the other holding a snifter of brandy. His cronies were especially loud tonight, a raucous welcome for him after his long absence.

He looked at them, each one in turn. Garding was acting like the lord mayor, taking credit for Magnus' presence.

Clarely and Hedgemont were their jolly selves, slapping each other on the back as if in congratulations on some stupendous achievement.

Magnus took a mouthful of mellow liquid and swished it around in his mouth.

"Come on, old man, let's see if you've forgotten how to play cards," one of them called.

"Anxious to lose some money, are you?" Magnus answered.

A round of laughs rang out. The other patrons glanced over, some of them recognizing the Earl of Rutherford. Magnus saw Frederick Cannon watching him with narrowed eyes. Raising his glass, he got no response. Just the glare.

He sat down at the table and called for the cards to be dealt and a fresh brandy.

"So Rutherford," Clarely said. "How do you find the state of marriage?"

"Blissful." Everyone laughed at his flat tone.

"You should see her," Garding said with a meaningful look to the others.

"Say, I am glad to see you're done with that wretched fever." Hedgemont grinned. "It's good to have the gang back intact."

"Oh, I am not recovered at all." Magnus looked at his cards, arranging them neatly in his hand. "And it was no fever. I am dying, it seems."

Silence and gaping mouths faced him when he raised his eyes from the pair of queens he held. He felt a deep sense of satisfaction. He didn't know where the contempt for these men came from, but he felt it now, welling up and taking over. Each and every one of them were idiots. How he had borne them for so long, he couldn't imagine.

"Ante up," Magnus said cheerfully, placing two tokens on the green velour table.

"Dash it all, Rutherford, you can't be serious!"

"Quite. Are all of you out already?"

Someone cleared his throat and threw in a pair of tokens. The others slowly recovered and the play resumed.

The gay humor dissolved, which Magnus liked. After all, he was hardly in a celebratory mood. His complete satisfaction was disrupted by how many times his thoughts turned to Caroline. Each remembrance brought a fresh bolt of pain.

Did she think she would deceive him forever?

She didn't need to, not forever. Just long enough to bury him.

What she hadn't bargained for was who he was. One would think his reputation would be enough. He was a beast, a barbarian, a heartless ravager of both business and society's morals, a rake for whom nothing was sacred or off-limits. He had debauched righteous women, cuckolded good men, stripped the mighty of their fortunes and never creased his cravat in any of it. He was, after all, the infamous Earl of Rutherford.

Good God, even he had forgotten it for a while. Who he was. What he was.

It was time he remembered. And time she learned.

Caroline had no idea who Constance Whittingdon was, or why she was here. When Gregory had announced there was a visitor waiting in the yellow parlor, Caroline wished she had the nerve not to receive her. However, it was not possible to do so without offending the woman. Without knowing who she was, Caroline could hardly snub her out of turn.

She had risen and dressed that morning with the knowledge that Magnus had not returned home last night. Her anger had kept her awake until the wee hours, but even the righteous strength of it could not overcome fatigue, an effect of her condition. Thus, she was tired and completely out of sorts this morning, hardly in the mood to entertain a stranger.

Entering the parlor, she was surprised to see Constance Whittingdon was a beautiful, and young, woman. Dark brown hair was piled attractively on her head and she wore an expensive green silk that was molded to her voluptuous form.

"Hello. I am Caroline Eddington."

Miss Whittingdon sat in a yellow horsehair chair. She did not get up. "Yes, I know. I saw you and Magnus driving around the city last week, but I had to wait until you were officially 'out' before I could call." The woman's plainspokenness startled Caroline, as did her air of blatant arrogance. She spoke with a sense of superiority that was grating. And she had referred to Magnus by his first name.

She was saying, "I know it is considered ill-mannered of me to call without an invitation, but Magnus and I are old friends," these two words were emphasized, "and I simply had to see him. Is he in?"

Caroline's heart was thumping from the innuendo of the pair of words. "No."

The other woman shrugged, tilting her head to one side as if she were flirting. "Then we shall have a chance to chat. Tell me, how long have you and Magnus been married?" There was an obvious drop in her gaze to Caroline's waistline.

"Several months," Caroline answered. She sat down, deciding not to offer this woman tea.

"Did you know him long before that?"

"Not long."

"Oh, Magnus always was one for quick romance. Never liked to linger, that one." Constance laughed as if remembering some private amusement. "I'm surprised he finally wed. He said he never would."

"Of course he never married," she quipped, smiling sweetly at the other woman. "How else could he have wed me if he had?"

The look Constance gave her was barely civil. "I suppose some women need marriage. I, of course, could never abide it. Too stifling. A woman loses all her freedoms."

Caroline guessed from the way Constance was looking at her like she would be pleased to claw her eyes out, that this was not completely true, at least not where Magnus was concerned.

"And then," Constance continued, "the wives have to sit patiently at home when their men tire of them, pretending they are unaware of their husbands' indiscretions. Oh, I shudder to think of myself ending up in such circumstances."

Only months ago, Caroline might have been reduced to a stuttering mess by such haughtiness.

"Yes," Caroline sighed. "So many men must dominate in order to feel important. That is why I am so relieved my Magnus has no such tendencies. He indulges me constantly and showers me with presents all the time." *That* had gotten her. Constance Whittingdon's complexion deepened three shades. Greed was something this woman could understand.

They both almost came up out of their chairs as a new voice cut in. "Of course I do, Cara *mia*. I live for you."

Caroline lost all her courage as her husband sauntered into the room, his last words echoing their double meaning. His smile was tight. His eyes were cold.

Unfortunately, it was painfully obvious he had not been home since last evening, since his black trousers and tail coat were rumpled and his cravat was askew. A dark blur of whiskers bristled on his face and his hair was more tousled than usual.

Constance was the first to speak. "Magnus, darling, I was just getting to know your charming wife."

"Isn't she adorable?"

Caroline had not realized she was holding her breath until now. She let it out, but it didn't ease her tension.

Magnus came to her side. He smelled of whiskey. To Constance, he said, "You've chosen a bad time to call. I am afraid my old cronies held me hostage last night, not allowing me to return to my bride, miscreants that they are." Turning to Caroline, he said, "I stripped them of their savings, darling, as just reward for such cruelty."

There was a hard knot in Caroline's throat that kept her from responding. Not too long ago, he would have spoken such a sentiment without the mockery.

Apparently, his subtlety was lost on Constance, for she gathered up her reticule and announced she must take her leave. On account of such bad timing, she said, but Caroline rather thought she looked like she might retch.

After they had seen her to her carriage, Caroline grabbed Magnus' sleeve and yanked hard.

"What the devil did you think you were doing last night?"

"Are we going to go through this again? I had no idea your brain suffered from such frequent lapses, Cara. *I* thought I was at White's, visiting with old friends—"

"Oh, shut up, would you!"

He stopped and gawked at her, stunned. She took a deep breath and said, "Did it ever occur to you that I might be worried? What if you had taken ill? How would I have known? Or what if you could not get to someone who could help you—what would happen to you?"

"Oh, please stop," he snapped, recovered from his shock. "You are making me want to weep. What a cad I was not to think of your concern."

She glared at him. "You are such a bounder."

"Yes," he purred, triumphant, "I am."

She shook her head and sighed in disgust. "I am wasting my time with you. I am going upstairs."

She was almost to the door when he said in a voice so chilling it made her blood turn cold to hear it, "Yes, do. I've left you a present on your pillow."

Chapter Twenty

She could feel him watching as she fled up the stairs. She wanted to stay and scream at him, but she was afraid she would cry. Her eyes stung and her throat felt strained, stuck, as if stifled sobs were caught painfully inside.

She forgot about his reference to having left her a present by the time she reached their room. Slamming the door behind her, she flopped onto the cushioned stool in front of the dressing table.

Her reflection stared back at her. She looked pale. Her eyes were dark and round, making her appear waiflike.

Lord, she was lost. What was happening?

Her reflection had no answer for her silent appeal. Restless, she moved to the window. As she passed her desk, she noticed a letter had been placed on the salver. A quick check at the address brought a feeling of comfort. It was from Switzerland.

Tearing it open, she read the words written in her mother's hand:

Dearest Caroline,
Thank you for your last letter. You cannot know the joy it is to me to know you are so happy with the

earl. He sounds like a fine man and is treating you well. Rest and eat and take care not to overexert yourself.

Caroline's heart constricted. She had written glowingly of Magnus when they had been happy together. So long ago, it seemed.

This shall be short, for I shall tell you all our news when I see you in person. James is doing so well, his doctors have given me permission to take him on a brief holiday. Of course, London was not to their liking, but it will be a short visit. Do not worry about money, we have plenty of funds for our trip, thanks to you. I cannot wait to see you again, my darling, and hope this letter finds you well and happy. I am always
Your Loving Mother

She closed her eyes and thought how wonderful it would be to have her mother's sage advice and loving nurturance. Now that Magnus was so much worse, she would have someone on her side, someone to help her think of what to do.

She folded the letter and placed it on the salver.

It was then she remembered Magnus' having said he left her a gift on her pillow.

He had said it with such savage triumph.

Dread infused her body. She turned to the bed, her steps slow, deliberate, almost reluctant. Nothing could have prepared her for what she saw spread out over the embroidered linen.

The diamond necklace. The lovely choker flashed fire, caught in a slant of sunshine coming through the window.

Caroline cried out, falling to her knees at the side of the bed and taking the necklace in her hand. Turning it over and over, she saw it was exactly the same. There could be no twin of this piece.

A sound alerted her to his presence. She whipped her head around, still kneeling, still holding the damning choker in her hands.

''Aren't you going to thank me for returning it to you?''

Caroline's voice came as only a whisper. ''Magnus, I...''

''What?'' He stood with his arms clasped across his massive chest, disheveled, wickedly handsome. His eyes were a dark, dark green.

''I'm sorry.''

''Most thieves are. When they're caught.''

She bowed her head, knowing she deserved everything he would say. At least she had her answers. The mystery of his mood the last few days was solved. Yet, the knowledge gave her no comfort.

''Aren't you going to offer me an explanation? I admit, I have been looking forward to it. My mind is positively confounded with the possibilities.'' He moved to the bed. Caroline watched every move, noting the cruel twist of his mouth. He was pretending to be civilized, but the undercurrents of danger were there.

He was aching. Instinctively she knew that, and while it should have broken her heart, it didn't. For some insane reason she couldn't fathom, it made her heart leap. Because it meant he wasn't indifferent. He *cared*. Sitting on the bed, trying for all the world to appear severe, the pain in his eyes was as clear to her as anything had ever been in her life. He had pulled away from her, ignored and insulted her not because of his own perfidy, or because he was tiring of her, but because he was tormented by what he had discovered.

The hope of this first discovery was quickly dashed by a second. Whether he had truly cared for her, whether his changed attitude was out of wounded pride and not disinterest, she *had* deceived him. She had stolen and lied to him, and a man like Magnus would never forgive.

"I am going to explain to you," she began. "And I will start at the beginning. The facts are easy enough for you to check, so you will know I am telling you the truth."

"Nevertheless, you will pardon me if I do not take your word for it."

"Of course," she muttered, stung. She took in a long breath. "I came to you because I needed money. That you know. When my friend told me about you and your offer, I couldn't believe such an excellent opportunity. I told you about being poor. To you that is just a word, Magnus. It denotes something unpleasant, but it is not real. Poor, when you live it, is pure terror. Terror because you might not have enough to eat, terror because you have to live in a part of the city that is full of crime, and most of all, terror that your young brother will die."

He had been giving her that look, the keen, intense one that never failed to turn her insides to quivering mush, but the last part of her statement penetrated his cold veneer. His head moved slightly to one side and his eyes narrowed.

She went on, "You never met James because James is very ill. He has consumption. When we lived in London, he rarely had enough energy to climb out of bed. At the Barrister's Ordinary, he began to do better, and the doctor said it was because of the country air and the medicine he received. That was where my money went, Magnus. To James' doctors. It was suggested, seeing how well James was responding, that he might experience a full recovery at a sanatorium. The fees were prohibitive. I needed money for the sanatorium. So I sold the necklace. Once he was there, the expenses kept mounting. I stole the other things to augment my allowance, to try to afford the treatments as long as possible.''

He had not moved an inch. She felt like she was cowering before him, hunkered down on her knees as she was, so she stood and smoothed her skirts. That small action made her feel better. Or perhaps it was the cleansing of her secrets.

''Let us not dispute your story,'' he said after a while. ''For now. Pray explain to me why you simply didn't inform me of your brother's condition and ask me to pay the fees.''

''I kept James a secret because I feared you would not want a wife burdened with another who was ill. I was afraid you would think it would detract from my commitment to you and that you wouldn't choose me.''

He looked thunderous for a moment, as if he had just been gravely insulted. His lips pressed together in a hard white line. ''Is that what you think of me?''

''At first, Magnus, I didn't even know you, except by reputation, which was hardly complimentary to your character. And…'' She paused a moment before deciding she must tell him all of it. ''You investigated my family, you know the stories about my father. Except there are stories you don't know. No one does but me. My father taught me well about the nature of men. And you, by reputation, certainly seemed no different. You were a reprobate, without apology. Would you have me pin my brother's life on such a man's goodwill?''

''But after. After everything else. You still felt you could not come to me.''

Damn! Damn! She hated herself for crying. The heat of

her tears left tracks of stinging flesh on her cheeks. "Oh, God, Magnus, I thought of it a thousand times. I wanted to. But I was afraid. I told myself you would never miss those things, that you were so wealthy it hardly mattered, and I tried to forget what I had done. If I had told you, then you would have hated me no less than you do now."

He shook his head. "No, you're wrong. I respect honesty."

She blanched, knowing he was right. "I didn't tell you because I was a coward. And because I didn't want to upset you, perhaps bring on an attack." She paused, fighting with her conscience. "But the main reason I didn't ever tell you was that I didn't want to give you any reason to put me aside. Before the child, I thought you might just be disgusted enough with me to do it."

"I might just have at that. I am fairly disgusted with you right now. But, you planned well. There is the child." He rose off the bed. "I shall have my things removed to another room."

The flare of pain made her gasp. "I don't want that."

"Why should you mind? Our bargain was struck, and we have both kept up our ends. You're swelling before my eyes and I have given you the means to save your little brother. Therefore, there is nothing to do but wait for me to expire."

"Listen to me," she began, her anger and fear of losing him making her bold. "That's not what I want. I don't just care about your money. I don't care if I ever see a penny of it. Oh, I wish you weren't dying. I wish James hadn't been ill. I wish you could know how I feel about you. Just you, apart from everything else."

He threw his head back. "Are you now going to tell me that you want *me?* Will you again protest to me about how much you *care?* You don't have to, you know. I'm not going to put you aside. Despite your light-fingered ways, you've met your duty by me. I admit we got carried away, but I suppose we can rectify that and return to the way it should have been all along. A business arrangement. That is all.''

''That's impossible, Magnus,'' she said. She had no idea where the courage was coming from for what she was about to say, but she didn't question it. ''I've fallen in love with you. Truly. And I have nothing to gain by saying so, if it were false. If I only cared about money, I would be glad to get off so easy and be content to have it be as you say. But I shall not be content, Magnus. I love you. And I am going to have to lose you soon enough.'' She was sobbing now. ''Please don't do this.''

Magnus stared at her for a long time. He had never looked so hard, so unreachable. He said nothing, didn't even move a single muscle, until at last he simply turned on his heel and walked out of the room.

Cold and hot, nausea, gripping pain all combined, brought Caroline once again to her knees. She hugged herself, weeping and rocking.

The most terrible part of it was she had no regrets. James was alive, not just alive but thriving. And it was her doing. She could have trusted Magnus, she knew that now, but there was no way to have known then. She had taken a chance, for James' sake, and she had lost.

She had lost it all.

''Magnus, why the devil didn't you tell me you were here? I have been waiting for you to let me know when you came to London, and I have to hear it from Clarely, of all people.'' David was too far gone in his own pique to notice his brother's dour look as he stormed into the library. He made no mention of the missing chair or the scar on the wall where an old portrait had hung. "I heard you cleaned their clocks at White's last night. Devil take you, you should have let me know. I would have enjoyed seeing that."

He threw himself down on a sofa. "I heard that Cannon fellow was skulking about, glowering and making threats. Doesn't he realize he only makes a further fool of himself the more he—"

"Caroline has been stealing from me."

David paled. "What the bloody hell did you say?"

"She stole some of Mother's treasures and sold them. I gave her Mother's diamond choker. The one she wore in her portrait. She sold that, too."

"Jesus!" David blew out a long, slow breath. "You caught her at it or did she confess?"

"Both. I confronted her, then she confessed."

"Damn. I thought... Well, I thought she was good for you. I had almost forgotten why she got into this in the first place. She was so concerned, genuinely so it seemed." He seemed acutely distressed. "It would have made this whole rushed marriage thing seem much more beneficial if she hadn't turned out to be an opportunist. Too bad."

"She says she did it for her brother. Says he's dying. He needed money for treatment."

"Bloody Christ." David was sweating. "What did you say?"

Magnus moved to the window, clasping his arms over his chest. "Nothing."

"Do you believe her? I mean, that's not so bad a reason to steal. Damned tragic, after all. She should have told you sooner, of course, but after all, it wasn't like she had some lover on the side she was funneling it to."

Magnus blanched, betraying the fact that that very

thought had occurred to him as well. "I'm having Green investigate it."

"Let me handle this. After all, it cannot be easy for you. And Green is a disagreeable fellow, as I have often said."

"I'll take care of it."

David appeared uncertain. Magnus wondered why he was so upset. Did his happiness matter so much to his brother as that? He hesitated, then said, "She... She tried to appeal to me, tried to make it right."

David was suspicious. "What did she say?"

Magnus paused. "She said she was in love with me."

His brother's next words nearly knocked Magnus off his feet. "Of course she is, any idiot could see that. Are you telling me you didn't know?"

"I guess this idiot didn't see it."

"Magnus, I would have thought you would have realized it most of all. She is devoted to you."

"I can hardly believe it is sincere. Do you expect me to trust her after she has lied and cheated me?"

"Well, you said she had a reason. And your reputation certainly wouldn't have encouraged her to come to you with her troubles."

Magnus grunted. "That's what she said."

"Do you love her?"

Magnus glared, staring hard so that David would regret his impertinent question and not press for an answer. He should have known better. David said, "Well, do you?"

"I am not the type of man who falls in love."

It was not an answer. They both knew it.

"So, what are you going to do now?" David asked.

The silence stretched long. The sound of the grandfather clock became a deafening rhythm. Finally, Magnus answered. "Damned if I know."

Chapter Twenty-One

Magnus had elected to meet Caractacus Green in his offices on Burton Street. A not so elegant part of town, but not shabby either.

The damn fool had tried to keep him waiting, a mistake Magnus had quickly rectified by storming into the man's office and telling his other client to get the hell out.

Green was outraged. "I don't get paid enough for this kind of harassment, even from an earl."

"You get paid plenty, more than my own solicitor. Now, where the hell is that report?"

Mr. Green grumbled as he sorted through stacks of papers. "I couldn't find anything. I did, however, manage to get the names of all of the men who proposed marriage to her during her two seasons. By the way, there was never the slightest hint of scandal during that time. All of the men involved were gentlemen of quality. No evidence can be found that they are involved in any way with the countess, even as far back as last year. You'll see—"

"Yes, it is all here," Magnus said, frowning as he flipped through the carefully scripted pages. "What about that one fellow I told you about?"

"William Linny? Perfectly respectable. Fifth son to a

duke, poor as a church mouse until he turned an old mill his father bought him into a decent moneymaker. Does well enough.''

"Tell me about the brother."

"James Wembly, yes. Seven years old. Been sick since he was a small child."

"Why is it this fact was not picked up in your initial report?"

Mr. Green gave as good as he got, staring at the irate earl without flinching. "They kept the boy away from people. As they did not socialize with their neighbors, not many knew. When I got hint of it, it was hard to track down. His doctor wouldn't talk to me, but I got a few gossipy neighbors to tell me about the Wemblys. Seems they weren't well liked in their neighborhood. People got the idea the Wemblys thought themselves too good for the east end.''

"East end! My God, man, that is where they lived?"

Mr. Green wrinkled his fastidious nose. "You should see it. My runner tells me it was positive squalor. Every cent went to the boy's medicine, you see. When they were in Cambridgeshire, there were folks at the Barrister's Ordinary that saw him, and report a boy in significantly better health than what was said about him in London. Now, he and his mother are at a sanatorium in Switzerland, but they are planning a visit to London.''

"Yes, my wife has mentioned they are coming." Actually, it was one of the few things Caroline had said to him in the last two weeks. Since he had challenged her, she had kept mostly to her room. He had moved to another bedroom. They avoided one another.

That wasn't completely true, he amended. She had made attempts to speak to him. And he had been unforgivably rude.

His fist crumpled the pile of papers Green had given him. "This tells me nothing I did not know already. I paid you handsomely, Green. I want information."

"I cannot help it if the information you already have is accurate. These are the facts." Mr. Green sniffed. "And you are not paying me all that handsomely."

This was the second time the man had said this. Was he mad? Magnus was distracted by Green's next words. "Did your wife tell you about her father?"

"I know he was a bounder."

"More than that, the man was of horrendous moral character. He had a sick child at home, and he spent all his money on women and drink. He left them destitute, which is how they ended up in the east end. Mrs. Wembly took in laundry while Caroline Wembly accepted a position as clerk at a bookstore. That was a rather well-kept secret, the laundry. But not much escapes notice when families live, literally, on top of one another. The bookseller's shop was respectable, though. It was from one of the countess' fellow workers I gleaned an interesting piece of information."

What he was hearing made Magnus cringe. He didn't like the way it made the coldness inside him ache.

Green leaned forward. "Lucy is a friend of one of my young apprentices. She told him that the countess hated her father so vehemently, she could barely stand to hear him even referred to."

"As well I can imagine," Magnus said.

"Yes, well, there was a particular comment Lucy remembers the countess saying, one which she could not recall in its entirety. However, she clearly remembers the countess making reference to her father keeping his hands to himself. Lucy was left with the distinct impression the countess,'' Green paused, a delicate womanly blush tinge-ing his neck, ''was referring to herself.''

''You mean her father—'' Magnus broke off the thought, not able to utter it aloud. His mind reeled. He knew that such things were, tragically, not unheard of. Not that he had ever thought much about it before. But now, the thought of Caroline in the hands of an incestuous father made him want to roar in outrage.

He stood. ''I've heard enough. We need to settle your fee now, for I won't be needing your services any longer.''

Magnus' brain was too befuddled to register the fact that Mr. Green's fee was, indeed, much lower than Magnus would have thought based on past transactions. After he paid him, he grabbed the report and stalked out of the office.

On the way home, Magnus read the entire report in the back of the carriage, glad he had arranged for a driver today. His stomach clenched as he read the part about Louis Wembly. He read it through again, very carefully.

On impulse, he directed his driver to go to the east end of London. The man gave him a dubious look, but Magnus did not have to repeat himself. They rode down squalid streets amid a stench so choking he could barely breathe.

''Find this address,'' he instructed the driver. Within minutes, they pulled up in front of a row of houses built in the Elizabethan style of each story overhanging the other so that hardly any sunlight reached the refuse-strewn street.

''Here, your lordship,'' the driver said.

Magnus stared, caught in the grip of incredulity and disgust.

He sat back, turning away from the window. ''Home.''

Louis Wembly had reduced his family to this. He had done worse than that. It was a good thing the wretched man was dead, because Magnus had no doubt he would dispatch him to the bowels of hell himself if the lecher had still been alive.

As sick as he felt on Caroline's behalf, Magnus was even more put out with himself. She had tried to tell him how her father had clouded her judgment when it came to trusting. Magnus had taken it personally, too wounded by her betrayal to see it. Yet, who could imagine such a horrible thing?

When he arrived home, he was actually reluctant to go inside. He felt as if he needed more time to digest the shattering discoveries of the last hour. As luck would have it, Caroline was in the yellow parlor when he entered.

"Early for tea," he said, hovering in the doorway.

"I get hungry more often," she said. He still could detect no change in her figure, other than a more pronounced fullness to her breasts. Her waist was still slim. It seemed like ages since he had seen her undressed. "Would you like to join me? I have your favorite Danish."

That bit of thoughtfulness made him smile. Against the proddings of that primitive isolate in the back of his brain, he stepped into the room and sat down.

"What's that?" Caroline asked as she poured him a cup of Indian tea. She motioned to Green's report. He had forgotten he still had it in his hand.

"Business papers," he said, tucking them under his seat. When Caroline passed him the tray of sweets, he noticed her hand was shaking. So she was nervous. Blast, so was he. It had been a long time since they were easy in each other's company.

"When are your mother and brother due to arrive?"

"In a week's time."

"I shall be able to meet James."

"Yes, he is an enchanting boy. I hope you will like him."

"I'm sure I shall."

Inane! He wanted to shout—*Caroline, tell me about what your father did to you. Is that why you couldn't believe in me?*

Or was it my own fault?

That was really the crux of it. He had railed against her not being willing to trust him. The true issue was—was he worthy of that trust? Would he have turned away a woman because of an ill brother?

He didn't know. The man he was recoiled in horror at such a thought. But the man he had been might just have been that selfish.

Caroline was watching him. "Magnus?"

He knew she was worried about his health. She always got anxious whenever he got pensive. It must resemble the early stages of an attack.

"I am fine. Just not hungry." He was surprised when she put the last morsel of one of the large, doughy pastries that were made up just for him into her mouth.

Noticing his look, she smiled sheepishly. "I'm developing a sweet tooth, I suspect."

"My son is the one with the sweet tooth, and he is making his mama give him what he wants."

She looked startled. It had been a long time since he had said something light and teasing. Her lashes lowered quickly, but not before he saw the sparkle of moisture in them.

Feeling awkward, he stood and retrieved the document he had stored under his chair. "I'm really not hungry after all. I have some work in the library I had better see to."

"Very well." She appeared stricken. He walked out,

fearful an emotional scene was about to erupt. He was not ready yet for that.

He had only closed his door for a few minutes when an earsplitting scream rent the air. Racing out to the hallway, he almost collided with Dorothy, a servant, who was standing in the doorway of the yellow parlor. He caught her up against him to avoid knocking her down.

"The mistress!" she cried, grabbing two handfuls of his coat. "In there. On the floor."

Simultaneously, Magnus' heart dropped to the pit of his stomach and his feet moved, racing past the terrified maid and into the parlor.

Caroline was lying on the carpet, curled up in a tight ball. She didn't move when he shouted her name. He dropped down beside her, frantically feeling for her heartbeat. His relief was tremendous when he felt the steady flutter at her throat.

"Send a footman to fetch a doctor. And none of the nincompoops who attended me. Find someone new. Now, woman!"

Dorothy was off in a flash, and Magnus scooped his wife up in his arms and hurried her to her bedroom, taking the steps two at a time.

He quickly loosened her clothing, not knowing at all if it would help. She was sweating and thrashing. She was hot to touch.

When she opened her eyes, Magnus said, "Cara, darling, it's me. It's Magnus. Can you hear me?"

He recognized the green color that had oozed into her face as a precursor of stomach ailment and managed to get a clean chamber pot to her before she succumbed. He held her head, murmuring soft words, telling her it was all right, that he was here and he wouldn't allow anything to happen to her.

When she was quiet, he stripped off her clothing and tucked her into bed. He had laudanum in his room, but hesitated to give her any. She seemed to be sleeping well without it. The sudden thought that perhaps she had slipped into unconsciousness made him shake her awake.

"What? Who…?" Her head lolled, her words were slurred.

"Cara, my love, it's Magnus. You are safe. Sleep now, I'm sorry I disturbed you."

"Magnus?"

"Yes, darling. I'm here."

"You don't hate me?"

His heart flipped in his chest. "No, Cara *mia,* I don't hate you. I never hated you, darling. I just didn't understand, that's all."

"I'm so sorry."

"Shhh, rest now, sweetheart. Rest."

She relaxed, soothed by his endearments and the softness of his voice.

She retched three more times within the next hour. By then Magnus had realized that Caroline's symptoms were precisely his own.

Mad, insane thoughts flooded his brain. He had never thought to ask if his ailment could be contagious. But that was absurd, heart ailments were not transmittable things.

Yet how could it be she was experiencing the identical illness? Then he remembered something, something that knocked the wind out of him and left him gasping for air.

Lord, it was so obvious, so utterly and completely plain to see, and he was experiencing the strangest inability to comprehend it.

Wait. Wait. He cautioned himself to push the implications aside. When the doctor arrived, he would ask him.

For now, Caroline was gravely ill, and he could barely think straight with his near panic over her and the child.

The doctor was not long in coming. A Josiah Hebbs. He seemed a competent fellow, and Magnus was immediately heartened at the short man's quiet self-assurance and concerned manner.

Magnus refused to heed the physician's gentle requests for privacy while he examined the countess. Not that Magnus openly rebelled. He simply ignored him until Hebbs went ahead and pulled down the coverlet. He listened to her heart, then examined her body for any marks. "How long has she been running a fever?" he asked.

"I don't know. I only just came home. Less than an hour ago. Maybe longer, I don't remember. We had tea. She looked all right then."

"Did she make any complaints?"

"Only of being hungry."

The physician nodded slowly. "It seems she may have eaten something that disagreed with her."

Magnus' insides twisted. His breath shortened as his blood pumped furiously in his veins.

The doctor continued, "Perhaps some spoiled meat, or a bad piece of fish."

"She was eating pastry."

"Pastry? If it had cream in it, it could have been spoiled. Hmm." Hebbs' voice trailed off as he shook his head. "Not the right symptoms, though. Similar, but not…"

"Mr. Hebbs." Magnus motioned him to the corner of the room, lest Caroline awaken and overhear. "My wife's symptoms are remarkably like my own when I am in the grip of one of my attacks. If indeed she ate something to make her ill, could it be," he paused, a plethora of hope balanced on the next word, "poison?"

The physician frowned. "Poison?" He looked over his

shoulder at his sleeping patient, walked slowly back to her side. He lifted her eyelids and listened to her heart again. When he lifted his head from her chest, Magnus could see a disturbed expression on the older man's face.

He came away. "It *could* be digitalis."

"Is it dangerous for her? For the baby?" Magnus felt as though he was holding onto sanity with a thread. *Please, dear God, you have been surprisingly generous with me so far. Just this one last thing.*

"It shouldn't be. Digitalis can be fatal, but she would be showing worse symptoms by now if it were a seriously large dose. She is sleeping peacefully, and her heartbeat is strong. As for the babe, it is too soon to tell. There is nothing to be done but wait and see if she begins to miscarry."

Magnus bowed his head, breathing hard against the terrible weight pressing down upon his chest.

"I'll look in on her first thing in the morning," Hebbs said, putting his instruments back in his black bag.

"I need to speak with you," Magnus said. The doctor looked at him as if he had been expecting as much. Hebbs had probably heard of his case from his colleagues. Magnus could see understanding in his eyes. Hebbs shook his head. "Not here, and I doubt you wish to leave her."

"No." Magnus glanced over at Caroline. She hadn't moved. "Tomorrow, then."

"Yes, my lord." He left, closing the door behind him with a soft click of the latch.

Chapter Twenty-Two

Caroline awoke confused and disoriented. When she saw Magnus sitting by her bed, she asked, "What happened?"

Magnus had spent his night pondering that very question. Sometime after midnight, he had forbidden his mind to dwell on it anymore. After all, he could not be certain his suspicions were founded. He wouldn't know anything until he talked to Hebbs.

"You were taken ill yesterday. The doctor says you ate something that didn't agree with you." Which was not a lie.

She lifted a hand to her head. "Headache?" he asked.

"A touch." She then took notice of her state of nakedness. Her eyes widened, and she blushed.

"I undressed you. The doctor examined you for bites or rashes that might have indicated why you were ill. He found nothing."

"Oh," she said, drawing up the coverlet to just under her chin. It amused him, this modesty she was displaying all of a sudden. Not only had he viewed every inch of her body, he knew it by heart. A joking comment was on the tip of his tongue, but he swallowed it just in time. He had almost forgotten the state of affairs between them.

That amazed him somewhat. The Earl of Rutherford never forgot a grudge.

"Are you feeling hungry?" She nodded. He rose and yanked on the bellpull.

"Did you stay here all night?" she asked. Her voice was timid. She didn't know quite how to take him.

"Yes," he answered without turning around. Dash it all, he wanted to fling himself at the side of her bed and bury his face in her breast and tell her how terrified he had been. How he couldn't bear to lose her.

But things had changed drastically between them from when he could have indulged such an impulse. Or at least, he thought they had. Caroline Wembly Eddington had married him for money, with that he had to become reconciled. Moreover, the pain of her betrayal was already starting to fade. Yet, a new kink had developed. He hadn't been just any wealthy man. He had been a dying wealthy man.

What would happen now if she found out he was not— as he suspected—dying after all?

"The doctor said he would come back this morning. He should be here soon."

"Thank you. Could you leave me, please? I need some privacy."

"Certainly."

There they were, like two polite strangers once again. Before Magnus reached the door, her voice stopped him. "Thank you, Magnus. For taking such good care of me."

He paused for a heartbeat. "You're welcome, Caroline. Now make yourself ready for the doctor. I'll send Lillian in."

Magnus went to his room for a quick sponge bath and a shave. Gregory came in to tell him the doctor was here and had already gone in to see the countess. Dressing quickly, Magnus was stationed outside Caroline's door when Hebbs emerged.

"Well? Is she recovered?"

Hebbs smiled. "She looks bright as a new penny, my lord."

"And the baby? Any signs of…"

"Nothing so far. She's a sturdy girl. She'll do all right." The physician cocked his head at Magnus. "You, my lord, have kept me awake all night. Shall we go have that talk?"

Magnus brooked no disrespect from anyone, but he didn't mind at all the way Hebbs spoke to him. He realized just now that the doctor reminded him of his father a bit.

Once they were seated in the library and Mr. Hebbs had declined tea or coffee, Magnus said, "So, tell me, sir. Is it possible I could be being poisoned?"

"Not just possible, my lord. It is, in fact, probable. The symptoms are exactly the same and quite consistent with the effects of digitalis."

"Then I am not dying." What an inane thing to say. The doctor had just said as much, and yet Magnus needed to hear the words uttered out loud.

"I would, of course, wish to examine you, but it's quite possible—indeed probable from what I can remember hearing about your case from my colleagues—that you are not dying."

A detached part of himself observed how odd it was that he felt nothing. One would think he would be over-joyed, leaping about and whooping with delight. He was *not dying*, dash it all!

And yet, strangely enough, he found it took a bit of getting used to.

He looked up at Hebbs. "Why didn't the other doctors suspect poisoning? Why were they so quick to diagnose me with a heart ailment?"

"Do not think too badly of them, your lordship. Poisoning is very hard to detect. Only the improbable coincidence of your wife contracting the exact same symptoms alerted us to the possibility. Had I been your physician, I would have made the same prognosis as the others. There is your family history, you see, and there is no denying that weakness of the heart function does run in families. A poisoning of digitalis would not have been a feasible consideration, not with so blatant an explanation available. However, even if one does consider the possibility of a toxic substance, the question would be why? If you are in danger from someone, why would they poison you intermittently? Why did they simply not administer a fatal dose? See? It would make no sense, so even without the familial indications, it would be an unlikely hypothesis by any doctor."

"I still don't understand."

The doctor sat up, elbows on his knees. "What you don't understand, my lord, is why. That I cannot help you with. Nor am I able to enlighten you as to the other, perhaps more pressing, question of who. Do you have any suspicions?"

"Not yet," Magnus lied.

"This is a matter for the authorities."

Magnus shot him a dark look. "I don't want to involve anyone else, at least not until I decide what to do."

"But, my lord, you are in danger," Hebbs protested.

"No," Magnus rubbed his hands over his lips. "If someone wanted me dead, I would be. Someone wanted me ill, that is all."

Dr. Hebbs gave Magnus a long look. "Then you do know who it is."

There was no point in denying it, yet Magnus could go no further. So, he simply ignored the question.

Hebbs stood, bending to retrieve his bag. "You are a peer of the realm and a brash man, and I shall not be able to dissuade you from whatever foolhardy notion you have in your head. So, I will take my leave. No, don't disturb yourself. I shall see myself out." He paused on his way to the door. "My lord, please do not make me come back here for any other reason but to deliver your child."

Magnus grinned. "I'll see to it."

"Good. In that case, I'll return in, oh, six months or so."

In the wake of his exit, Magnus stood. Simply stood, not moving a muscle, not blinking or swallowing or daring to breathe too deep. He had never felt more alone in his life.

His life. His life was no longer over.

And then it happened. Slowly, at first, a slow trickle of belief seeping in around the edges. Then the walls started to crumble. Those carefully constructed barriers he had erected to stave off pain and wanting and fear came crashing down as the trickle turned into a steady stream and finally a gushing flood.

He sank to his knees and buried his face in his hands. In the silence of his heart, he gave thanks to the Lord who had not abandoned him, though he had abandoned himself so very long ago. He felt like Lazarus. He felt blessed. And he felt wretched because he knew he didn't deserve it.

Once he had said to Cara that it was only in dying that he had learned how to live.

Taking a cleansing breath, he rose to his feet and looked about him. This room still bore the scars of his decimating rage only a few weeks before. The night when he had given himself over to his most base self.

Could he ever fight his way back?

He had his life again. He was not going to waste it on bitterness as he had done before. Living, truly living, took courage. He suddenly realized that despite all his bluster and bravado, he didn't know if he had enough courage to live as he had planned to die.

He would just have to find out, he decided. He was terrified Caroline would not want a living husband. She had wed him only for the imminent promise of wealthy widowhood. Yet, she had said she loved him. Had she merely pitied a dying man? Or did she truly want him?

That he wanted her was never in question. He had not liked it, he had tried to deny it, he had railed and fought against it, but it would not go away.

He closed his eyes. And for the first time since hearing the wonderful revelation, he smiled.

The week passed as Caroline gained her strength. Magnus seemed to be very busy, coming and going all day long, sometimes whisking a stranger into his library and locking her out. She was wildly curious as to what he was about. Fear dogged her, for something was afoot and she could not imagine that whatever it was boded well for her.

The only bright spot was her anticipation of her mother's visit. She was absolutely frantic to see James. She had missed him terribly and was anxious to see how he had progressed. Not being able to be with him, to see him getting well, had been terrible, but before, when things had been good between them, she had had Magnus. Now, without her beloved husband, she needed her family more than ever.

As the day of their arrival neared, she could barely withstand the anticipation. It affected her appetite, a heretofore unseen phenomenon since the start of her pregnancy. Her lack of interest in food did not escape Magnus' notice.

They were seated in the dining room, a pretty room done in yellows and blues. It was cheerful and much less daunting than either of the ones at Hawking Park. Caroline was sitting rigidly in her chair, simply staring at the sliced capon on her plate.

Magnus said, "Are you feeling ill?"

The sound of his voice startled her. She looked up to meet his emerald gaze. Her heart gave a single, sharp beat of regret. She missed him. She missed their easy companionship, their fun, their passion. This was only the second meal they had shared in over a week. And he hadn't touched her in almost a month.

"My mother is coming today. Sometime this afternoon." She was reluctant to bring up the subject of her family, cringing lest the mention of them remind him of how she had deceived and cheated him on James' behalf.

He seemed undisturbed by her reference. "That should be an enjoyable event. You look positively morose sitting there."

"I'm just anxious, that's all." She tried a bite, finding no fault with the food yet her throat closed and she put down her fork. She sighed. "I suppose I am being silly. It's just that I've missed them both."

Magnus nodded as if he understood. "I assume your concern for your brother is making you nervous. Has he been faring well?"

The question so stunned her, she took a full minute to respond. "Yes," she stammered, "from my mother's reports, he seems to be."

"How long has he been ill?" His tone was so unaffected, without any inflection of resentment, she could scarce believe it.

"He's been ill since he was three."

"They say that the consumption often improves in favorable climes.'' He looked down at his plate and began to eat again, dismissing their strange conversation.

Still dazed, Caroline sat and stared at her husband. He was no longer attending to her, absorbed in his own thoughts, thus giving her the opportunity to study him. His glossy curls gleamed in the sunlight streaming through the windows, casting off warm highlights. She wanted to feel the texture, the softness of it. Like a physical ache, the need to lay her hand against his smoothly shaven cheek made her fingers curl. A surge of longing brought a sting to her eyes, causing her avert her gaze before she fell to weeping right in front of him.

Gregory, the butler, came to the door.

''Madam, Mrs. Wembly is here to see you,'' he said.

Caroline stood so quickly, her chair toppled over behind her. Catching Magnus' eye, she detected a half-smothered grin. He nodded, as if to say, ''Go on.''

Gregory had put Audrae in the yellow parlor. Caroline ran into the room and straight into her mother's arms.

''Goodness,'' Audrae gasped, laughing and sniffing at the same time. ''Look at you. All dressed up and looking every inch the countess.'' She held Caroline at arm's length, her eyes sparkling as she drank in the sight of her beloved daughter. ''I've never seen you look more lovely. Marriage must agree with you.''

Nearly choking on the words, Caroline agreed that it did. There would be time for confidences later. ''Mother, you look wonderful, too. I love that dress!''

Audrae smiled, giving a half turn to show off the violet and silver creation. ''Not one of Mrs. Dungeness's,'' she said. ''I had a Swiss seamstress make it up for me. I have a job now. I secured a position with the sanatorium, sort of a companion-nursemaid. I read to the older patients and see to their care a bit. It's actually enjoyable. Much better than being idle.''

"Come sit and tell me all about it. And James, you must tell me everything about him. Where is he now?''

Arranging her skirts on the settee, Audrae gave her daughter a circumspect look. "I left him back at the hotel.''

"Alone? And why are you staying at a hotel? It is terribly expensive, and you must stay with us. Magnus knows about James now.'' At her mother's widened eyes, Caroline held up a hand. "I'll tell you about it later. Right now, I want you to take me with you back to your rooms, and we will collect James and have him here.''

"Quite right,'' Magnus said, striding into the room. He came directly to Audrae and took her hand, bowing over it. Audrae inclined her head, making Caroline smile. Her mother had always, even in the worst of times, maintained her dignity. This surprising homage from the earl, she took in as her due.

"You look well, Mrs. Wembly,'' Magnus said. He was relaxed, at his most charming. Caroline looked for signs of his infamous temper, a temper she had tested all too often of late, but he was apparently not going to broach any unsavory topics, namely Caroline's thievery, with his mother-in-law.

"As do you, your lordship. Exceedingly well. Caroline's letters tell me your illness seems to have been giving you a reprieve.''

Caroline's breath caught in her throat. No one, not even she, had referred to his infirmity so casually. Magnus, however, only smiled. His dimple appeared, a sign of his genuine pleasure.

"Yes, indeed, madam. It seems to have done so.'' Giving another bow, he said, "I have work to attend to. I only came in to pay my respects. And Caroline is quite right. You must stay at Eddington House."

"I thank you for your invitation, your lordship. And I would think it would be more appropriate for you to call me Audrae."

"Agreed. And you must return the favor by referring to me by my Christian name."

Caroline watched her mother consider this honor for a moment before nodding. "Very well. In private only, of course."

"Of course. Good day. Audrae. Caroline."

He left them alone. Caroline felt her tension ease in his absence. "Now, I must know about James, Mother. Please, tell me everything."

Audrae's eyes shone. "Oh, Cara, he is doing splendidly. Just last week he ran. *Ran*. He was walking in a meadow near the main building, and some animal or other caught his eye and he just bolted after it, not thinking. I was with him, and I chased after him. Oh, my darling, I don't need to tell you how worried I was, but he was fine. A bit winded, but he didn't cough, not even once."

"But that's wonderful!" Caroline exclaimed. "I must see him. Oh, Mother, let's go now."

Audrae reached up to grab Caroline's hand, pulling her back down in her seat. "In a moment, darling. I have come alone because there is something I need to tell you."

Afraid of bad news, Caroline waited. "Don't give me that look," Audrae said. "It's nothing terrible. At least I hope it isn't."

"Is it James? Is there something you're not telling me?" Caroline rushed.

"No, no. Nothing about James. All the news on your dear brother is only good, Cara. I promise." She hesitated, looking down at her hands, then angling a look at her daughter. "This news is about me. Cara, I have brought someone with me to London. Someone I wish you to meet. His name is Roger Carrey. He is the son of one of the patients at the sanatorium. Cara, Roger is a wonderful man. I want you to like him."

Caroline stared, aghast. "Mother, are you trying to tell me you are in love with him?"

Audrae said carefully, "Cara, darling, he has asked me to marry him."

"Oh!" Caroline exclaimed, leaping to her feet and flinging her arms about her mother's shoulders.

"Then you are pleased?" Audrae said.

"Well, I have to meet him first," Caroline exclaimed, "but if he makes you happy, then yes, I am very happy indeed!"

They laughed. Caroline sank to her knees in front of her mother, her hands entwined with Audrae's.

"Cara, he is a wonderful man. Kind, and generous. James adores him."

"Oh, James adores everyone."

"But most especially Roger. I've told him everything about us, and he is quite sympathetic. He is as pleased as I am at James' miraculous recovery." She sobered, leveling her eyes at Caroline. "And just as worried about you."

"Me?" Caroline said feebly. "Nothing is the matter with me."

A shift upward of her eyebrows spoke of Audrae's disbelief. "Your letters became less and less contented. I thought it was just a mother's worry, but Roger agreed with me, that there was something there in the tone, something subtle."

Caroline rose and took her seat. She sighed. "I stole some items from Hawking Park and sold them to make up the difference in James' fees. I also sold an heirloom Magnus gave to me, a necklace of his mother's. I knew he cherished it, but what could I do? I sold them to a London broker, and Magnus has found out.

"I don't think he'll ever forgive me."

Audrae was silent for a long time. "You had no right to do what you did, Cara. It was wrong. You know that, and I can see how remorseful you are, so I shall not berate you." Rising, she paced to the window, and turned. "If I know you at all, I know you are doing a better job of admonishing yourself than I could ever do. Besides, I understand why you did it."

"Mother, it was for James," Caroline whispered. "I hate that I betrayed Magnus, but I had to."

"Could you not have told him?"

Caroline's shoulders sagged. "I thought I couldn't. I don't know, not anymore." She closed her eyes, barely able to speak. "He used to be wonderful. It became so lovely between us, Mother. We talked, and laughed. He was so different than he had appeared at first. When he was ill, I tended him. He didn't want me to, but then he allowed it. It brought us close together. He's been hurt before, and he still carries the scars on his heart, but I thought, at least for a while, he had become almost…happy again."

"So, you've fallen in love with him."

Neither the plainspoken fact nor her mother's perception surprised Caroline. She pressed her hands to her cheeks. "Yes, Mother, I have. I love him so desperately. And he despises me."

"But he seemed quite congenial just moments ago."

Caroline gave a groan. "That's just it, he's *congenial.* Oh, he was furious at first. Then he settled into this awful politeness. As if we were strangers."

"Have you tried to speak to him?"

"What can I say? He knows what I did. He knows why I did it."

Audrae gave her a long, considering look. "Could it be you're afraid to ask him to forgive you? I never knew you to be a coward, Cara."

She opened her mouth to protest, then stopped. Her mother was right. If she tried to explain, to appeal to him, she would know once and for all if there was a shred of hope. If she failed, it would be absolute. She hadn't realized how much she was holding out against the longing that if she would just ignore it, it might fade away. He might forgive her all on his own. Her treachery would evaporate, almost as if it never had been.

She was a coward, it was true enough. She simply couldn't face the thought of losing him.

"He'll never forgive me," she said flatly.

Audrae's face drew into stern lines. "He is entitled to be angry. And he is entitled to an apology."

"I've said I was sorry."

"More than that. A full explanation. Darling, you must tell him everything that is in your heart, you must tear open those secret places you've never allowed anyone to touch and you must show it to him. Appeal to him, beg him if you have to. It's a great risk, I know, for if he spurns you then, you will be truly devastated. But you must do it, Cara. You must *fight*."

"I don't know if I can."

Audrae sat back down, leaning back against the plush upholstery. "Did your father hurt you that badly that you cannot show your heart to the man you love?"

Caroline's head came up. Audrae said, "No, I don't know your secret. Only that you have one. I see the closed look that comes into your face each time we speak of him, and I know it goes beyond what he did to destroy our family. Whatever he did, Louis was a sick, depraved man. You mustn't let him pollute your life, Cara. We cannot help the things that happen to us, or where we come from, but we can make choices. To hide, or to face it and get it behind us. Once and for all.''

Recovering from the shock, Caroline offered, ''I did tell Magnus I loved him.''

''And what did he say?''

''He said nothing. He left.''

''Then you didn't tell him enough.''

''Mother, I think he's planning to divorce me. He's been having all these secret meetings. What if he's drawing up the papers?''

''Divorce you? Are you forgetting that you carry his child? And forgive my crudity, but what need does he have for such a distasteful process as that when he will be leaving you a widow before too long?''

She was right. Caroline's fears had taken hold of her, defying reason to taunt her with her worst imaginings. ''It's too confusing. I don't know what to make of it.''

''Then let's give it some time to settle in our brains, shall we? Come. We'll visit James and you can meet Roger. Your brother gave me strict orders not to tarry and to bring you posthaste after you had gotten the news about Roger.''

Caroline tried a smile. ''So he's turning into a little tyrant, is he?''

Audrae laughed. ''Yes. It's wonderful.''

Chapter Twenty-Three

On the way to the hotel, Caroline's mother settled back in the hired cabriolet and told her daughter about Roger.

He was forty-nine, only a year older than Audrae herself. He lived in Herefordshire, in a small but prosperous manor house which had been in his mother's family for generations. He was a third son, and the manor was his only inheritance. He worked at it diligently and had turned it into a profitable enterprise. Devoted to his mother, he had visited Switzerland where she had gone to recuperate from chronic lung ailment, and he and Audrae had met while she had tended the woman, who was, incidentally, quite pleased with the union.

"So, is he handsome?" Caroline teased.

"Caroline!" Audrae admonished, blushing. "Actually, yes, he is. Very."

"He had better be every bit as wonderful as you say," Caroline cautioned, "because I shall not approve of him if he is less than you deserve."

Roger did not disappoint her. He was a quiet man, achingly sincere, and, from all visible signs, absolutely devoted to Audrae. Caroline felt a lump in her throat as she watched them together, the brush of his hand against her mother's as he took her cloak, the looks they exchanged and the soft smiles they had for one another.

Yes, she remembered what it was like to have that.

Roger was indeed good-looking. Tall and rangy, he had a pleasant face and an unruly cap of straight sand-colored hair. It made him look boyish and bookish at the same time, but it was an attractive effect.

Caroline was exceedingly interested in him, but could not spare him much of her attention for only moments after their introduction, James came bounding out of a back room, yelling, "Cara! Cara! Cara!"

There he was, bright and exuberant like…like an ordinary seven-year-old. Her heart surged into her throat, lodging painfully as she swept him into her arms.

"James, you are extraordinary!" she cried, smiling while she fought back tears. A little boy would never understand weeping at a joyful time like this.

"I am, Cara. Wait until you see what I can do! I can run."

"Perhaps later," Audrae said gently. Caroline looked up to see her mother standing by Roger. His hand rested on her waist. Quite improper, yet it looked *right*.

"Not too much at once, remember?" Roger added.

"Oh, all right," James agreed. He seemed a bit deflated, but it lasted but a moment. Brightening, he said, "I know you are going to have a baby."

The breach of etiquette in front of Roger should have been awkward, but surprisingly it wasn't.

Caroline nodded. "I shall make you an uncle before long."

"Oh, I hope it's a boy. I shall teach him how to sail a toy boat and how to line up soldiers like the battle of Waterloo."

"Splendid. Skills any child needs to know. If she's a girl, what shall you do?"

His little face frowned as he thought on that one. "I suppose I could read to her. And tell her stories, but no scary ones."

"Agreed. It wouldn't do to give her nightmares. The same is true if it's a boy. Boys can have nightmares, too."

"But boys are brave," he informed her, boasting further, "*I'm* brave."

Caroline held his face in her hands. "Yes, you are the bravest boy that ever was."

They laughed and chatted until it was almost the dinner hour. Caroline had no idea whether Magnus planned to take his meal with her this evening, so she reluctantly announced she had to leave. Roger went to hire her a hansom.

"So," Audrae whispered as soon as he was out of the room, "what do you think?"

"I think he's grand, Mother. I can see he makes you very happy. James, too. He seems quite fond of him."

Audrae was obviously glad to get her daughter's approval. "We were thinking of getting married while we are in London. So you could attend."

It was very quick, Caroline thought, though she didn't say so. "That's kind of you to think of me. Of course I wish to be there."

"Roger is going to apply for the license, so we won't have to go through having the banns read."

Just how Magnus arranged our wedding.

"Wonderful, Mother. I am very happy for you. And James... It's a miracle, isn't it?"

"Yes, darling. It surely is."

Caroline remembered her talk with Mrs. Bronson about

miracles. She had never thought to get one. Now, she needed two.

As if knowing where her thoughts had turned, her mother said, "Remember what we talked about. Think on it, Cara. You must do something. You owe it to the earl."

Caroline grinned, despite herself. "Magnus."

Her mother grimaced. "Oh, yes, I did forget. And tell him that I thank him for his generous offer to stay at Eddington House, but we are quite comfortable here and Roger has a suite on another floor, so he is close by. With things being what they are, I think you two should have your privacy."

"Won't you reconsider, Mother? I've missed you. I'd love to have you at the house."

Audrae gave her one of her no-nonsense looks. "You will see plenty of us. But you have something to do which requires your immediate attention. I suggest you get to it."

It was amazing how her mother could make Caroline feel like a child of approximately eleven years of age, even though she was twenty-two, married and about to have a child of her own. "Yes, Mother," she said dutifully, smiling.

Audrae smiled, too. "Now go. We shall send a messenger tomorrow to see if you should like to visit."

It was hard to know the precise reason for her reluctance to leave her mother and James. She had missed them, of course. Yet it was more a matter of dread. She must face Magnus as her mother had urged her to do, with all of her heart laid out for him to see. When Roger returned saying he had hired a carriage for her, she hugged her mother and brother tightly, fighting the urge to linger.

When she arrived home, Magnus was in the library. After waiting in the parlor for a while, she went up to bed

alone, relieved and disappointed at the same time that tonight was not to be the night of confrontation.

He was already gone when she arose the following
morning. This left her free to spend the day with her family. She met them at their hotel restaurant for luncheon,
then accompanied them as Audrae took Roger on a tour
of London. They purchased admission to the Royal Academy of Arts and strolled among the treasures. James did
an excellent job keeping up with them, though he began
to tire around teatime. Caroline left them off at their lodg-
ings and went home, hating to part company. Her mother
had not been pleased when she had told her that she had
not had time to approach Magnus. Thus it was with a
meaningful look that she bade her daughter goodbye.

There was a message waiting for her from Magnus, informing her he had invited Audrae and James to dinner
the following evening. He had already informed cook and
sent a request to the hotel.

Surprised by his thoughtfulness, Caroline was heartened.
It showed, at least, that he had thought of her. Then she
paused. He still never conversed with her, or spent any
amount of time in her company. Since they had arrived in
London, no—since he had found out what she had done—
he could scarcely abide to be in her presence for long. He
was kind, civil, *congenial,* but he was not loving. Not anymore.

He must have simply accepted the relationship on the
basis of the original agreement, Caroline decided. Purely
business. Money and a child. It merely meant that it ended
up precisely as it had been intended. And perhaps all the
rest of it—the passion, the companionship, the wondrous
feelings in each other's presence—didn't mean all that
much to him after all.

The arrangements for the dinner party required only one

thing from Caroline, and that was to inform cook that the number of guests should be increased to five, to include Roger. When the minor adjustment was made, Caroline gave the rest of the planning over to the staff of well-trained servants. Eddington House was used to running without benefit of a mistress.

Magnus did not return home until after dinner. Caroline, having spent the evening reading in the yellow parlor, heard him come in the front door and go directly to the library. Drawing a deep breath and squaring her shoulders, she put down her book and went to the library door. She knocked.

There was a short pause before Magnus unlocked and opened the door.

"Caroline." His inflection was flat, with neither any note of welcome nor undercurrent of irritation.

"Magnus, I wished to speak to you. May I come in?"

He looked behind him, paused, then shook his head. "I am in the middle of something right now. Is it urgent?"

Coward that she was, she readily answered that no, it was not urgent. She remembered to thank him for inviting her family to dine, then retreated. Halfway up the stairs, she heard the door close behind her and the lock turn.

Magnus wanted to go home to Hawking Park. As he stood at the window, staring out at Hyde Park, he longed for the more pastoral vistas of home. Carriages sped by, folks strolled along and a pair of boys dodged in and out of traffic, shouting and laughing. None of it penetrated his brain. He was lost in thoughts of what he must do.

He wanted his garden, the physical labor, to help exorcise his demons. But he had to stay in London a little while longer. His tormentor had to be dealt with.

David came in. "You wanted to see me?"

"Close the door." He turned away from the window.

"Ah, if you are staring out of windows, it means you are troubled. What is it? Have you gotten this dreadful business done with regarding Caroline?"

"No," Magnus said, taking his seat behind his desk. "It is not Caroline."

"Hmm. Cannon got you down? I hear he has been shooting his mouth off all over London. As the Americans say, he is 'gunning' for you."

Leaning back, Magnus laced his fingers in front of his chin, elbows on the armrests, and leveled a penetrating look at his brother. "Cannon doesn't bother me. What is of concern is right here in my own family. In fact, David, it is you."

"Me?" David attempted a laugh and dug his hands into his pockets. Magnus just looked at him. David said, "What is it, what have you heard? Has someone been spreading rumors about me?"

"No rumors. Simply a question. It is a rather large question, rather important to me, thus my distress. I hope you shall endeavor to answer it honestly."

Magnus could see the sheen of sweat appear on his brother's brow. David nodded.

"Why did you need money so badly that you would poison me?"

David looked no less terrified than if Magnus had pulled a pistol and placed the barrel against the younger man's forehead. He paled. Magnus could see his Adam's apple glide up and down as he swallowed hard. Then he gave one quick laugh. "Magnus, what is this? A joke?"

Magnus didn't answer. He watched David's eyes dart around the room, searching, it seemed, for aid from some quarter.

"Poison you? What the devil are you talking about?"

"Digitalis."

"What? I've never heard of the stuff."

"A doctor in Whitehall said he gave you digitalis. It seems it is you, not me, who suffers from the same heart ailments as Father."

"What doctor? He is lying." He darted a look to the door.

Magnus didn't move a muscle. "Then there are the books. I've been going over them thoroughly. During the periods of your stewardship, there are large amounts of money missing. Cleverly concealed, but close investigation has shown them to have been appropriated."

"You know I have no head for business," David protested.

"Mr. Green's fees are surprisingly smaller than I was led to believe. When you were in charge of contacting him, he was much more expensive than when I dealt directly with him. Could it be you took a little bit for yourself?"

"Fees are based on the services provided, Magnus, not on who one is."

"What about the Waterford bowl? And Mother's Chinese vase? Both are missing."

"You told me Caroline stole them."

"Caroline did not. She admits to the other items, but not those two. It seems we have had two thieves at Hawking Park."

"I don't see why you are accusing me!"

"Because I *know,* David. I know about the vase and the bowl, about Green and the digitalis and the embezzling you've been doing. I know I'm not dying. By the way, you have not reacted at all to the news. An odd reaction from so devoted a brother. Could it be you knew already?"

"I…" David paused, visibly weighing his options. His round eyes locked with Magnus' for a moment before he hung his head, muttering, "I would have never harmed you. It was just to make you sick for a while until I could pay off my debts."

Magnus forced himself to remain calm, but the intensity inside him was climbing. "Debts?"

"Haven't your wonderful sources told you about my debts? I'm in for over seventy thousand pounds."

"No, you aren't. Your debts are substantial, but not that great."

David gave a harsh laugh. "You want to know all of it? So you shall. The debts you know about aren't a tenth of what I owe. There is no way to estimate what I have already paid out just to keep the blasted creditors off my back. And keep me alive. I've fallen in with some unsavory fellows, Magnus. I suffered some losses at the gaming tables, and I had to make payment or else lose face. I went to a moneylender and borrowed the money to pay it off."

"You went to a moneylender, but not to me?"

"I didn't know it was going to turn out like this. It was only fifty pounds I needed. When I couldn't pay him, the amount I owed went up. It kept going up."

"It's called interest."

"It's called extortion. Before long, the fifty pounds had turned into two hundred, and I couldn't pay it. I kept gaming, hoping for a win. I don't seem to have your luck at the tables."

Magnus was confused. "What moneylender compounds interest that quickly?"

David looked away, washed in shame. "He was from Mecklenburgh Street."

"Mecklenburgh Street!" Magnus placed his palms on the desk and came up out of his chair. "Mecklenburgh Street!" he roared again. "My God, what were you thinking?"

"I didn't think, that's just the problem. I didn't want you to know, I couldn't bear that. You are a daunting enough fellow to try to live up to, what with your legendary prowess with women and your great skill at the tables and in business. The Midas touch in all things. How could I come to you a failure?"

Magnus almost growled. "Don't try to lay this at my feet."

"Oh, no, it could not possibly be your fault." David's face altered, his cultured veneer replaced by an ugly sneer. "Nothing you do is ever wrong. Mother adored you. 'My little poet.' And Father pined for the day you would come to your senses."

"Father despised me, and Mother never favored one of us over the other."

"Father could have come to me. I was not the one in London wasting my life, I was at home, being the dutiful son. He never once considered it."

Magnus came around the desk. "So you wish to punish me for that?"

"No. It wasn't about punishment. I just couldn't tell you. I have been so foolish. You know the type of people I became entangled with. I feared for my life. It's true, I take digitalis for my heart. I was warned about the toxic effects it could have if taken improperly, but in small doses it was harmless, even beneficial. That's when I got the idea. You are my brother, Magnus, and I love you. I would never have harmed you, never. It was just a little bit to make you ill, so I could get to the money. It was my life, for God's sake! You know the men I'm dealing with. It cost you nothing, just a touch of illness now and then."

He stopped, as if hearing the words spoken out loud made him realize what a terrible thing he had done.

Magnus watched him, steeling himself against the rage

of emotions in his breast. David turned and went to a chair. He threw himself into it, slouching and burying his head in his hands.

"Oh, God, what the devil have I become? I always admired you. But I hated you a little bit, too, I think. How could I have done it if I hadn't? I told myself you had been given unfair advantage by our parents, by birthing you first if nothing else." He raised his head. There was true anguish in his face. "I would never have given you enough to do harm. That one time, I saw you. You were so bad. I hadn't realized...I must have given you too much. It was awful. I swore no more, but then the moneylender sent these two apes to 'speak' to me, and I had to do it again, but only a little. That's why the attacks got milder and less frequent. I was going to stop. When I was safe, I would have stopped. I would never have hurt you, Magnus. Never."

Magnus thought perhaps he would stay silent, not speak the words screaming in his head, for if he begun to give voice to the horror he was feeling, he might not stop. He would lose control.

In the end, he started calmly. "You keep saying you didn't wish me to come to any harm. It's almost like a litany. I wonder if you yourself believe it. How could you have ever deluded yourself into thinking I was not being harmed?" His voice rose and his hands curled into fists at his side. "I thought I was dying. Dying, David. I looked at every day as it passed, each month, each season, and I thought I would never see another. *Do you know what that was like?* Do you know what torture it was for me to know every moment that my very hours were numbered? How could you think that you were not truly harming me?"

"But you changed," David protested in a high, whiny voice. "It was upsetting for you, I know, but you weren't really going to die. You just thought you were. I hadn't planned that, but the doctors told you so and suddenly you wanted to have a family. You stopped all your self-destructive ways and decided to settle down. I hadn't seen you that determined in a while, in years. It was good. And then you met Caroline, and I knew it was all going to be all right. She is so lovely, so kind, in every way a woman worthy of you. And now she carries your child. It would have never have happened if it weren't for me. You would have been miserable and alone forever, waiting for a miracle to cleanse you so you would be free. Don't you see, Magnus? In a way, I gave you that miracle. I set you free.''

Magnus could hardly believe what he was hearing. ''Is that what you tell yourself in order to sleep at night? That you were doing me good? Have you ever experienced the effects of digitalis? The nausea, being out of control of your body? The fever and the delirium, the terrible nightmare images that assault you in your weakened state?''

David spread his hands out in front of him, palms up. A gesture of pleading. ''I know it must have been horrible. I'm so sorry.''

''Sorry. Yes, that makes up for it.''

''But think about Caroline. You wouldn't have her, and you have to admit she is wonderful.''

Magnus felt a tight curling in the pit of his stomach. David had come to Magnus' own most profound concern. ''She is wonderful, David. And you are right—there is no possible way we would have even met had I never been fooled into thinking I was ill. But think about this, dear brother. Caroline married me for the money to purchase medicines and treatments for her brother. And the promise of wealthy widowhood. Now, her brother is on the mend and shall soon be in no need of expensive sanatoriums or doctors, and I am not dying. So tell me, what good does having a wonderful wife do me when she has no use for me anymore and I have outstayed my welcome in her life?''

Shaking his head, David protested, ''But she cares for you, Magnus. I can see it.''

''Yes, she cares for me. Enough to want me around for a lifetime? It's not what she bargained for. Therefore, before you congratulate yourself too heartily, think about the facts. You made me suffer untold tortures, of the mind and the body, and you took an innocent woman and put her in an impossible position. You have caused so much misery, even your pathetic lies to yourself about all the good you did can't make it better.''

''I know, I know.'' David began to weep. Magnus turned away from him in disgust, angry at himself for the effect those pitiable sobs were having on his resolve.

''Magnus,'' David gulped, ''what are you going to do?''

Magnus made him wait for a while before answering. ''Cut you off. Banish you from my households, rescind your stipend and take possession of your town house.''

''Wh-? I... You can't mean it. How will I live? Magnus, don't you realize they will kill me? These blokes don't play lightly. I wouldn't have resorted to such drastic means had I not been completely desperate. If you cut me off, I can't pay them back, and they'll break my arms and legs and throw me into the river. They told me so.''

Magnus stood rigid, immutable, hoping to appear impervious to his brother's pleas.

''Dear God, Magnus, you are condemning me to death!''

''You did that yourself. Would you rather I report you to the authorities? I will do it if you like, and ride out the disgrace to our family, if that is what you prefer.''

''No,'' he exclaimed. ''I wouldn't. But this, Magnus,

this is unconscionable. Think of how it would reflect on you, if nothing else.''

Magnus snorted, giving his brother a prize scowl over his shoulder. "I have no fears of sullying my pristine reputation.''

David rose, stepping slowly toward his elder brother. "Magnus, I'm begging you—*begging*. I'm as good as dead if you do this. *As good as dead.*''

Turning, Magnus laid a companionable hand on David's shoulder. "Take some advice from someone who's been in your shoes. Facing your own end square in the face has its rewards. You said so yourself. Think of all the good it will do you.''

He stayed only a moment to see David's face crumple before he walked away.

"See yourself out,'' he said as he strode out the door.

Chapter Twenty-Four

Even after all of the things Magnus had borne in his life, one of the hardest ordeals was sitting through dinner that evening and making pleasant conversation with Audrae and her fiancé. Roger was a pleasant fellow, someone Magnus would have thought beneath him at one time, a ploy he used with all people he met whom he perceived as good. He named them fools and basked in a false sense of superiority. The truth was, men like Roger, steady, kind, good-hearted, had always made him feel inadequate.

Thus, it was something of a revelation to find himself liking the man. It was gratifying to see Audrae so happy. He liked her, and after what he had found out about her first husband, she deserved to be happy. Caroline was nervous. He sensed it, and he knew it was because of him.

James, the mysterious and miraculously healed brother, was silent during the entire meal. Though Magnus didn't make a habit of keeping company with children, he had enough knowledge of them to know this behavior was exceedingly unusual. A curious child. Judging from the frequent covert glances he cast Magnus' way, the boy was intrigued with him as well.

It gave him an idea. After the meal was concluded, and

the ladies had arisen to adjourn to the parlor, Magnus invited James to stay with the men. The lad looked shocked. He appealed to his mother, then to Caroline. It was Audrae who nodded, as if it were the most normal thing in the world.

When the two women had gone, Magnus wasn't sure he had done a good thing. The boy looked painfully unsure.

"Come over here and sit," Magnus said, indicating the chair on his right. "Don't worry, I won't force you to smoke a cigar."

"Yes," James answered, his voice trembling a bit. "Mama wouldn't like it."

"Of course, most mamas don't care for that sort of thing. My mother, on the other hand, didn't mind at all. I had tasted seven kinds of wine before my tenth birthday and on that day she started me on hard liquor."

"How extraordinary," Roger said.

"It was her belief that a boy should learn to hold his alcohol, and if it was not thought of as some kind of reward one gets for coming of age, then one would not be tempted to overindulge."

Roger frowned. "I don't see the logic."

"Will you let your son drink before he is a man?" James asked. Magnus grinned, knowing the lad was too interested in the conversation to stay quiet for long.

"I'm in agreement with Roger on the matter. It was my mother's belief, not mine."

The boy looked relieved.

Acting on impulse, Magnus said, "Roger, would you excuse James and me? I feel like a stroll, and I imagine some light exercise would do the boy good. Feel free to relax and enjoy your cigar."

Roger nodded, not at all put out at being abandoned. It would not have mattered to Magnus if he were. He was still enough of his old self to disregard someone's feelings in a pinch.

"Tell the ladies we shall not be long. Come, James. Your mama will not mind."

This didn't allay the child's trepidations completely. His eyes were big and wide, his steps unsure as he followed Magnus to the cloakroom and then outside the front door.

"See," Magnus said as they walked to the end of the short driveway. He was pointing to the park. "We are very close to where the queen lives."

"I know. Cara showed us yesterday."

"Cara? Do you call her that as well?"

The boy looked up at him. He had an extraordinarily winsome face, Magnus noted, then thought how odd it was for him to have such a thought. "Yes. I always did. Do you?"

"Well, I always thought she was more of a Cara than a Caroline. Caroline is much more...stiff."

"She tries to be stiff, but she isn't," James observed.

Magnus smiled at the adept insight. "No, she isn't at all."

There was a brief, companionable pause as they walked along. The gaslights had been lit and there were others out on this mild winter night.

"Do you like her?" James asked.

"Who? Your sister? Yes, James, I like her very much."

"She likes you. She's worried you don't like her. She didn't tell me. No one tells me anything. I just know."

"Ah, the burdens of childhood. No one recognizes your worth, do they?"

James gave him a thoughtful nod and a smile. "I thought you didn't like me. That's why I had to be a secret. But I think you do."

"It's true. You're a fine boy."

''Why did you want to talk to me alone?''

Magnus shook his head in amazement. This child's perceptiveness was uncanny. ''I wanted to see you alone because Caroline has told me about how you were ill. She didn't tell me for a long time. She thought I wouldn't like it, that it would make me not have chosen her as my wife.''

''I know. She said you wanted her all to yourself.'' There was a tinge of mournfulness in his voice, not enough to be maudlin, but enough that even a thickheaded clod such as himself could not miss it.

Magnus pointed just up ahead. ''We'll go up to the corner and turn around, is that all right? Do you feel up to it? Good. Well, about Caroline, yes, she thought I would want her all to myself, but to tell you truthfully, James, it would have made no difference. You see, when I met Caroline, I knew she was the one I wanted. I knew it right from the start.''

''Golly.''

Magnus laughed. ''An apt term. In any event, the reason I wished to speak to you alone was that I wanted you to know I don't mind about you having been sick at all. I'm very happy to know you, and had Cara told me about you, I would have been glad to help in any way I can. So you are not to be concerned. I'm going to take care of everything from here on out.''

''Did you tell Cara? Because she's been worried. She's very unhappy. I can always tell because her smiles don't make her eyes crinkle in the corners. So, if you tell her, it might make her feel better.''

''You're right, of course. I should tell her. And I shall. I have been rather busy of late, but that is over now and I shall tell her the first chance I get.''

''You should,'' James said with a definitive nod. ''Women don't like it when you keep them waiting. I know. I've lived with Mama and Cara all my life. If you don't tell them what you're thinking, they'll imagine something worse. So, it's usually best to let them know.''

It struck Magnus at that moment that he was discussing his marriage with a seven-year-old. More incredibly, he was hearing some of the wisest reflections on women he had ever heard.

''Time to go in now. Are you ready?''

''Yes, thank you, my lord.''

''You can call me Magnus. I am your brother-in-law, you know. May I call you James?''

James giggled. ''Of course. That's my name.''

Just then, Magnus glanced up and there was Caroline standing in the doorway. His heart reacted, bumping up against his ribs with an erratic rhythm. She might have been poised on the deck of a ship, or on top of a cliff, with her loose hair dancing on the wind, her dress blown back to reveal the slightest of bulges beginning to take shape low in her belly. She had no wrap. Her arms were clasped around her, and she was shivering. Coming to the bottom of the three steps, Magnus put his right foot on the first riser and gazed up at her.

She stared down at him. A goddess addressing her petitioner from her oracle. Her face held no trace of expression, and her voice was devoid of emotion. He knew her well enough by now to know it meant her guard was up. ''I didn't know where you had gone,'' she said.

''Just for a short walk. Sort of getting to know each other. Man stuff. Right, James?''

''Right, Magnus.''

Magnus laughed at the way her mouth dropped open at her brother's familiar address. ''Come on, James, we should get inside. Your mama probably wants to get you home to bed.''

''All right, Magnus.''

* * *

Something had changed. Caroline could sense it, *feel* it sizzling around Magnus like the way the air gathers and tenses just before lightning strikes. He moved differently, exuding an aura of excitement and expectation. It was in the way he looked at her, his eyes dark, holding a tantalizing blend of unfathomable emotion.

Something had indeed changed. And something was about to happen. It filled her with dread.

After her mother and Roger left, the latter encumbered cheerfully with a dozing James, Caroline retreated to her chamber. There she paced, waiting, her mind racing while her stomach knotted.

This state was not good for the baby. It was this sensible thought that ignited her maternal instincts. She sat, forcing herself to breathe deeply, calmly. Her eyes darted around the room.

When the soft knock came, she nearly jumped straight out of the chair.

"Magnus?" she called. Her voice quivered.

He entered. Caroline's mouth went dry. He looked much as he had on their wedding night. His shirt was open, cuffs rolled up to bare muscular forearms. He still wore his dark trousers and polished shoes. She was hit with a wave of desire and sadness and regret. She tried to swallow.

"I want to talk to you," was all he said. She watched as he crossed to a pair of Sheraton-style chairs. He moved like a panther, she thought. He picked up one and brought it over, setting it down in front of her. Then he sat. Their knees were only inches apart.

His gaze held hers as he settled his elbows on his knees. "I want the truth, Cara."

Cara. The old endearment registered, sparking a flutter of her heart.

She nodded slowly, half fearing, half savoring the hope beginning to take form in her breast. His next words stifled the tender emotion.

He said, "Tell me about your father."

Chapter Twenty-Five

A small sound escaped her. A cry, as if he had struck her physically. The intensity of his stare didn't flicker. "Tell me, Cara, tell me the truth. If you can't bear it, then tell me so, but don't lie to me. For God's sake, don't lie to me."

Frigid fingers of terror tripped lightly up and down her spine. She wanted to flee. She wanted to stay.

She wanted to tell him.

"My father," she began, "was a bastard."

He waited. She dragged in a breath and closed her eyes. It was only when she did this that she felt the moisture on her lashes. Something deep inside her rose up, feeding her voice.

"He was never a loving father. Remote, self-centered in his early years, but anything good in him deteriorated into a disgusting evil man later. It was drinking that did it, but he was a rotter to begin with."

She couldn't look at his eyes, so she studied his hands. Those hands that had touched her, loved her, cherished her with passion and tenderness. "I despised him before he died. Afterward, when we found out about his debts, his other women, the way he mortgaged everything to indulge his base appetites when his son needed so much…'' She darted a glance full of appeal, begging for reprieve.

Magnus did not move. "What did he do to you?"

She waited a heartbeat, then the words tore out of her, almost not of her conscious volition. "He touched me. *Once*. And… He tried to…to kiss me. Like you do, not in the way a father should. I hit him. He was so drunk, he didn't feel it."

The words evoked no flood of memory, no connection to that terrible night. Only anger. It filled her, curling her hands into fists on her lap, spurring her breath into shallow pants.

"He was so loathsome to me, it never occurred to me to be afraid. I struck his hands away as he kept reaching for me, pleading in a way I can't describe. It occurred to me then that he was pathetic. I think that's what made the difference. I had this idea that he was so very vile because he was afraid of me, and he was doing this to despoil me, make me less fearsome to him. That may sound absurd, but it was what I thought. Perhaps it was what I told myself to give me strength.

"I told him how much I hated him. I spoke of all the things I had held in my heart. He cowed before me. My words came spilling out in a flood of loathing, and he couldn't bear it."

She did meet Magnus' eyes then. They were soft, she thought, wondering if she only wished it so. She continued. "After that, he never troubled me. He was no kinder, nor worse, merely beaten. He never looked at me and we never spoke. When he died…I was happy. I was relieved. Even being left destitute, it was better to have him gone."

He reached out his hand, touching her averted face. As soon as his fingers brushed her cheek, she grasped his wrists with both her hands and buried her face in the large palm.

"Did you think I would treat you so?"

"No, I never did. I just couldn't trust you, not at first. I mean, you *were* the notorious Earl of Rutherford. I didn't dare think you were an honorable man. James was depending on me for his very life. Oh, God, Magnus, I didn't know what to do."

He pulled her to him, nestling her on his lap.

"Magnus, can you forgive me?"

Magnus buried his nose in her hair, inhaling deeply. Forgive her? He should be begging her forgiveness for not understanding, not caring about the why of it all.

It didn't matter now. There was only one thing that mattered, and everything weighed on it.

The light pressure of her arms about his neck was sweet, calling him to the heady promise of a kiss, an embrace, a touch that would heal everything. Yet the most important fact of all remained undisclosed.

Magnus found he was trembling.

"Caroline, I have something to tell you. Something very, very important." He pulled her up so he could see her face.

"First, tell me you forgive me." He could never resist the appeal in those eyes.

"Cara *mia,* I forgive you. If you need to hear it, there it is."

Her teeth caught her bottom lip and she nodded. "Very well," she said. "Now, what is it you must tell me?"

He realized she was afraid. His mind fastened on a dozen things she could be expecting him to say, none of them good, he would wager. He would lay another thousand pounds she never, never expected what he was about to tell her.

He could barely form the words. He was afraid, too.

"It turns out I am not going to die, after all."

He hated the way it came out, blithe and light and not at all what he had wanted to say.

"I mean, I will, eventually. Just not soon." God, he was making it worse. But he couldn't bear that stricken expression on her face. His chest burned, and he felt a deep flush of shame for all of a sudden he had the overwhelming fear he was going to weep.

No. Don't let her be sorry.

Magnus knew the power of silence, but he couldn't still his tongue. "I was being poisoned, Caroline. I knew it when you fell ill. I realized the truth almost immediately, for you had eaten one of the thick doughy pastries that only I can stomach."

"I had a craving for sweets," she said in a small voice, as if he were accusing her. He knew by the flat, vacant tone of her voice that she hadn't really comprehended what he had said. He remembered how he, too, had had disjointed, strange thoughts as his brain had grappled with the startling revelation that he was not ill after all.

"Yes, I know. It was a terrible illness, and I regret you had to go through it. Scared me half into my grave, worrying about you and the baby. Then it dawned on me how similar your symptoms were to mine."

"I hadn't realized it." She put a trembling hand to her forehead, obviously still dazed. In a small voice, she added, "How stupid of me."

"The doctor confirmed my suspicions. I was being intermittently poisoned by varying doses of digitalis. That accounted for the differences in the severity of each attack and the unpredictability of them."

Her next words stunned him. "My God, Magnus. How awful for you. To think you were dying, to face that." Her hands came over his, clutching with a fervency that seeped into his bones and filled him with warmth. Her brow creased. "Who?"

His voice failed him when he attempted to speak. In all of this, the pain of his brother's betrayal was the one thing he hadn't dared yet face. He drew in a shaky breath and tried again. "David."

Gasping, she shook her head, murmuring, "No, it can't be. You must be mistaken. I don't understand any of this. Magnus, he loves you. He would never try to kill you."

"Do you think I would make such a mistake?" he said gently. "No, Cara. It was he. Not to kill me. To make me believe I was so ill that I had to give over the running of the businesses to him. He needed money. He had gambling debts, it seemed, and—"

"Magnus!" Her eyes were wide as saucers, her face as ghostly pale as a wraith. Her hands grabbed great fistfuls of his shirt and she curled into a tight ball against his chest.

His hands came to her shoulders which were shaking with her sobs.

"My God, I must be the stupidest woman in the world!" she cried. When she looked at him, her face was streaked with tears. Speechless, he let her gather his face in her hands. "You just told me you're not dying and I'm questioning you like an idiot! Oh, Magnus, you aren't ill. You are going to *live!*"

His voice came out only slightly better than a hoarse croak. "Then you are pleased?"

"Pleased? Pleased?" Her laugh was high-pitched and a little hysterical, not at all the pleasant sound he was used to. She was giddy, she was euphoric. No words could have told him more succinctly, or with more blessed clarity what lay in her heart.

The dam burst, flooding him with a surge of emotion

that left him weak. She was saying over and over, "I'm so happy. Magnus, I'm so happy."

Then she stopped, sobering all at once and giving him that stare that said she was wary. "Do you still want me? And the baby?"

He had never thought she would doubt it. Yet, he understood. Just as he had tortured himself with thoughts that she might not want to stay with him, she was afflicted with similar doubts. It wasn't the least bit funny. Nevertheless, his laughter rumbled out of him, loud and raucous and filled with joy.

He saw her look of consternation, a flash of drawn brows and a dropping of her jaw, before he swept her against him. Even as he let loose the wild delirium that tossed him on its heady ride, he felt a sting in the back of his eyes.

"My love, my precious, precious love," he said. Her head whipped around, bringing them nose to nose. "Can it be I fooled even you?"

Her smile appeared, filled with so much it was almost blinding. "Then, you want me?"

"Cara *mia,* I might as well truly be dead without you. Yes, I want you with me, always. You have given me everything." His voice faltered. Damn it, he would not back away from this now. If he did, then everything his father had accused him of would be true. And, strangely, it was not so very hard to say, "My God, Caroline, don't you know I'm mad for you?"

"Oh, Magnus, I love you," she declared. His eyes fastened on her lips as they formed those words. He let them seep into his soul before pulling her to him. His mouth closed over hers, claiming her anew. And she answered. Her mouth answered and her body answered and her arms twining around his neck, her hands splayed over the back of his neck to twist in his hair, answered every question that ever mattered.

He loved, was loved in return, as incredible as that was, and from this improbable eventuality a new life grew. Their child, made in passion. Had any man had so much?

"So, you will not hate our child, I trust." Her lips were against his, an impish smile playing on them. "Even if he has terrible temper tantrums or wants you to applaud his drawings?"

He grinned, loving the molten feeling those images pumped into his limbs. "I shall drool over every stroke and indulge him without conscience."

"And if she is a girl, you will teach her to dance and bounce her on your knee?"

"I will make her a princess."

A slow smile spread her lips. He loved her smile. He felt heat in his loins and he wanted to kiss her again.

"You are making me insane," he muttered, giving into the tempting curve of her neck. He heard her sigh. It was like music.

"You are a wicked earl. Now I know how you got such a reputation."

"Would you like to see more?"

"Mmm."

His hands shifted to her bottom, bringing her up to settle more comfortably on his lap. His arousal strained against his trousers, aching with need that made him grit his teeth and frown in concentration.

"David told me I was lucky to have faced death."

"What a terrible thing to say."

"He's right, though. It galls me to say it, but he is. It was only when I thought I was dying that I realized what life meant to me. And after all, Cara *mia,* he gave me you."

"What did you do to him?"

He paused, tracing the exciting valley between her breasts. He smiled when her breath hitched. "I sent him away without a farthing. His creditors will deal with him." When she was silent, he added, "At least, that's what I led him to believe. This afternoon, I had a messenger give him a banknote worth fifty thousand."

"Pounds?"

He chuckled at the expression on her face. "It's his settlement. He's never to bother us again."

"Oh, Magnus, I'm so sorry." The soft kisses she pressed on his brow, across the bridge of his nose were stirring his blood to near combustible levels.

"I also included a note," he said, sighing against the gentle pressure of her lips against his. "I asked him how beneficial he found facing certain death. It was small of me, I know. My temper is improving, but not that much."

"I love you just as you are."

"A curious affliction for such a sensible woman as yourself."

Her eyes danced. She delicately traced the outline of his mouth with her tongue. "We all have our failings."

He brought his mouth fully over hers.

She pulled back, still smiling. "And you are mine."

Letting out a low growl, he set her on her feet, only to sweep her into his arms, bearing her to the bed where he laid her upon the coverlet.

With aching slowness, he undressed her, then rid himself of the nuisance of his own clothing. Lying beside her, he placed first his hand, then his cheek, to the hard swell just beginning to rise in her abdomen.

"You are mine, Cara *mia*," he murmured, running his lips over her taut flesh. He could hear her breath coming in short audible gasps as his hands slid over her skin.

"Mine. You are my love, my life, everything that matters. I shall love you for eternity."

"Love me, Magnus," she said, pulling him up to her. "Never stop, not tonight, not ever."

He kissed her. He spoke words he didn't know he could, words that poured forth from his soul. He drank in her passion, her sultry movements, her murmured endearments and when it was over and they lay in each other's arms, he closed his eyes and felt, for the first time since he had been a small child, the blessed, sweet calm of utter peace.

Epilogue

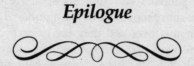

The morning was already warm enough to raise a thin sheen of sweat. It was a fine day for working in the garden. Magnus had stripped off his shirt and used it to wipe his brow as he surveyed his work. The roses were in bloom in an erratic explosion of pinks, salmons, yellows, whites and bloodreds. He looked about him in satisfaction.

Life was all around him, vibrant and real. His scalp tingled. He leaned on his hoe and squinted up at the sun. He smiled. Contentment filled him in one swift surge.

A sound made him turn around. Caroline was coming down the lane, holding tiny Esmine in her arms. His daughter spotted him and waved her arms excitedly, her cries of delight as sweet as birdsong.

His heart, that fragile part he thought would rob him of ever setting eyes on his child, constricted in a spasm of pure joy.

"Esmine has something she wants to show you," Caroline said. She set their daughter down on the grass. Esmine's bare toes curled, gripping the turf. Her fingers were wrapped tightly about Caroline's index finger as she played at lifting her feet.

"She wants to walk to her Papa," Caroline announced.

The child was only nine months old. Tolerantly, Magnus hunkered down and held his arms out. To his surprise, Esmine let go of her mother and toddled three good steps before lunging into his arms.

"She walked!" he exclaimed.

"Isn't she a genius!" Caroline clapped for their child's momentous accomplishment.

"No child has ever been so clever." He covered the cherubic face with kisses, making Esmine giggle.

She was the perfect blend of both of them. Her hair was flaxen, like her mother's, but it was curly, like his. Her eyes were vivid green. His eyes. Caroline's nose and her mouth, too. It wrenched his gut to think of that mouth as the child grew into womanhood. Well, he would just have to watch her like a hawk.

It was good he had such a damning reputation. Hopefully it would scare the daylights out of her suitors.

"What are you thinking?" Caroline came up to hook her arm through his. She was smiling at him.

"I was thinking of Esmine's beauty, and what a burden it will be to us. I am determined to terrorize all the young bucks of London."

"So you would keep her a spinster?"

"Would that be so bad?" He gazed once again at his adorable child.

"And cheat her out of the happiness we know? Magnus, really."

The good-natured reprimand made him sigh. "Very well. She may marry when she is thirty."

Caroline giggled. "You are a wicked earl. Come, Esmine, your performance is over. Papa must return to work and it's time for your nap."

Esmine went to her mother without protest. Caroline

reached up on tiptoe, brushing her lips much too briefly against Magnus' mouth.

"Esmine is going to nap," he said thoughtfully. "Are you in the mood for a ride, Cara? There is a spot I know, by the Witch's Cauldron. A beautiful spot perfect for making love."

He savored the flush that flooded her features. He would never grow accustomed to the beauty of his wife, or the response she could stir in him with the slightest provocation.

Her mouth twisted in a wry, good-natured grin. "Yes, I think an outing would be just the thing. Esmine, say goodbye to Papa."

The child let out a garrulous cry as Caroline bore her back to the house. Magnus went to the stables to order their horses prepared before dashing up to his room to change. It took only a few moments, for his anticipation made him hurry.

It was a beautiful day, he mused when he was at the stables, striding toward his stallion. Caroline waited, seated astride her mare with eyes bright with love and adoration and desire.

Oh, yes, a glorious day.

* * * * *

Harlequin® Historical

Love,
Americana Style

JOE'S WIFE
by Cheryl St. John

Available in February 1999
(29051-9)

THE TENDER STRANGER
by Carolyn Davidson

Available in March 1999
(29056-X)

Available wherever
Harlequin books are sold.

HARLEQUIN®
Makes any time special ™

My Secret Admirer

Savor the magic of love
with three new romances
from top-selling authors
**Anne Stuart,
Vicki Lewis Thompson and
Marisa Carroll.**

My Secret Admirer is a unique collection
of three brand-new stories featuring passionate
secret admirers. Celebrate Valentine's Day with
these wonderfully romantic tales that are
ideally suited for this special time!

Available in February 1999 at your favorite retail outlet.

HARLEQUIN®
Makes any time special ™

COMING NEXT MONTH FROM

HARLEQUIN HISTORICALS

Jasmine in sight. Then he realized what room she had disappeared into.

The ballroom. Of course that would interest her.

The urgent pull of business needled him to keep going. She could explore while he got things done. Problem solved. But there was also the worry that she would wander somewhere that she could get hurt. Not all the rooms were finished. Since they hadn't been expecting company, the dangerous areas weren't necessarily marked.

Then there was the question of her excitement and how he wanted to read it in her expression as she explored. He shouldn't care. The fact that he was even thinking about this meant he should keep going. Instead his steps took him back toward the open doorway.

The ballroom walls had been carefully stripped of ancient wallpaper to reveal intricate painted murals. They'd decided to clean and preserve them as is, rather than recreating them. Wear and tear showed in spots, but it was the kind of damage that one would find in an antique museum piece. It simply added to the charm. The crown molding surrounding the windows, murals and chandelier bases had been stripped and refinished in an off white. Eggshell, his mother had called it.

The elaborate crystal chandeliers had been refinished and rewired. The wood floor had been stripped of decades of dirt and grime and was waiting to be stained and protected with a thick coat of polyurethane. There was still a series of mirrors waiting to be hung.

The room was a showpiece in and of itself.

Jasmine twirled slowly in the center, taking in all the delights. She stopped as she came to face him. Some of his indecision must have come across as irritation in his expression, because her eyes widened for a moment.

Then a grin that could only be classified as cute spread across her face. "I can't help it," she said. "I need to see what I'm gonna have to work with."

"So you *do* approve?"

The expression he'd come to associate with her trying to figure out a way around him made a quick appearance. "Possibly." She turned away. The skirt of her dress swirled with her movements, giving him another glance at sculpted calves and pretty ankles. Didn't the woman ever wear pants?

"But I will need to see more before we know for sure."

Vixen. The minute the word crossed his mind, Royce had second thoughts. After all, he'd never thought about any of the other women he worked with, now or in the past, in such a way. It was surely inappropriate. But completely and totally true.

Jasmine knew exactly what she was doing—keeping him on his toes.

Resigning himself, he gestured for her to continue down the hall. "Everything else on this floor has been completed, except the kitchens." He hoped. "That's what I need to check on today."

As they made their way down the hall, he opened

various doors. She got to explore. He got to maintain forward momentum. Win-win.

Only every peek into a room elicited the same excitement as a child opening presents on Christmas morning. The first gasps jumpstarted his heart, even though he tried to ignore them—and his physical reaction.

"Are these fixtures original?" she asked.

He nodded, warming to one of his favorite subjects outside of business. He and his mother had had two things in common—antiques and cooking. Their shared interests had strengthened their bond.

"All of the fixtures are original, unless they were broken beyond repair. Some of the back rooms had busted windows and weather damage, so we had to do some extensive replacements there. Everywhere else, I had what I could refinished. Some of the electrical components had to be updated. But the feel of the original should be maintained wherever possible—"

He noticed her watching him and felt a moment of unfamiliar self-consciousness. "In my opinion," he added. An opinion he had only shared with his contractor and his mother when she was still alive. Not only was it no one else's business, Royce had always found himself extremely protective of projects that he was full-on enthusiastic about.

Projects that sparked his creativity and drive, instead of the logical side of his brain. Only certain people who shared that drive were let in. He wasn't ready to let Jasmine in. These softening tendencies she inspired in him made keeping things strictly business with her an absolute must.

After what seemed like hours, they finally made it to the kitchen. Jasmine took herself off to pepper the workers with questions while Royce checked in with the foreman. He almost laughed at how short and to the point their discussion was, compared to the last hour with Jasmine. He had a feeling he would hole up in his office when he got back and communicate only by email. He'd used up his allotment of spoken words for the day.

It wasn't until they were on their way back out that Royce's relief was busted.

Jasmine's frequent glances warned him something was up. It didn't take her long to get to the point.

"One of the workers said your mother lived here."

Ah. Well, it wasn't like he'd told them to keep it a secret. "Yes. She lived in the carriage house for a few years before she died."

"I'm so sorry."

Royce just kept walking. He didn't want to get into how much he missed his mother, or how he hadn't felt he'd done everything he could for her before she died. There wasn't much point to those types of conversations.

"Was she interested in the renovations?"

Maybe they weren't done with this subject. "She definitely was. I bought the property for her, and she helped plan every facet of the renovations before she passed away. She was a history and museum buff."

"My sister loves history, too. She teaches it at the

community college. She's the one who told me about this place."

The personal nature of the conversation set off alarms in his brain, but his sudden desire to talk to someone who understood the house and his love of it overrode his caution. "We discussed everything about the direction of the renovations. How much to save. How much to gut and start over on. She loved every minute of it."

He could almost feel Jasmine's warm gaze on his face. Then she said, "I bet she did. That must have been a wonderful thing for her."

He shrugged. "It was the least I could offer her. She was a single mother my entire life. She sacrificed more than any woman should. To make her comfortable and happy was a small gift in comparison."

He remembered watching Jasmine with her daughter, and how it had given rise to the uncomfortable memories of his own childhood. He'd told the truth. His mother had sacrificed a lot. So had he. Which had fostered his attitude on single mothers and the workplace.

As they walked back down the front steps, the burning question Royce had ignored for days finally surfaced. "Jasmine, do you regret being a single mother?"

She halted abruptly. The gorgeous, expressive face he'd been surreptitiously watching all morning shut down. He should have known—should have kept his mouth shut. Reason number two that he avoided social gatherings...he wasn't great at handling casual conversation.

Then her words hit him like bullets. "Never," she said. As she turned away, she added, "Without me, she'd have no one at all."

Jasmine sprinted around the corner of her regular event photographer's house, groaning when she saw Royce sitting in his car at the curb. She'd had her sister drop her off at the side of Dominic's, hoping she wouldn't have to explain how her morning had gone. The last thing she wanted to get into was why she'd needed a ride here instead of driving herself. Of course, the fact that she was fifteen minutes late and running in her heels probably raised eyebrows.

At least she'd texted Royce and Dominic to let them know she was running behind.

She took a few seconds to straighten her dress as Royce climbed out of his sleek car. The chaos of the morning made it a little harder to pull on her professional demeanor. She would blame that on the difficult circumstances rather than the effect every meeting with this man had on her.

Regardless, it didn't bode well for being in close proximity with Royce this morning.

Hopefully her smile wasn't strained enough to show the lack of sleep and worry. Rosie was teething again, so she hadn't slept well. Then Jasmine had worried about leaving her with Auntie when she knew her daughter would be more than a handful. And then… she'd gone out to find her car dead as a doornail.

Her frustration levels were maxed out.

She thought she'd masked her feelings pretty well,

but Royce's double take as he approached her told her otherwise. For once, she prayed he'd stick to his strictly business MO. Even if she'd felt inclined to share her situation, his attitude about single mothers and the workplace gave her pause.

Instead, she tried to concentrate on the bright sunshine in hopes it would chase away her worries and gloom. Other than a brief good morning, she remained silent as they waited for Dominic to answer the bell. Unfortunately, the one day she wished Royce would stick to his robot impersonation, he had to deviate from the norm.

"Everything okay?" he asked.

This must be payback of some sort for her nosiness...

"Yes." She knew her tone would give away that she was lying.

"You seem upset."

Lord, why did she have to have such an expressive face? Why couldn't she just hide behind a stone facade? Of course, that was against her nature and normal method of dealing with clients. She liked being on friendly terms and being perceived as approachable. Which was why everything about her business interactions with Royce had felt wrong.

Fortunately Dominic opened the door of the house before she had to respond to Royce. The photographer's enthusiastic bear hug covered a lot of her strain and helped her regain her equilibrium. She'd worked with Dominic a lot over the last few years. His sheer size made clients think twice about hiring him—he looked more like a bouncer at a bar than an artist—until they saw his portfolio.

He had an ability to showcase emotion in an image that was sheer genius.

His handshake with Royce was firm but not a masculine attempt to dominate. He held the door open for them to enter the historic slate-gray and white Victorian cottage that served as his office, as well as the home that he shared with his partner, Greg.

"I'm so sorry that I was late," Jasmine said, taking a deep breath and noticing the intoxicating scent of baking cookies.

"No problem," Dominic said, always easygoing. In all the time she'd known him, she'd never seen him angry, even when dealing with some pretty demanding clients.

"Dang, Greg must be cooking," she teased. "I could gain weight just breathing." Greg was a baker who created incredible cookies and meringues in the industrial kitchen at the back of the house.

"We try," Dominic said with a wink before leading them into a nearby office. "He probably chose what to make the minute he knew you were coming over. A little sugar for our Sugar."

"He knows me well."

Just following Dominic deeper into the house helped Jasmine relax a little bit more. She'd never been the corporate office type. Her one venture into cubicle-land had convinced her it was the ninth circle of hell. Dominic's office echoed her own, though they were two totally different styles. His was comfortable, with masculine elements of leather, grommets, wrought iron. Hers was everything fluffy and feathery. But both were designed to be lived in, played in.

Which just made the work more fun.

"So, tell me a little about what you're aiming for," Dominic said, leading them to a round table in one corner.

"That would be Jasmine's department," Royce said as he held out a chair for her.

Royce might be all business, but his mama had obviously made sure he was a gentleman.

Dominic tossed Jasmine a brief glance, but she could read a wealth of questions in the look. Like, what was this guy doing here if he wasn't doing the talking? But she didn't want to get into that right now.

"We're planning a masquerade event," she said.

The light in Dominic's eyes told her he was on board already.

"But we don't want just your traditional ball," she added. "We're also looking for other options for entertainment. I was thinking about that photo booth you set up for St. Anne's."

"A photo booth?" Royce asked, the doubt clear in his tone.

"Oh, it isn't your normal photo booth," Jasmine assured him.

Dominic eagerly reached for one of the large photo albums on the table. "Check it out."

He turned the pages slowly, giving them a chance to study the various options. "We created a background unique to the event and brought in props for the guests to use." He pointed to a group of people in a rowboat in front of a mural of a lake with a decorative bridge over it.

"I was thinking a mysterious castle," Jasmine offered.

The men batted ideas around for a minute. Against her hip, Jasmine felt her phone buzz. Since her family knew she didn't answer during meetings, she assumed it was a client and ignored it for the moment. When the buzzing started again after a few minutes, she stiffened, all her earlier tension returning.

Trying to brush it aside, she tossed out some more ideas. But the third buzz was her undoing. Slipping the phone from her pocket, she glanced at the screen. Two missed phone calls and a text from her sister Ivy.

911

She looked up to find both men watching her. Her smile was probably strained but she offered it anyway as she stood. "If you could excuse me just a moment, gentlemen?"

"Nothing wrong with that beautiful baby, I hope?" Dominic asked.

Seeing Royce's back straighten both unnerved her and ticked her off. "I certainly hope not," she said, unhappy with the quaver that had entered her voice.

But she wasn't backing down. She didn't know what his beef was with single mothers and families, but it wasn't her problem. There was no denying she wasn't a perfect mother. She had no delusions about that. The learning curve of the last six months had been steep. Still, she'd go above and beyond for Rosie and the rest of her family.

Family was the one thing that came before her clients, regardless of what they thought.

As she stepped back out to the porch, she prayed it was something like another stalled car or a burst water pipe. Things were replaceable. People weren't. Now that Rosie was a part of their lives, she simply couldn't imagine it any other way.

"Ivy?" she asked as her youngest sister answered the phone. "What's wrong?"

"I need you quick," Ivy said, her voice trembling and breathless. "I'm at Savannah General."

Jasmine's heart thudded in her ears, cutting off Ivy's voice. The hospital? So much for her day getting easier.

Six

Royce watched Jasmine disappear out the door with her phone and was surprised at his personal concern. Ordinarily, he would have been put out. He didn't have a problem with his employees dealing with life, as long as they did it on their own time. Normally he'd be formulating a few admonishing words after she'd kept him waiting this morning and then stepped out of a business meeting to handle what was obviously a personal call.

Instead, he sat here wondering what was wrong.

He turned back to find Dominic staring at the door with a frown on his face. The lines between his eyebrows said he was worried, too, but his expression turned more neutral when he caught Royce's look.

"Would you like to go over a few portfolios while

we wait?" he asked, his voice calm even though he seemed to have other things on his mind.

Eager for a distraction, Royce gave a quick nod. Besides, they were here on business. He needed to focus.

Dominic was quick thinking and smart, which gave him a leg up in Royce's book. He pulled out examples of things he thought might work from the limited knowledge he had of their plans. Royce was impressed. He kept looking through one of the books while they discussed some photo booth ideas. Still, the whole time, his brain was ticking off the minutes that Jasmine had been gone.

What was going on? Did she need help?

As if his very thoughts had conjured her up, Royce turned the page to see a grouping of photos featuring Jasmine and her daughter. There was also another woman in the outdoor portraits, which seemed to have been taken at one of the local squares. The fountain behind them was familiar. The greenery provided a lush frame for the women.

"Oh, I'd forgotten which book those were in," Dominic said, surveying the spread with a smile.

Despite admonishing himself to focus on the meeting, Royce found himself tilting the album farther toward him so he could study the group of women more closely. Jasmine was her usual elegant self, her summer dress full and flowing with a fitted bodice. This was his first time seeing her hair down around her shoulders. The thick mass blanketed her pale skin in soft waves, the sunshine creating glossy highlights in the dark color.

Rosie looked to be newborn, but there was no mistaking those black curls. The other woman looked down at the baby with a smile. But upon closer inspection, Royce thought he detected a pervasive sadness in the woman's gaze that belied her indulgent expression as she watched the child.

Royce detected another subtle difference among the three. The third woman seemed sick. Her skin appeared a little gray, a little more aged than Jasmine's.

Though the three were grouped close together on a picnic blanket in dappled sunshine beneath the trees, the other woman seemed to be more of an observer than part of the group. Still, Dominic was definitely talented when it came to composing a shot.

"The resemblance is remarkable," Royce murmured. All that dark hair linked the women together. No male could penetrate their bond. Only it made him curious about Rosie's father and whether she looked like him at all…

No. He refused to entertain any thoughts like that. It was too personal…too tempting…

"I know," Dominic was saying. "Hard to believe they aren't even related, isn't it? You'd never know Jasmine wasn't Rosie's biological mother."

Royce's gaze snapped up to the other man. "What?"

Dominic's eyes widened. "Well…"

Without me, she'd have no one at all. Jasmine's words came back to him, haunting his mind.

"What do you mean, Dominic?" Royce forced himself to keep his voice nonchalant. He kept all urgency out of the question. Even though, suddenly, he wanted to know very, very badly.

"I'm not sure I should share Jasmine's personal business," Dominic said with a frown. "I spoke out of turn."

"I understand. I just wondered because Jasmine seemed so natural with her daughter. I knew she was a single mother," he added, sprinkling in the truth, "but I never would have guessed she hadn't given birth to her."

Dominic seemed to consider his words. "You've seen her with Rosie?"

"Sure. She brought her to the office the other day." Royce wasn't going to reveal any more details about that visit…details that would make him look bad.

"Oh, yeah. Rosie's such a good baby. Jasmine can pretty much take her wherever and the little one is perfectly content. And will charm anyone within smiling distance."

Which just resurrected images of the sleepy child grinning in Jasmine's arms. They'd looked so perfect together, which made it hard to believe that Jasmine wasn't the birth mother.

Royce tried to assimilate the new things he'd learned into the old image, but it wasn't working very well. An odd feeling started in his chest. And feelings weren't a normal occurrence when he conducted business. Yet he seemed to be having them more and more often around Jasmine Harden.

He needed to get a hold on that…later.

"Is this Rosie's mom?" he asked without thinking.

Dominic paused again, then shrugged. "Yeah. Jasmine met her at City Sanctuary mission. I'm not sure about the details, but I know Jasmine's family took her in early in her pregnancy. Something went wrong and she asked Jasmine to take Rosie if anything happened." He looked down at the smiling women in the picture. "She never even hesitated."

Royce wasn't surprised. Jasmine was strong. She ran a successful business and had a great reputation. He imagined she'd tackled motherhood with the same determination and grace.

He should be ashamed of thinking any differently. Except now he wanted the whole story.

"Dominic, will you call me a cab, please?" Jasmine's voice quavered as she asked the question.

Royce hadn't even realized Jasmine had reentered the office. He glanced up. Her expression was calm, but Royce could see the strain around her delicate mouth and eyes.

Dominic stood. "Sugar, what's wrong?"

Jasmine visibly pulled herself together. "I'm so sorry to cut this short, but Auntie is at the hospital. She fell."

As Dominic made the appropriate remarks, Royce stood. This type of thing was totally out of his realm of expertise.

He watched as Dominic slid an arm around Jasmine's shoulders, feeling completely lost in this situation. That's when he realized he didn't need to do that part. Dominic had taken care of the comfort side of things. Royce could go straight to the logistics of the situation—which was his area of expertise.

"Where's your car?" he asked, his tone now brooking no arguments.

She wouldn't look him straight in the eye, but mumbled, "It wouldn't start this morning. My sister Willow brought me."

No wonder she'd looked frazzled when she arrived.

"Let me cancel my next few appointments and we'll head over," Dominic said.

"Absolutely not," she countered, although her eyes were starting to look suspiciously glassy. "Just call me a cab."

As they argued with each other, Royce argued with himself. So she had no car. She needed to go to the hospital. A cab would take forever.

He didn't want to get involved in her personal life.

But she didn't have a car.

And he was an ass for even debating this with himself. Finally, he cut them both off with, "It looks like I'm your ride."

For the second time that day, Jasmine found herself riding in Royce's car. Sitting next to him reminded her of all the reasons she shouldn't be here.

The subtly spicy smell of him. The sight of his sure hands on the wheel. The overt luxury of the vehicle.

It was too intimate. Too much. There were too many reasons she should stay far away from personal situations with Mr. Business.

But what choice did she have?

Taking Dominic away from his other clients didn't seem fair, though he'd been more than willing to help her out as a friend. A cab would have taken a while. She needed to get to Auntie and Rosie as soon as possible. It was her job to take care of her fam—

"Who is Auntie?"

It took Jasmine a moment to register Royce's words because she'd completely blocked out any chance of his asking her a question about herself. Their few personal interactions so far had seemed as awkward for him as they had been for her. Maybe she'd been wrong.

"She's not really my aunt," Jasmine clarified. "She was my mother's nanny when she was little and my grandmother's best friend. We moved in with her after...anyway, all of us girls still live together now."

Royce nodded. She could see the movement out of the corner of her eye, even though she refused to look directly at him. His presence was overpowering in the small space, especially in her vulnerable state. It was simply too close for comfort.

"She must be older," Royce surmised. "A fall can be pretty serious in those circumstances."

Which was a fact Jasmine wasn't ready to confront. They'd be at the hospital soon enough, and she'd deal with it then. "She helps with Rosie when none of us girls are able to be home."

"I know one of your sisters is a college professor. What does the other one do?"

"She's an executive assistant at the McLemore firm."

"That's good. I'm glad you all are close and you

have that kind of support. Rosie won't be alone when her mom's working."

Jasmine felt her body stiffen in defense, but something about the sad tone of his voice had her reconsidering. Before she could question it, he went on.

"Why didn't you tell me Rosie was adopted?"

The world swirled around Jasmine for a moment, disorienting her. This whole line of questioning was completely out of character for Royce. "I didn't realize you would care."

Why would he? Every encounter with her daughter, or even talking about her, seemed to bring a negative reaction from him.

As if he didn't realize the intent behind her answer, he mused, "You look so much alike. It never occurred to me."

Jasmine was getting more confused by the minute, but at least it kept her worry about Auntie at bay. It also loosened the hold she normally kept on her tongue in front of her clients. "I truly don't understand, Royce. What difference does it make? I'm her mother. I'm a damn good one. I would never deny her a home or neglect her to go out to earn a living."

"Why wouldn't you?"

The car came to an abrupt halt. At first, Jasmine thought she'd pushed too far. Then she realized he'd actually parked in a parking space. They'd arrived at the hospital more quickly than she'd expected.

Only as he was climbing out of the door did he answer. "My mom did."

As he softly shut the door, then walked around the

car, Jasmine sat in stunned silence. Not only because Royce had admitted something so personal, but because it contradicted everything he'd told her about his mother at Keller House. He opened the door and helped her out as if he hadn't just dropped a bombshell of magnificent proportions on her. They walked into the hospital in silence.

What should she say?

He'd taken care of his mother before she died. She'd lived in the carriage house for years. Her son was Savannah's youngest, and most mysterious, billionaire. Had whatever happened to his mother colored how he saw women, how he saw Jasmine?

His earlier comment made the answer obvious.

Before she could get a handle on her reaction, they reached the waiting area where Ivy was sitting with Rosie. Thankfully, the baby was sleeping, though her pudgy cheeks were flushed with the slight fever Jasmine was learning to associate with her teething spells.

Jasmine leaned over to carefully hug her sister around the sleeping child. "What did the doctors say?" she asked as she crouched in front of the pair.

"We're still waiting on the X-rays to find out." Ivy worried her lower lip, making her look a lot older than her twenty-three years. "I'm sorry you had to come here. I just didn't know what to do."

"No. It's fine," Jasmine said. Though asking Ivy not to feel bad was like asking Jasmine not to worry. "The last thing I would have wanted was for you to be sitting here by yourself dealing with all of this. It's no problem at all."

"But your car—"

"Driving over here wasn't a big deal," Royce interjected. "We were about done, anyway."

Ivy glanced at him, her eyes growing wide with surprise.

"You had to get him to drive you?" she breathed. "I'm so sorry."

"Car trouble always hits at the worst possible moment." Royce tried to reassured her.

It didn't work too well. Jasmine spied a slight sheen of tears in her sister's eyes before she dropped her gaze and placed a kiss on Rosie's head. It still amazed her that her littlest sister handled difficult clients with such ease at work. Jasmine still saw her as the child in need of her protection and care. But in this situation, they were going to support each other through whatever challenges they faced.

"Is everybody okay?" Willow rushed up behind them.

Ivy stood as they all talked over each other, trying to share what they knew and offer comfort. Though Jasmine still felt a touch of panic over Auntie's condition, it was better with both of her sisters here. Out of the corner of her eye, she spied Royce standing to the side, watching them. His expression was carefully neutral. With a quick squeeze of her sisters' arms, she walked over to where he stood.

"Thank you so much for bringing me here. I didn't intend to disrupt your day."

A slight frown snuck across his face, but wasn't there long enough for Jasmine to figure out what it meant. Ivy appeared at her elbow with a blinking Rosie. Jasmine smiled at the little girl and got a crooked grin in return. Taking her into her arms, Jasmine hugged her close for a moment. Then she turned her focus back to Royce. She definitely noticed how his gaze had settled directly on her, avoiding Rosie completely.

Without thought, she softly asked, "Why would your mother leave you alone?"

For a brief second, she saw a flash of pain in his expression that was so intense it took Jasmine back to the days and weeks right after her parents had been killed in the car accident. But within the space of a blink, the emotion disappeared. Had she imagined it? When he dropped his gaze to Rosie, it made her wonder.

Then a nurse called from behind him, "King family?"

Recognizing Auntie's last name, she handed Rosie over to Willow and rushed to the edge of the waiting area. But the nurse wasn't very helpful, and Jasmine found herself returning with a clipboard in her hand.

"What did she say?" Willow demanded.

Jasmine shook her head, blinking so tears wouldn't well up in her eyes. "Just that they were waiting to take her to X-ray, and in the meantime they needed this paperwork filled out."

Seven

Royce shifted uncomfortably as he watched Jasmine blink before looking at her sisters. He remembered the many brave faces he'd put on with no one there to take notice except his mother. Turning away from the reminder, he took a seat across from Jasmine's sisters in the waiting room.

Jasmine settled into a chair and started on the paperwork. Her sisters studied him with varying degrees of interest.

"Is there a problem, ladies?" he finally asked.

"Why didn't Jasmine take a cab?" Willow asked.

"It would have taken too long."

"One of us could have picked her up," Willow said.

This felt a little like a what-are-your-intentions interrogation, not that he had any experience with those.

Or with anything in this situation, really. Long-fallow instincts had kicked in when he'd seen Jasmine in need, overriding his usual laser focus on business.

"That would have taken even longer," he said, attempting to soften his clipped tone since they were just trying to look out for their sister. "Besides, my mother wouldn't have appreciated me leaving a lady high and dry."

The two women shared a look, one that should have made him very suspicious. But, like all good businessmen, Royce held his tongue. He knew better than to give them extra ammunition, especially when he wasn't sure what the bullet was actually made of in this instance.

Suddenly both women glanced down. Following their gaze, he took in how Rosie was snuggled up against Ivy. Her eyelids drooped. He could see the softening effect the little cutie had on Ivy and Willow, and even felt an echo deep inside himself. He hadn't dealt with so many emotions since his mother died.

Was it being in this place? The same hospital where they'd spent her last days? Or was it these women? Seeing their interactions, how they cared for each other, he found it fascinating. A little scary, too. Being the focus of their attention wasn't comfortable at all.

Like his mother, they seemed to be able to see past the front he presented to the world to the actual man beneath. He could almost feel the crack in his protective wall. He wasn't very comfortable with that.

Yet he couldn't bring himself to leave.

He reached out one hand to rub it gently against

Rosie's chubby, flushed cheek. "She feels a little feverish."

"She's been teething," Ivy explained. "Which means she's often fussy and not sleeping well, poor thing."

"Poor Mama," Willow added, giving the little girl a loving look. "I don't think Jasmine's had a full night's sleep in days."

Which explained why Rosie was so tired today. But Royce knew absolutely nothing about babies and teething, so he switched subjects. Anything to distract himself from the memories whirling through his mind. "So, what do you ladies do for a living?" he asked, even though Jasmine had already told him the answer.

Willow jumped in easily. "I teach history at the community college."

Royce nodded. "Any specialties?"

"American and local history. When you're descended from a pirate family, you can't help but immerse yourself in Savannah's colorful past."

"I'd imagine." Somehow he wasn't surprised to find Jasmine had some pirate blood in her. She certainly drove a hard bargain to get exactly what she wanted.

Ivy filled the pause. "I'm the executive assistant to Paxton McLemore."

That was interesting. "Intense guy to work for, isn't he?"

"At times, but I love it. Challenging but enjoyable."

Obviously they were a family of very smart women who were very good at standing on their own two feet, making their way in the world after losing their parents. He could relate. Impressive.

But, unlike him, they weren't focused only on making money. He thought over all the charitable causes for which Jasmine had coordinated events. The dossier his assistant had put together had been more than impressive.

As she rose and crossed the room to return the clipboard to a woman behind the desk, he couldn't help but think of all she'd dealt with at home while she'd been pulling off those events. Unlike Royce, she didn't go home, put up her feet and catch up on her rest after a hard day's work.

No, she worked just as hard at home. If not harder. She kept her family together and fed. Took on the role of mother. And apparently offered hands-on help to the charity she'd chosen to support with his event.

Her life had turned out very differently from his.

The women across from him went suddenly silent. Royce followed their gaze to see Jasmine slowly approach from across the room. Before he knew it, her sisters were on their feet.

Royce watched the baby pass from sister to sister with a kind of bewilderment and an incredible calm. Until inevitably the baby was passed to him, and he found himself standing alone in the waiting room with the child snuggled carefully in the crook of his arm. He watched as the girls disappeared around a column and joined their sister.

He glanced down at the baby now in his arms. She was so small. Yet when she was awake and her eyes were open, that small body came alive with personality. Even at her young age.

As Jasmine turned back toward the hall, the child gave a shuddering breath, evoking sympathy for how miserable she must be at the moment. She probably wished she was home in her own bed instead of being carried around a noisy hospital waiting room.

Though he knew she couldn't have heard it from where she stood, Jasmine froze. Then she whipped her head around to survey her sisters. "Where's Rosie?"

As if passing the buck, both women pointed in his direction. Jasmine's eyes went wide with shock. But as she glanced down to see Rosie still sleeping, the tears that she'd held back earlier finally overflowed.

As the women before him sniffled and hugged each other, Royce moved closer to stand outside their circle with the baby nestled in his arms. For a brief moment, something akin to panic welled up in Royce's chest. A feeling he hadn't experienced since he'd first realized he was completely alone in the world. As if these people he barely knew had abandoned him.

Crazy.

A noise caught his attention. He glanced down, meeting wide dark eyes. The one difference between Rosie and Jasmine. The baby's eyes were dark and oddly wise. But beautiful. Compelling. Royce found himself as mesmerized as he'd been by his first glimpse of her mother's bright blue eyes.

Suddenly he realized that he was bouncing the baby

slightly. It was a rhythm entirely seated in his bones, natural but unfamiliar. And he couldn't stop.

"King?" a nurse called from across the room. "The King family?" He looked up.

The women before him seemed completely oblivious. Stepping closer, he adopted a firm, no-nonsense tone. "Ladies, let's go see what the nurse has to say."

Immediately their tears stopped and they started across the room. "Purses," he reminded them.

They paused to rapidly scoop up all their stuff, then he ushered them across the carpeted floor to the staff member. She smiled, as if she were completely used to such a delay. He'd watched enough waiting room drama when his mother was sick to know she probably was.

Jasmine shifted impatiently as the nurse waited for all the sisters to gather around her. Then she said, "I wanted to assure you it's just a sprain…" She glanced around, meeting everyone's gaze. "It's a bad one, though. The doctor can explain more, if one of you would like to come back and speak with him."

"You, Jasmine," Willow said. "You'll remember more of the details than I will."

The nurse nodded, but Royce stepped forward. He kept his voice low, but firm. "Is there any possibility we could all go back with you? I realize the rooms are small, but the little one isn't going to do well without her mother."

The nurse took one look at Rosie and Royce could see her refusal melt on her tongue. "Poor baby. Is it a fever?"

"Just a low-grade one," Jasmine rushed in to answer. "From teething. She isn't sick."

"Oh, but that makes babies miserable, doesn't it?" The nurse cooed at Rosie for a few moments, gaining a gummy grin; Royce spotted just a hint of a tooth breaking the front skin. "Of course you need to be with your mama." Some semblance of a stern look returned to the nurse's face, but it lacked conviction. "But if it gets full in there, you'll have to wait across the hall."

"Not a problem," Royce said, eager to go now that he'd gotten his way.

The last thing he wanted was to split up the three women or find himself alone with the baby in his arms, which seemed to be drawing out all kinds of emotions he didn't want to handle.

Rosie was really good while they met with the doctor and received his instructions. After all of his experiences with his own mother, Royce knew that physical therapy wouldn't be easy for Auntie, but would be worth it for her to get fully back on her feet at her advanced age.

The half-jiggling, half-bouncing motion Royce's body had adopted worked wonders, but before long a little whimper erupted. A streak of panic burned through Royce, but he refused to let it show.

It almost slipped through when he found the women watching him. Royce had an uncomfortable feeling they were finally evaluating his child-holding skills and finding him lacking.

"What?" he asked in a soft tone.

"Aren't you the guy Jasmine said didn't care about

anything but business?" Ivy's blue eyes dropped to the baby in his arms.

He wasn't offended. "I'd say that would be an accurate description." Did he owe them an explanation? Did he even have one for why he was here right this moment?

As they stood around the tiny cubicle where Auntie lay in the hospital bed, Willow dug into the diaper bag she held. "Here," she said, holding out a ring-shaped toy. "Let's try this. Want me to take her?"

Royce took the toy but shook his head. "Actually, I want you to go get your car and pull it around to the entrance."

Willow glanced around. "But they haven't discharged Auntie yet."

"I'll help your sisters take care of that," Royce assured her. "You just bring the car around."

Willow nodded uncertainly, then kissed Auntie and went for the car.

Jasmine watched her go. "Why is she getting the car so early?"

"Because we're leaving," Royce assured her. "I want you to get Auntie dressed."

When she opened her mouth to question him, Royce simply shook his head. "Just do it."

Turning away, he went to find the nurse at her station. She watched him struggle with the now squirming baby; her teething ring was no longer keeping her occupied. "I know you have a lot going on around here," he said, "but we need to get this one home before we have a full-blown scene."

His only knowledge of babies was of them crying in restaurants and stores. He had no idea what would set Rosie off, but he'd use her to their advantage in getting Auntie released sooner.

The nurse cooed at Rosie, nodding her head. So at least he was right in one sense.

"I have my hands full with the ladies…all the ladies," he said with a smile. "Could you possibly help us out and get Ms. King released before things go downhill?"

Seeing the nurse snap into action, Royce had to wonder how much more he could accomplish in life if he had a baby as his wingman.

Less than twenty minutes later they were headed for the car. It was unprecedented in Royce's experience with hospitals, but he wasn't going to look a gift horse in the mouth. Willow was right up front, waiting for them.

The nurse who had wheeled Ms. King out got her settled into the front passenger seat with minimal effort while Jasmine supervised. Then Jasmine turned to look at him. She shook her head. "I can't believe you managed that." A gorgeous touch of pink lit up her pale cheeks. "And managed Rosie. That was incredible."

"Only to be thwarted by something as simple as a child's car seat," he replied as he nodded toward the contraption in the back seat.

Jasmine's eyes widened and she smiled. "Right. These things look way more complicated than they are. After all you've done, though, I think we'll overlook your shortcomings on that score," she said, taking the baby from him.

There was the sassy woman he'd come to know.

In two minutes, she had Rosie deftly strapped in and content with her pacifier. Closing the door, Jasmine again gifted him with a smile. Maybe he was tired after the morning drama. Maybe he was still feeling the effects from holding the tiny, innocent child in his arms. Whatever it was, this smile snuck through his usual defenses and hit his heart with unerring accuracy.

"I still don't know how you managed it," Jasmine said. "I was so focused on Auntie and my sisters and taking care of them. But we are very, very grateful."

And that's when he stupidly ran off at the mouth before thinking. "I'm glad to know all of my experience came in handy. My mother had a very long stay at this hospital before she died here."

Eight

Jasmine sucked in a deep breath as she saw Royce slip through the coffee shop door. Her stomach churned, forcing her to leave her café au lait untouched. She had no idea how to act after their last encounter.

No idea how to return to business as usual.

The week he had been out of town since Auntie's fall should have helped give her some perspective. Frankly, it hadn't. Because her thoughts of Royce had turned very personal and she had no idea how to combat that. Except to only talk about business.

She could do that, right?

But his smile as he sat down wasn't business as usual. It sped her heart up a little…okay, more than a little. This wasn't right.

She glared at the green ring sparkling in the sunlight for a moment.

"Everything okay?" Royce asked as he sat down with his coffee.

"Sure," Jasmine said, consciously forcing herself to relax. "I appreciate you coming."

Reaching down, she pulled several small poster boards from her bag. "I've put together some visuals for you to see what the decorator is suggesting."

"I'm amazed you're only letting me view pictures, rather than insisting I attend an actual meeting with her."

Jasmine froze for a moment. Was he complaining because she'd excluded him? "Well, with you out of town, then her going out of town, I just thought this might be easier."

To her shock, his hand lightly covered one of hers. "It's okay, Jasmine. I'm just teasing you."

"Teasing me?" She almost swallowed her tongue, because teasing had never been on Royce's agenda.

"Yes," he said, drawing the word out. "After all, you've stuck to your stipulation that I attend every planning meeting pretty hard. I can't believe you're letting me slide on this one…"

Feeling like she'd stepped into an alternate reality, one that tempted her with the idea that Royce might actually be human after all, she grinned. "Well, everyone should get time off for good behavior."

His laugh rang out, startling her. The sound was oh, so sexy. Over his shoulder, she saw several patrons glance their way, most grinning in response to his amusement. Only one didn't seem amused, a rather dour, expensively dressed man at a choice table by the window overlooking the river.

Jasmine would rather focus on the man opening up right in front of her.

She pointed out the various options depicted in the photographs. The dark purple-and-black color scheme was her favorite, with highlights of white and bright red. The elaborate table schemes included taper candles and crystals to mimic the chandeliers. Lots of rich fabric and sparkling highlights.

Event planning was her passion, so she could have gone on forever, but noticed the minute Royce's gaze started to glaze over. "Okay," she conceded, "I think I've tortured you enough."

"Honestly, give me the details of a ship's engine any day as opposed to decorating details. I only agreed to meet in the coffee shop so I'd have this to keep me awake." He lifted his coffee a few inches off the table. But it was the sheepish grin that got to her.

She'd never imagined seeing that expression on this driven businessman's face. Unfortunately, she liked it. Too much.

"So how are Ms. King and Rosie?"

"Oh, she'd just want you to call her Auntie."

He nodded, his expression remaining open in a way she wasn't quite used to or comfortable with.

"Physical therapy is going well, although she hates it."

Royce shrugged. "Who wouldn't? It's torture."

"Even more so for her, because she thinks it's a

burden to everyone that we're juggling her appointments with our jobs and Rosie's care. As if that matters to any of us girls."

"My mother was like that," Royce said, staring down into his cup. "She didn't ever want to tell me when she had a doctor's appointment or treatment—she felt it took me away from more important things."

When he looked up, his eyes were serious in the same way she'd seen at the hospital. "But she got over it after the one time she took a cab to the hospital for a chemo treatment. After that, she knew in no uncertain terms I would be there for every appointment, no matter what I had going on."

That had to have been a huge concession for such a driven man.

This led her to say what had been on her mind for over a week. "I really do appreciate all you did for us, for me, at the hospital. Especially knowing that there had to be a lot of bad memories associated with that place."

"It was nothing—"

"Don't."

When he finally looked at her, she reached out and cupped his hand where it lay on the table. "It wasn't nothing. No man in that frame of mind should have to hold a teething six-month-old for that long—it was a tremendous help to us. I won't let you dismiss that."

He glanced down at her hand over his. It wasn't until several moments later—moments of anticipation that caused Jasmine to shake inside—that he spoke.

"My mother, no matter how sick she was, always

had a kind word for everyone she came across at that hospital. She would help in any way she could, sometimes even pushing herself past what she was capable of to help her fellow patients."

"And you were there to help her?"

"As much as possible." Still he wouldn't look up at her.

She couldn't resist pushing a little farther. "But I don't understand. You say she took care of you, you took care of her, but also that she abandoned you. What happened?"

"It wasn't because she didn't want me…" His husky voice trailed off. Beneath her palm, she felt his hand curl into a fist. Then she noticed the shadow across their table.

Glancing up, she found the stern man from the far table standing over them. He didn't look her way or acknowledge her. His gaze was trained tightly on Royce as he said in a gruff voice, "Getting involved with your employees never leads to anything good."

Then he turned and walked away.

"That was my father. Guess he didn't want to stick around and be introduced."

The bitterness in his own voice made Royce cringe.

Jasmine glanced over her shoulder to watch the man disappear out the door. "I'm confused," she murmured.

Join the club.

"He looked familiar," she said with a faraway tone in her voice.

Though he never talked about him, just this once

Royce was happy to provide the basics. "He should. His name is John Nave."

He could see the light of recognition dawning in her sexy blue eyes. "That's right. *The* John Nave, from one of the oldest families in Savannah, and one of the richest."

"But I don't understand…" Jasmine said, her brow wrinkling in confusion. "He's your father?"

"My mother was his housekeeper." Royce hated saying it that way, because it sounded like he was defining his mother by her profession when she'd been so much more.

To her credit, Jasmine's expression didn't change. If anything, it turned a little stiff. "I'll be honest, I'm appalled he would say something like that to you, considering…"

She didn't know the half of it. "That's mild, for him. When he bothers to acknowledge me at all, he's usually pretty nasty."

"But isn't he married?"

"To one of the coldest women in the world," he murmured. "But that was a while after my mother had broken contact with him."

"How did your mother manage?" Jasmine whispered, her voice full of empathy.

"When she didn't get rid of me like he wanted, it took her a long time to find more work. But when she did, she worked her fingers to the bone, because the bastard made sure she couldn't get a judge in the county to award her child support."

Jasmine closed her eyes tightly, shaking her head.

When she opened them, he noticed the glossy sheen of tears.

Were they for him? No one but his mother had ever shed a tear over the way he'd been treated.

"I'd like to say it surprises me," Jasmine said, "but I've seen it often enough at the mission. Dads who simply couldn't care less about a child out in the world with their DNA. Men who would have preferred for them to die than take on any obligation in their own lives."

Oh, how well he knew that type.

She leaned back, studying him. He wasn't sure when she'd stopped touching his hand, but he felt the loss of contact keenly. "I'm not really upset about me," he said, waving the thought away as if it were a particle of dust in the air. "It's more about my mom. What she was left to deal with."

"That's why she left you, isn't it?"

He glanced over her shoulder instead of looking into her eyes and seeing the knowledge there. He nodded. "She had to work a lot to keep us afloat."

"And you made it up to her."

Royce sat a little straighter. "I did. She loved that house. She used to work there when she first started." He could remember long stories she would tell about the few parties she'd helped serve at, then caring for the house until it was closed. "I wanted her to be in a place she loved, so I bought it for her."

Jasmine covered his hand with hers once more. "That's wonderful, Royce."

"It's what she deserved after all of her sacrifices

for me. By damn, I was going to give it to her." He let a little smile slip out. "She was happy."

"She never fell in love again?" Jasmine asked. "Never wanted to have more children?"

"When would she have had the time? Nope. She loved me, but she wanted no more children to complicate her life. And I'll never have children, either."

Jasmine didn't draw up in shocked outrage the way he might have expected. She simply asked, "Why not?"

"I've made my choice. Business is a demanding mistress. I refuse to do both."

She pressed her lips together for a moment before letting herself speak. "It's a shame. You were good with Rosie."

"Raising a child is a lot different than holding one for thirty minutes."

She smiled, though there was a hint of sadness around the edges. "I'm learning that all too well. My mother died, too, when I was fifteen."

He'd gotten that impression but never asked the details.

"Both of my parents, actually. They were killed in an automobile accident." She absently ran her finger around the edge of her cup. "We came to live with Auntie. She took all three of us in when we had no other place to go. No other relatives. Not even distant ones."

"That's a big responsibility."

"Auntie said something to me then. Something I've never forgotten, even though I didn't fully embrace it at the time."

"What's that?"

"That children aren't everyone's cup of tea."

It made sense, especially to Royce.

Jasmine wasn't done, though. That sad smile returned as she added, "But some people should learn to be tea drinkers."

Nine

"I really don't see why we need to do this," Royce said as Jasmine approached over the cracked and broken sidewalk. "It's not necessary."

And here she thought she'd loosened him up a little. Especially after the surprisingly personal meeting at the coffee shop a few days ago. Of course, the way he'd conceded the design choices with a curt "You know better than I" should have reminded her he didn't want a say in everything.

"It's not necessary to educate yourself about the charity you are promoting with your big-ticket event?"

"I told you the charity was your choice."

She could just get right to the point, but why not enjoy teasing him for a minute? "What's the big deal?

So you spend a few hours down here on a Saturday. What else are you gonna do? Work?"

They shared a look, his blue eyes narrowing as if he was contemplating retribution for her sarcasm.

"Just consider this part of your job," she said. "Trust me, I've been to dozens of these charity events. You're gonna get asked lots of questions about City Sanctuary mission. Do you want to appear ignorant?"

"I could refer them to you."

"And still appear ignorant. Especially to the Jeffersons."

He grimaced, probably because he knew she was right. "It should be enough that I'm donating money."

"Don't sulk, Scrooge. You just might enjoy yourself."

His eyes widened just a notch at her tone, but she ignored it and headed for the entrance. The parking area was hidden from view of the building by a tall retaining wall that supported the elevated ground the original church had been built upon. Excitement filled her as they made their way to the break in the wall for the stairs leading to the lawn. There she caught the first glimpse of the ancient stone chapel. Though the additions made to the compound over the years didn't entirely match the architecture of the original building, which had stood since just a few decades after Savannah was founded, they didn't detract from the atmosphere, either.

Jasmine followed the gravel path with ease, having developed a familiarity with the place after years of volunteering here. She greeted the regulars as they passed.

She'd always felt safe here. The mission's destitute clients had never scared her. She'd experienced more fear among Savannah's elite, to be honest.

Everyone she greeted along the way to the entrance followed the same pattern: a smile and hello for her, then a quick suspicious glance at the man behind her. Strangers to the mission were often regarded that way, at first, but this was probably enhanced because she'd never been here with a man. Usually she was alone; only occasionally did she visit with her sisters.

They entered through the main registration lobby, where Jasmine paused. "This is the area where most public traffic comes in," she said. "Overnight guests are assigned their spaces, and those who need other services are directed to the areas or personnel they need."

She waved to the couple who usually handled the front lobby on Saturdays, then led Royce to the first large hallway. "The building was originally a church, and has been added to over the years. This makes it a little confusing for newcomers." She gestured to the left. "There are offices down here. A couple of class-rooms where we hold seminars or tutoring. And there's a closet at the far end where we store used clothing to hand out."

After giving him a minute to process, she turned right. "The main dining area is at the back. I'll take you there in a little while. It was the most recent area to be updated, because part of it collapsed during the last hurricane that came through. A tree fell on it, so we had to do some structural repairs."

They stepped through a set of double doors into a gymnasium with a scuffed but decent floor. Royce, who had been silent the whole time, took in the group of children playing basketball. "This looks nice."

"It is—we use it for some after-school programs and there's actually a men's basketball group that meets here. Anyone in the building is allowed to participate." She nodded toward the far corner. "But here's the problem. This room has to serve double duty."

"Are those beds?"

"Foldaway cots. We have a women's dorm in the back, which has a leaking roof. The old chapel serves to shelter small family units when necessary. This is the men's dorm. So every night we have to pull the beds out onto the floor and every morning they are stripped and put away."

"That's a lot of work," he murmured.

"It is." She took a deep breath, almost afraid to share her hopes for the fund-raising event. "The neighbors here were an elderly couple and they gifted their land to the mission upon their deaths. But there aren't any funds to build on it." She met his solemn gaze. "A fully functioning building with single-purpose sleeping quarters would make a big difference in this part of Savannah."

"Miss Harden! Watch this!"

Jasmine glanced over as one of her little tag-alongs, Oliver, jumped toward the basketball net. At five, he wasn't tall enough to make headway, but he had enough enthusiasm to make his jump impressive. "Great job!" she yelled back.

He dribbled the ball over to them, showing off his skills. "Look what I learned to do." He grabbed the ball up and rolled it across his outstretched arms and along the back of his neck.

Jasmine laughed. "Well, that's pretty cool. But how is it gonna help you play basketball?"

"Mr. Mike said it will help me learn dex—um, dexter—"

"Dexterity?" Royce offered.

"That was it."

"I see," Jasmine said. "You are well on your way to being a professional ball player, in my opinion."

The little boy stopped moving and gave her a cheeky grin. "Didn't you say you don't know anything about basketball?"

She brushed her knuckles against his cheek. "That's true. But I know determination when I see it, and you have tons of that, my sweet."

He giggled, then dribbled the ball back toward the court. She smiled after him. "He's such a cutie. His mama named him Oliver after a cocky, sneaky cat in a cartoon. I have a feeling he's gonna live up to the name."

Instead of a chuckle, Royce said, "My mother named me after my father's car."

She swiveled to face him. "What?"

"My father's Rolls Royce. He told her the only thing he'd ever loved was his car. Guess it was some kind of dig to remind him that a kid deserved love, too. Didn't work so well."

"Or maybe it was to remind her that she got the better end of that deal."

"What do you mean?"

"Cars don't give an awful lot of love in return, Royce."

As they turned back toward the main building, Jasmine spouted facts about the various aspects of the homeless mission's programs. Royce wasn't tracking. Her words from the gym kept ringing in his ears. He couldn't help but wonder—were they true?

"Jasmine, *ma fleur*. So wonderful to see you."

Royce forced himself to tune in as they were approached by a man in khaki pants and a polo shirt. Jasmine introduced him as Francis Staten, the director of the mission.

"So wonderful to meet you," Francis said with a firm handshake that matched his calm, competent expression. "We are so grateful for what you are doing for us."

Royce was having none of that. "You know I can't take the credit. Jasmine is the one who brought the need to my attention."

Francis smiled. "And *you* must know that with her running your event, it will be very successful."

"That's my sincere belief, also," Royce agreed.

Francis gave an appreciative chuckle. "Before she combusts from that blush, shall I show you around?"

Jasmine smiled in a sheepish way. "Well, we've already looked over the gym, front offices and lobby."

"Excitement got the better of you, huh?" Francis asked as they headed farther down the hallway toward the back of the building. "I've never had a more enthusiastic volunteer than Jasmine here. She was such a sad girl when she first came to us, and she has become the mission's biggest asset."

"All of our volunteers are," Jasmine insisted.

That blush sure was cute.

As they crossed through a large double doorway into a spacious banquet room, Francis explained, "This is our main dining area, with industrial kitchens on the other side of those serving tables. The kitchens were refurbished by a major pledge drive. We serve hundreds of meals per day. The kitchen updates made it so much easier to keep the food fresh, hot and plentiful."

The long room was broken up by rows of tables and chairs. Only about a third of them were occupied at this time on a Saturday. "We'll start serving lunch soon," Francis said.

A lady sitting at the first table with a group of her friends called out to Jasmine and waved. With a smile, Jasmine excused herself to go over to them. Royce and Francis watched as she hugged each woman in the small group.

"She's incredible," Francis said. "A young woman who lives her beliefs, rather than simply talking about them."

He glanced over at Royce, lowering his voice a touch. "Have you met Rosie?"

Royce nodded. His stomach flipped as he imagined Rosie in this environment. Her birth mother had been a frequent guest here, so Rosie would have grown up with no stable, secure home base. "She's a beautiful little girl," he murmured. "It's hard to tell she was adopted."

"Indeed," Francis agreed. "Jasmine had known Rosie's mother for several years. One thing you learn very quickly here—you can't force your own beliefs or preferences on those who aren't as fortunate. You can only offer them whatever you have. Some are on the streets because life has given them no other choices. Some are there because it is safer or more comfortable for them than the places they left behind."

"Was she very young?" Royce asked.

"Twenty-six when she died."

Royce couldn't bring himself to ask the obvious question.

"She confided in Jasmine one night. She wanted so badly to have the child, but knew her health wasn't all it should be. It took her a lot of courage to go to the doctor. By then, the cancer was too far advanced for treatment, even if they could have done anything while she was pregnant. When Jasmine offered to take her in, she agreed with great reluctance. She'd been on the streets so long, but she knew she had to overcome her fears for her baby to live."

"So she lived with Jasmine's family before the birth?"

"And after," Francis confirmed. "Her health declined rapidly. But she was smart enough to make sure

Rosie wouldn't end up on the streets. They'd barely finished the adoption process before she died."

Jasmine glanced their way. Her smile here had a different, softer quality. Instead of the take-charge woman he'd butted heads with, in this environment, her leadership abilities seemed to be subdued under a layer of compassion.

Francis cleared his throat, reengaging Royce's attention. "All that to say, Jasmine has volunteered here for years, but she's also changed her entire life to take care of someone in need. There's no doubt she loves Rosie. Her entire family loves her. But it was, and is, a huge sacrifice in one so young."

"Why are you telling me this?" Royce asked. After all, this was technically a business meeting.

Francis studied him for a long moment, a slight smile on his face. "Call it intuition or the prompting of the Spirit, but something tells me you need to know. Even if Jasmine is just your event planner."

Why did that last statement sound more like a question to Royce? And why was he trying to fool himself into thinking he wasn't interested?

"What about the children here?" Royce asked, eager to change the subject. He thought back to the boys in the gym. He hadn't failed to notice the worn lettering on their clothes and thinness of the soles on their shoes—and remembered the years that his own clothes had looked the same. "Is there anything special they need?"

"Right now, just the usual things that they always need. We have families who fund scholarships for some of our regulars in the after-school programs for disadvantaged families. Those scholarships and donors are coordinated by the Jefferson family from Savannah."

The Jeffersons. Instead of filing that detail away to use to his own advantage, Royce felt gratitude wash over him. They were doing so much for these kids. How much of a difference would it have made to him, to his mother, if he'd had the opportunity to participate in an after-school program like they offered here?

"We do have some other special programs we would love funding for, but I don't want to appear greedy."

Royce waved away his words. "It's not greedy when I asked. I'll have my assistant contact you for more information, okay?"

Francis nodded. "Thank you again."

"It's my pleasure." And Royce had a feeling he was going to have to admit to Jasmine that he'd changed his point of view. He wanted to be more involved in this charity event now. That had probably been her whole point in bringing him here: educating him for far more than just being able to talk knowledgably about his event's charity.

She'd done a thorough job of it, too.

Sure enough, they'd barely made it to the sidewalk in front of the cars when she paused and said, "Not as bad as you thought, was it?"

He turned to face her where she leaned against the moss-covered retaining wall. "You enjoy being right, don't you."

"Only with you." She grinned, her sassy joy drawing him out of his shell and into the sheer life she exuded. He found he was beginning to like her energy and enthusiasm—very much.

He shook his head, knowing he was going crazy. But for once, he didn't care about losing control. "You're incredible, you know?"

"Not really."

Royce leaned in close, propping one hand against the wall next to her glossy black hair. He swallowed hard against the emotions welling up despite himself. "To prove to my father that my life was worth something, I pursued wealth that would far surpass his."

For the first time, he let himself reach over and touch her thick hair. "To prove that life was still worth living after your parents died, you dedicated yourself to your family and taking care of others."

He stepped closer, bringing their bodies together even though he knew he shouldn't. "In the eyes of most people, that's incredible. Especially me."

Then Royce let his logical brain take a hike and brought his lips down on hers. Her taste was just as exotic as her name. Royce's craving shifted into overdrive.

If he'd thought it would just be a quick peck, he was mistaken. Instead, his body pressed closer. His mouth opened over hers. Her lips left a slightly sweet taste on his tongue, but it was the heat inside that he sought.

The catch of her breath sent a streak of sensation through him. He wanted to explore all the ways he could make her react. All the hidden places on her body that would make her gasp and moan. But for now, he focused on the heat of her mouth and the sexiness of her response.

After long, exquisite moments, Royce forced himself to pull back. To regain control. To think about Jasmine instead of his own sorry self.

Which meant he couldn't bring himself to look into those gorgeous blue eyes to see exactly how he'd ruined everything.

Ten

How in the world was she supposed to act after that kiss?

As Jasmine waited for Royce outside the nondescript building that housed one of the hottest restaurants in Savannah, she tried to shut her brain down. But the question wouldn't go away.

Not even in the face of her curiosity about the restaurant. She'd never been to After Hours before today. Word in elite circles was that it was incredible, but Jasmine had never been able to afford to eat here. And, to her knowledge, they didn't cater events, so she'd let it slide off her radar.

But Royce had insisted he knew exactly what he wanted done with the food for the charity event, and

After Hours was it. Since she didn't have to pry or coax the opinion from him, she'd let him lead.

"Are you ready?"

Jasmine jumped. Tightening her control, she forced herself to take a deep breath before turning toward Royce. "I'm not sure," she admitted.

Instead of leering, Royce faced her with a benign grin. He could have approached the situation any number of ways, considering how she'd sprinted for her car after he'd kissed her on Saturday, but he didn't appear to be messing with her.

Though there was something suspicious…

"What's so funny?" she demanded, hiding her embarrassment behind a sassy attitude.

"You," he admitted. "Seeing you off kilter is honestly a little fun."

She studied him a little closer, but still didn't see any signs of sexual innuendo. That was a relief, but she still had the urge to call him a brat. Even if Auntie would say it was unladylike.

Instead she let him lead her inside with a light grip on her elbow. Being on his territory was fun, but not nearly as comfortable as being the one in control. His confident stride and barely there grin said he definitely knew it.

The closed restaurant was dark, though sunshine tried to peek in around the drawn blinds. The hushed emptiness was disconcerting, though as much as she hated to admit it, the darkness evoked a sense of intimacy.

This meeting didn't have the same strictly business feel that their previous ones had started out with, even if they all ended up being out of the ordinary. Especially the last one—that kiss had changed everything for her.

Though she'd never admit it, even under threat of torture.

One of the tall silver doors at the back of the room swung open, revealing a tall, lanky guy in a white chef's coat. "Royce!"

"Marco." Royce stepped forward to shake the other man's hand with more enthusiasm than Jasmine had seen from him before. "Good to see you, buddy."

"I wouldn't miss this for the world."

"Marco, this is my event planner, Jasmine Harden."

The chef turned his smile in her direction. "Welcome to After Hours."

"Thank you for having us," she murmured, leaving out how she'd always wanted to see the inside of this place. Now didn't seem the time to fawn over something that was so far outside her middle-class budget. Instead, she tried to keep her demeanor as professional as possible.

"Why don't y'all come back into the kitchen first?" Marco asked.

Jasmine followed him, her heeled boots clicking against the Italian tile floor.

"Royce mentioned that you were unfamiliar with our restaurant," Marco said over his shoulder. "We serve fresh, local, organic food whenever possible. The focus here is a modern Mediterranean cuisine, though we can add some Latin influence, since I know Royce likes things spicy."

"Royce Brazier?" Jasmine asked, thinking of the by-the-book businessman she constantly butted heads with. "Are you sure?"

Marco simply laughed, even though Jasmine was only half teasing. And she was pretty sure she could make out the hint of a blush stealing over Royce's fair cheeks, despite the darkness.

Not wanting to embarrass him further, or draw out any discussion over how "spicy" he might like things, Jasmine said, "I wasn't aware After Hours catered." They'd never been on her list before today.

Marco grinned. "That's because we don't."

Jasmine looked between the two men. "I'm not sure I understand."

"We don't actually cater here, but I told Royce I would help him out for this event."

Jasmine was already shaking her head. "That's not a good idea." The last thing she wanted was an inexperienced staff working her star event.

"Don't worry," Royce said. "Marco did plenty of catering during school and early in his career."

"And I'm strictly a food man these days. So I've already partnered with Geraldine's to handle the catering service and staffing. You've heard of her?" Marco asked.

"Yes. I've worked with her on several occasions." Knowing that the logistics were taken care of helped calm Jasmine's panic.

Royce nodded as if that settled everything. "Well," he said, "let's show Jasmine what we had in mind."

Jasmine glanced over at him in surprise. That conspiratorial look was back again. For good reason.

When it came to food, Royce showed that he had a few surprises up his sleeve over the next half an hour. Instead of sitting back and only asking a few questions, as he had throughout most of their other meetings, the catering discussion brought out a passion in Royce she'd never seen before...or rather, only seen once before.

She'd more than seen it when he'd pressed his lips against hers.

She watched in unabashed awe as they tossed around menu ideas involving lobster, truffles and exotic spices. Royce certainly knew gourmet food. Jasmine had very little to add except for a few tips and tricks she'd learned throughout all the events she'd executed over the last five years.

Before long, Marco was shooing them to a table in the main room so he could assemble some sample plates for them. Jasmine grinned at Royce as they were seated. "He doesn't have to do this. I have a feeling anything that comes out of that kitchen is gonna be incredible."

Royce shook his head. "I never turn down the chance to taste anything Marco wants to make for me."

"You seem to know each other well."

"Since we were kids. We grew up not far from each other."

Jasmine wasn't sure if she wanted to broach the

subject of his childhood. To change the conversation from business to personal. Instead, she glanced around the elegantly stark room now that the lights had been turned up some.

"Is he the one who taught you so much about food?"

Royce only hesitated a moment before he said, "I learned to cook really young, because my mom was gone at all hours."

So much for avoiding the personal.

"She would also bring home leftovers from different events where she served. That's how I developed a taste for food that was far out of our budget."

"I can sympathize." Jasmine rarely sampled anything that could be labeled *cuisine*, except at her events. They were more of a down home food family.

Royce grinned. "I'll have to cook for you sometime."

Seriously? The guy could cook?

He must have read the thoughts on her face. "Let me guess. You thought I was only the order-in type."

"Instead of?"

"The mess-up-the-dishes-and-have-to-run-the-dishwasher type." He relaxed back into his chair. "I spend all day out. Believe it or not, cooking is very relaxing."

"Well… I wouldn't know," she admitted.

This time he was the one to look shocked. "You don't cook? I thought every good Southern girl cooked."

"I prefer to eat the fruits of someone else's labors, in this instance."

"Then this is perfect for you," Marco said as he approached across the room.

He deftly placed a couple of long, hand-glazed platters on the table, each filled with gorgeous little colorful morsels that smelled as good as they looked.

"Oh, my."

Royce glanced up at his friend. "I think she's sold without a single bite."

"Just wait until she tastes it," Marco said with a grin, then strode back toward the kitchen.

Jasmine surveyed the bounty. "I don't know what to try first."

"There's an art to it."

She raised a brow at him. This was the first time the tables had been turned—a nonbusiness situation where Royce gave *her* advice.

"Trust me?"

He waited for her nod before lifting a tiny lettuce leaf cradling what appeared to be a meat and vegetable mixture off one of the trays. "Start here."

Before she could lift a hand to take it from him, he'd brought the bite to her lips. Jasmine felt her smile disappear as she blinked. She could do this. She would remain professional.

Even though this felt far from professional.

She let her lips open. Just as she took the food into her mouth she glanced up and met the delicious heat of his stare. Their proximity reminded her of his kiss, his lips over hers. Talk about delicious.

Sudden flavor burst over her tongue. Cool, crisp lettuce. Spicy meat with an undertone of shrimp. A sweet drizzle that she couldn't quite identify. As she moaned, she could see a reflection of her own experience in his eyes. His grin said he knew exactly what she was tasting. He picked up a matching hors d'oeuvre and slid it between his lips.

"Just the right amount of sweet to balance the spice," he said after he swallowed. Lifting a wineglass from the tray, he washed the morsel down.

Jasmine did the same. Her inspection of the trays revealed several options for her next bite, but Royce knew exactly what he wanted her to have. Taste after taste, he walked her through the platters. Spicy butter glazed lobster skewers, meatballs spiced up with chorizo, jerk chicken mini-pizzas…her taste buds were in heaven.

"You were right," she admitted about halfway through.

Royce gave her the most suggestive look she'd ever seen on his face. "About what?"

"The food."

He feigned shock. "I did something right?"

"This time you did, smart aleck. This food will be the talk of the town for months after the event."

"Marco will be thrilled to hear it."

"But you won't."

He shrugged, sobering a little. "I really couldn't care one way or another. But if I can help him even a little with this, then I'll count it as a plus."

"That's a great thing to do."

He shrugged again, then searched the platter with renewed enthusiasm and chose another morsel. Jasmine thought she heard the buzz of a phone but couldn't bring herself to care as she helped herself to a hyped-up version of teriyaki steak that ravished her taste buds.

A good fifteen minutes later, Jasmine heard the phone buzzing again. This time it was accompanied by Royce's grimace. He pulled his cell phone from his pocket and read the texts. "It's Matthew."

For the first time, Jasmine wished that he would ignore his phone. For the first time, her reasons were personal.

The telltale buzz filled the space between them. Matthew wasn't giving up. "I have to go," Royce said.

For the first time, the regret in Royce's voice matched Jasmine's feelings.

"Too bad," she said, not caring that her voice had gone husky. "I was having fun."

His gaze met hers, bringing a return of the electric atmosphere from earlier. "Me, too."

"Isn't your business ever fun?" Deep down, she knew she was past the point of being strictly professional.

"I'm good at it," he finally answered. "But no. Business has never been fun…until now."

"So the ring is working!"

"No," Jasmine insisted, frowning at her youngest sister. "That is not what I said at all."

"Close enough."

Why had she even broached this topic? Jasmine should have known better. Her sisters—both of them—

had a tendency to take a notion and run with it. Auntie presided over the scene from her recliner in the corner of the breakfast nook. The mischievous look on her face meant there would be no help coming from that direction.

"I don't know why I tell y'all anything," Jasmine complained. "It's just—" But the word *business* wouldn't move past the constriction in her throat. She crossed the kitchen to stir the big pot of soup on the stove. Willow had chosen the perfect dinner for a rainy Saturday.

Though the chatter continued behind her, Willow appeared at her side. "Are you okay?"

While confident and decisive, Willow was also very sensitive to others. No one was more willing to lend a helping hand when she saw someone who needed it.

Jasmine lowered her voice. "I just can't forget how he talked about learning to cook because his mother was never home. And about being named after his father's car."

She absently stirred the soup, watching chunks of veggies appear and disappear beneath the liquid surface. The lack of sunlight in the room left the green jewel in her ring lackluster; Jasmine still had the feeling the jewelry was mocking her.

"I don't know what this is, but Ivy's right—it's not just business anymore."

Ring or no ring.

Willow gave a tiny squeal that she quickly silenced under Jasmine's glare.

"What about him? What does he think?" Willow asked, echoing Jasmine's own questions.

She didn't want to admit that Mr. Business was turning out to be someone completely unexpected. Jasmine could never have guessed that the stern CEO she'd met in his office that first day would be able to melt her with such a hot kiss. But hadn't that tattoo on his neck hinted at hidden depths? A tattoo she had yet to see in its entirety, now that she thought about it.

"From your silence, I gather Royce is showing signs of moving in a different direction, too," Willow filled in for her.

"Surprisingly," Jasmine mused. "I think so."

"So why not just go with it?"

Jasmine gave the soup a final stir, then peeked into the oven at the cornbread sizzling in a cast-iron skillet. It was a simple delaying tactic, since they all knew cooking wasn't in her skill set.

"It's not that easy." She glanced over her shoulder to check on Rosie, who was cooing at Auntie and Ivy from her bouncy seat. "Even leaving aside the fact that he's my boss...of sorts. How can I get involved? Royce definitely isn't the family type. I have Rosie..."

"She's six months old," Ivy said from right behind them.

Jasmine jumped. "How'd you move that quick?"

Ivy had a baby face, but her grin made her look even younger. "I have my ways." She shook her head, making her blond curls dance. "And I wasn't about to miss what all the whispering was about, now, was I?"

She linked her arm with Jasmine's and adopted the expression of a captive audience. "Now's the perfect time for you to live a little. Rosie isn't old enough to notice at this age. Later, you'll need to be more careful because she'll realize when Mommy is gone or bringing someone to visit."

"I don't know." Everything about this change in their attitudes toward each other had Jasmine off kilter. She and Royce had sparred from the moment they met. But now, something different was emerging. Something she wasn't sure she was ready to face.

Willow nodded in agreement with Ivy, but Jasmine didn't want to concede that her baby sister was right. She searched for a reply that didn't make her look like a scaredy-cat. From across the room, Jasmine's ringtone filled the air.

"Sweetheart," Auntie called. "It's that nice young man from the hospital."

Jasmine shared a look with Willow. The temptation to ignore the call was strong. Jasmine wasn't ready for the test she could sense was coming around the corner.

"Why don't you answer it?" Ivy teased. "After all, it's just business."

"Brat."

Willow was less about talk than action. She simply herded Jasmine in the direction of her phone. Jasmine removed her apron as she went. She caught the call right before it switched to voice mail. As she answered, she was acutely aware of her audience.

"Hello?"

"Jasmine?"

Even his voice sounded different. The cadence a little slower. The tone a touch deeper. How was that possible? "Yes?"

"Since our tasting session was cut short, I thought I'd make it up to you by cooking dinner for you."

That was more like Royce—straight to the point. It was the nature of his point she couldn't quite grasp.

She could feel the eyes of everyone in the room staring at her. Even Rosie seemed to be watching, still and waiting for her answer to an unknown question. Jasmine hesitated. Going to Royce's penthouse was definitely not business. She glanced back and forth between Willow's encouraging expression and Ivy's excited one. Jasmine forced herself to turn away, to lay the burden of other people's expectations aside for once.

Even as she paced a few steps and opened her mouth to answer, she wasn't sure what to say. Was she ready for this? Probably not.

But then she thought over everything she'd been through in the last year. Learning Rosie's mother was pregnant, that she would probably die. Bringing her to live here. Taking care of her family while learning to be a mother for the first time. All while holding down a crazy job.

What the hell—it was time to live for once.

Eleven

Royce knew he was in trouble the minute Jasmine walked out of the elevator into the foyer in one of those feminine, flowy dresses she wore. Only this one seemed to have a little more oomph—a little extra cleavage, a slit up one side. Or was his overheated brain imagining that?

He felt like someone had flipped a switch inside him, jumpstarted an electrical pulse that shot through him whenever Jasmine was near. It was like the exhilaration of implementing a successful business plan—only a hundred times harder and sharper.

He didn't want to fight it anymore. Didn't want to fight her.

Make love, not war. Wasn't that a phrase from days past? His mother used to say it. Not that it had gotten her far. Her inability to go to war against his father had turned her life into endless days of drudgery—until Royce had stepped in to change that.

Royce opened the door to his penthouse to allow Jasmine inside. Her heels clicked on the glossy black tile. She breathed deep. "Something smells incredible," she said. Her slight smile intrigued him.

Was she nervous?

When she swallowed, it confirmed his suspicions, though he had to look hard to notice. "You weren't kidding that you could cook," she said.

"I just need to finish a few last-minute things. You aren't averse to any particular seafood, are you?"

She shook her head, bringing his attention to the thick dark hair swinging around her shoulders.

"That's good, or else this would be a complete disaster," he said with a laugh that seemed to break the unexpected tension between them. "I'm finishing up some shrimp scampi. The sides and salad are ready. But I wimped out on the dessert."

"Not you," Jasmine mocked in her sassy way.

"I'm not a pastry chef. I figured since we didn't make it to dessert the other day, I'd go by Marco's and pick up a praline cheesecake."

The O of her mouth was encouraging—and sexy as hell. "Sounds awesome," she said. "But I'm surprised you would admit you can't cook everything."

"I realized a long time ago that there was no point in pretending to be something I'm not."

Her delectable body went still for mere seconds,

but Royce caught it. He should have expected a question to follow.

"Was it a problem? Early on?"

He waved her farther into the living area as thoughts swirled through his mind. He watched her take in the comfortably luxurious space. Royce had never wanted to live in a showplace. A few designers had tried to convince him otherwise, but eventually he'd found someone who understood his preferences. The magnificent space was in one of Savannah's formerly dilapidated shipping warehouses, now refurbished for people who could afford the best—although his "best" meant an awesome sound system, overstuffed leather furniture and a magnificent view. Not high-priced works of art and anemic, uncomfortable chairs.

Jasmine seemed to agree. "Wow," she breathed as she approached the wall of windows looking out toward downtown and the river.

The architect had pushed out the walls so the floor extended all the way to the stone arches that used to frame an old balcony for ship watching. The arches were now fitted with glass panes for an extended view from inside the unusual room.

"This is an incredible blend of old and new," she said. "I'm very impressed."

"It's relaxing when I finally make it home at night."

The black mirrored tile from the foyer gave way to glossy wood floors in the living areas. Royce walked over to the bar in the far corner. "Having you here gives me a chance to use the bar. I hardly ever have company."

He fixed the martini she requested while she strolled along the long wall of windows, skirted the corner bar and continued along the shorter wall. "Incredible."

"Thank you."

"And thank you for inviting me here." This time her look was more straightforward, promising.

Royce felt his insides heat up. "Well, thanks to you, I'm learning to mix business with pleasure."

She lifted the martini glass in salute. "Me, too."

If he let this go much farther, dinner would be burned beyond recognition. "I'd better finish up the food."

As he turned away, he heard her footsteps behind him. "Mind if I join you?"

He paused, giving her a chance to catch up. "Please feel free."

As they walked down a short corridor and into his designer kitchen, he had to chuckle.

"What's so funny?" she asked.

"I just realized." He paused, then let a long, slow breath ease out, surprised he was admitting this. "I just realized that, besides my mother and the cleaning lady, you are the first person to ever join me in my kitchen."

"Wow. Really?"

He watched as her blue gaze roamed over the mahogany cabinets with their black hardware, the cream ceramic appliances and the black tile on the walls. She made a beeline for the stools on the other side of the kitchen island. The large room was designed for social gatherings, but Royce had never used it as such.

"Yes," he murmured. "Really."

But what was even odder was how comfortable he felt with her in his space, if comfortable was even the word to describe the electrical connection that continued to surprise him.

But it wasn't the only thing that surprised him. He was also bemused by how completely at ease they were with each other. They ended up eating at the island in the kitchen, seated across from each other on stools. Her eyes sparkled just as much as her wineglass under the lights. Their conversation flowed naturally from the upcoming masquerade to other events they'd attended.

After exclaiming over the food with genuine enthusiasm, Jasmine took her wineglass and wandered back down the hallway to the living room. Night had taken full hold. The mature trees below and the climbing ivy overflowing the outer walls onto the windowsills gave the impression of being protected by nature as they looked onto the lights spread out before them. Savannah was a city of hard brick and lush greenery. "It really is beautiful, Royce." She half turned toward him. "I can't believe your mother loved the manor house more."

"She did enjoy the view here, but I think Keller House made her think of a time when she was happier, when life had possibilities."

Jasmine was nice enough to add, "But in the end, she was left with the knowledge that she had raised a fully capable young man who would take care of himself and her."

He glanced down into his glass, feeling a familiar mixture of sadness and pride. "She didn't have to worry anymore."

Suddenly he felt a brush of warmth on his arm. Through his dress shirt, he could feel the outline of Jasmine's hand. He couldn't count the number of times recently he had dreamed of how soft her skin would be against his. How those perfectly manicured nails would feel against his back. Or how the curves of her body would feel pressed against his.

She was offering comfort. He needed to remind himself of that.

Then she stepped closer. Any effort at restraint became exponentially harder. He allowed himself a glance, only to find her gaze locked on him. And it wasn't overflowing with sympathy. With just one look they both knew exactly where this was headed. "Will you stay the night?" he finally asked.

"Do you really need to ask?"

That amused him. "Sweetheart, with you I never assume anything."

Her smile was a concession to everything they'd been through so far. "Then let me make myself plain. Assume all you want."

Royce may have been cautious about getting to a more intimate stage, but when the time came, Jasmine found he was as focused in the bedroom as he was in the boardroom.

One minute they were facing each other, then he took a few purposeful steps to bring her within reach.

She barely had time to blink before Royce's hand was in her hair and his mouth once more covered hers. The heat that she remembered from their first kiss was there, this time underpinned by a purpose that made her insides melt.

He tasted spicy, which ramped up the temperature inside her. There was nothing tentative about his kiss. Instead, he conquered her with smooth glides and strong pulls. There was nothing more for her to do than enjoy.

When he pulled back, she was tempted to beg him not to stop, but she clamped her teeth over her lower lip to keep the words inside. Her body was anxious, aching for the race to be finished. But Jasmine wanted to savor the ride. She glanced up to find his gaze glued to the deep V of her neckline—a design she'd deliberately chosen with him in mind.

Then her own gaze dropped and she glimpsed the edges of his neck tattoo above the open collar of his button-down shirt. Curious, she let her fingers trail over the skin of his neck to push the material aside.

To her surprise, the elegant tendrils she'd often glimpsed above his collar gave way to a solid shield, an old-world symbol emblazoned with a brilliantly colored dragon. It stood for strength. Protection. Not what she'd expected, but somehow very fitting for the man she was coming to know.

Her smile gave him all the permission he needed. His palms slid from the back of her neck down over her collarbones, leaving warm trails that quickly faded.

When he finally reached her breasts, she gasped. Her nipples tightened in a quick rush, eager for attention.

He simply held them, each mound a handful. The heat from his hands soaked into her skin through the layers of her clothing. She couldn't stop her back from arching just a little. Then his thumbs began a dedicated exploration that made her wish her clothes would just disappear.

She had no recollection of ever needing someone to see her, touch her, this badly. It was scary—just as much as it was exhilarating.

After long, long moments of exquisite torture, his devilish hands moved down—tracing her generous curves. His touch wasn't simple. No. It was magic. The pressure and heat imprinted the feel of him on her skin.

How could a seemingly innocent touch make her knees go weak? Cause her bones to melt until she leaned forward, her hands braced on his shoulders as he knelt before her?

He eased off one of her high-heeled pumps. His thumbs traced the line of her foot before he squeezed hard into the arch, surprising a gasp from her. Maintaining the pressure, he slid his fingers along the silky surface of her thigh-highs. Too soon, he reached underneath her skirt to find the tops of her stockings and roll them down her legs.

Who knew being undressed could be such a sensual dance?

By the time both legs were bare, Jasmine's entire body throbbed. Royce looked up at her from his crouching position. "Take your dress off for me."

She knew where every tie was, every clasp. But she kept her movements slow, taking her time, building anticipation. It was worth ignoring her own need to see his eyes widen as she revealed a pale pink, lace-edged slip over matching bra and panties. When the dress finally puddled at her feet, he gripped her silk-covered hips and buried his face against her.

She thought she heard him suck in a deep breath. His hands tightened for a moment. Her tummy quivered beneath his cheek. Her throat went dry while she grew slick between her thighs.

Royce stood, only pulling his hands away at the very last minute. That small concession told her more than anything that he wanted her as much as she wanted him. Then he circled around her to take in the view from every angle. To her surprise, he turned her to face the window. That's when she realized their reflections stared back as if from an antique mirror. Hazy. Shimmery.

"This," he said, running a finger along one bra strap, then the lace that edged the top curve of one breast, "is very sexy." He pulled the straps down off her shoulders. Then he hooked his fingers in the material of her slip and slowly eased it down over her curves. "But it isn't what I'm most interested in seeing."

She had only a moment to catch the reflection of herself in the bra and panties before he picked her up and carried her down a longer hallway to the back of the penthouse.

With a quick sweep of her gaze, she took in the dim

bedroom with dark furniture and smoky walls before Royce arranged her on the comforter on her knees, facing him as he stood beside the bed. The soft moonlight from the bedroom windows revealed his outline, but the details of his expression were now lost to her. Once more he traced the edges of the clothes she had left before slipping his hands beneath the silk of her panties to cup her rear.

His touch was firm, with just enough concession to her softness. Pulling her close, he rubbed his fully clothed body against her. The fact that he was covered while she was practically naked left her feeling decadent. The pressure of his erection excited her. Her body went wet in anticipation.

Again, that firm grip guided her down until she lay on the bed. His mouth devoured hers, teeth nipping her lips, tongue delving inside to stroke against hers.

She lost herself in the sensations.

Then, somehow, his mouth was sucking at her naked breast, pulling cries from her straining lungs. He worked one nipple, then the other until they were tight and hard. Electrical pulses streaked through her. She lifted her pelvis against him, more than ready for some relief from the driving urges inside her body.

Deftly, Royce rose to his knees. His dress shirt was gone in seconds. He opened his pants to reveal the very thing she needed in this moment. He put on protection quickly, efficiently. Then, with a snap of his wrist, he broke through her panties. All barriers were gone. Finally his body covered hers.

She could feel the rub of his suit pants against the

insides of her thighs as his body searched for her opening. His fingers spread her wide, coating her with her own moisture to ease the way. Then they teased her, drawing out her cries of desperation.

Not soon enough, he entered her. She struggled for a moment to accommodate him. The pressure was exquisite. One lift of her hips and he slid inside.

There was no more waiting, no more savoring. They were both too desperate.

She clutched at his ribs as he pistoned into her, demanding her response. Indulging his own. Her cries mingled with his groans in the darkness.

All too soon, she needed more. Needed his utmost. She dug her nails into his buttocks, urging him to give her everything.

Then the exquisite pressure burst. The world turned white in a shower of stars. But the best part of it all was knowing that he followed her.

Twelve

Royce woke to movement on the other side of the bed. He opened his eyes. Though there weren't any lights on, he could see Jasmine walk around the end of the bed and out the door to the hallway. It was 1:30 a.m.

The normal debate he'd expect to have with himself never occurred. He simply acknowledged that he had no desire for Jasmine to leave. Getting up, he took a few seconds to pull on a pair of boxers—more for her comfort than his. Then he followed her to the living room.

He located her in one corner near the window by the light of her phone. She seemed to be reading from the screen. As he got closer, he could see that she'd pulled on her slip. Just the thought of that silky material over her naked skin sent him spinning.

Now he knew how someone could become addicted after just one hit.

"Everything okay?" he asked softly, hoping not to scare her.

She only jumped a little. Then she shook her head. "Yeah. I was just checking in."

The silence hung between them for a minute, but for Royce it wasn't the usual awkwardness that came with this situation. Though he could honestly say he'd never been in this situation before. He'd never fallen asleep next to any of the few women he'd bothered to let distract him enough from work to get to sex. Now he couldn't think of anything he wanted more than for Jasmine to spend the rest of the night.

That should have had him freaking out, but he wasn't going to analyze why it didn't.

"Need to go?" he finally asked.

Jasmine hesitated. If he'd been in her situation, he would have, too. Honestly, there was no way she could possibly imagine him wanting her to stay. After all, look at his past behavior.

Covering the few steps left between them, Royce let his body act on instinct. He reached out and cupped the cool skin of her upper arms. Then he rubbed up and down, aiming to warm her. But also to fulfill his own craving to simply touch her.

She stared up at him in the dark. Beneath his touch she shivered, then she shook her head.

For him, the answer was simple. "Then come back to bed."

When they got back to the bed, that first touch of

skin on skin exhilarated him. He rolled over her, covering her cool body with his warmth. Savoring the gasp of air that signaled her surrender.

Royce moaned against her neck, opening his mouth to feel her pulse against his tongue. Her taste was unique, almost floral, but sweet, too. His body responded by hardening, and he reached for her. *Holy smokes.*

"You are like a gourmet meal for me alone."

Jasmine arched against him. He breathed her in, nipping her ear and burying his hands in her hair. This time he savored her touch, too. The feel of her palms grazing down his sides. The light scrape of her nails across his ass. The softness of her lips beneath his.

Her legs slid apart, making a home for him between them. He rubbed himself against her most sensitive spot, wanting to shout because she was so wet for him.

Lifting himself a little, he regretted the space he had to create, if only for a moment. Quickly he covered himself with a condom, then worked his way inside of her. So tight. Incredibly hot. There was no way he could wait.

He was overcome with an instinct to imprint her with his scent, his touch, in case she ever thought she could walk away. Where the possessive urges came from, he had no idea. They were unique to Jasmine. He couldn't resist.

As he gave his first long, slow thrust, he rubbed his body up hers. Never had full body contact felt so good. He felt her slick skin, alert nipples, harsh breath. Most of all, the clasp of her around him.

He anchored his hands in her hair. Then he started to thrust in earnest. The strain in his thighs, the twist of his hips, didn't seem to be enough. Her nimble legs encircled his hips, urging him to thrust harder. Faster.

He attuned his senses to her body's responses. Not just her breath and the lift of her hips, but the subtle clutch of her muscles around his hardness. He nurtured every hint of ecstasy until she called his name in the darkness. They worked together until Royce thought his heart would explode. But he couldn't let go until she did.

Shifting his angle, he ground against the soft cushion of her mound with his pelvis. Her breath caught. Her neck arched. Her hold on him tightened. Then there was the extra force that threw her over the edge.

Her incredible cries filled his ears as her body clamped down hard and milked him dry. There was no denying the demand for him to join her.

Now or ever again.

"I haven't seen you in three days," Royce pointed out. With some men, the reminder would have been a whine. With him, it was a simple logical statement. Until he got to the question. "Are you trying to tell me something?"

In this instance, the complications were all on Jasmine's side. Not Royce's. Most men would have been trying to find ways to keep a woman at arm's length. Not this time.

Much to her surprise.

She wanted to sigh as she glanced over the planner on the desk before her. She wished it wasn't over-flowing with Willow's classes, Ivy's job and blocks of time that she really needed a sitter for Rosie. Facts were facts. She should have known life would inter-fere with the blissful two weeks she'd spent explor-ing the incredibly sensual side of Royce Brazier—but she couldn't keep business and her personal life sepa-rate forever.

She'd never been good at juggling.

But *business* wasn't even the right word. What she and Royce were doing in the luxurious bedroom of his penthouse had nothing to do with business. Still, she was doing her best to keep him and her family far away from each other. Royce had made it clear he wasn't in the market for a family. She was a single woman with a small child. The last thing she wanted was for him to think she was daddy hunting.

For a man like him, the title of *daddy* would never be an option.

"I just can't get away tonight." The planner clearly showed that Willow had a night class to teach. And Ivy had called to say she would probably be working late that night. Auntie was recovering nicely, but her abilities and stamina with a small child were limited. This left Jasmine between a rock and…well, a very lonely, needy place.

Royce hesitated for only a moment. "Would your family object to me dropping by?"

"Why would you?"

Silence greeted her unexpected question, but only

for a moment. Just long enough for her to feel mortified.

"Believe it or not, Jasmine," Royce said, without any of the angry heat she would have expected, "I do enjoy more about you than just the sex."

Jasmine almost choked.

"And they have met me before," he reminded her.

Not as a potential suitor. At least, in her eyes. This visit just might confirm what her family was expecting…except Jasmine knew her liaison with Royce could never live up to the romantic fantasy they would build in their minds.

When she finally answered, her voice sounded small. "It just didn't occur to me you would want to come by."

"Jasmine." His voice deepened, almost a reflection of the turmoil rumbling around inside of her. "I'm finding, to my surprise, that I'll take you any way I can get you."

Royce always was one to tell the truth, whether the other person wanted to hear it or not. The sheer enormity of his confession shut her up quick. They agreed on a time for him to drop by.

The bewilderment and need in his voice were still eliciting tremors later that evening as she waited for him to arrive. Mostly because they echoed her own feelings.

She found her attachment to Royce too close for comfort. Her craving for him only grew each time they were together. She wanted to bounce ideas off him at odd times. She even wished she could spar with him on occasion. Talking to him. Cooking with him. Making love with him. He never failed to stimulate her in some way—in all the ways that mattered.

But he wasn't a family man—had no desire to ever be one. So her need for him to be more than he could offer scared her more than anything.

Her hands still shook as she opened the door that evening. It should have been a scene from a romantic movie—a handsome man on her doorstep with blooming trees filling the background behind him as the sun set. Instead, it could have been the boogeyman at her door, if her feelings of trepidation were to be believed.

"Hey," she greeted him, her voice hushed.

"Hey, yourself." He matched his tone to hers as he glanced behind her. "Are we having a secret liaison on your doorstep or is there something I need to know?"

That would have been funny if she hadn't actually been keeping her family in the dark as much as possible since that night two weeks ago. Still, she tried for an amused grin, ignoring her nerves.

"No. Auntie and Rosie fell asleep."

Letting him in, she gestured toward the entrance to the family room, where Auntie could be seen lying propped up with lots of pillows on the couch. Rosie reclined against her, pacifier in place, blanket snuggled close. There was a cartoon on the TV turned to a low volume.

"They were watching television together. But Rosie seems to have caught Auntie's tendency to take cat naps now that she's having to rest her leg so much."

Royce studied the sleeping pair, though Jasmine couldn't read his expression. "She looks peaceful."

She assumed he meant Rosie. "She's a good baby. I'm very, very lucky."

He turned back. "So am I, hopefully."

Jasmine raised an eyebrow. "Trust me. There's not enough time for sex."

Royce quickly smothered a laugh. "I guessed that much. But is a proper hello too much to ask for?"

Jasmine's cheeks burned. Shame on her for accusing him of only having sex on the brain.

Leading the way to the kitchen at the back of the house, she busied herself putting coffee on to perk. Anything to give her blush a chance to subside. She'd learned that Royce was an avid coffee drinker. Caffeine didn't seem to faze him. He drank it at all hours of the day—not that he slept much, anyway.

Only after the task had distracted her from her embarrassment did she cross the room and kiss him. It was a little more than a peck, but not much more before she pulled back. "How was your day?"

Dang it. Though she'd asked him that before, in this setting it took on a different connotation. More of a "How was your day, dear?" connotation.

"The Jeffersons have received my proposal." He grimaced, staring off into space for a moment. That tiny frown between his brows when he focused on something was unexpectedly sexy. "I hope they find everything in order."

"How can they not, with all the hard work you and

your assistant put into this? And the masquerade will be fabulous. You're definitely gonna be noticed."

Even though she doubted he needed one, she gave him a hug. Her entire family were huggers. It served as greeting, comfort, reassurance, encouragement, celebration—like a language all its own. She and Ivy had talked at length about the difficulties of being a hugger in a business setting. It was a hard habit to shut off.

Finally, she leaned back to look at him. "Besides, I got good news today."

"What's that?" His voice had gone husky, warning her he was losing interest in business and moving on to far more interesting topics.

She couldn't help but smile. As much as she knew she shouldn't—she loved the effect she had on him. "I received an invite to the Sunday Salon yesterday. We attend on the fifteenth."

"Yes, ma'am. I'll be there with bells on, as my mama used to say." She couldn't help but notice that, even though the words were right, his eyes were trained on her lips.

"That would make a memorable fashion statement," she murmured, just before his lips found hers.

They'd just reached the gasping-and-fumbling-with-clothes stage when Jasmine heard a whimper from the other room. She stiffened.

Pulling back, Royce straightened his tie, then took a deep breath. "I'll just fix myself a cup of coffee," he said.

Leaving him to fend for himself, Jasmine rushed to

the living room where Auntie was still snoring softly and Rosie was rubbing her eyes.

After picking the baby up and soothing her with a soft swaying motion for a moment, Jasmine headed back to the kitchen, not wanting to disturb the older woman's rest. Auntie hadn't slept well since her fall. Simply finding a comfortable way to sit or lie down could be a challenge on the bad days.

As soon as she stepped into the kitchen, Jasmine ran into another problem. Rosie stiffened a moment when she noticed the unidentified male in the room. But it didn't bother her for long.

Jasmine was in the process of saying, "You remember Mr. Royce, don't you?" when the little girl threw her whole body forward in a swan dive. Right in Royce's direction. The move was so unexpected that Jasmine wasn't able to get a good grasp. Rosie would have slipped from her arms if Royce hadn't stepped forward and caught Rosie.

Jasmine didn't know if it had been instinct for him, but it saved her daughter from what could have been a nasty tumble to the tile floor.

As soon as she'd caught her breath, Jasmine exclaimed, "Oh, goodness. I don't know how that happened." Her panicked mind replayed the child's jump for Royce over and over.

"No problem," he said, sounding far calmer than she felt. He immediately righted the baby and positioned her in his arms as if it were something he did on a daily basis.

All Jasmine could do was blink and breathe.

Rosie, the little stinker, ignored the drama she'd caused her mama and immediately began to babble at her captive audience. Royce's colorful tie seemed to fascinate her. And Jasmine could swear the baby was actually flirting as she glanced up at Royce's face and bestowed a big, gummy grin on him.

It might have been funny if it was anyone but Royce. The man who wanted nothing to do with family.

"Here. I'll take her," Jasmine offered with a step forward.

"It's fine," he assured her.

Unsure what else to do, she waved toward the table. "Have a seat."

As he settled them in at the dining room table, Jasmine brought his forgotten coffee from the counter. She stood next to them for a moment, fascinated and embarrassed by her daughter's animated behavior— and Royce's ability to take it all in stride. When had this happened?

Before she could get a handle on the scene before her, Jasmine was mortified to hear her sister Ivy say from behind her, "Well, isn't this the perfect picture of domesticity?"

Thirteen

This was not how Royce had planned to spend his evening. Very few men would complain about being surrounded by a roomful of beautiful Southern women, being served delicious home cooking—and Royce wasn't going to be the one to start.

He'd simply planned to spend it with Jasmine. Alone. Preferably naked.

It took considerable self-control not to watch her every move with a hungry gaze, though baby Rosie's attachment to him had dampened his ardor significantly, as had the avid speculation on the other women's faces. He wasn't sure what was up with the little squirt, but she'd apparently decided Royce was her one and only adult tonight. She wasn't having it any other way. Any time Jasmine or her sisters tried to hold

Rosie or move her away from him, big tears flooded her little eyes and rolled down her cheeks.

Much to his chagrin, Royce was a sucker for it.

Her high chair had been set beside him with Jasmine on the other side. The setup felt unreal to him, as if his brain couldn't comprehend what he'd gotten himself into. But he also had no desire to hightail it for the front door—an odd development, to say the least.

Normally, he would have been the first one to hit the road.

As they ate, Rosie alternated between her baby food and sippy cup, and playing with the emerald ring on Jasmine's right hand.

"You wear that ring a lot," he said. "Where's it from?"

The table went strangely silent, as if he'd asked something completely inappropriate—or something they didn't really want to answer.

"It's an heirloom piece we recently found in an old jewelry box," Auntie finally said.

Royce could swear the women around him slumped just a little.

"The girls' family line goes all the way back to the origins of Savannah. Their ancestor was a pirate who turned respectable and married the daughter of one of the founding families."

Royce grinned at Jasmine over Rosie's head. "Respectable, huh? So that's where you learned to fit in with the elite crowd so well."

"It's in the genes," she confirmed, putting on a fake bravado.

"It's actually quite fascinating," Willow said before launching into a monologue about Savannah's origins.

"History nerd," Jasmine mumbled out of the side of her mouth.

Royce quickly smothered his laugh when Willow glared. "I would hope so," she declared. "Otherwise I'd suck at teaching it."

"That makes perfect sense," Royce said. "I'm sure someone who loves history makes it much more interesting for her students."

That seemed to mollify Willow—that and sticking her tongue out at her sister.

Royce felt himself relaxing even more. Dinner around the family table was an experience he'd never had. When he and his mother had eaten together, usually on Sundays, they'd sat next to each other in front of the television, eating off of TV trays. He hadn't expected to enjoy this when he'd sat down tonight.

Just then, a soft weight rested against his arm. He glanced down into the two soft brown eyes in Rosie's tiny round face. She blinked slowly, then rubbed her head against his arm.

"Um..." Royce glanced around the table, something akin to panic building in his core.

Willow giggled first, then Ivy. Auntie simply smiled.

Jasmine rolled her eyes, shaking her head at her daughter. "You big flirt."

"She is a woman, after all," Auntie said.

Royce glanced back down. The baby grinned, showing the first of her teeth in her otherwise empty gums. The panic disintegrated. A feeling he didn't recognize settled in its place. Something similar to how he felt when lying exhausted in Jasmine's arms. Almost like...peace.

"How about a change of subject?" Jasmine asked. "After all, I'm not sure how comfortable I am thinking about my six-month-old as a woman. Too early." She turned to Royce. "Shall we talk about the Jeffersons' soirée?"

"Oh, you get to go to that?" Ivy asked. "I loved the times I was allowed to go as Jasmine's guest."

Willow frowned. "Not me. Too many people and I had no idea what to talk about. I much prefer smaller groups."

"Which is why I'm going to the masquerade and you aren't," Ivy said.

"Have fun." Obviously Willow was not the social butterfly type.

Jasmine explained, "Willow is more of an introvert than the rest of us."

"My students are about as big of a group as I can handle," Willow said. "And even that exhausts me sometimes."

"I can sympathize, Willow," Royce said. "I'm a homebody myself. Comfortable only in my private spaces or the office. I don't often attend social events, but when I do, I try to think of these things as business meetings—just with more people present and a more fluid agenda."

"I hate to burst your bubble, but not this time," Jasmine said.

Royce glanced at her over the baby hugging his arm. "What do you mean?"

Her blue eyes were slightly somber. "The Jeffersons don't do business at these things. It's very socially oriented. That's why they are picky about the guest list."

"All of these social events are covers for getting business done. You may not see it, but it's there," Royce insisted. He'd been to enough of them to know, even if such parties weren't his preferred venue. "Otherwise, they'd be a big waste of time."

She was already shaking her head. "Not this time. While there are usually a lot of business people there, it isn't discussed directly. Remember my little talk about building connections, not just business deals? They're just as important. Trust me."

"Sure." *We'll see.* Jasmine was a smart woman. A whole lot more people smart than he was. But Royce knew business…and he was determined to advance his at every opportunity—no matter what she thought she knew.

Royce would trust his instincts. Every time.

Jasmine smoothed out the collar of her dress, then the skirt. It felt weird to be heading to a public event with Royce. They'd spent plenty of time together in private—delectable time. And, yes, they'd occasionally talked business or gone over progress for the masquerade, but this was different. Something they had never addressed.

Attending the Jeffersons' Sunday Salon with Royce put her on a path that left her with no distinct sense of how to act. Was this business? Was it a date? Would she look into his eyes and see the heat that often exploded between them without warning?

How should she react? Naturally? Or keep it under wraps? All the questions had her twisting her hands together in her lap.

Suddenly Royce pulled his car over and put it in park. Jasmine's stomach flip-flopped. But she swallowed against the tightening in her throat and asked, "Is something wrong?"

"You tell me. *Is* something wrong, Jasmine?"

"How did you know?" As if her stiffness this morning wasn't a clear sign. She'd been hoping he would ignore it.

"You're not at all your normal happy, mischievous self today."

She glanced over at him, realizing that was probably the first time she'd looked directly at him since they'd gotten into the car. No wonder he'd asked. Royce wasn't stupid.

"Sorry."

"Just tell me what it is and we'll figure it out."

He was right. Even though this was the last thing she wanted to talk about, what was the point of prolonging the torture that she'd been enduring for over a month? "I'm just not sure…" She swallowed, trying to loosen up her throat. This was something she'd never had to say to a client. "I'm not sure how you want me to act while we are here…out in public."

His grip tightened on the steering wheel as he nodded slowly. "I see what you mean."

"I know you hired me as your event planner. Attending this party was part of our business agreement. I'm just—"

Without warning, he leaned across the console to cup her face with his palms. The press of his lips to hers was so familiar now, almost as necessary as breathing. The fear, the uncertainty sparked by that revelation, was something she spent a lot of energy ignoring every day.

She opened her eyes to meet his, just inches away.

"I should have known this would be a problem," he murmured.

Her heart sank.

"I have no idea where this is going between us," Royce said.

This was it…he was going to dump her because she'd asked how he wanted her to behave in public.

He rubbed his thumb against her cheek. "But it's time we just accept that it's there and deal with it. Don't you agree?"

"Wait. What?"

"Surprised?" He granted her his rare grin. "Me, too."

As if he couldn't stop himself, he kissed her again. His touch was tinged with a gentleness that had tears burning behind her eyes.

"Listen," he said. "We don't have to be all over each other. We don't have to ignore what's happening between us, either."

Jasmine took a deep breath, searching his expression. "You don't care if people talk?"

"My mom and I learned a long time ago that talk can't hurt you if you don't let it. You and I started on this path with business as the sole purpose, but we left that behind a while back."

She sat stunned while he pulled back out onto the road. She'd been working hard to convince herself that her time with Royce was limited and would eventually end. That he could never accept Rosie or Jasmine's commitment to her family. All to keep herself from getting too involved.

He'd been so accepting of Rosie the other night. Jasmine hadn't tested it further, but seeing her daughter cuddle up to Royce's arm had done something to her. Made her wonder, for the brief moment she'd allowed herself to, whether this might actually be a possibility. Could this be another sign that what was happening between them might actually work? For real?

Silence reigned until they pulled into the long drive to the Jeffersons' palatial home. They lined up behind the considerable number of cars already parked out front.

It wasn't until Royce came around to help her out that he spoke. And he was so relaxed, it was as if there hadn't been a long silence between them. "So, you just be your beautiful, smart self, and I promise not to accost you when everyone is looking. Okay?"

"What about when they aren't?"

Again he reached out to her cheek, smoothing the pad of his thumb across it as if testing the texture of her skin. She heard the telltale note in his voice that always signaled his arousal as he said, "I'm sorry. I can't make any promises about that."

For the first time since she'd woken up that morning, Jasmine laid her worry aside and smiled. "I guess I'll have to live with that."

It was different, entering the stately house on Royce's arm. She'd been there over a dozen times before, and the Jeffersons had never made her feel anything but welcome. They did the same this time. Still, her smile was a little bigger, her confidence a little higher and her mood a whole lot brighter. Royce stiffened as they went in, but she chalked it up to adrenaline. She doubted Royce ever really felt nerves. But something had to power him through all those business negotiations and decisions.

"Royce Brazier, this is Don and Marilyn Jefferson, our hosts," she said, automatically attempting to put everyone at ease.

The man she'd respected for a long time shook Royce's hand without hesitation. "Welcome to our home. I believe we've met once or twice before, but always on more formal occasions," Don Jefferson said with his slow Southern drawl.

Jasmine was grateful to see Royce meet his gaze and shake his hand without any of the macho posturing she'd had to endure in some Savannah circles. "I believe so, sir. Thank you for having me."

"Always a pleasure. We're glad to see you, but would welcome anyone Miss Jasmine cared to bring with her."

"It was gracious of her to include me in her invite,

sir," Royce said, with a smile in her direction that lingered just a little longer than normal.

Jasmine warmed from the inside out, despite the sleeveless summer dress she wore.

"This is my wife, Marilyn. Please, call me Don. Now Jasmine, why don't you show Royce where the food is? Make yourself at home. We can talk after a while," Mr. Jefferson said.

Fifteen minutes of mingling, with Royce's hand at the small of her back and a mimosa or two, helped Jasmine get a handle on how to behave. She let Royce lead, but introduced him to a few couples he hadn't met before. Most were familiar with his meteoric rise in Savannah's shipping industry but were gracious enough not to grill him on his presence at today's party.

"So, what are you working on now?" Evette Pierce asked Jasmine. She'd been to several of Jasmine's events, and they'd worked together on a charity event last spring.

"It's gonna be so much fun." Jasmine knew she was gushing, but she couldn't hold her excitement in. "We're working on a masquerade night in late May. You'll love it."

"Sounds fascinating."

"It will be. And the proceeds will go to build a dormitory for the mission."

Evette raised her wineglass. "A cause very close to you, I know. You can count on me being there."

As they moved away, Royce leaned closer to whisper, "I thought this wasn't the place to discuss business?"

"She asked," Jasmine said with a shrug. "Besides, it wasn't really business. I was just passing her information about something fun I think she would enjoy."

"Po-*tay*-toes, pot-*ah*-toes."

She simply grinned. "Told you. Everything has a social spin."

"And you are the smarty-pants I should trust to know what she's doing?"

"Every time."

Royce grinned down at her. Movement in the doorway behind him caused her to glance over his shoulder. Don and Marilyn were greeting a man in the foyer. Suddenly Don looked toward her, a frown on his face as his gaze met hers. Only as the other man faced her did she realize who it was. And why Don looked so unhappy.

The man who had just arrived was Royce's father.

Fourteen

"I do want to apologize for the mix-up," Don said as he led Royce down an ornately paneled hallway into an office.

"What mix-up?" Royce asked.

Don let the heavily carved door close then studied Royce for a moment. He had a feeling this wasn't going to be a very comfortable conversation. And he could think of only one subject that would warrant this type of formality from his host.

"Of having your father here without any warning."

Bingo.

Don stepped into the room, gesturing Royce toward a chair while he took the one behind the large desk. "Not all of our guests are as courteous as Jasmine about letting us know who they are bringing with them."

Royce felt the unease that had been simmering since he'd first caught sight of his father rise a little higher. Not for himself, but— "I don't like the idea of him having access to Jasmine." Especially without him there to run interference.

Don offered an approving look. "We agree. Marilyn will be watching over her until you return. I assure you, she's quite capable of handling men of his ilk." He grinned. "Jasmine can, too, though she's often polite to a fault."

He studied Royce for a minute more before he asked, "Does he know about the two of you?"

"What?"

"That your relationship has become personal as well as professional?"

Royce wasn't sure he wanted to address that issue yet. Something had been bothering him since this conversation started.

"How did you know he was my father?" Royce asked. "That's not something I advertise."

"I don't blame you. He's not the kind of man I'd want to claim as a relation, either."

Royce met the other man's gaze in surprise. It wasn't often he had conversations with people who would admit to disliking his father as much as he did.

Don explained. "I'm a very thorough man. I know a lot about you, Royce. I've kept you on my radar for a while. With your meteoric rise on Savannah's business scene, it was inevitable we would do business with each other at some point. When your proposal came in, we had you investigated."

"Why?" But there was something Royce wanted to know more. "Actually, right now, I just want to know if my father has ever tried to do business with you."

Don nodded slowly. "He has attempted to work with us in the past. And, yes, I did investigate him just as thoroughly. But I didn't find the connection at that time."

He smiled at Royce. "I didn't need to investigate to see your relationship with Jasmine. It's all in her face, though she tries to hide it."

Royce could see it, too, every time she looked at him. He was deeply worried his own feelings showed just as clearly, and he wasn't ready for that.

Don leaned back in his chair, causing it to creak. "As to why we investigate the personal backgrounds of potential business associates, I like to know who we're working with. Not just what you're capable of in a business arena, but who you are as a person. Unusual, but that's just how my wife and I like running our company. It works for us."

Royce wasn't sure how he felt about that. He could understand the concern, but the idea that his personal life had been scrutinized wasn't something he was comfortable acknowledging.

"Of course, we don't usually share that knowledge with our employees or contractors," Don said, "but in this instance, I felt it was particularly important."

"Again, why?"

"Well, I doubt this will make you feel any better

about my snooping, but we happen to have taken a special interest in Jasmine Harden."

Royce wasn't above digging for his own information. This he wanted to hear. "My event planner?"

Don cocked his head to one side. "Is that all she is?"

"You tell me. You're the one hunting for info."

"Touché. You've just never been known to date much. She's never dated any of her clients."

This was getting more bizarre by the minute, but the fact that Don was concerned about Jasmine oddly reassured Royce. "I guess the real question is—is there a problem with anything you found out?" He might as well know if his history was about to stand in the way of his future.

"You've done very well for yourself—and in the best way possible. The only complaint I could find out about your company, or you for that matter, is that it isn't very child friendly."

"It's a business." *Not a day care.* But, for once, he kept that part to himself.

"I get that," Don conceded. "And a better understanding of a healthy work environment and happy employees will come to you with more life experience—but it's not a concern for us when it comes to doing business with you."

The proposal.

Don continued, "I'll be honest. I was skeptical at first. You see, we believe business should have a soul."

Royce shot his host a questioning look. The phrase sounded vaguely familiar. Royce wondered if it was something he'd read on Don's company website.

Luckily, Don was willing to enlighten him. "We believe that all of our business efforts should be done with our fellow man in mind wherever possible—helping take care of those who can't, keeping the environment stable and as unharmed by our work as possible, providing safe working conditions—and by extension, creating better living conditions for those who can't afford to do that for themselves."

Okay, this sounded familiar. The Jeffersons' company was known for its environmental stewardship and humanitarian working policies, in addition to its philanthropic efforts.

"When you first applied," Don continued, "I didn't believe this was a philosophy you readily embraced, despite your own efforts to make your shipping company as environmentally friendly as possible. Don't get me wrong—you've accomplished incredible things at a very young age."

Don grinned at Royce. "I can say that from my very advanced age and not sound Scroogy.

"Then I found out about your work with Jasmine. I know you have a charity event you are planning together. One we are much looking forward to, by the way. Sounds exciting."

Royce relaxed—a little. "Isn't anything Jasmine plans exciting?"

"Just about..." Don smiled. "She's an incredibly talented woman."

That was an understatement. Royce had learned more about the hidden depths of Jasmine Harden than he'd ever dreamed he would. She was smart, sexy, bold yet gracious, tenacious and amusing. And the first woman he'd ever wanted to stick around for longer than a night.

"My concern might sound a little old-fashioned. But I would never presume to insist that you marry her or stay with her. That's not anybody's place," Don conceded.

Royce acknowledged the sentiment with a nod.

"But she doesn't have a father present, and Marilyn and I are friends of hers, so I do feel a bit of a responsibility to request that you treat her decently. That's all any of us can expect."

"It's what any woman deserves," Royce said tightly, thinking of the man in the other room.

Don's nod was slow, almost contemplative. But Royce sensed it had nothing to do with studying him to get more inside information. Instead, the wisdom in Don's mature gaze told Royce he had more than an inkling about the hardships and poverty he'd suffered as a child…and why.

"I agree," Don finally said. "I'm glad to know we're on the same page."

Jasmine realized she was in for it when Marilyn smiled her way and asked, "So, Royce Brazier, huh?"

The older woman nodded sagely when Jasmine didn't answer right away. Instead she snagged them each a pretty mimosa off a passing waiter's tray. Jasmine sipped, grateful to have something to occupy her.

Under normal circumstances, she had no problem talking with Marilyn. They could cover a wide range of subjects without running out of steam. This time, she tried to act cool, but the blood rushed to her cheeks, anyway. She'd never discussed Royce like this outside of her family—and at home she was mainly deflecting her sisters' teasing.

His father standing across the room made her even more uncomfortable. She twisted the emerald ring round and round her finger until Marilyn laid a hand over hers. Jasmine met the older woman's understanding gaze.

"How did you know?" she asked.

Marilyn's expression showed delight that she'd guessed correctly. "I have a feeling about people. He isn't the first male client you've brought to our little get-togethers, but he's the first one you've looked at like that. Or who has looked at you the same way."

Suddenly Jasmine's mouth felt like a desert. She took a quick sip of the fizzy drink. "Like what?" she asked, almost afraid of the answer. So far, there'd been no one to see her with Royce except her sisters. And they were biased.

"Like he discovered a diamond in the midst of his sandbox. I remember." She leaned her head a little closer to confide, "Don looked at me that way, too."

"Really?"

Marilyn raised her glass. "I was his secretary," she said, then took a drink.

"No," Jasmine breathed. Somehow, she'd never thought to ask how Marilyn and Don had met. She'd just assumed Marilyn came from an upper-class family that wasn't from around here.

"Oh, yes, sweetheart. I married way above my class, which ended up being the scandal of the year. No one would mention it now, but they weren't afraid to criticize then. To Don's face, no less."

"I can't imagine." Jasmine felt privileged Marilyn was actually bringing up something this personal. "That must have been incredibly difficult."

"Don wasn't as powerful then—but he also wasn't as diplomatic. Or patient." Her smile was gracious, knowing. "People aren't quick to learn, you know. And Don doesn't enjoy repeating himself."

Jasmine doubted Royce would jeopardize his client relations to defend her like that, though she knew he wouldn't allow others to be disrespectful. She had no idea where his happy medium would be between the two stances—and had no desire to find out.

As if on cue, Royce's father appeared beside Marilyn. He wasn't as tall as his son, but their bearing was the same. Straight spine. Squared shoulders. Royce always looked as if he were bracing himself against whatever the world dared throw at him. His biological father looked like he knew what was coming and was prepared to take the hit. The gray creeping into his sandy hair reinforced the impression.

John Nave greeted them both but his eyes were trained on Jasmine. She shivered. Therein lay a key difference between the two men. Royce might be focused on his business, but his expression was still open. His father's was cold and closed down tight, not letting even a glimpse of emotion through. It was as if he evaluated her solely on what she was capable of providing him—and didn't care one bit about her as a person.

She'd never done business with Royce's father. And she hoped she never did.

One look at Marilyn and she knew her friend was aware of who he was—and possibly the story behind his connection to Royce. But Marilyn's smile as she turned to him was perfectly polite and diplomatic. "Mr. Nave, I'm surprised to see you here."

"These little get-togethers are good for business," he said, not bothering to look in Marilyn's direction. "Right, sweetheart?"

Shock shot through Jasmine. "Excuse me?"

"I said—"

"I heard what you said." Jasmine tightened the hand at her side into a fist, hoping it would help steady her... and her voice. "My name is Jasmine."

As if he didn't already know that. He nodded slowly, continuing to study her.

Jasmine glanced at her friend, who had let a frown break through her polite mask. Before she could say anything, John spoke again.

"There are also a lot of different kinds of distractions at these parties. Which are you?"

Okay, this was a bit much. She'd dealt with the public since she was a teenager and wasn't about to be walked all over—no matter who he was. She gifted them both with the sweetest smile she could muster. "I think distraction is good for you every now and again."

His eyebrow shot up, vaguely reminiscent of Royce

when he was being obnoxious. "Not if you want to achieve success."

"Depends on the type of success you're aiming for," she countered.

"Very well put," Don said, as he and Royce joined them. Jasmine had been so focused on John that she hadn't noticed their approach. "I couldn't agree with you more, sweet Jasmine."

The endearment sounded so much nicer like that.

Don gave her a direct smile and an encouraging look. "I've always maintained that your intelligence is way above average—just like my dear Marilyn's."

Don stepped through the middle of their little gathering to gift his wife with a kiss. Jasmine was relieved to have a break from John's stare, though her tension was still through the roof.

"Darling, the caterer was looking for you," Don said. "Shall we?"

Marilyn nodded, smiling her goodbyes as Don settled her hand in the crook of his arm and led her away. Jasmine couldn't help but notice Marilyn didn't glance toward John. She was probably afraid she'd stick her tongue out at him.

Jasmine wanted to flip him the bird.

After the Jeffersons left them, Jasmine noticed that John had turned his stare toward his son. "I'm disappointed in you, Royce."

Heaven forbid we should make polite, pleasant conversation...

Royce wasn't daunted, though. He cocked his head

to the side, looking down at the older man. "I'm not sure why you're bothering to think of me at all."

"As my only progeny, you'd be surprised how often you come to mind. Though I'm disappointed after our last meeting."

"Why?"

John shifted his gaze to Jasmine for only a moment. She could feel her thunderous emotions start to play out in her expression.

"I see you didn't take my advice."

"This is beginning to feel a little surreal," Royce said with a quick look around. "This conversation makes no sense whatsoever. Since when have I ever listened to anything you've said to me, on the rare occasions when you've said anything? Why would I start now?"

John shrugged, not seeming the least offended. "I've always hoped my genes would prevail."

"I believe the better genes did. My mother's."

Hear, hear.

"You can go so much farther, even farther than me, if you remain unattached. I mean, she's pretty," John said with a lazy gesture in Jasmine's direction. "And I'm not saying they aren't fun to play with…"

"Wow." Jasmine was amazed at the scene playing out in front of her…with her as the object of attention. Or, rather, derision. And she was done being a passive bystander. "Royce, let me say I agree with you. The better genes do prevail in you."

His father turned his hard gaze her way once more, but she wasn't backing down.

"It's a good thing your opinion doesn't count. At least, not for long."

Royce stepped forward, crowding into John's space. "Actually, her opinion counts for a whole lot more than yours—and it always will."

Fifteen

Anger pushed Royce to drive mindlessly. He sped out of the Jeffersons' long drive with a little more acceleration than was necessary. But the squeal of the tires on the asphalt gave him a brief moment of satisfaction.

He remained silent, teeth clenched, because if he spoke, the rage of years past might spew out on someone who didn't deserve it. So he locked himself down tight, his fists clenched around the wheel. His gaze was narrowed, focused solely on the road before him.

Only when they got to the parking garage of his building and he opened her car door did he tune in Jasmine. Her stillness. Her silence.

I'm not the only one involved.

He'd forgotten. It had been years since he'd had to worry about a woman's feelings, a woman's reactions.

He remembered how his mother had internalized everything, taking the burden of whatever they'd endured onto herself as if she simply deserved it.

Jasmine certainly hadn't taken anything his father had dished out passively, though she'd maintained her ladylike demeanor better than his father had deserved. Now she sat looking up at him from the passenger seat, but she made no move to exit. Her posture was almost expectant, but his mind wasn't in a place to comprehend what she was waiting for.

"Something wrong?" he asked.

"I've been wondering if it was safe to ask you that."

As if realizing he was losing patience, she got out of the car but lagged behind as he strode toward the elevator.

"What?" He winced when his voice echoed off the brick and concrete walls of the garage, and he heard just how impatient he sounded.

"Do you really want me here?" she asked.

Her confusion and the lost note in her voice were finally breaking through his self-absorption. He softened his tone. "Unless you don't want to be here. I can't stop you from leaving, Jasmine."

"You already have."

Royce glanced around in confusion. "What?"

"My car isn't here," she pointed out, exaggerating her enunciation, probably hoping he'd catch on.

That's when he remembered picking her up at her house. He squeezed his eyes closed and cursed under his breath. How had he let that man get so far under his skin?

Jasmine.

Royce opened his eyes and looked at her expression, which was now slightly amused. Though he could still detect some concern lingering around the edges.

This was why he'd gotten so upset. So angry.

Royce had become immune to his father's reprimands and insults throughout the years, though his conversations with his father were few and far between.

Just the way he liked it.

So this anger wasn't about him. More than anything, Royce didn't want Jasmine hurt by his father. He didn't even want her touched by anything his father said or did.

Now he understood why his mom hadn't fought very hard. It wasn't like she'd had a lot of options. Certainly no lawyer in town had been willing to let her set foot in their firm.

Officially, it had always been her word against his father's. Those close to the situation had known the truth. But his mother simply hadn't wanted to be in the same room with the man who could treat her so disrespectfully after she'd served her purpose. The man who would threaten her and her son so he didn't have to part with the paltry sum it would have taken to lift their lives above poverty level.

Better to cut that person from her life than to allow him to destroy her, piece by piece, over years of contact.

That hadn't been an option for Royce, if he wanted to be any kind of businessman in Savannah. But he'd done his best to ignore John over the years. John seemed to prefer it that way, too. Now it seemed his father had taken some kind of interest in him.

Royce refused to let that dictate anything about who he was or his actions.

Reaching out, he took Jasmine's hand in his. But he just stood there. He didn't rush upstairs. Instead, he let his eyes close once more and let the early summer breeze carry her scent to him. When he opened his eyes and his gaze found her face, he took in how she was patiently waiting. He offered a sheepish smile.

"Would you like to come up for a while?"

"Only if that's where you want me."

Silly woman. "I can't think of anything I want more right now."

"Me, either."

That's when he noticed the slight strain in her smile, the tightness around her eyes. Their encounter with his father had affected her almost as much as it had him.

But he waited until much later, when he held her tight against him in his bed, to ask, "What did he say to you before I showed up?"

The delicious lassitude that fitted her perfectly to his side drained away. He felt her body stiffen, though she didn't retreat from him. "Honestly, I'm doing my best to forget. Let's just say, your dad is very much a sexist pig."

"First of all, he isn't my dad. He's the sperm donor."

His tone was light, and sure enough, she laughed. Unfortunately, the sentiment came straight from his heart.

"Second of all, it amazes me how he knew anyone willing to bring him. As you can tell, he isn't the most personable of people. But money talks."

"It must, because I can't imagine how that man ever got married." A shiver shook her body.

Royce hugged her closer. "I agree. Although, from the rumors I've heard, she's just as cold."

"Then why bother? I don't understand."

Neither did Royce. "It's marriage as a business merger. They're the perfect example."

"An example of what not to do," Jasmine murmured.

"I guess it works for them." He shrugged. "I'd rather be alone than endure something that emotionless."

She patted his chest. "That's because you actually have a heart…and human emotions."

"I know a few people who wouldn't agree with you," he said with a chuckle.

"*I* might not have agreed with me a month ago."

"And I wouldn't blame you for your assessment."

She snuggled closer. Her breath was warm across his skin. She was silent for so long that he began to wonder if she'd fallen asleep. Then she whispered, "So why be that way?"

It's safe. There was no way he was offering that explanation. Not even to Jasmine. Instead, he said, "It's what I know."

"What do I wear to the ball? Cinderella's eternal question shared by women everywhere."

Jasmine glared at her little sister as she walked past,

her arms overflowing with formal dresses. Ivy's words made Jasmine even more stressed. The store owner helped Ivy arrange her potential choices on a rack before she headed down the hall to a dressing room. Jasmine's arms were still empty.

They'd been looking at dresses for the masquerade for over half an hour already at a small local boutique where Jasmine usually bought her formal clothing. Ivy was attending the masquerade with her. She loved parties. Willow was more than happy to help pick out everyone's attire, then stay home with Auntie and Rosie.

The three of them had done this on quite a few occasions. Many times Ivy had assisted Jasmine at her events so she had an extra pair of hands. This time, her little sister was coming because what Jasmine and Royce had put together was totally cool.

But Jasmine had never had a problem finding a dress. Today was the exception, apparently.

She knew what the problem was, but she didn't want to acknowledge it. What difference did it make what dress she wore? After all, Royce had seen her naked on more than one occasion. But her stupid feminine psyche seemed stuck on finding *the perfect* dress. The dress that would wow Royce, make him proud to have her standing next to him.

At least, she assumed that's what she would be doing…when she wasn't conferring with caterers and waitstaff and Dominic, among others. Royce hadn't actually spelled that part out yet.

But she wasn't going to live with the same angst she'd had before their visit to the Jeffersons' Sunday

Salon. They'd gone out to dinner a few times since then. She'd felt safe assuming they'd present themselves as a couple, of sorts. By now she knew Royce wasn't the type of man who needed her on his arm the entire time. But when they were together, she knew he wouldn't ignore her.

Still, she hoped she got to have at least one dance with him…

"So, what's the problem?" Willow asked.

"I just can't find what I'm looking for." Jasmine glanced once more across the rows and rows of silky fabrics and sequins.

"What *are* you looking for?" Willow asked, the confusion in her voice echoing Jasmine's own conflicted emotions.

"I haven't figured that out, either."

Luckily, Willow didn't lose patience quickly. "At least we know where the problem is."

Jasmine tried to explain. "I don't want it to be too sexy, because I'm also there in a professional capacity. But I also don't want it to be too businesslike, because…"

"Royce won't find that sexy?"

It took her a minute to admit it. "Well, yes."

"Where are these nerves still coming from? Y'all are great together."

And Jasmine knew that was true. In every single way except one: Rosie. After seeing Royce with his father, she knew better than anyone why he limited his time around children. A conviction that deep wasn't going to disappear overnight. She felt like she had to protect at least part of her heart, when what she really wanted was to jump in with both feet and leave her worries in the dust.

"I really enjoy being with Royce," she began.

Ivy stuck her head out of her dressing room. "Of course you do."

"But I just don't know that it can ever be something permanent."

Willow seemed to get this, although Ivy rolled her eyes. "Don't you trust Royce?" Ivy asked.

"In just about every way."

Willow peeked at her solemnly over the stack of dresses she'd started loading into her arms. "Then what is it that's holding you back?"

"Rosie."

"Why?" Ivy asked again.

"Babies are a big responsibility."

Ivy shrugged. "He seems to do fine whenever he's with her."

"But the occasional cuddle here and there isn't the same as living with a child. Royce has…issues."

"This is true," Willow confirmed.

Ivy, however, wasn't convinced. "What kind of issues?"

Jasmine forced herself back to her task, listlessly sifting through the racks. She wasn't sharing Royce's secrets. They were his to share, not hers. Willow reached over her to pick up dresses she'd overlooked.

After an uninspired search, they wandered toward the dressing rooms with just a few items. "Did the

Jeffersons give you flack because you're dating your client?" Willow asked.

"Nope. Which surprised me a little. I wasn't sure how they'd feel." Jasmine glanced over at Willow and lowered her voice a little, even though they were the only ones there at the moment. "Turns out Marilyn used to be Don's secretary."

Willow's green eyes went wide. "Wow. Never would have guessed that one. Every time I've met them, she just seems to…fit."

"I know. From admin assistant to billionaire wife. She has always seemed the perfect person to be at Don's side."

Ivy called from her dressing room. "Ooh, maybe I should join the trend…"

Jasmine was standing in the hallway not far from Ivy's curtained alcove. "It isn't as easy as you think."

"Why not?"

Jasmine couldn't tell if Ivy was being serious or just giving her older sister a hard time, which she liked to do on occasion.

"What if it ends?" Jasmine finally asked. "You're in the position of needing a new job then. If just one of you decides it isn't working, it can get messy. How do you act in front of people?" Jasmine was up close and personal with that particular situation, which was made even trickier because her business was dependent on appearances. "How much do you tell? How much do you keep to yourself? It's just very complicated."

"True. Still…"

Willow leaned closer but didn't bother to lower her voice. "Have you seen Ivy's boss? He's dreamy. He might actually be worth the risk."

"Well, if Ivy thinks it's worth it, *she* can have this ring." It was just complicating Jasmine's life. Though she'd never admit it to her sisters, the ring had indeed done its job. She couldn't deny that she wanted Royce forever…but a big part of her still doubted she would actually have him that long.

"Maybe the night of the masquerade," Ivy said, "especially if I wear this—"

She came out of the dressing room in a formal green dress. It faithfully followed her curves. Jewel chips formed flowers across the bodice and down one hip. The fit was gorgeous on Ivy's petite yet rounded figure. The color perfectly complemented her dark blond hair.

"Wow, Ivy," Jasmine breathed. "That's beautiful."

"Considering he's never seen me in anything but a business suit, I certainly hope *my* boss thinks so…"

Sixteen

Jasmine hung her dress in the alcove off the ballroom of Keller House, once again amazed at its brilliant blue color. The off-the-shoulder style and intricate beading were perfect. A fitted bodice flowed into a layered, full skirt that showcased her shape. Thank goodness the owner of the shop had stepped in and found an answer to her dress conundrum.

If only everything else were that easy.

The next two days certainly wouldn't be. She was at Keller House today to oversee the final setup. Most of tomorrow would be spent in preparation for the masquerade tomorrow night, and then there would be the event itself. Sunday she was hoping for a lazy sleep in, but as little as poor Rosie had seen of her this week, she wasn't holding her breath that the munchkin would cooperate.

She could at least have a lazy Sunday at home, though.

She made her way through the finished hallways to the incredible kitchen Royce had had installed. It was up and running, the catering staff currently finding a home for everything. She could see Geraldine laying out her plan and giving instructions on how to execute it. Having worked with the woman before, Jasmine didn't think there would be any problems there. Geraldine was as thorough and organized as Jasmine.

It would all work. The food was one area Jasmine didn't have to worry a lot about, but she couldn't stop herself from going over her checklist.

"Dominic, are you bumming samples?" Jasmine teased when she found the photographer in the kitchen.

He grinned. "Busted."

"We can always use an independent taste test," Geraldine said.

"Then you are a more generous woman than me." Jasmine smiled. "Of course, I know exactly how much he likes the sweet stuff. Doesn't Greg keep you in good supply at home?"

"Don't give away my secrets," Dominic said in a mock whisper.

"Okay… I'll distract you with a video, instead."

"Miss Rosie?" he asked.

"You bet."

Jasmine pulled out her phone and cued up the video Ivy had sent her from the night before. She'd been in the other room on the phone, confirming the catering list. Her sisters hadn't wanted to yell and distract Rosie, so they'd videoed it while they could. Thank goodness for modern digital technology.

Dominic gasped when Rosie started to show off her new crawling skills. "She's been rocking for a couple of weeks now..." Jasmine explained.

"And she just took off?"

Jasmine nodded. The excited conversation attracted the attention of the caterer and the kitchen staff, who converged on the phone to see Jasmine's daughter's new and exciting prowess.

Dominic shook his head, eyeing Jasmine with a mischievous look over the crowd. "Oh, you are in trouble now, girl."

"For what?" Royce asked as he entered the room. His business voice was one she rarely heard anymore—the no-nonsense, almost stern tone he used to command and commandeer. She and the entire kitchen staff jumped.

Dominic ignored them. "Check out this video of Rosie, Royce."

Jasmine suddenly felt like a kid caught with her hand in the cookie jar. The phrase *not a day care* roamed round and round in her brain. Not only had she been discussing her daughter in detail during work hours, but she'd distracted the staff with the video, also.

She was disrupting their productivity and focus...

Surprisingly, Royce did look at the video...actually,

he frowned. To Jasmine's shock, he then swiped a finger across the phone and started the video over again.

Finally, he said, "She crawled? Even though she's so little?"

Royce's gaze met hers, and she could see her own feelings mirrored in his eyes. Awe, excitement and a touch of fear.

Dominic said, "Cool, isn't it?"

"She's actually crawling right on time," Jasmine said, unable to quell her need to chatter. "Seven months. The doctors had worried about issues with her motor skills after..." Jasmine swallowed hard, trying to push back the memories of Rosie's mother struggling with drugs early in her pregnancy to ease the pain of her cancer. But the moment she'd known Rosie was there, she'd never touched anything her doctor didn't approve. "But she's a little trouper."

Royce shook his head slowly back and forth. "I'd be afraid of stepping on her or losing her."

Jasmine and Dominic shared a smile. "Well, it's not like I'm suddenly giving her free rein in the neighborhood or the keys to the car," Jasmine teased.

Dominic nodded in her direction. "Trust me, it's time to invest in some baby gates. She'll be into everything, as curious as she is."

"How do you know?" Royce asked.

Dominic puffed his chest out. "Proud, loving uncle to five nieces and nephews."

"Five?" Royce's surprise amused Jasmine.

"That's right," Dominic confirmed. "Five. And this little cutie is gonna be a handful. I guarantee it."

"I'd rather you didn't," Jasmine warned.

Despite her concern, Jasmine felt the glow of maternal pride. It was still fairly new, though less tentative than when Rosie had been a newborn. It had taken a while to give herself permission to feel it, to embrace it. Even though she'd legally been Rosie's mother from day one, it had taken time for her to grow into the role. She'd shared the daily responsibilities with Rosie's biological mother until she hadn't been able to help anymore. Her health had gone downhill rapidly after Rosie's birth. Her death had thrown Jasmine headlong into the reality of being responsible for such a small being's life.

Dominic winked. "Oh, before you know it, she'll be standing beside you at events like this in her own ball gowns."

Jasmine was shaking her head before he even finished, the words causing a distant panic to mix in with her pride. "Let's get through the challenges of potty training first…for now, back to work."

More than anything, she didn't want to push her luck with Royce. He'd been pretty understanding about this whole thing, had even participated in the conversation, but she was holding up progress here. Any minute he might remember that.

With a quick wave and a chorus of goodbyes from the kitchen staff, Jasmine headed back down the hallway to check out the formal living area where they were setting up carnival-type booths. Albeit for a very fancy carnival, that was for sure. Royce suddenly appeared at her side. For several moments, Jasmine maintained their silence.

She could tell Royce wanted to ask her something. She was simply afraid of what it was.

"Why weren't you there?" he finally asked.

"Where?"

"Watching Rosie crawl."

Jasmine froze, feeling as if someone had just punched the air from her lungs. She took a deep, extra-heavy breath, then said, "I was in the other room, confirming the menu with Marco."

She could feel her body stiffening, bracing herself for his derision.

"I'm sorry," he said simply.

What? "No *I told you so*?" Even though she kept her tone mild, Jasmine knew the words weren't. But frankly, she was tired of playing a guessing game. Now was as good a time as any to figure out where Royce stood on the subject of her and her child.

Even if it might burst her romantic bubble.

To her surprise, Royce reached out to rub his thumb across her left cheekbone. "My mother would say you've given me a wonderful gift."

His soft tone, his happy expression, reduced her question to a whisper. "What's that?"

"Helping me to see that women do whatever is necessary…which isn't always the same as what they want."

For a moment, Jasmine held her breath, afraid she might cry.

"What is it?" Royce finally asked.

"Your words are a gift to me, too."

Later that evening, everyone but Jasmine had finally left the restored mansion. She could almost feel the emptiness as she made one last check of the areas of the second floor that would be open to the public at tomorrow's masquerade.

In midafternoon, Royce had finally left to take care of some things at his office. Dominic had finalized the process for photographs and finished setting up the incredible photo booth. The backdrop was a doctored photograph of the house itself, looking mysterious draped in gray fog under a full moon struggling to be seen. Guests would sit in an elegant open carriage polished to a fine shine. Even Jasmine couldn't wait to have her picture taken.

She'd made the last touches to the flower arrangements on the side tables and in the seating areas. The ice sculpture would be delivered tomorrow, along with the centerpieces for the dining tables.

On her way back to the ballroom, Jasmine checked the long parlor along the front of the house where the carnival booths were set up. The whole length of the house had been beautifully restored, lovingly repainted with gold leaf accents. The chandeliers were original crystal period pieces and the long parlor had vintage wallpaper that Royce's contractor had ordered from overseas. But there was only one place in the house that caused Jasmine to hold her breath when she stepped in: the ballroom.

It was hard to believe people had homes with literal ballrooms in them anymore. But Royce's made Jasmine feel like a princess whenever she walked over the threshold. One entire side featured a series of large mirrors hanging in gilded frames. The rest of the walls had panels of hand-painted murals of lords and ladies from centuries past. Jasmine had only seen them in a horrible, degraded state. The experts Royce had brought in had restored them to their former glory as closely as possible.

Jasmine walked across the refinished floors, the click of her heels echoing. She went directly to the far wall where there was a hidden door in one of the panels. With a simple push, it allowed entrance to an alcove, but getting the right spot without knowing it beforehand was almost impossible. The room might once have been a ladies' sitting room, a place for women to catch their breath on elegant chaises, fix their hair and check makeup in the mirror of the old-fashioned vanity, or simply stare out the window over the back gardens.

Jasmine had a sudden itch to see her dress in the ballroom mirrors before tomorrow night's crowd cluttered the view. After stripping to her underwear, she took the gown carefully down off the hanger and stepped into it.

Only half of the chandeliers were on in the ballroom, giving it an even more magical feel. Jasmine had kept her heels on, so only the barest hint of the bottom edge of her dress touched the floor. Once, twice, she absently twirled before the mirrors.

The lights sparkled off the bodice and the tiny jewels adorning the edges of each layer of the skirt. Definitely princess material. She couldn't quite bring herself to pretend she was dancing, but the skirt flared out elegantly as she turned around and around in a circle. On one twirl, she spotted a shape in the doorway. Her heart jumped, throat closing for a moment until Royce stepped out into the soft light. Her pause was involuntary. It was as if everything stilled, waiting for him to lead the dance they'd come to share.

Royce walked slowly toward her, the look in his eyes nowhere close to businesslike. He was wearing his everyday suit, not a tux, but he pulled off a princely demeanor, anyway.

Feeling the pressure to fill the silence, she said, "Your mother would love what you've accomplished here. This house is magnificent."

He kept his solemn expression as he moved closer to her. "She'd appreciate it far more than my business accomplishments. I'm sure you would agree."

"Actually, Royce, I'm a businesswoman myself. While I love what you've done with the place in your mother's honor, I realize you couldn't create something this incredible without being successful in your professional life."

"She didn't approve of my work in many ways, didn't want me to follow my father's path."

Which he'd done wholeheartedly...until now. "But you haven't really, have you? You aren't your father."

He nodded slowly, as if he were thinking over his answer. "Maybe not."

Finally he stood before her, studying her with dramatic effect before stepping close to take her into his arms. But before he moved, he used one crooked finger to lift her chin so she could meet his look.

"Jasmine, I'll be so proud to have you by my side tomorrow."

Then he started to dance her around the room. There was no music, just the rhythm created by his body. Several times Jasmine caught the surreal sight of them in one of the mirrors. An elegant man and lady moving in time with each other. The fabric of her brilliant blue dress swirled and brushed over the legs of his pants.

But it was the look in his eyes that held her enthralled.

She'd been through so many changes this year. She'd lost a friend. She'd gained a child. She'd embarked on a journey as a mother. But, for the first time in a long time, her doubts were quiet and she was completely happy.

Maybe he will *accept all of me.*

Seventeen

Royce couldn't quite believe the woman in his arms was his. Soft. Sweet, with just enough spice. And he had no doubt that she was giving herself to him fully in this moment.

Was it possible to feel humbled and powerful at the same time?

He'd certainly never had the heady experience before, but he wasn't going to waste it. With the expert skill he'd never thought he'd need, he waltzed Jasmine in a full circle around the room, coming to rest near the alcove door. Knowing the house had been cleared of workers, he didn't bother leading her to a more secluded spot.

Privacy wasn't as important as their hunger for each other.

He thanked the universe for the opportunity and crowded her against the wall with his body. Her eyes widened. Her breasts plumped above the edge of her dress. Her skin was pale against the deep blue. Royce wanted to explore every inch, but for tonight, he would taste her right here.

His lips stroked over hers. He savored the mewling from her throat as their tongues entwined. She tasted of surrender, though he knew her strength; she had tested him with it more than once. And would again in the future.

But, for tonight, she was his.

She wasn't a passive princess. Her deft fingers unbuttoned his jacket then slid inside to spread warmth to his ribs through his thin dress shirt. Her touch sent a surge of need rushing through him. His hips pressed closer. She gasped.

He had to taste more of her.

Bending low, he placed his mouth right below her ear. One of the most tempting things Jasmine did to him every day was wear her hair up. It was gorgeous down, and it was pure pleasure burying his hands in its thickness. But when it was pulled up into a twist, a bun or, hell, even a ponytail, he couldn't resist the length of her neck and the sensitive skin he knew was there.

She clutched at him once more as his mouth covered the pulse point below her ear. Her breath hitched as he suckled lightly. The tension invading her body drove his own need higher. The fact that he knew how to make this woman ache with pleasure brought him the most satisfaction of anything he'd experienced thus far in life.

It was addictive. Necessary.

Slowly, he let himself meander the familiar but exciting path down her straining muscles. Her skin was smooth. Her body was responsive on every level. He lapped at the hollow at the base of her throat, savoring the rapid beat of her pulse. Her cries filled his ears. He knew without a doubt that she was ready for him.

But he wasn't taking things any further without sampling the top curve of her breasts, slightly salty from her day of work. He pulled her closer and lifted her higher with his hands at her waist. The tender flesh plumped beneath his lips. He couldn't stop working her until he nuzzled one tight nipple. Her textures and flavors amazed him.

He drew on her carefully, knowing how sensitive she was here. Her cries grew loud enough to echo off the walls. Strange how satisfying that was to hear. Royce played for long moments, feeling her fists clench and pull at his shirt.

Now. He needed her now.

With more haste than finesse, he scrambled beneath the layers at the front of her dress until his hands found skin. Then he followed the trembling muscles of her thighs to her damp underwear. Quickly he stripped it from her.

Mine. Mine.

He readied himself, practically tearing open his fly and fitting on a condom. He lifted one of her legs, making a place for himself between them. The moment that he slid inside, her head fell back against the wall. He captured her open mouth as he forged into her. The thrust and retreat was exquisite. His hips drove hard as she gasped out his name.

The feelings were too intense to last long. In a flash, they were both consumed. He gave one last thrust and her body clamped down on his with a demand of her own. And he obeyed without protest.

In the throbbing, heated aftermath, Royce knew a part of himself was now forever tied to this woman. For the first time, he could admit that he had no desire to fight the pull.

Jasmine's heart thrilled at the sight of hundreds of masked attendees in line to enter the mansion. The dark tuxes and formal gowns befit the setting, taking her back to a bygone era when this house was a mecca for Savannah society. The masks ranged from plain and simple to elegant affairs adorned with sparkles and feathers. They lent just the right touch of mystery, even when Jasmine knew who the wearer was.

Excitement filled the air as guests made their way inside. The chatter of each group transformed into oohs and aahs as they discovered all the wonderful entertainments available in the various rooms.

After most of the guests had arrived, Jasmine turned to the next person in line, only to discover Francis Staten. His long hair had had a slight trim and he sported a smooth new tux. She smiled. "Well, don't you look spiffy?"

His grin was a little shame-faced. "I was just gonna

dust off the old suit, but Royce had this delivered. I feel almost guilty wearing it."

"Don't." After years of seeing him in his khakis at the mission, she completely understood. Still... "Let him do this for you. Represent the mission tonight, in the midst of these people, with pride in all you do every day."

Jasmine knew how much more confident and comfortable she was among Savannah's elite when she dressed the part.

"I don't want people to think—"

"No, Francis. No one will think you are using the mission's money to buy yourself a suit. If they do, they won't understand what we're trying to do there, anyway. Just enjoy yourself, have a glass of champagne and talk us up."

"At least I'm comfortable giving speeches. Unlike wearing this bow tie."

He pulled at his collar as he walked away, but Jasmine was glad to see him join a conversation almost immediately. She didn't want him to feel alone all evening. Royce paused for a few moments to greet Francis, then made his way back to Jasmine's side.

His black tux and matching half mask set off his blond hair. Jasmine could have watched him walk toward her all day. He was so incredibly sexy...and all hers.

"Everything is going very well," he said, as he bent to kiss her.

"Thank you," she murmured against his lips.

He pulled back a fraction. "For what?"

"Francis's tux," she said, nodding in the other man's direction.

Royce glanced over his shoulder before turning back to her. "I figured it would help him feel more comfortable here. If he had the money for one, that's certainly not what he would spend it on."

"How did you know that?" Because Royce was exactly right.

His dark gaze was intense behind the mask. "I know a few things about people, you know. Even if I've never put them to good use in social situations before."

"Well, thank you for seeing that."

"Thank you for taking me to the mission so I could see it."

Before Jasmine had a chance to savor his words, the Jeffersons appeared before them. "Jasmine," Don said, "you have gone above and beyond this time. This masquerade is incredible."

Marilyn Jefferson's eyes sparkled behind her purple feathered mask. "And this house! I didn't even realize it was being renovated."

"For several years now," Royce said. "In honor of my mother. She loved this place."

"I'm sure," Marilyn said with a soft smile. "I just hate that she didn't see it like this. In the glory you've worked so hard to achieve."

Jasmine explained, "She lived in the carriage house for a few years as the renovations began."

"The final version that I executed is almost identical to the plans she drew up herself," Royce said.

"Congratulations, Royce," Don said. "Tonight will

be a smashing success, I know. For you and the mission. On Monday, let's make an appointment. To talk."

Jasmine knew Royce wanted to smile big, but he kept it under wraps pretty well. Still, she could feel the jolt of excitement that ran through his body. "I will set that up. Thank you, sir."

After the Jeffersons had walked away, Jasmine kissed Royce hard and long, not caring who watched. "Congratulations," she finally murmured.

The evening was as successful as Don Jefferson had predicted. Preliminary counts said they had earned more than enough money to pay for a nice, large building with sleeping quarters on the mission's campus and some additional upgrades, as well.

It wasn't until after the big announcements late in the evening that Jasmine even realized Royce's father was there.

She recognized that analytical gaze easily, despite the plain black mask he sported. Just the feel of him looking in her direction made her stomach clench and bile back up in her throat. Yet, for the next half hour, she saw him everywhere she looked, no matter what she was doing.

Finally she was able to break away from her hostessing duties and find Royce. To warn him. But she arrived only seconds before his father did.

Royce glared at the man over her shoulder. "You're not welcome here."

Jasmine turned to find John completely unmoved by Royce's anger.

"I bought a ticket," he said with a shrug.

"And I'll happily refund your money."

John cocked his head to the side, studying Royce as if to figure out exactly what he needed to say to get through to the man before him. "If word got around that you threw me out, that might hurt donations."

"We don't need any more." Royce's expression was undeniably proud. "But if we did, I'd make it up out of my own pocket."

"That's not good business, Royce. You know that." John shook his head as if Royce were behaving childishly. "You cannot let your emotions rule over money."

"Tonight's not about business," Jasmine insisted.

But the look John turned her way reminded her she wasn't speaking for herself. "You sure?"

Suddenly she remembered Don Jefferson's invitation to set up an appointment with Royce. The real reason he had started this venture so long ago. But before she could respond, Ivy appeared at her elbow. "Jasmine, the catering lady has a question. She's looking for you."

"Right," John said, "Go on back to work now."

Royce stepped firmly between her and his father, brushing a brief kiss over her brow. "Go ahead," he murmured. "Don't worry. I'll handle dear old Dad."

Eighteen

So Jasmine left, but forty-five minutes later, she realized that Royce was nowhere to be found. Oh, the party was in full swing without him, but that didn't defuse the worry that settled in her gut.

She knew he wasn't in the front parlor, because she'd just been through there. Everything was running smoothly and the vendors had given her very positive feedback. But there'd been no sign of Royce.

Next, she checked the ballroom as best as she could. Between the dancers and those milling around listening to the small orchestra, it was a little too crowded for an accurate reading. But she didn't see him. The kitchen and dining rooms were also a bust.

Though he could have stepped outside to cool off, that didn't feel right. Besides, Jasmine wasn't familiar enough with the grounds to trust herself to go looking around in the dark.

Instead, she climbed the back stairs. Several rooms at the front of the second floor had been opened for guests to tour, including a grand sitting room and a couple of bedrooms. There were other completed rooms on this floor that weren't open for viewing. One she knew to be an office that Royce had set up with equipment in case he needed to be reached or do something while he was out here—which he often had been during the last month or so.

As she reached the top of the stairs, muffled voices reached her. Alert that there was someone in the office, she approached the closed door with trepidation. Why would Royce have brought his father up here? Or was it just someone else he'd wanted to talk to?

She didn't want to interrupt business. But the thought that he would be taking a business meeting in the middle of their event was upsetting.

At first she thought the door was closed, but as she reached it, she realized it was cracked. The voices filtered through enough that she recognized Royce... and his father. She should have just turned away, gone back downstairs and left Royce to handle it. Instead, she reached out and pushed the door back an inch, allowing her to see a small sliver of the scene inside.

John Nave flicked a silver lighter, then used it to light a thin cigar. He puffed a few times, causing the tip to glow red. "I, more than anyone, know how disruptive women can be," he finally said.

Royce turned to him. The lamp nearby allowed Jasmine to read the surprise on his face. Unconcerned, his father blew out a stream of cigar smoke. "Yes, your mother wasn't the first. But she was the only one I made the mistake of getting pregnant."

"I wouldn't consider myself a mistake."

John paused in that way he had, as if he considered every word before speaking it. "I did, at the time. But I've checked in through the years. You've turned out well. Still, I felt it was best if I married after that."

Royce scoffed. "I wouldn't call what you have a marriage. More like a business arrangement."

"I call it the best of both worlds. I handle the business. She handles the house and our image. And takes the edge off when I really need it. What more could I want?"

Jasmine waited for Royce to say *love*, but he remained silent.

"You've made a terrible misstep, son. I've seen the way you look at her. You're going soft. Besides, that woman has a baby, for Christ's sake. One that's not even hers."

"How did you find that out?" Royce stalked closer to stand over John's chair. "Never mind. I'm sure I can guess. A better question is, why do you care?"

"Because *you* should," John insisted, gaining his feet to meet Royce head-on. "You should care that her middle-class family is going to suck your focus away from your business. Why would you let someone like that stand in the way of achieving all that you can?"

Royce's voice hardened. "I have never let anything

stand in the way of my success. I'm not about to start now."

John extended his hand to shake Royce's. "Good. I'm glad to hear that."

Jasmine's last look showed Royce and his father standing close to each other, hands clasped, the picture of power and business acumen.

There was no place in that picture for family or all the tender, passionate emotions Royce inspired inside her. Emotions he obviously didn't return. Had he been pretending all along?

Turning, Jasmine fled back along the hall and down the staircase, holding her quiet sobs inside and lifting her skirt just enough to keep her from tripping and breaking a bone.

She rushed along the hall behind the kitchen, her only thought that she needed out before she broke down completely. Then she ran smack into someone tall and solid.

"Sugar, what's the matter?" Dominic asked.

Just hearing his voice brought reality back in a rush. Jasmine clutched at the front of his jacket, dragging in deep breaths in an attempt to get herself under control. Unfortunately, that just made the darkened hall whirl around her. "I feel dizzy."

"Come here."

Dominic clutched her to his solid chest as he led her to a small storage room where he pulled out one of the folding chairs they were using for seating in the dining room and settled her into it. Then he opened one for himself and sat next to her.

"Now, tell me what's wrong."

Jasmine shook her head, unable to put into words the pain she felt. "I trusted him."

"Who?" Dominic asked, laying his large hand against the bare skin of her upper back. His heat calmed her, centered her focus on that one spot. Oddly enough, it made her realize that the rest of her body was chilled, inside and out.

"Royce. I thought…" Why had she thought that she would be enough to make the leopard change his spots? "I thought maybe he might be different."

"Was he ugly to you? Did he hurt you?"

"No." *He simply chose business over me.* "I just overheard something I shouldn't have."

"Maybe you didn't hear enough."

She hadn't wanted to hear more. She shook her head. "I don't know if I can do this."

Dominic's hand flexed against her, drawing her focus away from the pain in her heart. "You can," he said. "Tonight is your crowning glory, and it's almost over. Ivy and I will help you finish what you need to, I promise."

Jasmine just hoped that would be enough.

Royce concentrated hard on the feel of John's hand against his, letting the sounds of the party in the house disappear. He'd never touched his father before. He'd never wanted to be this close to him.

Just as he'd expected, the grip was firmer than it needed to be—a competition to see who could outman the other. It wasn't the recognition and respect Royce had exchanged with men like Don Jefferson. Men who were high achievers in their businesses, but who were also intent on contributing to the greater good in their families, their communities and the world.

Royce tightened his hold before stepping in, mere inches away from his father. He had to admit the slight advantage he had in height made him feel superior, even though it was a petty sentiment that shouldn't have a place here. Then again, his father preferred for this meeting to be about strength, and probably his own superiority to his son. Apparently, he'd come here to school Royce in how he should live.

But he had no lessons Royce needed to learn.

He found himself leaning close to his father's face, looking him dead in the eye and acknowledging the biological link between the two of them. Then he grinned, because he didn't have to base his life and decisions on that biology. Or, rather, he'd prefer his maternal biology to any genes this man had passed on to him.

"That's right," he said, his voice low but clear. "I've never let anything stand in the way of achieving my goals...only my goals have changed."

John's eyes widened as Royce's grip turned punishing. After a few seconds, Royce turned away. But he wasn't done proving his point. "Success isn't defined by money, *Father*, despite this belief system that you've built your life upon. I've seen many examples in the business community of men who care just as much about their fellow man as they do about themselves."

"And they're poorer because of it," John insisted.

"How much money do you really need to live, John? After all, you can only drive one Rolls Royce at a time."

The other man's gaze flared at Royce's words.

"I'd rather have one or two fewer cars and build a dormitory for homeless men at the City Sanctuary mission. I'd rather make a little less money on a shipping contract and know that people are getting life-saving supplies that they need. After all, I only require one place to live."

He gestured around the luxury office he'd built here at Keller House. "All of this is simply surplus."

Royce returned to his post behind the large mahogany desk but didn't sit down. Instead, he faced his father—businessman to businessman. "But most important, John, I'd rather have the love of a good woman and a family as my legacy than the money to build a huge mausoleum for all the people who couldn't give a rat's ass about visiting my grave after I'm gone. That's *my* definition of success."

"You're wrong."

"Am I? Because tonight I have my money, my woman and a child with the sweetest smile in the world. A child who deserves a chance to achieve her own success, no matter who contributed to her biological makeup. What do you have besides your money, a wife who couldn't care less about you and a big, empty house?"

Royce braced his hands on the desktop, staring the other man down. "Now, while this little family reunion has been very enlightening, in the future, you will not contact me. If you see me in public, you will walk the other way. If you see my future wife, future child, employees or anyone associated with me, you will keep on walking. If you don't, I will make sure you regret it. Because I don't need you in my life."

It was almost amusing to see his father draw his body straighter, even though he was facing defeat. "I doubt you can do that."

"Oh, I can. You see, I know what you value the most, *Father*. And while I'm sure you had plenty of cronies to help you disavow me and leave my mother poverty-stricken while she raised your child, this is a new day. A new culture. And news of the steps you took to ruin that woman and your biological child won't go over nearly as well in today's business climate—especially coming straight from that child himself. Who is now a very successful man in his own right."

Royce smiled, though he knew it wasn't a pleasant expression. "So I will warn you again—you keep your mouth shut. That is, if you want me to do the same."

Nineteen

Jasmine kept herself busy. Since she knew she would need to leave sooner rather than later, she quietly made preparations to disappear once the midnight unveiling had happened. For the first time ever, she had no plans to stay at her event until the last guest had left and the last plate was packed.

Ivy seemed to have disappeared while Jasmine was upstairs, and she wasn't answering her phone, so Jasmine went to the point person in each area to make sure they were covered. Plans had been made to close the party at 2:00 a.m. Every staff member knew what was expected of them. A cleaning crew would be here tomorrow.

She'd hoped her sister would stay behind as her eyes and ears, but she'd make do as best she could.

Who knew how long she'd be able to hold all these emotions inside? And the last thing she wanted was to make small talk with Royce while wondering if he was simply humoring her to get her into bed.

There was nothing she wanted more than to get out of this dress and be home with her family. That was the difference between her and Royce. They were her comfort, her sustenance. Royce would have to settle for sleeping with cold hard cash if his success meant so much to him.

Jasmine's hypervigilance allowed her to spot him when he came down the stairs. John wasn't with him. Luckily, Royce paused with some guests, so she headed in the opposite direction. It wasn't like she didn't have plenty to do.

The waiters started to circulate throughout the ballroom with fresh trays of champagne while staff informed guests throughout the house that it was almost time for the midnight unveiling. Jasmine had been so looking forward to this part of the night. That romantic moment when masks were discarded, when the true person behind the mask was revealed.

Even though she and Royce recognized each other behind their masks, she'd still looked forward to meeting his gaze in that moment.

Now the last thing she wanted was to look at Royce without the protection of her mask hiding her expression.

She saw his sandy-blond head as he entered the ballroom. Even from this distance, she knew he was looking for her. And she couldn't handle it. She simply couldn't.

As she backed slowly away, her hand made contact with the wall behind her. That's when she realized the panel where she stood was actually the door to the private ladies' alcove. She hadn't revealed the existence of the little room to the guests. Jasmine took a quick look around to see if anyone was watching, but they'd all turned their attention to the MC preparing the crowd for the pinnacle of the evening. So she opened the door and slipped inside.

Only seconds after she'd quietly closed the door, her phone vibrated. It was her sister.

"Ivy, where are you?" she whispered frantically.

It wasn't as if there was anyone in the room to hear her, but she couldn't help it. Her rapidly beating heart felt as if it was calling out across the room. What if Royce found her here?

She wasn't sure she could face him.

"I'm so sorry, Jasmine," her sister said from the other end of the line. "I left."

"You what?"

"I left…with someone."

Even though Jasmine should have been questioning her sister or concerned for her safety, she could only respond with panic over her absence. "I need your help. Right now."

"I'm on my way to Paxton's apartment."

"What?" Oh, that was a bad idea. A very bad idea.

"I just… I want this, Jasmine."

"Please don't. I'm telling you, Ivy. This is not a

good choice." Jasmine knew that for certain. Now more than ever.

"But it's my choice," Ivy said softly. "And I'm going to make it."

"Ivy!" Jasmine cried, but her sister had already hung up. "Damn it."

Why wouldn't her little sister listen to her? She was getting her own heart broken over a client right now. She knew just how dangerous those working relationships could be.

But Ivy, as the youngest, had been trying to prove she wasn't a child for a while now. This act of rebellion might end up costing her more than her job.

As the sounds of a trumpet heralded the coming of midnight in the ballroom, Jasmine quickly gathered her purse and keys, a plan forming in her mind. She'd slip from the room while everyone was distracted and make her way to her car. She could send Ivy back to Keller House for the rest of her stuff tomorrow.

Right now, she just needed out.

Away from the fairy tale she'd thought was happening and home to the day-to-day drudgery and chaos that was her life. She'd find magic again, someday, but she'd learned her lesson. Never date a client. Never get so close you think you're seeing behind the facade, only to learn the facade had been the reality all along.

Time to go.

Desperate to get away, Jasmine jerked the door open, only to find herself face-to-face with the one man she never wanted to see again. Well, maybe he wasn't the only one. She'd be happy never to see his father again, either.

"Jasmine, where have you been?" Royce's hard business tone scraped over her nerves.

"I could ask you the same thing," she choked out.

"What are you talking about?" He frowned. "I've been looking everywhere for you."

"Why?" A small spark of her normal sassiness finally made an appearance. "Are you unhappy with my service in some way?"

"What?"

She shook her head, grief overwhelming that tiny spark.

"Jasmine, what is it?"

The words simply wouldn't come. She had no idea whether to lay into him, scream and cry, or simply skulk away from the humiliation of knowing he'd lied to her. Granted, he hadn't turned into some kind of super-involved family guy. If anything, at times he'd seemed lost.

But he hadn't retreated, hadn't rejected Rosie completely. And he'd made love to Jasmine with a passion she'd never experienced before and hadn't been strictly business outside of the bedroom. Memories of him holding Rosie at the hospital, helping them get Auntie taken care of, talking about his mother's death…he'd opened himself up to her and her family.

Had the confrontation with his father washed all of that away?

I have never let anything stand in the way of my

success. I'm not about to start now. No. She wasn't strong enough to find out.

Around them the crowd erupted in applause. The lights dimmed for a moment, then the orchestra struck up a lively tune. But Jasmine and Royce remained frozen in their silent battle. Without permission, Royce reached up to touch the mask she'd had made to match her dress. His other hand found the ties at the back of her head.

He was so close, his touch so intimate, that she was transported back to the night before, when he'd shown her in no uncertain terms just how much he enjoyed her. Only now, their encounter felt dirty, tainted by motives she could only guess at.

It wasn't until the strings came loose and Royce pulled the mask away that Jasmine felt the tears spill onto her cheeks. Royce's eyes widened and what looked like panic washed over his expression. But all Jasmine could feel was the humiliation of knowing she was crying over a man who would walk away from her whenever business demanded.

So she walked away first and didn't look back.

Royce looked down at the paper Matthew had handed him and cursed. Jasmine's final invoice.

She hadn't wasted any time. It had only been three days since the masquerade. Three days in which she wouldn't return his phone calls or text messages. He'd even gone by the house once. Auntie had answered the door, holding Rosie, only to tell him that Jasmine wasn't home. From her worried expression, he assumed she was telling him the truth.

But she'd also refused to tell him anything else.

He'd learned nothing about what had upset Jasmine that night, though he suspected it had something to do with his father's visit. As far as he could tell, they hadn't spoken to each other alone. She could have overheard something, but what?

Royce was an astute businessman, but when it came to women, especially upset women, he was more than a little lost. He'd have given anything to have his mother there so he could ask her advice. Did he confront Jasmine? Leave her to stew for a while? What?

"I just don't understand, Matthew," he said, more as a way to express his frustration than anything.

"I know. She was perfect for you." As soon as the words left his mouth, Matthew must have realized what he'd said, because his assistant's eyes went wide and worried.

"You're right. She is."

Matthew started to shake his head and back away. He was probably wondering where the heck his real boss had gone.

Royce was beyond caring about keeping things professional. He ran a rough hand through his hair, no longer worried what it would look like afterward—or who might see it messed up. He was no longer the consummate professional. Jasmine had stripped the superficial facade away. "But I can't fix what's wrong until I know what it is."

Matthew studied him for a moment, then cautiously offered, "Obviously you aren't trying hard enough."

"What? I've texted, called, gone by the house."

"Come on," Matthew admonished, the tension in his body easing up some. "Where's the guy who beat out every shipping company in Savannah to get Jefferson's contract? I'm pretty sure you stepped out of your comfort zone to accomplish that."

Boy, had he. "But this is a woman."

"No different…except you might need a little more finesse. Use some of those personal negotiating techniques Jasmine taught you."

"A little more finesse, huh?"

Royce thought about that the rest of the day. Jasmine's techniques had really just been about seeing people for who they were, treating them with respect as human beings. She'd drilled that into him, but he still needed a little more work in that area.

Starting now.

Even though it was about an hour before he normally left the office, Royce headed for the door. "Take the rest of the day off, Matthew."

He had to smile at his assistant's gasp. Those words hadn't been uttered in Royce Brazier's office, well, ever.

So why was Royce grinning as he got into his car?

Today was a Thursday. Jasmine always volunteered at the mission on Thursday evenings. She had for the entire two months he'd known her. Why not use that knowledge to his advantage?

As he drove toward the mission, he experienced

an unfamiliar sensation of freedom. So this was what playing hooky felt like.

Of course, it didn't hurt that he had some business to discuss with Francis Staten. Royce hadn't changed his stripes *entirely*.

He walked into the mission's large dining area just as the line was forming for dinner service. Sure enough, Jasmine stood behind the steam tables. Their eyes met across the room. He could read the jolt in her body, even from this distance.

The pull to go to her was strong. He wanted to be near her, beside her. But he had to make things right first.

So he crossed the room to find Francis, instead. The director stood with several visitors, chatting before the meal. He greeted Royce with a smile and a warm handshake. "So good to see you here."

"Thank you," Royce replied. "I wonder if you would spare me a few moments of your time."

"Absolutely." Francis said his goodbyes to the others, then gestured for Royce to follow him out of the room. "I hope this isn't bad news."

Royce was quick to reassure him. "Definitely not." But he waited until they reached Francis's office before filling him in.

"Everything has been tallied and totaled, and we had some very generous donors at the masquerade," Royce said.

"That's good," Francis said with a smile. "And I can't remember ever enjoying an evening so much. What you and Jasmine put together was pure magic."

"Yes, it was, wasn't it?" He and Jasmine were magic together, too, if only he could get her to see that.

"Now, why do the two of you both turn so solemn when I say that?" Francis's gaze was a little too astute.

And here Royce had thought he was going to be able to stick to business, at least for this part of the evening. "Just a little misunderstanding that I'm hoping to clear up."

"I hope so, too. Jasmine deserves to be happy. And so do you, young man."

"Happiness never factored into the equation for me before," Royce said with a sigh. The happiness he'd found with Jasmine would leave a hole in his life if they weren't together. *Please let me be able to fix this.*

"What about now?"

Now, Royce was determined to make Jasmine the happiest woman on earth. If he had to give up every dime to do it.

But instead of saying that, Royce simply smiled and returned to the original subject. "The truth is, we made far more than our goal at the masquerade."

"Oh?"

"It will mean you'll have more to work with when you build the men's sleeping quarters. But I have an idea I would like to propose."

Francis beamed at Royce as he explained his plan. The money he gave wasn't going into this man's pocket, yet it still made Francis happy because it meant he could help more people every day. That humbled Royce.

"There isn't enough to cover all I'm suggesting, but

I'm willing to donate the additional funds myself," he said, waving away Francis's protests. "But I have a confession to make."

Francis was all ears.

"I'm going to need your help."

Thirty minutes later, Francis was more than on board.

Twenty

Jasmine watched the men approach, her mouth dry and her heart pounding. Her hands shook as she tried to maneuver the hot pan of food into the empty slot on the steam table.

They sure looked chummy.

Not that she wanted Francis to be angry at Royce. She'd deliberately told no one except her sisters about the break because the responsibility was hers. Royce had told her, warned her in many different ways, that he wasn't built for family or forever. She'd chosen to listen to her heart, instead. And she'd paid the price.

Now, part of her felt violated that he was here, in her space, her territory. Not that she owned the mission. The feeling was ridiculous. But it was there, nonetheless.

She also needed to face the fact that she might be seeing a lot of Royce during the upcoming construction. Or maybe not. Certainly if he returned to his normal way of conducting business, it wouldn't be a problem.

He'd just put someone in charge and go on his way.

But she never would have imagined him coming to the mission of his own accord, so anything was possible. And something in his expression told her that he was going to choose a hands-off approach.

"Jasmine," Francis started, "Royce brought delightful news today."

Her smile felt unnatural, like hard plastic. But it was better than crying.

In contrast, Francis looked ecstatic. "We're not getting just one new dormitory, but two."

Shock rippled through her. "Excuse me?"

"Royce himself is donating the cost of a new women's dorm—in full. We will be able to provide better accommodations and turn the original housing into small private rooms so families can stay together while they're with us."

"Um…" Speechless didn't begin to touch it. This was a dream she and Francis had discussed for several years but they'd figured it was forever out of reach.

"And he wants you to work with him on it."

Whoa. What? "I do events, not buildings."

"But you know more than anyone what these women need," Francis pointed out. "You could offer great insight into planning and utilization of the space to meet those needs."

Why wasn't Royce saying anything?

"You two talk about it. Then come see me." Francis laid a hand on Jasmine's arm and gave her the same comforting smile he'd been offering since she first walked through the door at fifteen. "Just consider it."

Jasmine forced herself to tell the woman working next to her that she needed to take a break. Then she stripped off her gloves and headed out the back door to the small lawn where Francis maintained his beloved rose bushes. Royce could follow if he wanted.

Her thoughts whirled ninety to nothing. When she couldn't stand the chaos anymore, she turned on him. "Seriously? What is this? Some kind of ploy?"

"Actually, it's an apology."

Surprise left Jasmine speechless for a moment. There'd been way too much that left her speechless today. She crossed her arms under her breasts and summoned the firm tone she used when the boys in the afterschool programs decided to act the fool. "Explain."

"It's an apology from me to Francis...and to you. And a decision my father will hate—so it's a win-win."

She raised a brow, completely uninterested in talking about John Nave.

Royce stepped closer. Jasmine was glad she had her arms crossed in front of her. It lessened the temptation to reach out and touch him. "It's an apology for acting out of greed."

Jasmine found herself holding her breath as he met and held her gaze. "I started all of this in an effort to make money, Jasmine. Now, on the other side of it,

I realize how wrong that is. You were right. I wish I could say I did the masquerade in an effort to help people, to help the mission. But I honestly didn't care about the mission's needs."

His next step brought him just inches from her. "But I was right about one thing."

"What's that?" she whispered, then cleared her throat.

"You were the heart of all we did together."

She couldn't push him away when he leaned down to kiss her, but she couldn't pull him closer, either. The conflict inside of her refused to die.

And he refused to move away. "Now, tell me what happened, Jasmine."

This time she was silent because she wasn't sure what to say, not because of sheer stubbornness.

"I'm used to the sexy, strong woman who set me straight in her own sweet and sassy way. This silence is scary."

"Well, it's easier to be sassy when there's nothing big at stake."

"Is there something big at stake now?"

Jasmine turned away. She just couldn't bear to face his intent gaze. "Just leave it alone, Royce."

"I didn't get where I am by walking away."

That sparked her temper. "I'm not a business deal." Her voice rose as she tossed the words back over her shoulder.

"And I'm not a robot. Next to losing my mother, nothing has impacted me like losing you."

She wanted to believe that, but she couldn't ignore what she'd heard. "Then why would you do it?"

"Jasmine, I'm afraid I need more to go on."

"I overheard you with your father, Royce!" Jasmine whirled around to confront him. "How could you shake that man's hand and say 'I have never let anything stand in the way of my success. I'm not about to start now'?"

"Because I needed to speak in a language he understood."

The confusion on his face frustrated her. She groaned, then stomped away. How could he dismiss this so easily?

"I'm going to guess from your reaction that you didn't stick around for anything further?"

This time she faced him from the safe, much more comfortable distance of a few feet. "What more could be said after that?"

"How about—I'll do whatever I can to achieve success…but my definition of success has changed?"

His answer was so unexpected, she almost couldn't get her question out. "To what?" she whispered.

"Jasmine, you've taught me so much over the last couple of months," he said, shaking his head as if he still couldn't believe it. "Not just you, but Don and Marilyn, Dominic, your family. The problem with immersing yourself in business is that, after a while, that's all you see."

And that described the Royce she'd met that first day.

He went on, "My mother tried to warn me, but I refused to listen. I just knew that I had to prove myself, and my father's measuring stick was money."

"But you had your mother."

"I did," Royce conceded. "And I took care of her as best as I knew how. But emotionally…emotionally, Jasmine, I'm not nearly as savvy as I am at business." He stepped carefully into her personal space. "Actually, I'm in desperate need of someone to teach me what I need to know."

"Teach you?"

He nodded, but it was the look in his eyes that took her breath away. "I think it's time I conquered a new arena."

"What's that?"

"Love. Family."

Was this really happening? Jasmine was almost afraid to believe.

"Would you and Auntie and Rosie and your sisters be willing to take on a workaholic CEO and teach me how to be…human?"

Yes, this might actually be happening. "I think your mother would have liked that."

"I know she would."

With the gentlest of touches, Royce cupped his hands around Jasmine's face. As his lips touched hers, she again felt the magic of connecting with him.

After long minutes, he murmured against her lips. "I need you, Jasmine. Please help me become the man I should be. A husband. A father."

Was it possible for your heart to explode, simply

from emotion? But Jasmine couldn't give in to the mushiness too fast. "On one condition."

"What's that?"

Jasmine dragged in a deep breath before she said, "That whatever we do...we do it together."

"That's a deal I'll never turn down."

* * * * *

*If you liked this story
pick up these other novels from
Dani Wade!*

*HIS BY DESIGN
A BRIDE'S TANGLED VOWS
THE BLACKSTONE HEIR
THE RENEGADE RETURNS*

Available now from Harlequin Desire!

And don't miss the next
BILLIONAIRES AND BABIES *story,*
*BILLIONAIRE BOSS, HOLIDAY BABY
by Janice Maynard.
Available October 2017!*

*If you're on Twitter, tell us what you think of
Harlequin Desire! #harlequindesire*

*If you enjoyed this book, you'll love
CAN'T HARDLY BREATHE,
the next book in* New York Times
bestselling author Gena Showalter's
ORIGINAL HEARTBREAKERS *series.
Read on for a sneak peek!*

DANIEL PORTER SAT at the edge of the bed. Again and again he dismantled and rebuilt his Glock 17. Before he removed the magazine, he racked the slide to ensure no ammunition remained in the chamber. He lifted the upper portion of the semiautomatic, detached the recoil spring as well as the barrel. Then he put everything back together.

Rinse and repeat.

Some things you had to do over and over, until every cell in your body learned to perform the task on autopilot. That way, when bullets started flying, you'd react the right way—immediately—without having to check a training manual.

When his eyelids grew heavy, he placed the gun on

the nightstand and stretched out across the mattress only to toss and turn. Staying at the Strawberry Inn without a woman wasn't one of his brightest ideas. Sex kept him distracted from the many horrors that lived inside his mind. After multiple overseas military tours, constant gunfights, car bombs, finding one friend after another blown to pieces, watching his targets collapse because he'd gotten a green light and pulled the trigger...his sanity had long since packed up and moved out.

Daniel scrubbed a clammy hand over his face. In the quiet of the room, he began to notice the mental chorus in the back of his mind. Muffled screams he'd heard since his first tour of duty. He pulled at hanks of his hair, but the screams only escalated.

This. This was the reason he refused to commit to a woman. Well, one of many reasons. He was too messed up, his past too violent, his present too uncertain.

A man who looked at a TV remote as if it were a bomb about to detonate had no business inviting an innocent civilian into his crazy.

He'd even forgotten how to laugh.

No, not true. Since his return to Strawberry Valley, two people had defied the odds and amused him. His best friend slash spirit animal Jessie Kay West...and Dottie.

My name is Dorothea.

She'd been two grades behind him, had always kept to herself, had never caused any trouble and had never attended any parties. A "goody-goody," many had called her. Daniel remembered feeling sorry for her, a sweetheart targeted by the town bully.

Today, his reaction to her endearing shyness and unintentional insults had shocked him. Somehow she'd turned him on so fiercely, he'd felt as if *years* had passed since he'd last had sex rather than a few hours. But then, everything about his most recent encounter with Dot—Dorothea had shocked him.

Upon returning from his morning run, he'd stood in the doorway of his room, watching her work. As she'd vacuumed, she'd wiggled her hips, dancing to music with a different beat than the song playing on his iPod.

Control had been beyond him—he'd hardened instantly.

He'd noticed her appeal on several other occasions, of course. How could he not? Her eyes, once too big for her face, were now a perfect fit and the most amazing shade of green. Like shamrocks or lucky charms, framed by the thickest, blackest lashes he'd ever seen. Those eyes were an absolute showstopper. Her lips were plump and heart-shaped, a fantasy made flesh. And her body...

Daniel grinned up at the ceiling. He suspected she had serious curves underneath her scrubs. The way the material had tightened over her chest when she'd moved...the lushness of her ass when she'd bent over...every time he'd looked at her, he'd sworn he'd developed early-onset arrhythmia.

With her eyes, lips and corkscrew curls, she reminded

him of a living doll. *Blow her up, and she'll blow me.*
He really wanted to play with her.

But he wouldn't. Ever. She lived right here in town.

When Daniel first struck up a friendship with
Jessie Kay, his father expressed hope for a Christmas
wedding and grandkids soon after. The moment Daniel
had broken the news—no wedding, no kids—Virgil
teared up.

Lesson learned. When it came to Strawberry Valley
girls, Virgil would always think long-term, and he
would always be disappointed when the relationship
ended. Stress wasn't good for his ticker. Daniel loved
the old grump with every fiber of his being, wanted
him around as long as possible.

*Came back to care for him. Not going to make
things worse.*

Bang, bang, bang!

Daniel palmed his semiautomatic and plunged to
the floor to use the bed as a shield. As a bead of sweat
rolled into his eye, his finger twitched on the trigger.
The screams in his head were drowned out by the
sound of his thundering heartbeat.

Bang, bang!

He muttered a curse. The door. Someone was
knocking on the door.

Disgusted with himself, he glanced at the clock on
the nightstand—1:08 a.m.

As he stood, his dog tags clinked against his
mother's locket, the one he'd worn since her death.

He pulled on the wrinkled, ripped jeans he'd tossed earlier and anchored his gun against his lower back.

Forgoing the peephole, he looked through the crack in the window curtains. His gaze landed on a dark, wild mass of corkscrew curls, and his frown deepened. Only one woman in town had hair like that, every strand made for tangling in a man's fists.

Concern overshadowed a fresh surge of desire as he threw open the door. Hinges squeaked, and Dorothea paled. But a fragrant cloud of lavender enveloped him, and his head fogged; desire suddenly overshadowed concern.

Down, boy.

She met his gaze for a split second, then ducked her head and wrung her hands. Before, freckles had covered her face. Now a thick layer of makeup hid them. Unfortunate. He liked those freckles, often imagined—

Nothing.

"Is something wrong?" On alert, he scanned left… right… The hallway was empty, no signs of danger.

As many times as he'd stayed at the inn, Dorothea had only ever spoken to him while cleaning his room. Which had always prompted his early-morning departures. There'd been no reason to grapple with temptation.

"I'm fine," she said, and gulped. Her shallow inhalations came a little too quickly, and her cheeks grew chalk white. "Super fine."

How was her tone shrill and breathy at the same time?

He relaxed his battle stance, though his confusion remained. "Why are you here?"

"I…uh… Do you need more towels?"

"Towels?" His gaze roamed over the rest of her, as if drawn by an invisible force—disappointment struck. She wore a bulky, ankle-length raincoat, hiding the body underneath. Had a storm rolled in? He listened but heard no claps of thunder. "No, thank you. I'm good."

"Okay." She licked her porn-star lips and toyed with the tie around her waist. "Yes, I'll have coffee with you."

Coffee? "Now?"

A defiant nod, those corkscrew curls bouncing.

He barked out a laugh, surprised, amazed and delighted by her all over again. "What's really going on, Dorothea?"

Her eyes widened. "My name. You remembered this time." When he stared at her, expectant, she cleared her throat. "Right. The reason I'm here. I just… I wanted to talk to you." The color returned to her cheeks, a sexy blush spilling over her skin. "May I come in? Please. Before someone sees me."

Mistake. That blush gave a man ideas.

Besides, what could Miss Mathis have to say to him? He ran through a mental checklist of possible problems. His bill—nope, already paid in full. His father's health—nope, Daniel would have been called directly.

If he wanted answers, he'd have to deal with Dorothea…alone…with a bed nearby…

Swallowing a curse, he stepped aside.

She rushed past him as if her feet were on fire, the scent of lavender strengthening. His mouth watered.

I could eat her up.

But he wouldn't. Wouldn't even take a nibble.

"Shut the door. Please," she said, a tremor in her voice.

He hesitated but ultimately obeyed. "Would you like a beer while the coffee brews?"

"Yes, please." She spotted the six-pack he'd brought with him, claimed one of the bottles and popped the cap.

He watched with fascination as she drained the contents.

She wiped her mouth with the back of her wrist and belched softly into her fist. "Thanks. I needed that."

He tried not to smile as he grabbed the pot. "Let's get you that coffee."

"No worries. I'm not thirsty." She placed the empty bottle on the dresser. Her gaze darted around the room, a little wild, a lot nervous. She began to pace in front of him. She wasn't wearing shoes, revealing toenails painted yellow and orange, like her fingernails.

More curious by the second, he eased onto the edge of the bed. "Tell me what's going on."

"All right." Her tongue slipped over her lips, moistening both the upper and lower, and the fly of his jeans tightened. In an effort to keep his hands to himself, he fisted the comforter. "I can't really tell you. I have to show you."

"Show me, then." *And leave.* She had to leave. Soon.

"Yes," she croaked. Her trembling worsened as she untied the raincoat...

The material fell to the floor.

Daniel's heart stopped beating. His brain short-circuited. Dorothea Mathis was gloriously, wonderfully naked; she had more curves than he'd suspected, generous curves, *gorgeous* curves.

Was he drooling? He might be drooling.

She wasn't a living doll, he decided, but a 1950s pinup. *Lord save me.* She had the kind of body other women abhorred but men adored. *He* adored. A vine with thorns and holly was etched around the outside of one breast, ending in a pink bloom just over her heart.

Sweet Dorothea Mathis had a tattoo. He wanted to touch. He *needed* to touch.

A moment of rational thought intruded. Strawberry Valley girls were off-limits...his dad...disappointment... But...

Dorothea's soft, lush curves *deserved* to be touched. Though makeup still hid the freckles on her face, the sweet little dots covered the rest of her alabaster skin. A treasure map for his tongue.

I'll start up top and work my way down. Slowly.

She had a handful of scars on her abdomen and thighs, beautiful badges of strength and survival. More paths for his tongue to follow.

As he studied her, drinking her in, one of her arms

draped over her breasts, shielding them from his view.
With her free hand, she covered the apex of her thighs,
and no shit, he almost whimpered. Such bounty should
never be covered.

"I want…to sleep with you," she stammered. "One
time. Only one time. Afterward, I don't want to speak
with you about it. Or about anything. We'll avoid each
other for the rest of our lives."

One night of no-strings sex? Yes, please. He wanted
her. Here. Now.

For hours and hours…

No. No, no, no. If he slept with the only maid at the
only inn in town, he'd have to stay in the city with all
future dates, over an hour away from his dad. What
if Virgil had another heart attack?

Daniel leaped off the bed to swipe up the raincoat. A
darker blush stained Dorothea's cheeks…and spread…
and though he wanted to watch the color deepen, he
fit the material around her shoulders.

"You…you don't want me." Horror contorted her
features as she spun and raced to the door.

His reflexes were well honed; they had to be. They
were the only reason he hadn't come home from his
tours of duty in a box. Before she could exit, he raced
behind her and flattened his hands on the door frame
to cage her in.

"Don't run," he croaked. "I like the chase."

Tremors rubbed her against him. "So…you want me?"

Do. Not. Answer. "I'm in a state of shock." And awe.
He battled an insane urge to trace his nose along

her nape…to inhale the lavender scent of her skin…to taste every inch of her. The heat she projected stroked him, sensitizing already desperate nerve endings.

The mask of humanity he'd managed to don before reentering society began to chip.

Off-kilter, he backed away from her. She remained in place, clutching the lapels of her coat.

"Look at me," Daniel commanded softly.

After an eternity-long hesitation, she turned. Her gaze remained on his feet. Which was probably a good thing. Those shamrock eyes might have been his undoing.

"Why me, Dorothea?" She'd shown no interest in him before. "Why now?"

She chewed on her bottom lip and said, "Right now I don't really know. You talk too much."

Most people complained he didn't talk enough. But then, Dorothea wasn't here to get to know him. And he wasn't upset about that—really. He hadn't wanted to get to know any of his recent dates.

"You didn't answer my questions," he said.

"So?" The coat gaped just enough to reveal a swell of delectable cleavage as she shifted from one foot to the other. "Are we going to do this or not?"

Yes!

No! Momentary pleasure, lifelong complications. "I—"

"Oh, my gosh. You actually hesitated," she squeaked. "There's a naked girl right in front of you, and you have to think about sleeping with her."

"You aren't my usual type." A Strawberry Valley girl equaled marriage. No ifs, ands or buts about it. The only other option was hurting his dad, so it wasn't an option at all.

She flinched, clearly misunderstanding him.

"I prefer city girls, the ones I have to chase," he added. Which only made her flinch again.

Okay, she hadn't short-circuited his brain; she'd liquefied it. Those curves...

Tears welled in her eyes, clinging to her wealth of black lashes—gutting him. When Harlow Glass had tortured Dorothea in the school hallways, her cheeks had burned bright red but her eyes had remained dry.

I hurt her worse than a bully.

"Dorothea," he said, stepping toward her.

"No!" She held out her arm to ward him off. "I'm not stick thin or sophisticated. I'm too easy, and you're not into pity screwing. Trust me, I get it." She spun once more, tore open the door and rushed into the hall.

This time, he let her go. His senses devolved into hunt mode, as he'd expected, the compulsion to go after her nearly overwhelming him. *Resist!*

What if, when he caught her—and he *would*—he didn't carry her back to his room but took what she'd offered, wherever they happened to be?

Biting his tongue until he tasted blood, he kicked the door shut.

Silence greeted him. He waited for the past to resurface, but thoughts of Dorothea drowned out the screams. Her little pink nipples had puckered in the cold, eager for his mouth. A dark thatch of curls had shielded the portal to paradise. Her legs had been toned but soft, long enough to wrap around him and strong enough to hold on to him until the end of the ride.

Excitement lingered, growing more powerful by the second, and curiosity held him in a vise grip. The Dorothea he knew would never show up at a man's door naked, requesting sex.

Maybe he didn't actually know her. Maybe he should learn more about her. The more he learned, the less intrigued he'd be. He could forget this night had ever happened.

He snatched his cell from the nightstand and dialed Jude, LPH's tech expert.

Jude answered after the first ring, proving he hadn't been sleeping, either. "What?"

Good ole Jude. His friend had no tolerance for bull, or pleasantries. "Brusque" had become his only setting. And Daniel understood. Jude had lost the bottom half of his left leg in battle. A major blow, no doubt about it. But the worst was yet to come. During his recovery, his wife and twin daughters were killed by a drunk driver.

The loss of his leg had devastated him. The loss of his family had changed him. He no longer laughed or smiled; he was like Daniel, only much worse.

"Do me a favor and find out everything you can about Dorothea Mathis. She's a Strawberry Valley resident. Works at the Strawberry Inn."

The faint *click-clack* of typing registered, as if the

guy had already been seated in front of his wall of computers. "Who's the client, and how soon does he—she?—want the report?"

"I'm the client, and I'd like the report ASAP."

The typing stopped. "So this is personal," Jude said with no inflection of emotion. "That's new."

"Extenuating circumstances," he muttered.

"She do you wrong?"

I'm not stick thin or sophisticated. I'm too easy, and you're not into pity screwing. Trust me, I get it.

"The opposite," he said.

Another pause. "Do you want to know the names of the men she's slept with? Or just a list of any criminal acts she might have committed?"

He snorted. "If she's gotten a parking ticket, I'll be shocked."

"So she's a good girl."

"I don't know what she is," he admitted. Those corkscrew curls...pure innocence. Those heart-shaped lips...pure decadence. Those soft curves...*mine, all mine.*

"Tell Brock this is a hands-off situation," he said before the words had time to process.

What the hell was wrong with him?

Brock was the privileged rich boy who'd grown up ignored by his parents. He was covered in tats and piercings and tended to avoid girls who reminded him of the debutantes he'd been expected to marry. He preferred the wild ones...those willing to proposition a man.

"Warning received," Jude said. "Dorothea Mathis belongs to you."

He ground his teeth in irritation. "You are seriously irritating, you know that?"

"Yes, and that's one of my better qualities."

"Just get me the details." Those lips...those curves... "And make it fast."

CAN'T HARDLY BREATHE—available soon from Gena Showalter and HQN Books!

Get 2 Free Books,
Plus 2 Free Gifts —
just for trying the Reader Service!

◆ HARLEQUIN *Desire*

HDI7R2

Want to give in to temptation with steamy tales of irresistible desire?

Check out **Harlequin® Presents®**, **Harlequin® Desire** and **Harlequin® Kimani™ Romance** books!

New books available every month!

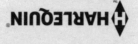

LOVE Harlequin romance?

Join our Harlequin community to share your thoughts and connect with other romance readers!

Be the first to find out about promotions, news, and exclusive content!

Sign up for the Harlequin e-newsletter and download a free book from any series at

www.TryHarlequin.com

CONNECT WITH US AT:

Harlequin.com/Community

 Facebook.com/HarlequinBooks

Twitter.com/HarlequinBooks

Instagram.com/HarlequinBooks

Pinterest.com/HarlequinBooks

ReaderService.com

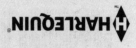

ROMANCE WHEN YOU NEED IT

While he stood in line, mute, Dani fussed over the contents of the cart. "If the baby wakes up," she said, "I'll hold her. It will be fine."

In that moment, Nathaniel realized he relied on her far more than he knew and for a variety of complex reasons he was loath to analyze.

Clearing his throat, he fished out his wallet and handed the cashier his credit card. Then their luck ran out. The baby woke up and her screams threatened to peel paint off the walls.

Dani's smile faltered, but she unfastened the straps of the carrier and lifted the baby out carefully. "I'm so sorry, sweetheart. Do you have a wet diaper? Let's take care of that."

The clerk pointed out a unisex bathroom, complete with changing station. The tiny room was little bigger than a closet. They both pressed inside.

They were so close he could smell the faint, tantalizing scent of her perfume.

Was it weird that being this close to Dani turned him on? Her warmth, her femininity. Hell, even the competent way she handled the baby made him want her.

That was the problem with blurring the lines between business and his personal life.

Don't miss
BILLIONAIRE BOSS, HOLIDAY BABY
by USA TODAY bestselling author Janice Maynard,
available October 2017 wherever
Harlequin® Desire books and ebooks are sold.

www.Harlequin.com

HARLEQUIN Desire

*It's almost Christmas when Dani is snowed in with her
too-sexy boss—and an abandoned baby wearing a note
that says he's the father! Nathaniel needs Dani's help,
but playing house means finally facing the desire they
can no longer deny...*

Read on for a sneak peek of
BILLIONAIRE BOSS, HOLIDAY BABY
*by USA TODAY bestselling author Janice Maynard,
part of Harlequin Desire's #1 bestselling*
BILLIONAIRES AND BABIES *series.*

This was a hell of a time to feel arousal tighten his body.
Dani looked better than any woman should while
negotiating the purchase of infant necessities during the
beginnings of a blizzard with her brain-dead boss and an
unknown baby.

Her body was curvy and intensely feminine. The
clothing she wore to work was always appropriate, but
even so, Nathaniel had found himself wondering if Dani
was as prim and proper as her office persona would
suggest.

Her wide-set blue eyes and high cheekbones reminded
him of a princess he remembered from a childhood
storybook. The princess's hair was blond. Dani's was
more of a streaky caramel. She'd worn it up today in a
sexy knot, presumably because of the Christmas party.

HDEXP092017